QUEEN OF THORNS

MICE AND MEN BOOK 2 (THE WAR OF ROSES UNIVERSE)

LANA SKY

Queen of Thorns

Queens of Thorns By Lana Sky

Copyright © 2021 by Lana Sky
All rights reserved.

ACKNOWLEDGMENTS

Thanks so much to everyone who supported this draft along the way, including the many beta readers who provided encouragement! Please keep in mind that this story includes dark, graphic, and explicit content matter that is not suitable for readers under the age of 18—or for readers who are uncomfortable with the following subject matter: age gap relationships, explicit sex, mentions of sexual abuse, and graphic depictions of violence.

DON

I was fourteen the first time I ever killed someone. It was a sloppy hit, done at point-blank range with a stolen 9mm. Later on, I found out that was intentional on the part of the man who put me up to it— throw off suspicion by making it seem like a reckless, random robbery.

I'd merely been a pawn in a game I'd been too damn young to even guess the scope of. Such is the way of the world.

Everyone is a fucking pawn.

I don't recall much of that day, though I sure as hell remember the messy aftermath. Namely, the blood splattered all over the pavement and the pile of puke I left alongside it. Shaking from head to toe, I could barely grip the gun in my hand. Rather than dispose of it like a seasoned hitman would, I turned tail and ran, leaving both the body and the weapon there out in the open, a rookie mistake.

I don't even remember the poor bastard's name. As far as I knew, he had been an enemy of Mr. Rossi, a mobster I'd pledged my loyalty to, and that was all that mattered.

Loyalty.

It was my one talent, and what I thought would cement my status as a member of the *famiglia,* age be damned. Until I learned a lesson they don't bother to teach in schools, that is. A boy doesn't become a man the second he commits murder.

No, my old boss and leader of the *famiglia,* Giovanni Rossi himself, told me the truth from across his desk that night. Later, as I washed the blood from my hands, I realized that some lucky bastards never learn it.

Becoming a man relies on knowing one universal certainty. Understand it, and even the poorest, dumbest son of a bitch can become whatever the hell he wants, be it a doctor, a teacher, or a fucking crime lord.

So what is it? This—*all* men have the same capacity for evil. No matter what he does. No matter what he wears or says. No matter how good his upbringing is, or how much money he has in the bank...

Everyone is the same underneath.

The true question of morality is whether they choose to embrace the darkness or suppress it—though the Bible tries its damn hardest to muddy the waters. I grew up with the lies, reading every classic moral lesson, which typically ended with all sin leading neatly back to the devil.

A good, God-fearing Catholic woman, my mother abided by every warning and did her best to teach me the same. The only problem? I knew early on that it was all bullshit.

The devil isn't real. Greed is. At his core, every man is little more than a creature born of sheer *greed*. A priest and a mobster are both one and the same—a snarling, vicious animal out to satisfy the most basic urges. Strip him down to the bone, and he'll do whatever it takes to eat. To fuck. To shit. And…if necessary, kill.

God rest my mother's soul; I wish things were different, though. I wish a simple prayer could cure every act of evil.

The death.

The violence.

The blood.

I wish I could still blame my sins on the devil—though maybe I can. Just one of flesh and blood who goes by another name.

Mischa Stepanov.

He's the reason I'm here—driving up the west end of Hell's Gambit in a stolen car with a kidnapped woman in the trunk. I barely remember the how and why. My skull throbs as I pick through the scattered memories, each one as blurred as the last.

Mischa let himself be played by faulty information. He came after me. Vin got attacked…

I left the villa, I think, though I didn't go see the man I should have.

No, I went right to the source of the lies. The man who tried to have me killed and then framed me for an attack on the Stepanovs. Antonio Salvatore.

I broke into his fancy manor and tried beating any information I could out of him. After that, I strangled him with my bare hands and used his own daughter as a human shield to evade the remnants of the *famiglia*.

Then I went back to Havienna and…

Groaning, I take one hand from the wheel to rub at my temples, but the grainy images don't get any clearer. At least one fact is answered—if all of what happened was real, then there are *two* bodies in the trunk—one being just a child, kidnapped from her own home.

Fuck. I laugh out loud and meet my gaze in the rearview mirror. Ironically, I look like hell. Bloodshot eyes. Hair mussed to shit and dripping with a substance that sure as hell ain't water. One hard sniff and I can peg the acidic stench—lighter fluid.

That's right. I doused myself in it.

Maybe *I'm* the devil in this tale?

If only reality were as neat as the Bible. I'd confess my sins and accept the punishment. God knows, I've been down this road before, and the good Donatello, the man I've strived to be… He would turn around. Do the noble thing and bend the knee to those who wronged him.

Fall on his sword like a repentant bastard.

I can't say the idea isn't tempting. I'm so damn tired. Breathing is a struggle, let alone driving. The car veers from lane to lane as the steering wheel bucks against my grip. My lungs ache with every breath I take, and even blinking hurts. I just want to sleep. I'm so weary of running, and scraping, and suffering. I'm so exhausted of hiding from the past.

From Safiya.

Why not surrender to both in one fell swoop? Let the past have my pathetic soul and allow Safiya Mangenello her pound of flesh. As it stands, I should have died seven years ago, anyway.

Or…

I could say "fuck that" to mercy. I tried the good boy routine once, and it cost me the only damn thing in the world I care about. The only person whose life truly mattered. Vincenzo…

Every time I think of him, it feels like I'm the one taking a bullet to the skull. Over and over again.

I see his face everywhere I look, hovering before me, my smiling boy—only he isn't smiling now. His dark eyes blaze, his lips moving wordlessly, demanding an answer to just one question—*how could you fail me, Don? How?*

I swear I see him right now, standing in the middle of the road.

"Vin!" I wrench on the wheel just to avoid him, sending the car into an arc. Mud flies up, speckling the windshield as the tires squeal in protest. Deep down, I know I'm being insane, but the second the car screeches to a halt, I scan the landscape for any sign of life.

Predictably, he's gone. In his place is just an endless fucking road and a swath of trees looming beyond.

I'm drunk. In my right mind, I'd never be driving, especially not here. It's what the city natives deem the no-man's-land —a swath of hills on the outskirts, hugging the bay. There are no guardrails this far out, and my heart races as I glance over to where the shoulder ends—at a cliff. Somehow, I'd managed to hit the brake without driving right off the edge. Though fuck, I should.

A sigh rips from my throat as my toes twitch over the pedal, easing up, bit by bit. Bouncing over the uneven terrain, the car lurches into motion, barreling toward the edge of the drop. Slowly. Faster. Faster…

Right when the momentum picks up, *one* thing has me slamming my foot on the brake again—self-pity.

A death dashed on the rocks below is too good for me. In my soul, I sense I'm destined for something far worse, an end worthy of a monster.

Giovanni Rossi met his via a heart attack on the eve of his daughter's wedding. Imagine that. A week before, he pulled me aside, as if he'd seen it coming. In his typical gruff baritone, he imparted one last piece of advice to me, his heir primed to take over.

Life, for all its pretentious bullshit, is just a game, sonny, he said. *You can be a coward and cringe from battle. Or you declare fucking checkmate. At all costs, you go for the checkmate. You pound your fist on the damn game board if you have to. Don't you ever give up. The second you do, someone's already beaten you. It's game over.*

To him, everything was just a round in an unending game with every player fighting his way to the top.

Thanks to Mischa Stepanov, my time playing is nearing its end. Giving up now would be forfeiting everything to him, the ultimate checkmate.

Though, what else could I do?

As if Giovanni himself sent me a reminder from the grave, I sense something around my right hand and hold it up to the light. It takes several blinks before I can focus on it— delicate strands of golden hair looped around my fingers. I bring them beneath my nose, inhaling the scent I swear they still carry.

Roses and hatred.

I can clearly picture the source—a head of golden hair, framing a face crowned by watchful dark eyes. Wrapped around my fingers, their presence alludes to the violence that resulted in them being there. Fighting her off. Shoving her aside. Putting her in the trunk…

I catch myself eyeing the direction of it in the rearview mirror. When I lower my hand, a new emotion takes hold, and I gladly let it. *Rage.* Along with it comes a new perspective. Mischa may have won the last round, but as Giovanni used to say at the *famiglia's* lowest moments, *the war is far from over.* Especially when I have in my possession one of my enemy's very own pawns.

Willow Stepanova herself could be the perfect tool to ensure that no one wins in the end.

And there are a million ways I could wreak my vengeance through her. Brutal, sick fucking shit I would have never thought myself capable of doing, even at my darkest. My fingers twitch against the steering wheel as the possibilities cross my mind.

I could rip her apart limb from limb.

Tear that beautiful body to pieces.

Torture her. Torment her. Then send the aftermath to her father, wrapped with a bow.

The truly sick part? My hand is already inching into my pocket, closing over the handle of a dagger I don't remember carrying. It's hers, small enough to fit her grasp with the word *Mouse* etched into the hilt. I run my thumb over the metal's edge, surprised by how sharp it really is.

Sharp enough to slit a throat.

Slowly, I reach for the door handle next, but my fingers shake too badly to grip it. Out of guilt? That's right. I made a vow once. Hell, I swore it over Olivia's grave. To redeem the Vanici name. To never return to my old ways. To set a good example for Vincenzo and leave a legacy they both could be proud of.

I've failed two of those vows, but I can still fulfill one final pledge. I can make the Vanici name worth speaking again—even if feared.

Mischa Stepanov will pay for what he's done.

Wrestling my hands into submission, I finally push the door open and yank the lever alongside my seat that unlocks the trunk. Slowly, I climb to my feet, bracing one hand against the car while the other returns the knife to my pocket.

It's slick as shit out, with nothing but gravel and mud underfoot. Even now, a spitting rain speckles my skin, coating everything in a slippery, silvery layer of frost. On top of that, my balance is shit. As I try to take a step, the world rocks beneath me, and I vaguely remember drinking from a bottle stolen right from Antonio Salvatore's minibar.

This whole thing could be some booze-induced hallucination. Still, I start forward.

As I round the back end of the car, a faint rustle draws my notice, and I freeze mid-step in grim anticipation. Will she jump out to meet me? Try to fight? My knuckles twitch, until both of my hands form fists so tight my own nails cut into my palms.

I wait, but the top of the trunk doesn't budge.

The booze still in my system might be to blame for the feeling that comes over me next. Weightlessness. I stagger forward, but it's like I'm watching a stranger curl his fingers beneath the rim of the lid, wrenching it up in one go.

Thick cloud cover obscures the sun, leaving only a faint bit of light to see by. Even so, I have no trouble making her out, curled on her side at one end of the compartment, the Salvatore girl on the other. Golden hair fans out around her, shrouding the pale limbs bared by a thin yellow dress. If I had to imagine how she'd appear, I'd assume afraid, trembling fearfully in anticipation of what I'd do next.

One look at her shatters that fantasy. Her dark eyes meet mine head-on, fiery in the grayish daylight. In them, I see a challenge portrayed so brazenly it might as well be branded across her forehead—*What will you do, Donatello?*

The answer is as elusive to me as it is to her. Her knife is still in my pocket, but all I seem capable of doing is staring. Remembering.

Her...

More obscure images from last night flash across my mind. Us, together in my old study, her body struggling against my grasp. A groan revs in my throat as I recall why—I'd been ready to set the entire house on fire, myself along with it.

Only one force had been able to stop me.

Her.

I remember her wrestling the matches from me, and my broken psyche adorned her with a million different embellishments then—that of a vengeful angel clothed in gold, condemning me to live another day out of spite.

In broad daylight, there is no hiding from reality.

She isn't flawless like a soldier of divine mercy would be. No. She's battered and pale, her yellow dress askew, her eyes as bloodshot as mine are. Liquid slicks her hair to her skull, reeking suspiciously of accelerant. That's not all. A necklace of dark bruises encircles her fucking neck. Irrational anger flares at the sight of them, and I'm already wracking my brain for the identity of who could have possibly hurt her.

Only a monster…

Not even a heartbeat later, I catch sight of my wrist, and I realize that I don't have to look far for the culprit—*me*. I did this to her.

My hands shake, outstretched before me, bruised and bloodied. In contrast, she looks so small.

And so dangerous.

"Is this what you wanted?" I direct the question toward her, still inspecting my fingers. An assortment of cuts and bruises mar each digit, but not enough to cause the amount of rust-colored liquid encrusted beneath each fingernail. There's no shying from what the substance really is. Blood.

Mine.

Antonio Salvatore's.

And Vincenzo's.

"Why?" The shout echoes throughout the narrow clearing this part of the road runs through, bellowed and broken.

But how does she react?

When I finally look at her again, she's just staring.

And staring, and staring...

There's no answer reflected in those dark irises. No hate. No fucking emotion.

Not even when I lunge for her, grasping at whatever I catch. Warm flesh trembles beneath my palm as I find myself tearing back through the trees, dragging her with me.

"You wanted to punish me, is that it?" I say in between pants. "Well, now we can both find our retribution."

Giovanni was right. Why give up when you can ruin the game? And what better way to circumvent Mischa's inevitable win than to aim straight for his heart?

I'll do more than pound the damn game board. I'll break it.

The woman resists, digging her bare heels into the earth with every step—not that there's much she can do. I'm heading for the edge of a sheer drop, overlooking a section of gray water churning beneath. A fall from here would be deadly. If the height alone doesn't do the trick, then the rocks down below should.

Two birds with one stone—a fitting end for Donatello Vanici, and a fitting punishment for Mischa Stepanov.

I take another step, and the woman by my side goes still, her gaze fixated on the drop.

Watching her triggers another memory, but one that occurred years ago rather than hours. Someone younger had been in her place, her dark eyes just as fearful, though the drop, in that case, had been the edge of a pool.

She couldn't speak, but I had no trouble reading her mind. Her face was so expressive; she couldn't keep anything secret from me even if she tried.

"You're afraid," I told her with a smile. "Don't be. As long as I'm here, you've got nothing to be afraid of. Just close your eyes and jump. I've got you…"

No! I bare my teeth against the past, forcing myself back to the present. The woman struggling in my grip bears resemblances to that little girl—but it doesn't matter. She should have no other identity than who she is now. An enemy. A means to an end. Willow Stepanova, daughter of the man who took everything from me. Everything…

And yet for someone so consequential, she doesn't look it, so small she barely comes up to my shoulder when I shove her forward.

My grip on her arm is the only force keeping her upright. With every twitch and gust of the wind, she staggers, her feet scrambling for balance on the uneven ground. Beneath that tattered yellow sundress, she's so slight that one strong breeze could blow her away.

All I'd have to do is let go.

So I do.

Alarm flits across her face for an instant, widening her eyes and parting those pink lips. Her impending death is a slow, morbid dance of slender limbs against relentless gravity. Her right foot loses contact with the ground first, followed quickly by the second. Left with no stability, her entire body jolts backward, that hair swaying in the wind.

Even as she starts to fall, her eyes shoot up to mine, and her brave façade cracks. Beneath it, I see her fear. The grim realization that I'll let her die.

She knows I will…

"Fuck!" The curse slips from me, as my hand shoots out before my brain can fully process the motion, gripping the neckline of her dress. Grunting, I yank on the material, hauling her back over the edge. As I let go, her fingers fly to the rocky outcropping, using it for stability to drag herself up.

She falls to her knees as a monstrous sound rips through the silence. Booming and guttural, it's seconds before I realize it's coming from me. Laughter. Manic, unstable laughter.

The emotion tearing through my chest isn't amusement, though—far from it. Just sheer, dizzying confusion.

"Why are you here? Did you come to distract me so your father or one of his men can finish the job?" I demand, spinning around as if expecting another car to appear on the road at any moment. "Where are they? Don't tell me he's watching from the shadows, pleased with the show? Because he sent you, didn't he? He sent you here..."

It's the only explanation that makes sense. Either that, or she wanted him to save me for herself, so she could be the one to drive the knife into my chest.

But then why stop me?

Her eyes flicker toward me and away, giving me the answer.

"You came on your own." I sound as incredulous as I feel. It seems insane to even consider—that she snuck from Mischa's fortress of a home. Made her way to Havienna alone. Made her way to me.

For what?

Voice rasping, I propose the obvious answer, "Did you come to watch me die, Safiya?"

She should sneer in confirmation. Instead, a muscle in her jaw twitches, and I imagine her clenching her teeth behind those pink lips. In anger? I hunt her gaze for an answer, reminded of another moment from the past. Those same eyes in another lifetime. So dark, they'd seem to touch on red whenever their owner felt enraged.

The day I left her behind, they blazed...

Now? They're too dark to interpret clearly. I just see defiance. *You don't control me,* they declare. *You lost that right.*

"You're mine now," I snap, turning away from her. Fuck the past. *This* is all that matters. Who she is now and what she's done...

She's mine.

And I don't have to kill her to enact my revenge.

I grab her arm, dragging her back to the road. The second we near the car, I shove her in the trunk beside another figure I've almost forgotten. She's curled in a ball, staring from behind a curtain of black curls. Antonio Salvatore's little girl, her eyes glazed over.

Both figures watch as I slam the trunk closed over them. Shaking, I reclaim the driver's seat, moving on autopilot as I put the car back into drive. A U-turn later, I'm speeding toward Hell's Gambit. I don't know where I'm heading at first. My brain churns sluggishly, fighting to catch up with my body's impulse.

Then it comes to me—I'm going home. How does that saying go? Things have a way of coming full circle. When I've hit rock bottom, what better place to complete that descent than the very location I rose from at the start of it all?

I still remember the whirlwind of those early days after I'd freshly joined the *famiglia*. Old Giovanni Rossi kept a public front in the heart of the city—a casino that Antonio Salvatore took over after ascending to the top of the outfit. Apart from that, the old man mainly did business in a small restaurant, but his pride and the true heart of his operation was located about an hour outside of the city proper.

Only his most trusted lieutenants knew of it, and even fewer were allowed to set foot there. From that old complex, Giovanni conducted his true business, using the place as a headquarters for the real source of his money—cocaine. A hell of a lot of cocaine, sourced directly from the most vicious Colombian cartels. I doubt Salvatore dumped that part of the operation. Given the lavishness of his mansion, the fucker has been enjoying the benefits of such an enterprise.

Who knows how much of that fortune remains. But even if Antonio spent every last penny, I know a way to garner more.

Enough to rebuild an empire all my own and destroy any hold Mischa Stepanov has on Hell's Gambit. I think we're more alike than either of us would admit. I valued the life of my son more than anything, enough to forfeit it all…

How far will Mischa go for his own daughter?

I'm willing to find out.

2

WILLOW

*A*rt glorifies even the most grotesque aspects of human nature and perpetuates a devious lie.

That it can be controlled. Harnessed. Made beautiful. Those of us who study music are especially vulnerable to that belief. Under the spell of a particular concerto, or haunting song, we become naïve to whatever tragedy inspired it, so entranced by every note.

And we sometimes fail to question the mindset of the man who wrote it.

One of my professors used a certain term to describe only the most complex pieces and the eccentric composers who crafted them. *Depraved.*

To him, those men were so lost and consumed by emotion they embodied it in every piece they created—though he didn't make it sound like a bad thing. In his opinion, true madness could craft the most esteemed works of art.

Maybe that beautifying of humanity's darkest aspects is what drew me to music in the first place. I could find a reprieve from my past as I played, drowning my reality in dazzling noise. As a pianist, I could appreciate those works both as a caution and something to aspire to.

Now, I know the innocent folly of that admiration—madness isn't beautiful.

It's terrifying.

The men capable of honing such insanity are arsonists with no aim in mind other than to burn. To watch the world burn. To them, pain is a tool.

It's fuel.

It's fire.

Donatello Vanici is *depraved*; no other word describes him. Instead of music—pain, agony, and hate form the notes of his own horrifying melody. His symphony is one of vengeance and terror, and only God knows how it ends.

And in this case? *I'm* the instrument being ruthlessly played.

My neck throbs with the imprint of his fingers, and I can't stop myself from tracing each mark in the dark. Neither one hurts per se. They merely sting, but the intent behind them is more alarming than any physical pain.

Tears burn behind my eyes as a sudden thought bites deep. Seven years of hating him never left me prepared to feel anything else. I've replayed the moment of him leaving me behind over and over. His retreating back. His parting words.

But never—not once—could I see him doing anything more than that.

Until now. My legs smart from scraping against the ground, as my heart still pounds with residual fear. I've never felt that terror before, so potent I could taste it.

Still can—copper like blood.

I will never forget the look on his face. One devoid of any shred of recognition. No hate. No anger. In that moment, I knew in my soul he would do it.

Let me fall.

Watch me die.

He betrayed me once, but for some naïve, childish reason, I always explained the act away as selfish cruelty.

Not hate. As pitiful as it sounds…I never expected him to hate me.

Ignore him, a part of my brain hisses. *Focus on where you are. Form a plan.* If Mischa were here, his advice would be simple—*run. Escape. Don't give in to fear.*

If only it were that easy.

Mischa, for all of his experience, couldn't imagine a moment quite like this one. Shrouded in darkness, I have every reason to be terrified. The most prominent example?

I'm still in danger. My eyes burn as my lungs contract to expel the stench of the accelerant dripping from my hair. The acrid smell fills the confined space of the trunk and beside me, a tiny figure coughs, overwhelmed by it.

Her presence presents another horrifying reality I can't acknowledge just yet.

So I put everything I have into the only task that matters —*escape*. Blindly, I extend my hands, feeling along the smooth interior of the compartment beneath me. It rumbles with the motion of the vehicle—the only clue I have as to the driver's intent.

To be as reckless as possible.

He's driving erratically, making it hard to get my bearings. Every jolt of the car, rams me against the narrow body beside mine. She whimpers, recoiling as much as she can while I try to create a mental map of the space.

It's small. My fingers tremble so badly it's hard to tell the softer material coating the inside of the trunk from the metal of the car's frame. Clenching my jaw is the only way I can keep my teeth from chattering, not that it matters much in the end. I'm shaking all over. I could blame the chill seeping in from outside, or acknowledge the unease gnawing at my resolve.

I'm panicking.

No matter how hard I try, my thoughts keep returning to the man in the driver's seat. Namely, his final threat to me, uttered in a voice gruff with malice. *I'm going to break your wings, little bird...*

And after that? His threat became even more specific.

That I would give him an heir to replace Vincenzo...

Something hard brushes my palm, snapping me back to the present. Cautiously, I curl my fingers around it. Something round and firm that gives slightly with a bit of pressure. An emergency release?

Any triumph I may feel, however, goes to war with common sense. I know better than to pull it now. We're moving quickly. Too fast. Way too fast. My heart lurches up my throat as I try to picture where he's heading in this state. Unfortunately, only one destination comes to mind—him speeding toward one of the cliffs overlooking the harbor—but I shut my eyes against it.

Focus! Instead of Donatello, I channel Mischa and the stoic mindset he drilled into me since childhood. *Focus, Mouse!*

Obeying the mental plea, I go still, breathing in through my nose and out through my mouth. With every breath, some of the fear gives way to logic.

If running is out of the question now, then the only course of action left is…

To fight. I curl my fingers into fists and wrack my brain for any available weapon. Apart from the girl beside me, the trunk seems to be empty. For the first time, I turn to her, straining my eyes through the darkness to make out what I can.

She's young, and my heart clenches with terror at that realization. She is so young. Dark curls glimmer in the absence of light, the only detail I can make out. Her soft breaths scrape on the air, adding a chilling backdrop to the engine's constant hum and the roar of rushing air rebounding off the vehicle's exterior.

God, he's driving even faster now. Suddenly, the car lurches, shaking violently as if the road switched from the smooth pavement of a main highway to a rougher texture. Stone? Gravel? Whatever the surface, it's uneven. Hissing traction comes from the wheels, making me suspect that we're traveling steeply up an incline.

That vision of the cliff returns, sharper in clarity.

Would he really do it? The answer terrifies me—I know nothing about this Donatello.

Nothing at all.

Fortunately, the only things a musician needs to play any piece, are their hands and an instrument

All I need to kill Donatello is a weapon.

And this time, if I get the chance…

I won't falter.

3

EVGENI

A man in my line of work abides by a simple code—if he wants to keep living, anyway. Loyalty should be his most prized asset. Only survival gets second priority. Leave the political games to politicians, and finally, never get too close.

To your employer. To anyone.

After a decade without dying yet, I've never questioned that creed once.

Until the moment I'm faced with an empty bedroom and a missing charge, that is. For a second, I consider a nice retirement somewhere far away from murderous employers and their sheltered daughters. The thought is a warning sign —I've failed the last bastion of my code already.

The missing daughter, in this instance, isn't some nameless mark. I've watched her grow up from a stoic little girl into an accomplished woman who lacks the spoiled apathy of most with her kind of privilege.

I know firsthand how power can corrupt families, and how the sins of the father can easily infect a child. At least until now, Willow proved to be an exception to that rule. Shunning the violence and brutality of Mischa's realm, she sought shelter in the mundane future of a quiet pianist.

I'd never admit as much out loud, but I always admired that drive in her. Some aren't so lucky as to choose a differing path from the world they grew up in. While it comforts some to separate men in terms of good or bad, morality has nothing to do with it. In a sense, it's only natural, no less tragic than a wolf pup learning the ways of a predator. Darkness begets darkness. Murderers beget murderers.

Monsters go on to sire even more brutal monsters...

Few can break that cycle. By forging her own path, Willow was braver than I could ever hope to be—though Mischa is the kind of man decent enough to allow his children the freedom to grow into their own.

Most aren't, and most children never escape the crushing weight of their forebearer's shadow.

It's a line of thought I try to avoid, and for a good reason. Control is an asset a man like me comes to cherish— namely, because it's so rare and fleeting. I lose my grip on my thoughts for a second, and they scatter. Instead of Willow, I see another face. Just as pretty, her hair darker, eyes rounder. She never got the chance to live out a life following some innocent future endeavor.

Because I failed her too.

The guilt I feel is a knife slicing at my splintering control—but a simple mantra is enough to repair it. *Loyalty first. Survival second. Stay focused on the job at hand and never lose sight of your task...*

I repeat that creed until my mind clears, but I'm no less ashamed by my own failure. Gritting my teeth, I express the irritation the only way I can. "*Fuck.*"

That curse says it all—this is my fault. My responsibility.

"There's been no sighting of her at all since last night?" I demand of the man beside me. The question—as is our presence in this very room—is a mere formality. It's already been hours since the alarm went up, with the mid-morning quickly approaching.

It's not a question of *if* Willow is missing but for how long —and who might be involved if she left willingly?

There aren't many options given the size of her social circle —her family's manor, or her closeted school in Vienna. Two teams of my men are out scouring the nearby road, as well as four key locations, but given their lack of contact, I doubt they've found anything useful yet.

And they might not.

Time is ticking. Who knows how far she's gotten by now. Or what state she's in…

"Yes, sir," one of the men replies, drawing up to my side. Fairly young, he's a new recruit, and I spot his hands fidgeting with the sleeve of his gray uniform jacket. I know how he feels, but just months into the job, he hasn't gotten it yet—our most important work is done in these quiet moments, far from gunfire.

Even if it feels as useless as twiddling thumbs.

"Tell me what you've deduced so far," I command, facing him directly.

He clears his throat. "She's not on the property. Left alone, it seems. No signs of forced entry," he adds. "If you plan on sending out another team, I'm ready."

I ignore the suggestion, though I'm just as anxious to get moving. Do something.

Damn, Willow. She's not like the other coddled heiresses I've dealt with. A beautiful girl with a wealth of secrets behind her silence. What in the hell would make her run?

There's always the possibility that someone breached the manor and took her—but I secured the premises myself. Two teams of ten patrol at all times, covering every inch of the property, not to mention the state-of-the-art surveillance. I'm fairly confident that God himself couldn't break into this manor.

But a certain sheltered heiress could find a way to sneak out, if she were so determined.

Before I know it, I'm questioning yet another tenet of my tried and true creed. What use is loyalty to a family wrought with secrets? How can I protect what I can't even begin to understand?

I know the answer—my intuition hasn't failed me yet, and it's telling me that this has everything to do with one man and one man only.

Donatello Vanici.

What is his tie to the Stepanovs beyond the obvious? Mischa rarely gives in to impulse, but he drew first blood against Vanici without even waiting for better intel. Only God knows what can of worms he might have opened as a result.

And I'm the fool left to wrangle the mess with no clue as to the nature of it.

"Sir?" the man beside me questions.

I wave him off. "Give me a moment."

Setting aside any suspicion, I refocus on the room itself. There has to be something here. A clue. Anything. I start with the bed. It's been left fully made, the sheets undisturbed. The only means of exit, other than the door, are the windows, both closed. I test the latch of one, finding it locked. Not to mention it's too high from this floor to climb down unseen.

"She didn't leave from here," I state out loud.

Which makes one possibility all the more likely—though I have enough tact not to say as much. Not until I've left the rookie behind and retraced my steps throughout the house, finally entering a study on the first floor.

Sympathy is an emotion I tend to shun, but if any man deserves it, it's Mischa Stepanov.

I don't think he's slept for days. Seated behind his desk, he could be mistaken for a ghost. Pale skin and windswept blond hair only add to the effect, and I wouldn't put it past him to have patrolled the outskirts of the property himself on foot.

All night.

One look at him, and I feel compelled to bend those boundaries I've steadfastly maintained.

"Mischa…" On second thought, I suppress the urge in favor of doing the one useful thing I can.

Stay professional.

"Sir," I say instead, pausing near the threshold of the room. Spacious, with a view of the west lawn, it's a prime position to spot any traffic in or out of the manor. I can't resist scanning the expanse of road, hoping to see a *mafiya* van on the horizon, Willow in tow.

All I find are the gray sky, fields, and the trees beyond.

"You've rechecked the property as I asked?" Mischa asks without looking up from his clasped hands. The muted response is a world apart from his initial reaction hours earlier—a fact that would terrify anyone who knew the man personally.

His anger may be legendary, but he's at his most dangerous when calm.

"Yes, sir," I say in answer to his question. "There is no sign of forced entry. I have my men in two teams out looking, but Vanici's residences have been cleared out. There's been no sign that he's left the city, and—"

"She couldn't have gotten far on foot," Mischa interjects, turning to stare from one of the windows.

Like me, I suspect he's merely going through the motions, voicing the expected questions when the answer is painfully obvious.

"Yes, sir," I reply anyway.

"She left on her own, didn't she?" There is no despair in his voice. No anguish.

I've never seen a man so drained of everything but pure exhaustion.

Standing at attention, I don't mince words. "My guess is that she left on her own but impulsively." I can't disguise the irritation in my voice.

Willow could be calm and reserved well beyond her nineteen years—but at her core, she's still nineteen. A child.

Mingled among the reports from her detail overseas in Vienna would be anecdotes of her sternly exposing a professor who insulted her or reprimanding anyone who dared to treat her any differently due to her disability.

"She's strong," I say finally.

"She's impulsive," Mischa snaps. "She's stubborn."

He's right—and she has no fucking clue as to the way things really are, or how far some men might go to gain leverage over her father.

Mischa's worked hard to keep his family safe. In the process, he's also kept them sheltered from the reality of their status. Willow never understood one truth. She isn't a normal woman—she's a pawn in a game of power.

"Fuck, I should have known better than to leave her alone," Mischa snarls, curling his hands into fists. "Hell, I should have locked her in her room and thrown away the key. I knew she couldn't leave him—" He breaks off, but I can suspect what he doesn't say. Who.

So I voice it for him. "You mean Donatello Vanici."

He says nothing, but the look he sends my way is a clear warning to tread carefully.

Well, I'm tired of tiptoeing. "If she went after him, I need to know why. What happened between them?"

Still nothing.

"Sir, it's only a matter of time before he retaliates if he isn't already planning an attack," I point out. "We need to stay on guard. Track his allies. Maybe he's contacted someone in the *famiglia*. We need to—"

"Enough." Mischa swipes a hand through the blond stubble speckling his chin. From this position, I have a glimpse of paperwork stacked haphazardly before him. What could be so important he'd pick now of all times to read it? As if aware of my attention, he shoves the stack aside, further from view. "I will handle Vanici."

"Alone?" I raise an eyebrow. "Sir, maybe if I didn't let you go after Vanici *alone*, we might have been able to avoid—"

"Are you challenging me, Evgeni?" His eyes cut in my direction as his raised voice echoes throughout the room.

"I'm just asking a question, sir," I say softly. Though I couldn't disguise the annoyance from my tone if I tried. Mischa went and kicked the proverbial hornet's nest, attacking Vanici's nephew. And for what? All on shitty intel and a reckless whim.

But I know the man. In six years, I've never seen him act without an ironclad cause.

Unless it's personal. Emotional. Only then can his instincts sometimes tend toward…irrational.

"Vanici's left his villa," I add, voicing what little intel I've managed to gather in the aftermath. "His associate, Fabio Botelli, has gone underground. There is no word on the status of his nephew, though we've assumed the worst. Finding Vanici should be our top priority."

Not playing hide and seek with a girl we both know is long gone. And yet, Mischa inclines his head to glower at the grayish sky, stubbornly silent.

It's been a game we've played since Mischa had the man removed from his daughter's ball. A verbal round of tag in which I ask more potent questions about Vanici and his history with the Stepanovs, and Mischa avoids answering every single one.

I can't fathom why. Mischa certainly isn't known for being demure—neither am I—and now isn't the time for coyness when Willow's life may be on the line.

So damn tact. "Can I ask why, sir?" It's a question loaded with a million others left unasked. "Why attack Vanici with little more than hearsay to go off of? Why was Willow found in his home after her first disappearance?"

The questions get more unsavory from there, but I'm not stupid enough to voice them now.

Why is she drawn to him?

Why has Mischa eschewed his usual tact and restraint where Vanici is concerned?

Why is he playing so coy with the answers?

And why is he hampering the efforts to find his own daughter by keeping me in the dark?

"I need you at the hospital," he says tiredly. "I want you stationed near my wife. Only you."

I nod, smothering my irritation. For now. The concern in his tone takes precedence, and I know he wouldn't ask this lightly. "Any improvement in her condition?"

He winces. "Eli is stabilized enough to possibly come home tomorrow," he says, referring to his son. "The baby could be released in a week."

But as for his wife? His silence says for him what he can't. Her condition is unknown, so tenuous the prognosis changes daily.

"Go," he demands, turning his back to me. "Vanici could attack the hospital next."

I nod, starting for the door. As I toe the threshold, however, I hesitate.

"What about Willow?" I ask. "I have my men searching Vanici's known properties as we speak. But if I knew more of their history... Even more about what happened after the debutante ball—"

"I will handle Vanici," Mischa growls.

But what could happen in the meantime?

Especially if the man has Willow. I have no delusions about what he might do to her. I've known men like him. Hell, I've worked for them. Be him a mercenary or a crime lord, the breed is the same. If he doesn't kill her—or worse—then he'll attempt to make contact soon, if only to sell her.

"Sir, time is of the essence," I insist.

"Evgeni..." When I look over my shoulder, his gaze meets mine with an intensity that would make the rookie upstairs piss himself. "Are you refusing a direct order?"

"No," I say—which should end the conversation. My feet twitch against the floor, but I don't move.

Despite my better judgment, I can't let this go. Sending me to the hospital now would be the equivalent of shoving me to the sidelines.

Why?

"I think I could be of more use to you here—"

"Ellen is the one who has *use* of you." He whirls around, bringing both hands hard over the surface of his desk. The resulting thud resonates through the room like a gunshot. A warning.

"I meant no disrespect—"

"Go," he commands, dismissing me with a wave of his hand. "That wasn't a request."

"Sir." I nod, finally reentering the hall, clenching my jaw against another retort.

Or an accusation—is this really the time to withhold information? Especially whatever might prove vital to anticipating Vanici's next move. Though a part of me sneers that the real question is a different one entirely.

How much is Mischa willing to pay for his daughter's life?

I'm sure that will become clear soon enough.

4

DON

*W*est Helm Lumber. An unimpressive facility with an even less impressive name—and by design. No one would ever suspect the seat of the *famiglia's* power rested in this sprawling, nondescript complex in the hills surrounding Hell's Gambit.

Which is the point.

Giovanni loved the juxtaposition of, instead of the casino or the restaurant, the true heart of his establishment residing someplace far different. *In a Podunk hellhole,* as he liked to joke. The man could be poetic when he felt like it.

It's been seven years since I've made this drive, but it still looks the same. Sort of. Leading off the highway, the asphalt road switches to beaten dirt, as old and worn as the day I came here as an eighteen-year-old kid, over four years into my career.

I'd been blindfolded that very first time, herded into the back of a van by the men more senior to me. It was tradition to make a big fucking deal of it all, if only to drill in the importance of what coming here meant—you were trusted. In the fold.

Part of the family…and how did I repay that trust?

By turning my back on the organization entirely—a mortal sin in our world. You don't just leave the *famiglia* and come back.

Still, I can't help but taunt myself with that fucking cliché at the sight of the battered sign appearing up ahead, pointing the way forward.

Home sweet home.

It even smells the same, a stench that seeps into the body of the car, despite the windows being rolled up. My nostrils flare to inhale it all. Damp wood, dirt, and musk.

Up ahead, the gate's entrance looms, a simple twisted wire fence outfitted with more security cameras than some military bases. Whoever is manning them has seen me coming for a mile now—but, oddly enough, they haven't mustered the cavalry to meet me.

Yet.

A battered metal speaker is affixed to a pole, easily reached from the driver's seat, and I wrench the window down, craning my neck.

"You know who I am," I say into it as a weak smattering of raindrops pelts my head. "Either let me in or put a bullet in my head now. I don't fucking care."

I mean it, and I close my eyes in grim anticipation of a response. If fate would have it that my story end here, then so be it. What a pathetic finale, but at least I'd have some ounce of peace. I might even see Olivia again on my way to hell…

It isn't long before an answer comes—not a gunshot. Rattling metal and the telltale whine of turning gears cut the silence instead. I open my eyes, resigned to the sight I find.

The gates slowly drift apart, clearing the way—but it's not the greeting one would expect in the old days. No men appear to line the road, and no warning comes from the speaker. Both signs don't bode well at all. Either the *famiglia* has become more welcoming to visitors, or I'm heading straight into a trap.

Though, hell, it's not like I have any other options. Sighing, I grip the wheel and drive.

It could be the fact that I'm viewing everything through a cracked windshield smeared with mud, but the landscape doesn't look quite how I remember it after all. Gone are the meticulously maintained fields and hints of regular patrols. Nature's returned with a vengeance, swallowing every inch of available land in thick weeds, and I don't see a guard or van in sight. Not only that, but the fact that I've made it this close without being met with gunfire speaks for itself.

Trap or not, one thing is apparent. Antonio let the place go to shit.

The overall layout still resembles a large rectangle with the main headquarters residing in the center, three outbuildings on the perimeter, and a lumberyard in between. A layer of grime shrouds the landscape, and if I didn't know better, I'd assume the property was abandoned. Most of the equipment appears rusted with disuse, and the piles of lumber stacked out in the open look suspiciously as though they've been there since the days of Giovanni.

The old man is turning over in his grave. Maintaining the sawmill was one chore he always insisted on, no matter how much money his empire amassed. Everyone, including him, worked at least some part of the business. In his words. *You forget the upkeep; you might as well forget your freedom. All the power in the world can't buy you a good cover.*

Because the sawmill is just a front. *Beneath* the property is where the real business lies—an underground warehouse with direct access to the river.

Though who knows what state the enterprise is in now.

With every inch I gain on the winding road leading to the main building, Antonio's influence becomes more obvious —primarily in the row of luxury vehicles parked amid a yard of overgrown weeds and sparse gravel. Apparently, he and his cohorts have taken the money for themselves rather than use it to maintain the façade.

And it shows.

Only five men stand on the steps of the building up ahead, weapons drawn—a fraction of the men Giovanni kept around at a given time. They look trained enough, despite wearing a mismatched array of jeans and casual shirts, another breach of protocol that would catch Giovanni's ire.

None of them move as I park and climb out. They just stare. As I spot my reflection in the glossy black paint job of Fabio's car, I realize why.

I look like hell. My hair is a fucking rat's nest, my clothes rumpled, drenched in booze, and lighter fluid.

Or maybe it's the blood that has their attention? Reddish smears streak my hands. My wrists. My chin. My clothing is stiff with it, like armor against the judgment of anyone watching. I start to tug on my collar, only to let my hand fall. Instead, I jerk my chin without adjusting a damn thing.

Let them stare. I may look like an animal, but they're no different.

"Keep your hands where I can see them." The man in the center of the pack steps forward, keeping his pistol trained over my chest. A formality, I suspect, given he had every chance to stop me at the gate. I recognize his face. Luciano. Hours earlier, he watched me stroll out of Antonio Salvatore's mansion.

"You have some nerve coming here," he says. His tone gives me nothing to go off of, his expression blank. I'm impressed despite myself—as far as poker faces go, he's damn good.

Which a bad sign if I intend to navigate this meeting peacefully. Looking at him, it's impossible to guess his motive—mainly why he let me go in the first place. Not to mention why he hasn't shot me now. I could always go the intimidation route to gain answers, but as I spy the blood on my shirt, I lose the urge.

Instead, I drop all pretense, facing him with my arms outstretched and nothing held back. Whatever he sees makes him grimace, though it doesn't take a stretch of the imagination to guess what impression I've made—that of a crazy motherfucker covered in blood.

He'd be better off opening fire—but he hasn't, and as the seconds tick past, he never gives the call to attack. Even his men don't seem to understand why, trading questioning looks between them.

It's easy to conclude that on this battlefield, Luciano is the only one worth confronting, so I turn my full attention to him.

"You haven't shot me yet," I finally point out, but there could be a multitude of reasons why, none of which being a desire to reconnect with an old ally. One real possibility is that he has Mischa already lying in wait inside? Admittedly, I didn't think this far ahead in terms of returning to my old outfit. Coming here at all could be neatly summarized as a suicidal death wish.

As I observe the mouth of the gun, I'm forced to admit that could very well be the reason. Why? I don't feel a shred of fear.

I don't feel a damn thing.

Luciano's expression reveals nothing either way. Without a word, he eyes my hands, and a muscle in his jaw twitches, but I doubt it's the blood alone that has him so wary. Sure enough, his eyes flicker toward the trunk, giving me a clue as to what might be behind his restraint.

Surprisingly, it might be as simple as basic human decency.

His next words leave no doubt. "Where is Kisa?"

Kisa Salvatore. The child I took from her home still dressed in her nightgown after strangling her father before her eyes.

From the man's tone alone, I can tell exactly what he thinks happened to her—I, *the Butcher, Il Mostro* himself, killed her.

Rather than answer him out loud, I circle around to the car.

"Why are you here, Donatello?" Luciano snarls as I run my fingers along the side of the driver's seat, finding the lever for the back. "Come to finish us off the way you did Antonio? Did you hurt Kisa too? Answer me! Don't think I won't fucking put a bullet in your skull—"

"Kisa," her name tastes like blood. I spit and realize that the flavor isn't all in my head—I must have bitten my lip sometime during the trip here. The warm moisture I feel dribbling down my chin must be the reason why Luciano backs up a step as I shoot him a glance over my shoulder. "Is she why you haven't attacked me yet?"

He keeps his face blank. "Did you kill her? I wouldn't put it past you—"

"If you believed I was a threat, you wouldn't have let me through the gates," I point out. "And if you really gave a damn about Antonio, I don't think you'd be interested in chatting to his murderer."

His eyes narrow a fraction—I hit a target, though I'm not sure which one. Maybe the fact that he obviously wasn't as loyal to Antonio as he wants me to think.

But he does care about the girl—and if he truly thought I'd hurt her, he probably wouldn't be so friendly.

"You let me go," I add, raising an eyebrow. "Why? Did you think the *famiglia* needed a change in management?"

"Fuck off." He spits on the ground, his gaze unreadable. "Maybe we didn't think you'd be so fucking dumb as to come here alone. It's five against one, Don. All I have to do is say the word."

"Then say it," I snap to no response.

The silence alone proves my hunch was correct—so much for staging a trap. Despite the show of force, Luciano isn't willing to risk an outright firefight. He's concerned for the Salvatore girl, or maybe that's his excuse. Objectively, he doesn't have much to mount an attack with, assembling barely enough members to form a welcoming committee.

"I'll tell you why you haven't shot me," I declare, thinking out loud. "You can't take the risk. Sure, I killed Antonio, but he wasn't in the running for boss of the year, I'm assuming. The *mafiya* isn't known for being the most welcoming of outfits. Mischa would consume the *famiglia* rather than align with it. Which means that you aren't in a position to be picky when it comes to allies."

How tragic. As stoic as he tries to be, Luciano's narrowed gaze proves I'm right. I'm not the only one who's been diminished in the shadow of the *mafiya*. Without Antonio's leadership, the best the *famiglia* can look forward to is being picked off by a rival faction or making a power play of their own. To do that, they need leverage—something I might have. Either way, another potential ally, even a murderer covered in blood, is better than nothing.

"You need me," I say, to sum it up nicely. I don't know why, but I can't silence a laugh at that realization. It rings out hollow, echoing on the morning chill only to trail off as I approach the trunk and hook my fingers beneath the lid. I lift it slowly, hissing through my teeth as light falls over the two small bodies curled within the compartment, one blond, the other dark-haired.

They're lying side-by-side, the girl whimpering while the blond…

I tense, expecting her to lunge at me, nails drawn, like she had during our first meeting. Instead, she grabs the child's hand, a simple motion that conveys more than any words ever could. She has enough space to jump from the trunk and run if she wanted to. I've seen her in action; she's more than capable of making a decent attempt at escape on her own.

Instead, she's focused on protecting the weaker entity.

From *me*.

I blink as if struck, and it takes a second to dull the guilt slicing through my chest—a long, fucking second. In the end, I banish it with a sharp shake of my head. Then I reach for the smaller girl, grabbing her opposite wrist. She whimpers fearfully, her bottom lip trembling.

As the blond stiffens, I catch myself snapping, "Let go."

Her eyes flit up to mine, and I can practically see the battle taking place beneath her skin. Muscle straining against restraint. Logic warring with instinct. Her lips pull back from her teeth in a feral expression I doubt she's even aware of. She wants to fight.

I know the feeling.

A second ticks by. Then another before she finally lets go.

I tug the girl out without resistance, easily pulling her into the men's line of sight.

"Kisa Salvatore, safe and sound," I snarl, releasing her.

Some of the tension leaves Luciano's jaw, an observation I note for later. Meeting his gaze, I ask, "Are you going to invite us inside?"

Luciano stiffens, an eyebrow raised. "I thought you were an upstanding businessman," he sneers, sarcasm dripping from his tone. "Better than all of us. You stepped down for a reason, correct? Only to return like a prodigal son. And what? We're just supposed to fall into fucking line?"

He has a good point.

Without answering, I turn on my heel, rubbing at the stubble on my chin as I try to decide the truth for myself. The booze is wearing off, making my thoughts clearer. Why am I here? Why now?

Amid the swirling chaos and pain in my brain, one coherent thought tumbles out. Revenge. Retribution. Petty rage. Whatever the fuck it's called, I feel it in the pit of my very soul. I think I always have, but I won't run from it like I have for the past seven years.

God, I want to indulge in it.

I need to.

This, I realize, is the only thing keeping me going —payback.

Taking a glance around the yard, I home in on the rotting, dried-out husks of lumber stacked haphazardly across the place. The more I look, the more painfully obvious the state of disrepair becomes.

If I hadn't already killed Antonio, I'd strangle the bastard a second time. Only an idiot would shoot himself in the foot by neglecting the main financial arm of his operation. To be fair, I'm the bigger dumbass who left him in charge.

Irritation aside, at least he did leave one useful thing behind, something that might help turn the tables on Mischa. I slip my hand into my pocket, finding the small device I managed to salvage from my successor. In it, hopefully, lies the key to finding out who he ordered to put a hit out on the Stepanovs.

And if not?

I haven't thought that far ahead.

"Don't let me interrupt," Luciano snaps. "It's a beautiful fucking day to waste my goddamn time. You've got balls, I'll give you that—"

"Tell me something," I say, directing my voice toward the men behind him. "What has the *famiglia* become under Antonio Salvatore? Don't tell me that four fucking men is all you could muster to guard the very heart of the operation." I don't even have to look at their faces to know I hit the truth on its head.

I only have to inhale. Shame has a certain stench to it, more potent than lighter fluid and blood.

"You've lost your standing," I say, raising my voice. "Your position in the world, forced to kowtow to someone like Mischa Stepanov for a seat at the table. All while Antonio pillaged the coffers and spent your money on his fancy-ass mansion. Pathetic."

"Antonio wasn't the only one pining for a seat at Mischa's table," Luciano points out coldly. "We've all heard the rumors about how you've chased his protection."

I put my back to him, facing the side of the car, and my own reflection once again. He's right—and as I stare into a pair of soulless dark eyes, I realize what a foolish act that had been. To grovel at the foot of a monster and demand mercy.

In this world? There is only violence and power, and it takes both to survive.

The proof of the first is written across my skin in various streaks of blood.

As for power? A symbol of my own appears before me, much like the angel I'd compared her to earlier. She must have climbed from the trunk, clinging to the side of the car for balance. It's the only clue of instability she gives. Otherwise, with her head held high, blond hair streaming down her shoulders, she seems untouchable.

Murmurs of alarm go up from our audience at the sight of her, though. Bravery aside, she looks even worse now than she had before. A divine being marred by bruises and still reeking of lighter fluid.

"What the fuck?" Luciano snarls from behind me. "You couldn't stop at shoving one girl into your trunk? Maybe you should go talk to the Saleris if trafficking is your thing."

"And Antonio wasn't into it?" I counter from over my shoulder. "Don't tell me he drew the line there."

"Antonio was a dumbass," Luciano says. I turn to find him descending the steps, gun still drawn. "He thought he could take on the *mafiya* himself, but what makes you any better? From what I heard, you forfeited everything you have to Mischa without so much as a fucking whimper. Are we supposed to see you as some kind of savior now?"

"No," I rasp, eyeing my battered hands. The blood on them speaks for itself. "I'm no one's savior."

"So, I repeat the question—why are you here?"

"Because I want to be," I say, letting my hands fall to my side. "We used to own this city—*us*. Mischa sits at the head of the table now, but in my opinion? He shouldn't even have a fucking seat."

"So what do you suggest?" Luciano counters, cocking his head skeptically. "We break into the man's house and slaughter him in front of his children like you did Tony?"

I don't even wince at the suggestion.

"No." Sarcasm aside, that would be too easy. Nowhere near punishment enough for what he's done. Mischa deserves so much more than that.

He should know the pain of reaching rock bottom with nothing to show for it. Not only that, but I want him to know that pain on a first name basis—Donatello Vanici.

"I don't want to kill Mischa." As the words leave my mouth, my gaze comes to rest over the slight figure before me, and I can't resist a gnawing suspicion as to what she's thinking. Does knowing that comfort her?

Her dark eyes watch me without a shred of emotion, and I turn away, ignoring her altogether.

"So, what do you want?" Luciano demands, sounding closer. I turn to find him behind me, but his gun is pointed at the ground. For now.

"What do I want?" I echo, tilting my head to eye the gray, colorless sky above. It's only been a few hours, but the loss of Vin has already changed everything so damn much. The grief is like putting on glasses that rob the world of its beauty. Its laughter. Its joy.

Without it, the world reverts back to the game board Giovanni always taught me to see it as—territory ripe for exploitation.

"Antonio spoke of having allies," I say, scoffing at the notion. One look at his supposed headquarters, and I doubt he's cultivated much. However… "He would be an idiot to try and frame me without thinking he had an insurance policy. Either that, or he was being used as a puppet by someone with a greater interest. Though, with his track record, I don't think he had many friends to pick from."

Luciano's frown proves it.

"Just the Saleris and the local MC," he admits. "Seeing as how you killed Antonio, I think only one of those options is in play for you."

Or neither. Another plan unfurls in my head. One so twisted, so wrong… I cringe in the face of it. Then I remember Vin and all the things playing on the right side of the law got me—nothing.

"I'll let them come to me," I finally say. "I have a feeling they might anyway once word gets out."

"That doesn't sound arrogant at all," Luciano says with another scoff, but considering he doesn't storm off, I already have his attention. "What are you even talking about? 'Word' about what?"

"That I have Mischa Stepanov's daughter as leverage against the *mafiya*."

I wait, and predictably Luciano swears. "Are you insane—"

"Not to mention that I still own the city's port," I say over him. "I'm willing to divvy up my share to anyone ready to collaborate."

"You own it? I thought—"

"If you plan to kill me, you might as well do it now," I suggest. "But if you boys are tired of playing games and want to win, then we have work to do."

Silence lasts for barely a heartbeat before Luciano sighs. "With Antonio dead, it's not like we have much of a fucking choice. So what is your plan?"

I inhale and exhale slowly before returning my attention to my only real leverage. If I wanted to find her cowering, she denies that fantasy.

She fucking smashes it into pieces, facing me boldly. I hate that her beauty draws my notice, even now. Not in a sexual way, either. The emotion swirling in my gut at the sight of her standing in defiance could be grim admiration. Respect, even.

Grown men have shown less resolve—but that doesn't mean I won't treat her the same way I'd treat anyone else who dared to challenge me.

But she's not just anyone, a voice in my skull taunts.

I blink, cutting off any memories that threaten to replay. Shake my head. Blink again. The longer I stare at her, the more unfamiliar she seems.

Just a snake with the face of a ghost.

Someone to crush.

Someone to kill if it comes to that.

She's nothing more than a pawn.

"Use one of your men to get a hold of Fabio Botelli. Now. Tell him to cancel any transfer of any assets to Mischa Stepanov. And inform him that he is no longer on my accounts," I say.

"And then?"

"Then… I have information from Antonio that might come in handy." I can't resist running my hand along my pocket merely to feel the shape of the cell phone there. Hopefully, the son of a bitch was as stupid as he was greedy, and the device holds proof that he was the one behind the attack on the Stepanovs.

"Information?"

Looking up, I meet Luciano's questioning stare with a shrug. "If it proves what I think it does, then we go to Mischa directly."

If only to ask him one question—how much is his daughter's life worth?

It takes a surprising amount of effort to turn off the small bit of my soul that might shy away from this line of thought. What might one woman go for on the black market these days? Add to that listing her hair, and those eyes…

I'd go so far as to assume she'd fetch a nice price, even without the caveat of being Mischa's daughter.

Though you could always kill her now, a part of me warns.

My fingers twitch as I size her up. It would be so easy to grab her.

But I don't.

Instead, I face Luciano and head for the front of the building. "Bring them inside."

"And put them where?" the man snaps. "I know you haven't been here in a while, but we don't exactly keep a dungeon on this property."

I stop for a second, running through the various rooms I remember. "The office," I say finally. "Put them in my old office. The one with no windows."

And, more importantly, no obvious escape.

5

WILLOW

*Y*ou can hate someone so much you create a reflection of them to fixate on. A phantom that takes on a life of its own, dwelling in your head. It mimics the source of the rage, sometimes so perfectly that you confuse the two—until you start to believe that you can predict the actual person. Their every action. Their every move.

You learn them inside out, convinced they'll never be able to hurt you again.

The fantasy merely lulls you into a false sense of security, though. Because the moment you finally meet the real being again in person... Only then do you realize just how unprepared you really are.

Donatello in the flesh is a different animal than who I've spent seven years picturing him as. He ambles toward the nearest building, dressed in a rumpled, bloodstained suit, unsteady on his feet. One good push seems liable to knock him down for good, and yet it's unquestionable the hold he has on those around him who quickly fall into line.

And it's laughable just how wrong my memories have portrayed him—confident, like a cartoon villain, evil, and callous. Someone easily shamed by his past, an opponent I could undoubtedly defeat.

All I had to do was face him once and for all.

The real man, however?

He's broken. Exhausted, disheveled, and battered. With nothing left to lose, he's an even more dangerous foe than the figure who abandoned me all those years ago. It's impossible to confront an opponent who can't even look at you.

I have Mischa Stepanov's daughter as leverage...

As he growled those words, his voice conveyed malice that terrifies me if I let myself dwell on it. It was the same tone someone might use when referring to an object. A toy. Someone not even worthy of the attention an enemy would command. Just a pawn.

Though should I be so surprised?

He never saw me as anything else.

"Get them inside," the gruff baritone draws my attention back to him. Head held high, he shoulders open a metal door and enters the building, clearly expecting everyone to follow. Which they do, almost in sync like some eerie, physical concerto.

My first instinct is to resist and do the only smart thing I can in this instance—*run*. Impatient, my feet twitch against the muddied earth as I scan the nearest line of trees, a few yards away.

I could make it…

But after that? I don't even know which direction I'd head in. We could be miles from the city, let alone my family's manor. Without proper clothing, or a weapon, it could be more dangerous to wander alone. Though, for all I know, Mischa could already be on his way…

"Keep moving," one of the men nearby warns as if reading my mind. He's tall, though I could probably outrun him. Gray eyes enhance his cold expression, however, and with his gun trained on the ground, he's intimidating enough.

Would he shoot an unarmed woman? I can't tell.

Warily, I turn back to the building, weighing the decision to bolt even as I take a step toward it. I shouldn't stay. Every ounce of common sense in me tells me that if I enter beyond those walls, I may never leave.

But my life isn't the only one in danger. A pale figure catches the corner of my eye, putting everything painfully into perspective.

The little girl huddles in the rain, shivering in a white nightgown, her bare feet caked in mud. Among these towering men, she looks even smaller, and a sense of protectiveness finally spurs me into action.

Rather than head for the trees, I inch closer to her and away from any route of escape. Her hand finds mine, and I grip it tight in return. I can't suppress the panic that rises in my chest as the other guards fall into step behind us both. They're silent, watching on with the intensity of dogs herding wayward sheep.

Or wolves.

Staring past them all, I find my attention resolutely drawn back to the figure in the lead. Framed in the doorway, bathed in the glow of fluorescent lighting, he moves like a man apart from the rest of the world, alone on an island unto himself. The slow, deliberate pace of his steps stirs a painful memory.

I used to be so awed by the rare moments when he revealed this side of himself—the leader. The figure my biological father and others deferred to as "boss." Typically, I only saw the playful Donatello who hardly ever raised his voice. One instance, though, sticks out, a time when his subordinate intruded on our game of tag.

My silly Donatello transformed before my eyes, losing the charming grin I knew in favor of a cold, calculating expression. His eyes seemed to darken, revealing a chilling intensity that could reduce the strongest foes to their knees.

In the years since, I used to placate myself with the idea that his wrath couldn't affect me anymore. I could face that piercing stare and never flinch.

I was wrong. His stare wasn't the worst aspect of him to contend with. It's this—watching him walk away, unable to make a sound. Do a thing. Hit him. Fight him. Scream.

It's the second time I've been faced with his retreating back, and my thoughts feel no different than they had years ago. Childish.

The reason? It's even more pathetic. I've been silent my whole life, but no one has ever made me feel invisible. Ignored.

Insignificant.

Focus! I bite my lower lip until I taste copper, desperate to adhere to the mantra Mischa taught me. *Escape.* Nothing more.

I replay his words over and over, but it's as if the child in me is screaming in a way I never could out loud, demanding to be seen. Heard. Acknowledged.

By him.

I dig my nails into my palm in a desperate attempt to stay calm. Regardless, rage infects my entire body until I'm shaking, almost too badly to do the one thing I should in this situation—pay attention.

Beyond Donatello expands a sprawling two-story building with blurred windows, some cracked, and gray metal siding rusted in places. It looks industrial—not a building someone might live in. A warehouse?

Two metal doors guard the entrance, opening onto a wide lobby painted gray with utilitarian tile flooring and fluorescent lights above. The windows are large, but too high up to reach unassisted, and at a glance, no other doors seem to lead outside. Still, I scan every inch of the interior, making a mental map as I go.

Up ahead, two hallways branch off the main space, presumably heading deeper into the building proper. Donatello goes left, but one of the men meets my gaze and inclines his head, indicating the opposite direction.

My fingers throb, crushed by the grip of the little girl. I can't even look at her, but to her credit, she's still standing, smothering her whimpers. When I move, she falls into step beside me as I scour the hallway for anything that could assist during an escape.

The further down the corridor we travel, the more I feel a sense of *déjà vu*. I think I've been here before, maybe as a child. Something about the water-stained ceiling above triggers a memory. Sitting in a corner, counting the square tiles over and over to pass the time…

"This way." This dark-haired man stands further down the hall beside an open doorway. "You'll stay in here."

The room is a small office devoid of windows. A desk cluttered with paperwork dominates the center of the space, illuminated only by the light from the hall. At a glance, there are no exits other than the door.

Warily, I step inside, sensing the girl on my heels. Mischa's advice echoes clearly through my skull—*Lay low. Devise a plan. Keep your head.*

But my head is spinning, filled with mistrustful thoughts. Of Mischa himself. Of *him.*

I still see his expression, mocking me. Taunting me.

Those eyes. That voice.

I'm going to break your wings, little bird…

The thud of the door slamming snaps me back to the present. I hear a lock engage, and the light vanishes, robbing me of the chance to gain a better idea of the layout. In the resulting silence, all I can hear are the soft, smothered whimpers of the girl.

Painful recognition hits like a lance, and I try to resist the memories triggered. Cowering in the presence of Nicolai, knowing that Donatello had left me there. Abandoned me.

My sole consolation is that I'm not bound this time. I can walk. Move.

And I can fully plot my escape.

6

DON

Giovanni thrived on power. I've never met anyone more calculating. You gotta be born with a head for business like that, though he did his best to teach me how to think as he did. Coldly and methodically.

Whether that meant retaliating against a rival by slaughtering their prized thoroughbred, or by showering allies in lavish gifts, each method relied on one detail to succeed—optics. Why get your hands bloody when you could put on a show and get the same point across?

The office he kept here is a case in point testimony to his preferred style. The layout is designed specifically so that whoever steps foot through the door would see themselves first, sweating and nervous, reflected in a huge ass mirror hanging on the wall. To cap off the experience, their next sight would always be the old boss himself, seated behind his desk like a king on a throne.

Talk about fucking *optics*. From that position, he could survey his prey while they grappled with having their own fear thrown back in their face. You couldn't buy a better setup than that.

The mirror is still here all these years later. It's antique, I think, about as old as this entire damn building. Dust coats the surface, blurring the glass, as I approach.

For a second, in my place, I see Giovanni. *A man should do nothing that he can't face himself in the mirror afterward*, the old boss used to boast.

Suffice to say, it didn't temper his cruelty any. In his heyday, he was known to sign a death warrant in the morning, kill a man in the evening, greet his children with a smile and check his teeth without flinching, all before this same mirror.

Every now and again, he'd call a man into his office and quiz them on who they thought they saw in their reflection. *Do you see what I see, Donatello?* he once asked me. *I see a leader. A man who can lead these sons of bitches to greatness if he wants to…*

I look on the surface of the glass now, and I see a shadow of that younger man, covered in blood. My hands shake as I swipe a finger through the grime, bringing the image into clearer focus. It's funny… Giovanni always looked the same to me, no matter what brutal deed he'd just committed. The man I see now, though?

He's a monster.

"So let's see it," a voice prompts from behind me. Luciano, absent his gun. He swaggers through the doorway, but I don't doubt for a second that he's still a threat. The fact that he hasn't shot me is due entirely to what Giovanni praised above all—power.

I don't have much left—but I have enough.

"What's this leverage, *besides* the kidnapped woman?" he demands. "I'm going to pretend you never said her name, by the way. Though, fuck. We're dead anyway. What's pissing off the entire *mafiya* but the cherry on top?"

"Here." I reach into my pocket and deposit the item I took from Antonio on the desk. As I do so, a mirrored version of myself copies the motion. Our eyes meet, but it's like staring at a ghost. Nothing at all is going on behind those dark irises. He's a creature moving solely on impulse, no better than a snake.

"A phone?" Luciano remarks, advancing with an eyebrow raised. His tone draws me back to the present, putting everything into perspective.

Revenge aside, I need a plan. Willow Stepanova is a fitting bit of leverage—but only if I can clear my name first. Doing so relies on finding proof that Antonio ordered the hit. Even if that means trudging through the bastard's cell phone.

Sighing, I take the leather seat behind the desk, leaning my head back.

Fuck, it's been a long damn time since I've sat here. This room was the most spacious of them all, with a view of the lumberyard. Surprisingly, Antonio kept much of the original furniture, down to this desk. I swear, Giovanni's coffee stains still mar the old wood. Mine too. As I run my fingers over them, I spot a name plaque encased in gold. I spin it to reveal the initials A.S. engraved on the front.

Guilt could be the name of the emotion lancing through my skull. Either that or I'm sobering up. Either way, I don't think it's really sunk in until now. Antonio Salvatore, the dumb bastard who couldn't find his ass with a map, was in charge of the *famiglia*. I left him in charge.

Giovanni would rise from the grave if he knew, just to kill me himself.

"Do you hear me, Donatello?" Luciano snarls.

"Huh?" With a wave of my hand, I knock the plaque from the desk and into the wastebasket on the floor beside it. Only then can I look up.

"Your ace in the hole," Luciano continues, nodding toward the device placed before me. "Your secret weapon to get us back on the map is a cell phone?"

"Antonio Salvatore's phone," I correct.

Lowering my gaze, I spot the topmost drawer, and I pull it open. Fucking predictable. A few loose cigars roll across the compartment, and I grab one along with the gold lighter resting nearby.

"It's password-protected," I add before popping the end of the cigar into my mouth, lighting it with a flick of my thumb. It's the good shit, and I drag on the damn thing so hard I nearly suck it down. When I finally exhale, Luciano's watching me, waiting.

"Might have the number of whoever he contacted to target the Stepanovs on it," I say. "Can you find a man to crack it?"

He blinks as if torn between bitching some more or getting down to business. Finally, he shrugs and steps forward, his frown still skeptical. "Antonio wasn't exactly Fort Knox. He tended to use the same password for everything. Let me see…"

He grabs the phone, and it turns on, revealing it's still on its last few bars of battery. After he taps a few keys on the screen, it unlocks with a musical chime. Scoffing, he turns it my way, revealing what the bastard had on the home screen —his own fucking picture.

"I thought so. The passcode was his birthday," Luciano says in disgust. "But I don't see how it helps. Trust me, if Tony had something he could use to get back in anyone's good graces, he would have used it—"

"Can it be tracked?" I ask. If Mischa's already put the pieces together about Antonio's death, it's only a matter of time before he settles on a prime suspect.

Luciano fiddles with the screen. "Not anymore. Blocked the GPS signal. It's still pinging with the cell tower, though as far as I know, you need a warrant to access that kind of shit—"

"Hand it over."

He slaps the phone onto my outstretched palm. "So what now?"

"These contacts," I say over him as I scan the most recent calls. "Any of these sound familiar?"

I hold up the screen to him. Squinting, he reads the first few names, and his eyes narrow.

"Paulie Vanetti," he says. "But... He's a fixer but crazy as fuck. Tony rarely used him. He could be sloppy, and expensive as hell—"

"Sloppy enough to cripple a child and attempt to murder a pregnant woman?" I ask.

"Shit!" His eyes widen, and he shakes his head, whistling through his teeth. "He didn't..."

"So you can see why I paid Tony a visit last night," I say, flicking the cigar to knock the ash on the floor. "The fucker tried to frame me. Did frame me."

He nods. "But I wasn't kidding about expensive. Likes to be paid upfront too. If you can't tell, Tony liked to play the big shot, but he couldn't amass that kind of cash on a whim. If he was working with Paulie, you can bet your ass someone else was footing the bill."

"Makes sense," I say.

It isn't unheard of for a bigger player to cover his tracks behind a patsy. If Antonio needed cash, how badly? Badly enough to play the role of a puppet. The real question is, who would have the balls to put him up to it...

I've been out of the game for a long damn time, but I doubt either the Saleris or any of the local gangs would have the capital to pull something like this off. An outside player?

"This Paulie," I say. "You know where to find him?"

He shrugs, crossing his arms. "No, but you have his number. Call him."

I weigh the benefits of doing so now. "Any other day, that might sound like a setup. Think he might be expecting my call?"

"Fuck me." Luciano laughs, raising his hands in mock defeat. "I doubt he knows Tony's dead, if that's what you mean. We've kept it under wraps, so far. Kept the staff from his house. Covered for any meetings he had today. Just until we can come to...an arrangement."

"You've bought time," I say, impressed despite myself. Maybe they all aren't as dumb as Antonio.

"At least a day, maybe two tops," he says, nodding. "The boys know to stick around. No one comes in. No one goes out."

I know what he has the tact not to say—he's done it for morale. To keep what little is left of the *famiglia* from scattering and to stave off any vultures who might come sniffing around whatever Antonio left behind.

If I were a gloating man, I'd state the obvious. As fate would have it, my old outfit needs me just as much as I need it.

"Call him," I suggest. "On Antonio's behalf. See if you can lure him here. Discreetly. And do what you can to keep the tragic news from breaking a while longer."

"And what will you do?" he demands. "I can only buy us another day at most. Someone will notice when Antonio isn't swaggering around town, throwing money left and right. And I'm sure he kept me out of the loop on many of his dealings."

"Me?" I turn my head just enough to see myself in that damn mirror. The longer I stare, the less I recognize the figure looking back. If Vin could see me now, he'd make some dumbass quip. *"You look like hell, Uncle Don. Sober isn't a good look on you. I'd stick to the booze..."*

God, that kid would have never made it past Giovanni's doorstep. The old man would have smelled the goodness on him. Rather than fight, Vin's primary instinct in any situation was to crack a joke. Aim for a laugh. Where some men saw only power and control, Vin saw a world in need of saving.

But when it came down to it, I couldn't even save him. Hell, I can't even face knowing if he's still alive...

"Don?" Luciano waves his hand in front of my face. "You with me, here?"

While dragging on the cigar, I stare down at my own hands, flexing them in and out of fists. These fingers can kill. Maim. Bleed. Yet, when it came down to it, they couldn't even feel Vin's neck for a fucking pulse.

I reach over and fish Antonio's name plaque from the trash and use it as a makeshift ashtray, setting the cigar on top of it.

"Don?" Luciano prods.

"Give me a minute," I say, flattening my palms over the armrests of the chair.

He scoffs. "Because we have all the time in the fucking world to just sit around and—"

"That wasn't a request. A minute."

He holds my gaze for only a second before turning on his heel. "You've got it. Take your minute. I'll go feed our 'guests,' and then contemplate if I've just cosigned the entire *famiglia* to the whims of a fucking madman."

He slams the door while I lift the cell phone and type out a number by heart. Like a fucking coward, I still hesitate before finally starting the call.

Unsurprisingly, it's answered after only one ring. "Botelli."

I suck in a breath at the sound of that voice. He sounds so fucking old. Not only that, but I can tell he's been chain-smoking from the hoarseness. I feel like I'm channeling Vin as I say, "You need a drink, Fab."

"Don?" He curses, and a wave of commotion comes from the other end as if he just knocked something over. "Fuck! Mary Mother of God. Where are you? Do you know how fucking worried I've been? What the hell were you thinking, sending some punk ass to inform me I'm off your accounts. You owe me more than that—"

"I know. I know," I snap. Still, I can't escape the shame I feel like a bitch slap. I've never heard him this fucking frantic. "Just, please... Tell me how Vin is."

"Vin... He's still alive," he says hoarsely. "But I won't lie to you, Donatello. He needs more care than I can provide him. He needs *you*."

"More care?" My head is spinning. "I thought you had a doctor."

"I do," he says. "But he needs a safe facility to operate in, and a skilled staff—more people than I can easily blackmail. Mischa and his allies are on red alert. I know they're tracking me. Hell, I'm surprised they haven't dragged me before him by now, thinking I know your whereabouts."

"Fuck! Have they tried an attack?" I ask, already rising to my feet. What the hell could I do from here? I don't know. But there has to be something. Anything.

"Not yet," he says cautiously. "But he's commandeered the best hospital in the city for his own family. My doctor can keep him alive, but it will be hard to get Vin the care he needs otherwise."

"The hospital…" There's only one nearby worth going to. Mercy, I think, is the name. If Mischa has it on lockdown, there's no way in hell they'd admit a Vanici. Not to mention it's in the heart of Saleri territory. Even as the cons mount up, I know there isn't another option. "I'll find a way to get him there."

"Fine," Fabio says absently. "But you know what he requires the most? An uncle who isn't riling up the *mafiya*, doing God knows what else… Don—" His tone shifts as if he suddenly realized something. "This isn't your number. Where are you calling from—"

"If I can get you a better facility. Would it change anything?"

I know deep down it won't. I'm torturing myself, playing with hope. Fuck, it's all I can do.

"Don… I… It might," he admits. "But where are you? If the worst does come to pass, he needs you here."

"You'll be hearing from me as to when you can move him," I say, barely able to keep up with the plan forming in my head. If I can convince Mischa to allow Vin into the hospital, fuck anything else. I'll beg the man on my knees if I have to.

But I don't. Not if I can leverage a worthwhile bargaining chip.

"Wait for my call, Fab. Until then, you lay low. Put an extra security detail on yourself. I mean it. I'll be in touch when I can." I don't realize I'm setting the phone down until I hear Fab's voice, distorted from the other end of it. "Don, wait!"

I hang up and wind up hunched over the desk, my face in my hands. The terms of the game have changed again.

If I can save Vin's life...

I'll do whatever it takes.

Even if it means making a deal with the devil himself.

Eyeing the door, I call out, "Luciano?"

He reenters the room not even a second later, giving credibility to the idea he might have been listening in this whole fucking time.

Ignoring the suspicion, I ask, "Is the old apartment still available?"

He nods. "Tony didn't use it much, though."

Because unlike Giovanni, Antonio didn't give a shit about the energy and forethought it takes to truly run the *famiglia*. Giovanni warned me before I even took over, the toll such a mantle could take on a man.

"This fucking apartment? Get used to it. You'll see these sheets more than any other property you own. They'll start to feel more familiar than your own wife's body does at night."

And he was right. The title as the leader—and the responsibility that came with it—took me from Olivia well before she died.

"Don? Where are you going?" Luciano demands as I stand, circling the desk with my back to my reflection.

I shrug. "I need to shower."

He laughs, watching me with an incredulous expression. "You're on the verge of war with the *mafiya* who, by the way, outnumber us three to one. You've murdered Antonio, who, while a dick, still controlled more men than you have on your own. All of that and you just decide to—"

"Shower? Yes." I rake my hand through my hair and grimace as my fingers come away slick. "See if you can find me some clothes."

"Should I order you some coffee while I'm at it? Some donuts for the boys? We might as well be well refreshed, right? Can I get you anything else this fine evening?"

I nod. "I want that fixer. Now. If not tonight, then by tomorrow."

He sighs, stroking his chin. "The man's hard to get a hold of—"

"Is that too difficult for you?"

He shakes his head. "I'll send a message through Tony's phone. That might lure him here, if he thinks his payment might be in question. What is another fucking piss poor decision to cap off my life? But first, I need to know your plan. Ransom the girl to Mischa? He'd send an army on your head before you could finish naming your price.

Besides, what's to stop me from killing you now and trying that idiotic plan myself?"

He has a point. Though Giovanni liked his mirror for more than one reason. From this position, you had a clear view of the man standing before you. Namely when they're shuffling nervously from foot to foot despite the bravado in their voice.

"You don't have the balls," I point out. "Besides, I have a better idea than that. Do you want me to say the customary words? Fine," I tell him. "Trust me. But before you go off, I need you to do one last thing."

He hesitates for seconds before finally answering. "What?"

"Make sure no one else so much as looks at the girl. She's mine." My voice breaks over that fucking word. I'm disgusted to hear it out loud—and not for the first time either.

She's mine in the only sense that matters. *My* stolen toy to barter with. Mine to break.

A shower can wait. I should see her first.

"Should I be alarmed by your plans for her?" Luciano wonders, his eyes on my face.

I'm startled by the chuckle that escapes my throat. It almost sounds genuinely amused. When I picture my "plans" for the woman secured somewhere within this very building…

They're anything but humorous.

"Not if you don't want to end up like Antonio," I tell Luciano.

His laugh sounds more strained this time. "Just don't make a mess. You hurt her; you deal with her. I told Antonio the same damn thing with his little flings. We aren't the Saleris."

"You can sleep free of nightmares," I assure him. "Put the word out to the rest of your men—only I can touch her. See her. Smell her. Breathe the same air. No one else. No one else so much as enters the room she's in. Are we understood?"

"Very," he says tersely. "They've been fed for now. As for *your* woman…she's beautiful," he adds on his way out of the office. "But I've learned that the beautiful ones bring the most trouble."

He doesn't even know half of the trouble this woman could bring.

On the other hand, if I could trade her life for Vin's, I'd crawl on my knees to do so—nothing else should matter. A smart man would keep her hidden and bide his time to make a deal.

There's no point in seeing her face to face. Watching her squirm. Wanting to know why the hell she came back at all.

Only a fool would confront her now.

But the truth as it's kept, I've done worse. Once, years ago…I had to convince myself to do the unthinkable. Feed myself lies. Wallow in the horrific aftermath with the hopes that one day I might atone for it.

There is no prayer for atonement now.

No expectation of forgiveness.

After these long, cold years, I've made peace with who I am.

Whatever her reason for coming back, this woman should face that man.

If only to learn once and for all, never to challenge him again.

7

EVGENI

*M*ercs aren't known for being picky when it comes to employment—that being said, few would work for Mischa Stepanov willingly. Ignoring our little spat from this morning, I can see why some might hesitate.

The pay is decent enough. While fearsome, I've had employers with a far worse reputation. Even the *mafiya's* dubious line of business would give few pause. Regardless, any guard worth his salt would avoid the Stepanovs for one reason, and one reason only.

Self-preservation.

A good job should be as uncomplicated as possible. Most are. No amount of money is worth more than that. You study the target. You study your employer even more. You get the money and come out on top always.

Mischa Stepanov, however, guards his secrets as closely as his family. In a word? The man is the definition of *complicated.*

In six years, I've never understood him, nor his past fully. Even the murky origins of his seemingly happy family are shrouded in secrecy—like the paternity of his firstborn son, and that of Willow, his adopted daughter. Logic dictates that those details shouldn't matter as long as I can do my job and do it well.

And they haven't.

Until now.

I suppose I can only blame myself for staying, though, to be fair, the job has been relatively boring prior to a week ago.

Donatello Vanici has brought an avalanche of drama upon the normally quiet household.

The aftermath of his attack on the Stepanovs has repercussions reaching far beyond the manor's limits. With Willow's disappearance thrown into the mix, our already strained resources have been pushed to their breaking point. Assigning me here could be interpreted as Mischa aiming to get me out of his hair, my expertise aside—but I'm not so petty as to ignore the bigger picture.

Protecting his wife is just as big a priority to him. The fact that he would station me here is a sign of trust, especially considering the job itself is no easy task. A squat four-story complex on the city's outskirts, Mercy hospital is a challenge within itself to secure—including the private wing and dedicated team of staff commandeered by the Stepanovs.

Nearly an hour from the manor, the location isn't ideal—in the heart of Saleri territory—and there is always a possibility that anyone with money and power can buy a guard or doctor to their side. All it takes is one faulty piece to topple a house of cards.

With that in mind, I take my time circling the building's perimeter as the evening progresses, scanning the outside for any potential areas of breach. This armored van is one of four, each patrolling a different section of the parking lot. It's mind-numbing work in comparison to the frantic search taking place for Willow. I don't doubt they'll find her; it's only a matter of when.

And how much of her will be left when they finally do…

The thought gnaws at my focus, distracting me from the monotonous task at hand. While uneventful, it's important given the week's recent events. The last thing the Stepanovs need is another attack to go unnoticed.

Blinking, I force my attention through the passenger window of the patrol van, inspecting the horizon. A light rain drenches the landscape, rendering the outer complex virtually deserted—though even a torrential storm wouldn't stop anyone determined enough to mount an attack.

"All clear, sir," the man in the driver's seat says. Mario, one of my best, hand-recruited after joining the manor's retinue. He was a damn good informant in a previous life, capable of finding dirt on anyone with only a name to go off and little else.

Given Donatello Vanici's pervasive reputation, I suspect finding information on him would be child's play. If I had the time, I'd delve into the mystery myself. As it stands, there's only so much I can do on my own.

"Ev?" Mario prompts. "Did you want to go around again before heading in?"

I wrestle with indecision for only a heartbeat. His primary focus should be Mrs. Stepanova—nothing else. Still, no one can garner better intel.

Willow's life is well worth the risk.

Placing my hand on his shoulder, I incline my head, prompting him to switch off the headset affixed to his ear, linking our position with the other six guards spread throughout the perimeter.

"Sir?" he asks, his expression unreadable in the dark.

Sighing, I cut right to the point. "I need you to do something for me, but we keep this between us. Understood?"

He nods. "I hear you."

"Here—" I reach into my pocket, retrieving a handful of rolled bills that I place in his hand. "I want everything you can get me on Donatello Vanici and the *famiglia*. Skip the basics. I know the surface level information, but there has to be more."

"Such as...?"

I exhale in a rush. Fuck it. "I want to know if he ordered the hit on the Stepanovs, or if someone else did."

"Shit." Mario whistles through his teeth, cagily eyeing the money. "Ev, if you're asking what I think you are, though I have to ask... Why go through me?"

"Mr. Stepanov has enough to worry about," I say, opening the door to the van. A cool wind throws the rain in my face like a bracing slap. In the end, the shock only helps solidify my decision. "I'll take the risk if anything comes of it. Think of it as nothing more than classic intel."

He nods, but I can tell from his raised eyebrow alone that he doesn't buy the explanation. "Anything else? The more specific, the better."

I grit my teeth, again weighing the risks. Willow's face appears in my mind, quashing any remaining doubt. Mischa may have barred me from the search party, but there are other ways I can assist. After all, it's better to ask for forgiveness than for permission.

"I especially want to know if Vanici ever had any dealings with a young girl," I say.

He grunts in surprise but hides it well. As long as we've both been in the business, nothing should shock us when it comes to the proclivities of men with power.

"How young we talking?"

"Any age. Any type of relationship. Give me whatever you can. I'll pay the price."

In more ways than one, if Mischa takes offense to my little quest for intel—a barrier I'll deal with later.

"On it," Mario says, nodding. "Otherwise, the birdcage is secure. The dove is resting. No update from the doctors as of yet. Kristoph is on watch. Nothing else to report from my end."

"Good," I reply, switching to a normal tone. "What about from base?"

He shakes his head with a sigh. "I've heard nothing from the Wolf—" our codename for Mischa. "But if anything major goes down, I'll phone you from here."

"Right." I step out, drawing my hood low, though I'm sure Mario caught my expression anyway. I can't shake the irritation that I've been shoved to the sidelines for a reason. Mischa's private security is composed of some of the best men I know—many of them hand-picked by my recommendations. Even so, I'd go so far as to say that none of them care for Willow more than me. Why? It's an entirely selfish reason—I'm the only one with a personal investment in her future.

Once she's safe and sound, living out her sheltered life as a pianist, mine will finally mean something. What's the word for it? Redemption.

I refuse to stand by as another innocent life is destroyed. Not this time.

"You okay, Ev?"

I blink to find Mario staring at me. "Yeah," I say. "I'm fine."

"Well, take care, then." He rolls his window up, and I watch him drive off, presumably to repeat the same route until I return.

Alone, I enter the building through a locked stairwell that leads directly to Mrs. Stepanova's wing. A key card gives me access, one of a few assigned to this wing. Even the hospital's regular staff can't enter these halls unaccompanied.

It's a strict level of security well warranted by the number of *mafiya* enemies who might be looking to make their mark. Suspects who come to mind include Vanici and the *famiglia* or their associates.

All outfits not necessarily helmed by a woman.

The second I enter the hallway, my nostrils twitch, catching a whiff of floral fragrance. Alarm shoots down my spine, setting every nerve on alert as I inhale again. This smell...

It violates the hospital's strict ban on perfume, for one. Not only that, but this fragrance is rich, definitely expensive, reminding me of the high class escorts an old client of mine used to cycle in and out of his home regularly.

The telltale scent of a viper.

Warily, I palm my weapon as I ascend the stairs. A pair of double doors open onto a narrow hall, accessible by only the medical staff assigned to Mrs. Stepanova and her security detail. As expected, only one man stands positioned near the entrance, his stance alert.

"Did you let anyone past?" I ask as I approach.

He shoots me an odd look, alarmed by my tone. "No one. I mean… Just a doctor."

"A doctor? I thought the last update was earlier this morning," I say. "Which one?"

He eyes his clipboard. "Uh… Rachel Main."

The OBGYN assigned to Mrs. Stepanova's case. A woman in her forties who usually visits in the morning. Never have I heard of her making an evening visit.

And I definitely don't recall her wearing perfume.

"You didn't call to confirm the visit with anyone?" I ask as the man sputters. "Has there been a change in Mrs. Stepanova's condition?"

"No… But—"

"Describe this doctor."

He squints before licking his lips thoughtfully. "Blond. Mid-thirties, I think. Attractive."

"Shit." I push past him, sensing the unease in my gut fester.

"She had a badge, sir." His voice chases me down the hallway. "Her name was on the list—"

"Stay back," I snap over my shoulder. "Get ready to call for backup if I shout for it." Without looking to see if he obeys,

I round the doorway of Mrs. Stepanova's room and instantly feel my eyes narrow.

The woman sitting beside the lone hospital bed lacks the stoic demeanor of the other medical professionals I've interacted with. With her back to me, she leans over the bedside, her golden hair falling freely down her shoulders. She doesn't seem to notice or care as I approach the foot of the bed. A glance at the head of the bed reveals Mrs. Stepanova resting, seemingly unharmed apart from the tubes and medical equipment attached to her at all ends.

As for her visitor, other than a white lab coat, the woman's resemblance to Dr. Main is tentative at best.

"Turn around," I demand. "Keep your hands where I can see them and tell me your name."

Her laugh catches me off guard. Warm and icy at the same time.

"Now," I insist, pulling my gun from the holster at my hip. "Slowly."

Another laugh teases the air as she swivels to face me, her head cocked.

I don't recognize her.

As relayed, she's attractive, with bright blue eyes and delicate features—but it's those features that alarm me. Confuse. Those eyes and that mouth don't belong to her, but the woman lying in the bed behind her. It's an uncanny resemblance, and I have to eye Mrs. Stepanova again, just to make sure they aren't one and the same.

"Who are you?" I ask the stranger.

She shrugs. "Just a visitor."

Her voice is nothing like Mrs. Stepanova's, lacking any hint of sweetness. It's a low, husky purr like that of a cat. The accent is crisper, reminding me again of those pricey escorts. They sounded the same way, tailored to mimic the posh lilt of the aristocratic.

Either way, she definitely doesn't belong here. A decoy, perhaps, sent by Vanici? A round of questioning should give me my answer.

I reach for my headset, aiming to contact Mario. To the woman, I say, "I'm going to have to escort you out."

She smiles, but something in the expression makes my finger still, poised to strike the call button. Those curled red lips portray confidence at a glance—at least to anyone not skilled enough to see her throat quivering in the same motion.

Not exactly the response of a trained assassin or even an escort. Before I can pursue the thought further, she stands and stalks forward. Were she anyone else, I'd have my gun trained on her in seconds.

For whatever reason, I don't move. Perhaps it's the tilt to her head, desperate to convey bravado—but her hand shakes, though she runs it along her hip to disguise the motion. Up close, it's apparent that she stole the lab coat. It's large on her, drawn partially closed over a red dress that pairs with her heels. She's as slight as Mrs. Stepanova, and I think I can pinpoint why my usual reflexes are slow to deploy.

Fuck, they could be twins.

"I'm leaving," she says in that husky purr, slipping past me unchallenged. "Though what has the world come to when a woman can't even see her own sister?"

"Sister?" I demand, spinning to keep her in view.

She doesn't head for—what should be—the sole entrance to the suite. Instead, she heads for a service staircase, opening it quickly.

"Who the hell are you?"

She laughs, but light on her feet, she darts through the doorway, slamming it shut before I can reach her. Through the metal comes a muffled taunt, "My name is Briar Winthorp."

I tug the handle, hissing to find it locked. She must have found some way to circumvent the security—a deficit on my part. I reach for the headset again, prepared to send up the alarm and alert the rest of the team about the breach.

My finger twitches against the call button, prepared to strike it. Instead, I find myself returning to Mrs. Stepanova's room. She's breathing, her vital signs seemingly stabilized, not a hair out of place.

I could raise the alarm and only heighten Mischa's paranoia.

Or do my job and handle the situation for now.

It takes just seconds to decide. I make a mental note to switch the guard, but I leave to take my post without calling anyone else.

Whoever the stranger is, I'm sure I can handle her alone.

In any way necessary.

8

WILLOW

I never realized how disorienting darkness alone can be. It's endless. Impenetrable. Terrifying. Without a clock or even a view of the sky, I'm all but blind. Very few sounds reach this room to give me any clue otherwise. There are no footsteps. No voices, either.

No way to track the passage of time. Apart from the gray-eyed man appearing briefly to deliver a tray of food—sandwiches we ate in the dark—we haven't been disturbed by anyone.

Forget the relief I felt before. I'd rather be bound if only to have *some* connection to the outside world. My only sense of direction comes from running my palms along whatever I can reach. A smooth wall. Gritty floor. Over and over, I retrace my steps from this narrow corner to the sole door.

There's no use trying to escape this way. The material is too solid to kick through or dent, and the lock too sturdy to pick. Though getting it open would only solve half of the equation.

The real key to winning any battle is to anticipate your enemy—and therein lies the problem—I know nothing about this Donatello. I can't predict him. Can't anticipate him.

So instead, I aimlessly wander through the dark as my mind races. Mischa would snarl in anger if he saw me now. I can clearly envision what he'd say—*Don't sit quietly waiting for your throat to be cut! Find a way. Any way.*

Guilt stabs through my chest whenever I try to imagine what he might be doing. I'm sure they've discovered my absence by now. Does he know how to find me? Does he even want to?

My knee strikes something hard enough to knock me off my feet, interrupting the chain of thought. Flailing, I scramble for something sturdy enough to break my fall. I find it in a firm material that feels flat. Immovable. Like wood.

The desk, I think. It's large, overflowing with paperwork. Letters. Stacks of documents. In the absence of light, they have no purpose. Still, I feel through the various materials, searching for a lamp. My fingers brush something rigid instead, partially hidden beneath a sheet of paper. Whatever it is, it's hard. Metal. Thin. A letter opener?

Hopeful, I swipe my finger along the edge. It's not sharp, but pointed enough to serve as a weapon anyway. Tucking it against my palm, I retreat to my previous position.

A soft cough breaks the heavy silence, and I stiffen, heart in my throat. That's right…

I'm not alone. The girl is on the opposite end of the room, huddled against the wall, only discernable by her stark white nightgown. Another cough and a muffled whimper consist of the few sounds she's made since we came here.

My throat aches with the weight of my silence. I've never been so acutely aware of my own limitations until now. I wish I could say anything, if only to comfort her. Instead, I head in her direction, reaching out until my fingertips hit warm skin. Almost instantly, a small hand finds mine, gripping tightly, and I sink down beside her.

She seems so young. Too young.

Much like another little girl who, if she had a voice, might have cried in a moment like this. Robbed of sound, all she could do was wait in the dark at the hands of a stranger as a million different thoughts crossed her mind.

Fear of what might happen next.

Disbelief.

Hate for the man who ruined her innocence and plunged her into chaos.

In the end, that little girl was spared the worst fate imaginable, rescued by an unlikely source, Mischa Stepanov.

For all I know, that same man could be on his way here now. God, I hope he is.

Straining my ears, I wait for any sound. Any sign of hope.

When none comes, my thoughts turn darker. I think I've stopped myself from reliving that moment until now—when Eli and Ellen returned to the manor in a bloodstained van, barely conscious. Despair is a noose around my neck at the thought that they could have died then. Still might…

And I wouldn't even know, because I decided to run right to the very man who might have hurt them. Mischa thought as much. A good, loyal daughter would trust his judgment. Trust him.

Not the memory of a man who no longer exists. A figure who, even at his worst, could never commit that kind of crime.

Though the girl beside me is proof enough of how very wrong I could be.

I don't know how long we sit like this before footsteps finally pierce the quiet, advancing toward this room. That fragile hope floods my chest, only to quickly die at the cadence of the figure's walk—slow. Unsteady. Heavy—not Mischa's.

Paces from the room, the steps stall, and my heart stutters. Tension teases the air, enhancing every passing second until…

A sharp sound breaks the quiet, alarmingly close. The doorknob? I crane my neck, blinking until I swear I can see it. Turning. Slowly, slowly…

The door itself opens without warning, ushering in a sliver of blinding light.

I blink rapidly, fighting to take in whatever I can. A blurred shape. A person?

"You," he says, dispelling the mystery. That gruff voice is unmistakable. "Come."

He walks away, but I don't budge from my seated position. The light from the hall is enough to illuminate this small corner. Beside me, the girl watches on, her eyes wide as her tiny fingers grip mine tighter.

Our visitor is already gone from what I can tell, his steps advancing away. For a second, I contemplate running, taking my chance now. Cautiously, I rise to my feet, pulling the girl with me, gripping the letter opener in my free hand. We creep forward, but with one look past the doorway, I realize the folly of running. The hallway beyond this room forks into two, but both exits are dominated by one man standing with his back to me.

My heart pangs at the sight of him. He hasn't changed, even though it must be hours since he brought us here. He's still wearing the same filthy suit, his appearance even more haggard. Disheveled. Going off the slow, heavy way he moves, I bet I could outrun him, even with the girl in tow.

Before I can go as much as a step, he inclines his head, the warning clear. *Don't even try it.* As if confident I won't, he continues down the left-hand hallway at that deliberate pace.

I grit my teeth, torn between logic and impulse. The further away he moves, the clearer my way becomes. From what I remember, the main entrance is through the right, and I flick my gaze in that direction.

"Don't." His voice is so soft, not even a shout, barely audible.

I go still regardless.

"Don't run. You wouldn't make it far," he adds.

I swallow hard. The threat isn't what makes me stop short. It's his tone, as chilling as a smattering of off notes on a piano. There was no inflection. No passion—just malice. The way I figure a shark would taunt a bobbing, bleeding fish in its orbit.

He's all but daring me to run, if only so he can give chase.

Because *that's* what he really wants.

Despite knowing that, it takes everything I have not to bolt anyway. It's painful, achievable only by digging my bare heels into the cool tile flooring as hard as I can. Then I loosen my grip on the girl and guide her back into the room, shutting the door behind her.

"Come," Donatello warns, still paces away. Patiently, he waited until now merely to drive one point home.

We're alone. My throat goes dry at the realization. Even with the distance between us, I notice the small details I hadn't been aware of before. Like the fact that I'm wearing only a thin cotton dress. My hair feels slick, and the stench of lighter fluid itches my nostrils with every breath. As much as I want to deny the fear seeping through my veins, I can't.

All I have against him is a dull secretary's tool.

He has…time. It looms, as threatening as any weapon whenever I look at him. That face, the catalyst of so many memories. His hands. Even his steps trigger a painful recollection.

Luckily, pride is a bitter antidote to his poison, potent enough that I can hold my head high and take a step toward him, unaffected. Another. Another.

I can't tell if he's moving too slowly or I'm just gaining on him too quickly, leaving myself little time to take notice of our surroundings like I should.

Breathing deeply, I try to focus, eyeing the length of the corridor. There are no exits within easy distance of the room we're being kept in. Still no windows, either. The only markers we pass are the fluorescent lightbulbs mounted in the ceiling above, casting swaths of darkness that swallow Donatello the further he goes.

Whether due to his intent or mine, the distance between us lengthens, putting me well beyond his reach. Again, the urge to run rises up. I could always fight. Overpower him.

The letter opener is still in my grasp. My pulse surges as I glance down, spotting the delicate strip of silver peeking between my fingers. It could be a useful weapon.

Even so, I don't move to brandish it. Yet. Sweat drips down my spine as I keep walking, tucking the weapon against my skirt.

I almost miss the moment he stops, disappearing through a doorway.

I have a second to glance inside before my toes brush the threshold after him. It's small. Narrow. We're even more secluded from the others, judging from how little sound reaches here—just the buzzing of electricity feeding the lights above.

The room itself doesn't contain much, obscuring his reason for bringing me here. There is a couch in the corner, composed of battered brown leather. A small table is across from it, positioned before a sight that makes fresh hope rise up my throat—dust-streaked windows overlooking a sea of trees. *Finally.* It's dusk, I think. Early evening? Apart from the glimpse of moonlight, the windows themselves look wide enough to break or escape from.

I only need a chance...

"Look at me."

His voice casts a spell over my body, banishing any thought of escape. My limbs jerk, maneuvering without input from my brain. Against my own will, my head swivels, bringing into focus the lone figure standing near the center of the room.

Up this close, it's even more stark how different he is from the man in my memories. Different from the figure I faced just a few days ago, even—a rival who barged into my family home under the pretense of attending my debutante ball.

This Donatello does nothing to disguise who he is at his core. A tortured man. A bleeding man. An empty soul.

"I want to hear you say it..." He trails off, laughing to himself.

The coldness of the wall against my back is a shock before I even register backing away—but I didn't move toward the doorway like I should. A few feet of space separate me from it, more than enough for him to cover in a single stride. I'm trapped as he moves to block my only path.

"I want to see it on your face for myself," he says, amending his request. "The happiness. The satisfaction. After all, this is what you wanted, isn't it?"

His stress on that word paints a morbid picture. *This.* Vincenzo dead, and my father at his throat.

Is it?

The question is so callous I can't even decide how I feel. Insulted? Though if I had to ask myself a better question, I doubt I could answer it either—why did I leave my home in the middle of the night to find him? Why did I go to Havienna alone? Why?

My head hurts, so rather than think, I watch him. It's surprisingly easy to meet his gaze without flinching, as long as there's a sizable distance between us. Every yard brings clarity. Bravado. I can comfort myself with the lie that he won't touch me.

He won't...

"You hate me, fine. I deserve it," he admits in a growl. "But Vincenzo? Did he deserve what your father did to him? A bullet to the fucking head. Did he deserve that?"

I look away, my face on fire. It's a cruel line of attack, but I humor it with an honest answer, anyway, at least to myself. *No.* Vin didn't deserve what happened to him.

While my captor has been vague as to the details, I can guess. Mischa, assuming Donatello was behind the assault on Ellen and Eli, attacked him out of revenge. Sweet Vincenzo with the crooked glasses and wry smile...

It's hard to even fathom that he might be dead. Donatello's betrayal darkened some memories of my past, but not all of them. The ones starring Vin still stand out, filled with mirth and warmth, untouched by hate. Tears prickle my eyes at the thought of them. My old birthday parties. Our petty squabbles that always ended amicably in the end. All of those years we spent together, playing as closely as any real siblings...

It kills me that Mischa could have been responsible for what happened to him—but another emotion quickly seeps into my chest, dulling the pain. Anger. It's a soothing balm that eases my own guilt, directed solely at the man before me.

Vincenzo's death or otherwise isn't my fault.

And only a coward would use that to negate everything else.

"Ah, little hellcat…" Donatello cocks his head as a low, gravelly sound resonates through his throat. A laugh? Or a pained groan. "You think I'm pathetic for mentioning him." He nods as if I spoke out loud, and I can't help it. My eyes swivel toward him narrowed with alarm.

The knowing tilt to his head is the same way he used to look years ago, while accusing me of ignoring a chore or stealing a treat with no other shred of evidence. He only had to see my face and know. To him, I always was an open book.

"Oh yes." He laughs again. "You're brave, I'll give you that. But while you may be silent, your face alone is enough to —" He breaks off, as his expression shifts too quickly for me to track. Horrified? He staggers as if struck, his eyes widening and narrowing in quick succession. When I finally peg the emotion twisting his mouth into a snarl, it's already too late.

Rage.

The next second, he's across the room, his outstretched fingers aiming for my throat. I go rigid. The air in my lungs escapes in a single gasp, and all I can do is watch him.

And wait.

His anger is a wild, ravaging thing, almost musical in nature. The creeping crescendo of a haunting melody that comes from nowhere, as much as a surprise to the person performing the piece as it is to the listener. There is no rhyme or reason to it.

Just pure violent emotion.

"Your face…" His chest heaves as he flicks my chin with the pad of his thumb. I flinch, but he does it again, sloppily, scraping delicate flesh with his nail. And again, applying more and more pressure until I finally meet his gaze.

His eyes flicker as if he's reading my thoughts word for word. I'm *that* vulnerable to him.

"Fuck…" He inhales through his teeth as a realization dawns over his face, transforming the frown into a gaping, formless shape. "I thought you might have done it out of hate. Implicated me on purpose. All for revenge. Revenge. Revenge!" His voice grows more bellicose with every word, bellowing throughout the room untamed. The look in his eyes is what sends ice through my veins, though. Wide, staring, angry, flashing irises, and dilated pupils. It's like he's demanding something from me. Pleading for it.

But I can't give it. Even worse, my own eyes water in response, confusing me further. I don't know what he wants.

"But it wasn't that, was it?" The pad of his finger shakes, grazing over my mouth. He presses hard against my bottom lip, bringing his taste against my tongue. Blood, and violence, and accelerant. A cough rips up my throat, silenced as he slams his palm against my mouth entirely, sealing it shut.

"You don't want revenge," he croaks, seemingly alarmed by the fact. "No. No... You don't even know what you want, do you? You're just a child. You're just a fucking child. *Fuck*!"

He lets me go, bracing himself against the nearest wall. His shoulders heave, his body shaking, a low sound ripping from his throat. At first...

I think it's sobbing—until I catch that telltale wavering note that identifies it for what it really is. Laughing. Uncontrolled, hysterical laughing.

"You're a little girl in a world of wolves," he grates in between the unstable notes. "Fuck. You probably don't even know why you came to me, do you? For a pat on the head? A goodnight kiss? I fucking sold you!"

He whirls around, brandishing a fist, his face so wet I assume he's found more lighter fluid at first, dousing himself in it. But no...

The longer I stare, the more the harsh fluorescents reflect off the signature droplets. Tears. They mirror my own. Burning, hot, painful tears that rake down my cheeks unchecked like slashing claws.

"Fuck, what did you expect from me?" he demands, slamming a fist against the wall. His knuckles leave scarlet smears on the white paint, a vibrant illustration of what he's capable of. "What? The truth? Fine."

The look in his eye warns that it's the last thing I want. An irrational sensation washes over me. Like I'd scream if I could. Slam my hands over my ears. Anything to make him stop.

I can't hear this.

Regardless, he says it. "I sold you for ten thousand dollars. Did you know that?"

I didn't, and I'm sure my expression reveals as much. He could have punched me, and I doubt my reaction would be any different. Lips parting, breathing heavy and broken. The amount stings, thrown in my face as though it were pennies. Change. A worthless sum that mattered little in the end.

Because it didn't.

"I didn't fucking care how much," he adds to twist the knife. "I didn't. I think I spent it on a horse race or some shit. *That* was your worth to me. It could have been ten dollars, and I still would have done it. You meant that little to me."

And it's the truth. His cold stare proves it even before he says the words, "I just wanted you gone. But you were lucky... Mischa," he spits out the name. "He gave you the life I never could." His red eyes sweep over me, and he sighs, swaying on his feet. "He kept you sheltered, Safiya. Sheltered and innocent with no fucking clue as to the way the world works. You thought you could see me again and what?"

He throws his arms out as if expecting the answer to fall from the sky.

"That everything would magically right itself? You'd get your revenge and ease the hole in your fucking heart? No. No..." He shakes his head with pity—but the worst realization creeps in as he sighs again. It's genuine. Eyes downcast, he says, "No, Safiya. The world doesn't work like that. You need to go home. Go back to your pretty little life and forget that you ever left that cage. You belong there."

There, safe in Mischa's beautiful family, where I only ever felt out of place. A misfit dove in a world of swans. I try to bat the thought away—the same way I have for seven damn years. But I can't. The truth claws at my chest until I finally acknowledge it—I only ever felt safe with him. Only felt like I ever belonged at Havienna.

And he knows that.

He's relishing in it, denying me the home I never really had.

Sending me away now isn't mercy. It's a pathetic way to assuage his guilt. Mischa's manor is far enough away from him where I can safely be ignored. Thrown away a second time. Branded with a word that stings worse than *tigre,* or *hellcat,* or even a *bitch* he could hate.

Child.

Someone too pitiful to fit in his world.

An innocent too stupid for him to acknowledge.

A ghost.

"I'm sending you back. I'll call Mischa. Take you there now." He runs a hand through his hair, and I realize he means it. With no fanfare. No ransom. He'll send me back with a slap on the wrist. The worst part? He thinks of it as a mercy. "You don't belong here…"

His voice trails off, distorted as if someone turned the volume down. I see him heading for the door, and I don't know what possesses me to move. I gain on him. Step, by step, by step…

Alarmed, he inclines his head toward me at the same time my hand lands against his exposed cheek with a sound so startling I flinch. Vicious, slapping noise. He grunts, and belatedly, I see the letter opener in my fist, glinting in the light. See a flash of crimson splatter the floor next.

And then I see Donatello, frozen mid-lunge. He blinks, struck dumb—only for a second. The next, my wrists are in his grasp, and he's herding me back against the wall with a brutality that snaps everything into motion again.

Confusion on him is torment. He sways, another agonized grunt slipping loose—but it's his eyes that disturb me the most. For once, they meet mine openly with none of the rage. No pity. Just sheer puzzlement that knocks years from his age.

He's just a broken man unsure of what the screeching little girl tugging at his pantleg wants. I'm that much of a mystery to him.

"You hate that I could ignore you," he says. "Are you that fucking childish? You are…" He scoffs at the idea of it. "What? You want me to grovel and beg for your mercy? I won't."

Anger rips through me so fiercely I'm shocked by the force of it. Because he's right.

He *should* be begging.

My teeth clatter together as I fight his grasp, but he's too strong, easily bending my arm behind my back.

"Do you think I won't hurt you?" he demands, his breath hot on my neck. "Is that what you fucking want? To drill it home? You only ever were a goddamn pawn! Haven't you realized that yet?"

I think I haven't stopped asking myself the same question since our uncanny reunion. Could he uphold the twisted boast he made? Sell his precious Safiya a second time? Break her wings?

Doubt circles my skull like an itch I can't scratch, growing all the more irritating by his nearness. Yes? No? Yes…

Yes, yesyesyesyes!

His eyes convey the true answer, glaring deep into my own. I can't escape them. My only defense is to rear back while holding his cold, lifeless stare and inhale.

Then I breathe out, my cheeks hollowing as spit flies from my mouth to splatter against that stern jaw. Triumph rips through me, but it's short-lived. Sparks that die in reality's cold chill.

He reacts like a man stuck in slow motion. His fingers brush at the liquid as he swivels toward me. The next second, his hand is in my hair, latching onto my scalp. Wrenching. He uses the leverage to draw me against him so quickly he doesn't even seem to realize he's done it.

"You were always so damn stubborn—" Once more, he breaks off, stopping himself from committing what seems to be the ultimate sin.

Acknowledging my existence.

Admitting the truth.

Seeing me for who I am.

Because this pathetic, stubborn, childish part of me wants to hear him say it.

He hurt me. He hurt me. He hurt me.

And that matters.

The tattoo on his chest implies that it does. I saw it once, etched in red ink as sloppy as if he did it himself. Carved every letter. Every twist and curve.

Safiya Mangenello meant *something* to him. But only as a lie he could comfort himself with. The real girl? She means nothing.

I see that now; his fuzzy, hazy expression blurred by tears is the only evidence I need.

"I'm done with your mind games," he says, dismissive once again. Releasing me, he starts to turn on his heel, but my hand flies out, snatching a fistful of his collar before he can.

It's still damp, a shock that reinforces our present circumstances.

We both smell like lighter fluid. His eyes are bloodshot, his hair a tousled mess.

The evidence of who we really are is all around us—the dust from Havienna on our clothing. The haunting memories of the past. The fact that he can take one look at me and know my thoughts so easily.

"You thought I was bluffing, did you?" He shoves me back, using his bulk as a battering ram to pin me flat against the wall. Air escapes my chest in a rush, as his hands find my waist, so large his fingers almost meet across my stomach.

A million different adjectives flood my mind in a rush to describe how he feels—*warm. Big. Too big. Heavy. Infallible.*

Strong.

So strong…

Once, these hands used to hold me. Comfort me whenever I felt alone or afraid. Never would they creep over me with a boldness that takes my breath away. His thumbs rasp over my belly button as his gaze lowers, and I'm riveted to his every reaction.

Dilated pupils. Flared nostrils. Wrong. The way his tongue flits across his lower lip almost too quickly to track is *wrong*.

And I can't stop it...

For the first time, I feel something itching through my skin I've never felt before. Ever. At least when it came to him. Still, I recognize it instinctively the way any woman would.

Fear.

The kind of fear you can only feel when a layer of fabric is the lone barrier shielding you from a man with nothing left to lose...

"Donatello?" The voice shatters the tense silence. Male? A face appears in the doorway, his gray eyes familiar. The man with the gun, only he's unarmed now.

Donatello shoves me aside so suddenly I go down hard, tasting copper as my teeth catch my lower lip.

"What is it?" he demands, his breathing heavy. "Fuck! What is it?"

"You have a visitor," the man replies, inclining his head. "I doubt you want to keep him waiting."

9

DON

For seven years, Safiya Mangenello has haunted me, a specter dwelling inside my goddamn head. I let her live there. I fed into the lie that as long as I continued to do good, it might somehow make up for my crime against her. Hell, I think I even believed it.

There are no lies to hide behind now.

She's dead, and nothing will ever change that. Whoever Mischa saved, she's someone else. A little girl howling that I atone for the sins of the past as though we're all living in some fucking fairy tale where wrongs can be righted with the wave of a wand.

But this is no fairy tale.

And I'm done fucking atoning.

"Don?" The voice hooks into my thoughts, tugging me back to the present.

"W-What?" I croak, turning to face Luciano. He's gaping at me, mouth wide open, like I'm insane—not that I can blame him. Fuck, I feel like it, shaking my head as though I'm resurfacing from minutes spent submerged underwater. I'm breathing just as heavily as if I were drowning.

Or, in this case, lost in a pair of dark fucking eyes ten times deeper than any ocean. With every glance, they suck me in, demanding something I don't know how to fucking give. An answer? But there isn't one good enough to satisfy that curiosity.

So they'll suck my lungs dry instead.

She'll drain me of every-fucking-thing...

"Don? I said he's here."

"Who?" I say, staggering toward him, fighting to stay standing. The figure I leave behind doesn't move, still on her knees, huddled against the wall. Blinking, I keep going. As long as I don't look at her, I can think. *Focus.*

The man observing the show raises an eyebrow but has the sense to keep his fucking mouth shut. Pushing past him, I brace one hand against the doorway and suck in a lungful of air. Exhale it slowly. Try to refocus. He came here for a reason.

A visitor...

"The man Antonio spoke with?" I ask, craning my neck in his direction.

He nods. The fact that he's wearing a different shirt and jeans betrays how late it is. How long did I sit in that damn study, gathering the nerve to see her?

"That's why I'm here. He should be passing through the gates any minute now—"

"Have your men detain him," I say, standing upright. I take a step, and my thoughts get clearer. Another and I can breathe normally again. The further I get from her, the better I feel. In control.

"Wait." Luciano raises a hand before I can leave the room behind entirely. "First… I think you need to explain what the hell you were doing." He inclines his head in a direction I refuse to look, his eyes blazing. "Assaulting the daughter of the *mafiya* head? Are you suicidal? Is that it? Fuck, man! Feel free to take yourself out in a rain of hellfire, but leave the *famiglia* out of it—"

"Are you done?" I ask, raising an eyebrow.

He blinks in shock rather than answer, as if he can't decide whether I'm truly insane or just foolish.

Maybe it's a bit of both.

Reentering the room, I spot a leather couch and collapse onto it. It's uncomfortable as fuck, but it provides enough support for me to ignore the rest of the world and think. My fingers find my chin, stroking the stubble there as I do so.

My first priority is finding proof that Antonio set me up. Though why would he even go through the trouble? Sure, he was a selfish fuck, but seeing the state of the *famiglia* for myself, I doubt control of the harbor would be enough to change their fortunes around. There had to be more to it.

I don't know exactly how much time passes before Luciano loudly clears his throat.

"I'd hate to interrupt," he snarls. "But I don't know, maybe you can relax another time? When we aren't on the verge of fucking Armageddon."

"You don't trust me," I point out, tilting my head to face him directly.

"Frankly, I'm wondering if you're any different from Tony," he warns, cutting his eyes away from me. "You two seem to have a lot in common."

In my peripheral vision lurks a figure clothed in yellow, still hunched on the floor. *Fuck...*

Gritting my teeth, I ignore her.

"And yet you're still here," I say to the man before me. "Don't pretend like you wouldn't be cutting and running like hell if you really thought I was crazy. You're still here, which means you're smarter than you pretend to be."

"Or I could be just as fucking crazy as you are," he retorts. "Perhaps it's the allure of it. I've heard the stories. The big bad Donatello who singlehandedly fought the Hortega Cartel and made off like a bandit with the spoils of war. You were a legend. Though, hell, they could have been just stories."

"Stories," I scoff. "Because Antonio's done so much better than I did—"

"Antonio was a dick, but he wasn't stupid. We always keep an ear to the ground, and you, Donatello? Mischa's been gunning for you like hell. It's all over the fucking city. The real question is, what do you plan to do next?"

I lean my head back as I contemplate that very problem. The good Don? He wants to wallow in his agony and pretend this isn't happening. Forget. Ignore. Repent.

As for the other part of me that isn't drenched in misery?

It only craves power. Revenge, the pettier, the better...

Above that? Vin's safety. If there's any chance of him staying alive, I'll crawl over glass if I have to. Whatever it takes. Luckily—or not—for me, every motive circles back to my captive little Stepanova. Funny, given only a few minutes ago, I'd been ready to let her go.

"I wanted to sell the girl," I admit, ignoring the fact that she's here in this room, listening to every word. "Use the money to challenge Mischa, or barter the threat to make him back down."

Luciano whistles through his teeth, but when I look over, he has his head inclined thoughtfully. "She's pretty enough to catch a nice price, but I don't think you're doing it for the money."

"No." I brace my hands against my knees, surprised by the laugh that rips from my chest. "Not for the money."

But he's right. Her youth and face alone would fetch a hefty amount, even before her identity came into account. Some crime lord would take her, eager to feel like a big man by breaking someone so seemingly innocent.

Though, a part of me scoffs, *what makes you any different?*

I try to envision it—her at the mercy of someone else. Their hands mauling that pale skin. Their fingers imparting new bruises around her neck. Another monster forcing his way inside her... The hot sensation flooding my skin isn't glee at the prospect.

"In that case, you should try the Saleris," Luciano suggests, oblivious. "They may not give you what she's worth, but if you want her to suffer... They'll ensure that. The boss' son, Mateo, is a sick son of a bitch. The shit I've heard he's into would make even your skin crawl. As far as I know, they have no ties to Mischa. I tend to avoid the crazy motherfuckers, but Antonio had a contact he used when he got in the mood for an exotic girl."

I can't tell if he's being serious or playing along. I look over, spotting my reflection in the glass of the nearest window. The frown I find shocks the hell out of me. It can't be remorse at the thought of selling her. No. It must be greed. She'd fetch a pretty penny on the market, but why let someone else have the privilege?

Doing the deed myself would be the sickest jab at Mischa. Cold hard revenge. A truly evil act that would kill any hope of redemption for good.

"Or maybe you just plan to sit here and wait for Mischa Stepanov to track you down," Luciano taunts. "I don't think it will take him that long to figure it out. It's not like you have an abundance of allies."

"Ah, but that is exactly why the *famiglia* will be the last place he'll think to check," I counter. "Men like Mischa are all about pride and honor. It takes pride to walk away. In his mind, he wouldn't envision a scenario in which I'd come crawling back."

But I'm not crawling now.

"Take me to this Vanetti," I say, rising to my feet. "Have one of your men record everything he says. You got that?"

Luciano doesn't respond, his attention elsewhere. When I clear my throat, he jerks his chin toward the corner. "What about your guest?"

I can sense her, lurking just beyond my line of sight, those eyes staring fiercely in anticipation of what I might do next. My gaze finds her without permission from my brain, riveted to that body with a magnetic focus.

Gone is the angry little girl. It's the way she holds herself that transforms her. Stoically facing forward, her lips pursed, hands gently smoothing her dress back into place.

Even Luciano's wary scowl fades in the face of her.

I'm too damn tired for jealousy. Too old. Too bitter. But if I could still feel it, the sensation might resemble the pinprick of fire in my gut, searing the longer his eyes trace her shape.

"Let's go." I head for the door, but I can't escape the reality of her presence. I should tie her up, lock her in a cage.

Reinforce her only identity that matters to me—that as a prisoner.

Instead, I exit the room without even looking at her—but I'm sure she'll follow. Even if she doesn't, I may not need her after all. Throwing proof of his stupidity in Mischa's face could be payback enough, sweeter than dangling his daughter's life over his head. With that in mind, I pause to direct just one request at Luciano.

"Get me a knife."

WILLOW

A good captive would play her role and hide. Better yet, I'd use Donatello's absence as an excuse to scour the area for any weakness to exploit. Or escape while his back is turned. A smarter woman would run.

I walk instead, following him and another down a narrow hall that opens onto a set of stairs leading to a lower level. Donatello stalks down them with purpose, the other man on his heels. Neither seems to notice me, but I never do the smart thing and take advantage of the moment.

I can't even take my eyes off him.

It's the way he moves. Assuredly, emboldened with confidence that the man I found on the floor of Havienna lacked. I don't know where he's headed—the other man mentioned a visitor—but I doubt joy, or happiness is the factor driving him. Not, I suspect, even revenge.

No… Whatever sustains him now is something I recognize. I feel it too. Desperation. Despair. Hate. A need to rage against everything and everyone, feeding an internal flame. The hotter the fire, the easier it is to ignore the rest. The pain.

If only for a little while. But few things can feed that blaze for long—like sustaining any fire, you need fuel.

My heart pounds with unease as I try to imagine what source he might choose to utilize in this instance. Me? His request for a knife echoes loudly in my mind. He's already bruised my throat. What next?

There are other ways a man can harm a woman…

My body still burns from his touch, that feeling, the look in his eyes—all of it so different from any memory I can call upon of him. The old him. Maybe the only feeling akin to it was the crippling heat that assaulted me when he stripped me in Havienna. When his finger slid inside me, and I knew, if only for that moment, that any past importance I had to him ceased to matter. In that moment, I was a stranger.

At his mercy.

I shake my head to banish the memory as my foot strikes drastically different flooring from the tile before. Concrete? All this time, I've still been following him.

The room we're in now is unfamiliar. A cavernous space with metal siding, naked floors, and a vaulted ceiling. A massive opening at one end of the building allows moonlight and fresh air into the area, but otherwise, there are no windows, and a single door connects it to the hallway we came from.

Four other men stand in a semi-circle nearby. In the center, a man is on his knees wearing a navy suit, his dark hair slicked back to his skull. He was handsome once, with a stern jaw sporting a burgeoning bruise and a straight nose gushing blood. What seems to be a tie has been shoved into his mouth as a makeshift gag, and at the sight of Donatello, he issues a stream of muffled noise.

"This is him," the man walking behind Donatello says. "Paulie Vanetti."

The name isn't familiar, though I doubt he's a friend given Donatello's cold glance in his direction.

Both men draw even with the crouching figure, and I suck in a breath, recognizing the way Donatello cocks his head. Exactly how a hawk might when sizing up a promising prey item. Calculatingly.

He steps forward, drawing all attention to him. "So this is the man Antonio contracted?"

"It's him," the other man says. "He's been cagey on the work he did. I don't think he'll tell us freely."

"There is no need for threats." Sighing, Donatello crouches on one knee and looks the bound man in the eye. They're quite the pair, and one would think the man caked in blood wearing a rumpled suit would look worse in comparison. He doesn't. From this angle, I can only see the periphery of his expression. Those eyes. That wry mouth twisted in concentration.

Still, his posture leaves no mistake. He is the one in control here.

"Was it you?" he asks softly, flicking his thumb along the other man's cheek. "The Stepanovs. Were you the man Antonio hired to do his fucking dirty work?"

Dirty work. The attack on Ellen and Eli? Curiosity has me inching forward before I can realize my mistake. Dark eyes cut in my direction, and I'm sure he knows exactly what's on my mind.

Is this man responsible for what happened to my family? For the chaos that came after, resulting in Donatello stowing a little girl in his trunk before trying to set himself on fire? Is this figure the source of the blood and violence? That pain.

Watching him, I don't know how I feel. What to feel. A million different emotions swarm my body all at once, and it's like my heart is too exhausted to decide which one to internalize. It just aches. Throbs. Swells in my chest until every thump of my pulse wracks my entire body.

The only way I can seem to dull it? Watch. Stare. Listen to the cold, stern baritone that cuts through the confusion, alarmingly clear...

"Were you?" Donatello prods.

"Ah!" the man mumbles, his reply distorted by the gag, but Donatello nods as though he understood every word.

"Oh? It wasn't you? You mean you weren't the sick son of a bitch who nearly killed a pregnant woman and her child?"

His cruel narration triggers a wave of memories. Ellen bleeding and pale. Eli, limp and lifeless…

"I hope the money was worth it," Donatello warns. The anger in his voice reverberates through the open space, and those nearby tense in response. It's too raw. Too intense. A shudder rips through me as I instinctively take a step back. Could this man be responsible for the attack?

Of course, a part of me hisses. *It wasn't Donatello. But you've known that all along…*

"Let's hear it," Donatello demands. He grabs one end of the gag and cruelly yanks it free. "Speak. Were you the lapdog Tony sent to do his bidding?"

Sputtering, the man croaks, "Go. To hell. Where the fuck is Tony? I'll teach that son of a bitch to—"

"Tony's dead." Rising to his feet, Donatello flicks the discarded gag aside and clasps his hands behind his back. That simple motion unnerves me for reasons I can't explain. Maybe the dark intent behind his eyes is what has me swallowing hard. It's another layer of cruelty, further separating this man from the figure in my memories.

He could be lying, but the blood painting swaths of his body from head to toe speaks for him. He's killed someone.

He takes *pride* in having killed them.

"You answer to me," he says, towering over the captive man. "Did he hire you to do it?"

"The fuck is this?" The man's eyes continue to dart warily around the room. "What the fuck is going on, Luciano?" he snarls, referring to the gray-eyed man beside Donatello.

"Answer the man." Luciano shrugs. "I don't think he's in the mood for an argument. Did you do it or not, Paulie?"

Paulie's shifty eyes twitch from Donatello to the men nearby and back again. "Tony paid me over a hundred grand for it, but I just did as I was told, okay? It wasn't nothing fucking personal."

"Personal." Donatello's laughter churns my stomach. It's as beautiful as it is disturbing, rivaling the most heart-rending crescendo. "Oh, but this *was* personal. If you won't take my word for it, then take hers."

He inclines his head to me. "This is the man who attacked your mother. The reason why your father tried to kill my son. Did you know that?"

He waits as if for the magnitude of his statement to strike me. When I don't react how he seems to expect, he assumes why out loud. "You knew. Didn't you? Is that really why you came running to me, little *principessa*? Guilt?" Genuine curiosity leeches into his tone. "Let us not forget... I didn't drag you here as my captive. You came to me."

His eyes blaze, betraying just how angry that makes him. Enrages him. In his thinking, I came crawling back, if only to see the mess left behind for myself. Like he said, it was childish.

But the truth goes beyond that, itching away at the back of my skull the more I try to deny it. Leaving the manor is all a blur—but one emotion sticks out. Fear.

Given the way he's scouring my expression, he should see that—but he's already returning his attention to the man kneeling before him.

"You may have been doing Antonio's bidding," he says coldly, "but in the process, you implicated me. My name. Donatello Vanici took the blame. Do you understand that?"

"Look, man," the bound figure says with a nervous laugh. He squirms but can barely keep himself upright, wavering on his knees. "I was just doing what I was told, okay? It was all Tony. He called me up—"

"Do you have proof of that?" Donatello demands.

"Check my accounts, for fuck's sake! Tony wired me the money personally."

"Can you do that?" Donatello asks Luciano.

"Already on it," he replies, fishing a cell phone from his pocket. "Tony only ever used one accountant for any transfers."

"There. Proof," the bound man says. "Now you gonna let me fucking go?"

"No." Donatello's voice rings out so softly I have to strain to hear it. The note resembles the ominous moment nearing the chorus of a thrilling piece of music. The pivotal point on which the entire melody turns on its head. "I'm not going to fucking *let you go*."

He turns around, and I shiver instinctively even before his gaze falls over me. I feel exposed. Like there's only air between us, and I'm without anything to shield myself behind. This thin fabric means nothing—he can see all of me regardless.

Every thought and fear to flicker across my mind.

Even the dark ones.

"But you knew that," Donatello continues. The corner of his lip quirks, but it's the furthest thing from a smile. More like the grimace of a man so far gone he no longer remembers what humor is. All he can do is relish the few things that bring him joy in its absence—power.

"I want to kill you," he declares, and my heart stops cold. Only the slight tilt of his head implies that he's still talking to the man. Not me. "I want to gut you like a fucking pig—after I make you squeal what you've done on the record so there can be no mistake. I'd string you up, let you die slowly. That would be a start. No, a mere drop in the bucket to atone for the damage you've caused me."

The pain in his tone is unfaked and undeniable. I'd have to be made of stone not to feel something in response. My breathing catches, my throat on fire. Any tears that may be building are kept at bay, though.

I'm too distracted to let them fall.

The musical comparisons return in full force, and I'm reminded of one of my most favorite compositions. It starts off innocently with a beautiful array of delicate notes before the tempo changes, becoming increasingly erratic until the final booming finale.

His rage is like that, a symphony composed of the most devastating instruments—a voice like thunder perfectly accompanied by eyes like fire.

He turns to me again, and I don't know what to expect. Not for him to crack a slow, lopsided smile.

"You feel it too," he declares, his head cocked, an eyebrow raised. He takes a step, and even with him a few inches closer, the effect resonates throughout my whole body. Goosebumps come to life, prickling my skin. I lurch back on my heels.

He advances another step.

"Hate," he continues mid-stride, even closer than before. "That sick need for revenge—and not mere 'justice,' either... You want pain. You want him to suffer, just as you suffered. Am I wrong?"

The men around him stare amongst themselves, obviously confused. Whether he cares or even notices, Donatello doesn't turn his attention from me for one second.

"I can see it written all over your face," he says with a knowing nod. "The hate—and not just for me, either—" he flicks his gaze toward the man at his feet. "How should we punish him?"

My stomach lurches at his choice of words. *We.* A deliberate shift in culpability. Almost as if he's proposing a game, like the many we used to play in what feels like another life.

His version of hide and seek involved water guns, and every board game always had small pots of money at stake.

But something in the pit of my soul warns me that this "prize" won't be so innocent.

And no matter what, no matter what he says or does…

I cannot play.

"Don't deny that you want to," Donatello scolds, advancing another step on me. "So what will it be? A slit throat? A beheading? Name your choice, *principessa*. You wanted to play in our world, so play."

He's serious. His low, stern tone conveys as much. So I don't leave it to chance, emphatically shaking my head so there can be no mistake. I don't want him to do anything.

"No." His nostrils flare, eyes flashing. "You don't have the option to abstain from this little vote. He threatened your family, your mother, your brother. You want more than just his pain. You want more than justice, don't you?"

My heart pounds ominously as images sneak into my skull unbidden. This man, just as broken as Ellen. As terrified as Eli.

No. I close my eyes, fighting them back. *Focus!*

"Look at me," Donatello warns. His voice is inescapable, rebounding off the inside of my skull until I finally open my eyes again.

The look on his face... I've seen it before. The most notable instance? The day he left me to die.

He wears it proudly, standing tall, his head held high as he extends his hand. Harsh, his voice rings out, "I asked for a knife."

"Here." One of the other men watching steps forward, presenting a gleaming weapon on his palm. It's small, about the same size Mischa trained me to use. Reverently, Donatello draws his thumb across the edge, and I swear I see blood streak it after.

Nothing in his expression or posture reveals any hint of pain. His back is rigid as his hand assuredly manipulates the weapon, brandishing it in the air.

Alarm grips my spine, rendering me paralyzed—I know the stern tilt to his jaw. The confident stance of a man in complete control. But as he sinks to his knees and presses the knife against the man's throat, one thing is painfully apparent.

I don't know this Donatello.

And he doesn't know me. If he did, he wouldn't play this game. He'd read my fear. Back down. Anything but smile conspiratorially as if our thoughts are one and the same.

"You're going to tell me how to kill him," he says to me. "Every cut. Every scream. It will be all on you. Your face tells me everything I need to know. Your eyes... I see the hate in them. You want this—Don't!"

He lashes out with an outstretched hand, pointing a finger at me accusatorially. "No. You watch me. You watch all of it. Now..." He crouches down again, but there's a predatory grace in the movement. His muscles ripple, creating patterns against his skin. Despite everything in me warning me to turn away, I'm riveted.

"Where should we begin? Ah, of course. We need a name," he suggests, toying with the blade. "Should we start with his tongue?"

His quarry comes to life, squirming so badly he nearly falls onto his side. "What the hell?" His breathing quickens, his eyes so wide I see myself reflected in them. A shockingly small figure gaping on in silence.

"Look at me," Donatello warns the second my attention drifts. I obey, but his eyes gleam so brightly, I turn away again.

"Look at me." His tone raises the hair on the back of my neck. Guttural and raw, but one note, in particular, unsettles me. It's a hallmark of the very last emotion someone should feel in a situation like this. Glee.

Excitement. It lurks beneath the deep baritone, adding a musical tilt to the words.

"I said watch me, Safiya." His eyes are narrowed, daring me to look lower. See what he's doing.

Something responsible for the sharp, inhuman shriek coloring the air next.

"This is your game, after all. Tell me where to cut him. Play your role. Look at me!"

The act is futile, but I purse my lips anyway as if preventing any sound from escaping. I'm sure that every move, every breath, doesn't go unnoticed by him.

I can't think. Not about revenge—like the man writhing in the agony he inflicted on my family. A missing tongue would be nothing. A pittance. A mercy...

No, I banish the thought, aware of the gaze piercing through my own.

Regardless, Donatello nods, raising his weapon menacingly. "His tongue, then—"

"Wait!" the man gasps. "Fucking... Wait! You want a name, okay! I never saw the motherfucker, but I know he was working with Tony. I think the hit was his idea."

Donatello blinks like a man waking from a dream. "Who?"

"The bastard just went by J.W. That's it! That's all I know. I swear to fucking God—"

"How did they contact you? How did you know where to stage the hit?"

"Tony fed me all the information. I never spoke with the man directly. I just knew he was footing the cash. Tony didn't have that kind of dough to throw around."

"So you attacked a woman and her child based on the say-so of a bastard like Antonio Salvatore and someone you never met?" Donatello roars. "What did they promise you? It had to be more than money. No amount in the world would be worth pissing off the *mafiya*."

"They talked a big game," the man says, his eyes on the knife dangling precariously above his head.

"Like what?"

"Like taking over all of Hell's Gambit for one. Divvying up the city on a platter to anyone who took part. They said..." His eyes flicker nervously in my direction. "They said they'd cut Mischa down to size. Rip control right from his hands."

"Sounds familiar," Luciano remarks snidely. "I guess you aren't so fucking crazy after all, Donatello."

The man in question doesn't answer, his gaze turned inward, triggering another chilling instance of *déjà vu*. It's an expression I remember from the days of crouching beneath his desk watching him work. It could be beautiful seeing him mull over a dilemma or problem. He would stroke his jaw much like he is now, until finally, he'd nod only to himself, seeing a solution where no one else could.

"Mischa was the target," he deduces finally. "They wanted him out. Why?"

"I don't know! Jesus! Just let me go." The man again tries to wriggle free of his bonds, but the heel of a boot slams against his chest, knocking him backward.

"Why the hell would I do that?" Donatello demands, aiming his foot to deliver another kick. He moves so fast. All I see is a spray of blood before a gash appears across the man's face.

He howls, spitting crimson onto the floor as he struggles to move. His attacker is ruthless, crouching over him, the knife poised above.

"Why frame me?" Donatello bellows. "If he wanted to take on Mischa himself, he had every right to. Why get me involved?"

"The harbor. Needed... Had to import something."

"Import?" the man behind Donatello interjects, his head cocked. "What the hell could they need to import that would require the use of the entire harbor?"

Paulie issues a stream of wailed curses. "I didn't ask fucking questions!"

"No, you didn't," Donatello growls. "You shot at a pregnant woman and a child. You got my son shot in his fucking head. You set me up to take the fall."

"It's just fucking money! I didn't give a shit who they were."

I can't control it. I see them—Ellen and Eli. The blood. The pain. The fear.

"You feel it, don't you?" Donatello rises to his feet as if sensing my rage before I even feel it creeping beneath my skin. He crosses to me, his victim forgotten. Once close enough, he captures my chin against his palm.

"You're angry." His eyes narrow further as he tilts my head toward him. "You have every fucking right to be. But you're suppressing it. Bottling it up nice and neat. Why?" He leans closer, bringing his mouth near my ear. Every movement of his lips sends a jolt through my earlobe, dizzying. "Your father isn't here."

I jump, but he grabs my wrist, locking me in place.

"You've played the role of a good girl for so damn long you don't know how to operate outside of your mask," he snarls, but his tone turns deceptively soft. A mocking perversion of gentle. "What has that gotten you? A life as a pretty doll?"

He steps back, dragging me with him. As we near the center of the throng, he shoves me to my knees. Wincing, I realize I'm kneeling right before the man bleeding all over the floor. Up close, he's pitiful, his fancy suit stained red, his face mutilated.

"You think he deserves your mercy? Why? Because it's the 'right thing' to do? Was it the *right* thing for your father to shoot Vincenzo? Should I show you that same mercy?"

I see his shadow move across the floor before I feel it—fiery pain teasing the base of my throat. Careful, deliberately applied pressure, hard enough to slice flesh, but not enough to bleed.

"He deserves to be punished. You know that as well as I do. So where should we start?"

The blade withdraws from my skin, and I exhale the breath I didn't realize I'd been holding—only to inhale sharply as a firm object presses against my fingers next. I glance down, alarmed to find the handle of a blood-covered blade. He slams it against my palm, forcing my fingers to curl around it.

He's too strong, easily overpowering my attempts to resist. With force, he snatches my hand. Then he makes me press the knife against the man's collar. Hard. Harder.

I can feel his heartbeat through the blade. His eyes bulge, his lips frothing with spit as he bites back a scream. My body takes over, bucking against the man controlling my movements. Fighting.

I'm sweating with the effort, but he doesn't even loosen his grip.

"I could make you fillet him," he warns, his palm shifting over the back of my hand to guide my hold on the handle. "I'd make you gut him. You'd be the one holding the knife. I could…"

To prove it, he makes the knife dance inches from the man's skin. I recoil, wrenching against him until my shoulder throbs.

"You're not a little girl. *Look* at what you're doing. Feel through your fingertips. Do it." His voice sneaks into my skull unbidden, and I catch myself obeying. I see my fingers entwined with his, squirming against the unfamiliar shape of the weapon. The harder I try to pull away, the more he tightens his grasp.

"Stop," Donatello grates, but for a second, his tone loses the cold edge. He's a teacher trying to reach a stubborn student —though this lesson is far different from any Mischa taught me. In his world, survival was all that mattered. To Donatello? It's inflicting pain.

It's retribution.

"We both know that's what you want," he says, speaking to my thoughts directly. "Revenge. If I let him go... If *we* let him go, do you think he'll learn his lesson?"

The man's wide, fearful eyes speak for him.

"No," Donatello says, lifting our combined fist to let the blade catch the light. "He'll just find another contract. Kill another woman. Another man. Another child. You know it as well as I do."

He taught me that lesson himself—the inherent cruelty of some men. It's a world apart from the simple system of actions and consequences the Stepanovs live by. One of their children may beat another or steal a toy. They are punished. Forgiven. The cycle repeats.

Men like this one operate in the same way, but their actions aren't childish impulses. They're violent. Brutal. They end lives and destroy them.

Over and over again.

"Stop living life in a fairy tale." Donatello's fingers graze the back of my hand, and in horror, I realize he's withdrawing.

But I'm left holding the knife. It shakes, the tip wavering in the air aimlessly before twitching in the direction of the sputtering man's throat.

Only for a second, just one—but in this moment, I know nothing is guiding the blade but me. *My* intent. My will…

To perfectly narrate the moment, Donatello's voice slithers against my ear. "You're no better than I am."

No! A heartbeat later, horror kicks in. I force my fingers apart, letting the blade fall to the floor as I recoil, kicking back until I'm well beyond that pool of scarlet.

He lets me go, pushing past me.

"So you choose to be a puppet. Fine. You can watch. Hold her," he snaps to one of the men who grabs my arms. "Don't let her turn away. Not for a fucking second."

He returns to Paulie, picking the knife from where I must have dropped it.

Then he lunges.

And I have no choice.

I watch.

He runs his knife across the man's throat like he's cutting through butter. Blood spurts in a waterfall, bathing the floor.

But all of the macabre details are secondary to *him*—Donatello. Through it all, his eyes never leave mine.

And in them, I see my own reflection gazing back without an ounce of fear.

11

EVGENI

*B*riar Winthorp...

That name haunts me well into the morning—even though I know there's no way in hell she was telling the truth.

That name carries the same mystique as the Tooth Fairy or Santa Claus in the Stepanov household, just without the inherent goodwill attached.

She is a rumor, whispered about in passing. The children have never met her from what I know. Even Ellen rarely mentions her, her mysterious sister and remaining member of one of the wealthiest families to exist this side of the continent.

I've heard horror stories about the Winthorps, known for their wealth and international investments. Their fortune bankrolled many a criminal enterprise, including the *mafiya* once upon a time. At least until seven years ago when their empire came crashing down after Mischa killed its head,

Robert. Supposedly the rest of the family scattered to the wind after that.

Even if the woman were lying, why that name? It leaves a sour taste in my mouth as I arrive at the manor.

It's the early afternoon, but the place is already a hive of activity. Armored vans mill in the stone driveway, but I don't recognize the men gathered around them. They're professional, watching warily as I march past.

An unfamiliar vehicle sits at the center of the chaos—a sleek black limo.

A visitor, I suspect, but one not cleared through me. As far as I know, I wasn't given any warning, either, or the typical rundown that prefaces any meeting. Warily, I look at the man standing guard by the main door. The second I draw even with him, he inclines his head but never meets my gaze directly. "Mr. Stepanov is in his office."

His tone alone warns me not to ask questions. Biting back an argument, I enter the manor and head straight for the study. I can smell the stench of cologne before I even near the room. For once, the door is closed, sealing off the space from the rest of the house in a way I haven't seen in years. I knock once.

"Come in."

The second I push the door open, alarm tightens my spine. A man standing in the corner draws my notice first, tall, built of pure muscle—obviously a bodyguard.

Seated across from Mischa must be his employer, a bulky man, his expression caught between a grimace and a frown. Gregori Saleri. I know him only from his reputation. An ally of the *famiglia,* his outfit is known for dealing in only one kind of commodity—women. The kind of women who don't *willingly* choose their profession.

As far as I know, Mischa has no business with them—and his wife certainly would prefer it that way. In Ellen's absence, has he tried to get in on the skin game, even with his daughter in danger?

I doubt that.

Seated behind his desk, Mischa watches me without offering an explanation. His face was always harder to read than most—usually, his eyes held a clue as to what he truly thought. Dark, heavy-lidded, and guarded, they give away nothing now. Who the hell knows what he's thinking? It pisses me off to realize that, in this rare instance, I don't.

"I hope I'm not interrupting something, sir," I say as I move to take my place beside him, spinning to face the seated man.

"Gregori was just leaving," Mischa says, nodding to his visitor who stands. Both he and his bodyguard exit, and I step aside, fingering the headset attached to my ear. "Guests leaving now. Follow them out."

"Already on it, sir," comes a reply. The response just cements what's been painfully obvious from the start. Mischa arranged this meeting without me.

Am I alarmed?

Definitely.

As I approach the desk, I strive to keep a neutral tone. "Was that meeting important, sir?"

"Evgeni..." Mischa sighs, interlacing his fingers over the surface of his desk. He's changed into a pair of black slacks and a shirt, leaving his hair to drape his shoulders. "I was enlightening Gregori as to why it would be in his best interest to avoid the *famiglia* and alert me if Donatello Vanici tries to make contact."

I feel my eyebrow shoot up. "You think he went back to them? The *famiglia*?"

It would make sense. A man on the outs would be desperate for allies. In a bid to outplay the mafia's reach, he could seek to return to the fold of his old organization.

"I know there is no love lost between him and their leader," Mischa admits. "But I'd put nothing past him."

"But that wasn't the only reason why you met with Saleri, was it?"

It's funny how well you can get to know a man just by existing in his orbit for years. I've seen Mischa at the heights of emotion, from the birth of his children to the death of his mentor. I've seen him at his happiest and at his worst, but even I can admit that I've never seen him quite like this—stewing.

It's a quiet emotion, alarming in intensity.

"You're wondering why I met with him without you, is that it?" he questions, leveling me with a piercing gaze.

I don't flinch. "Usually, you like to coordinate security when we have visitors."

"I won't play word games with you," he says. "I *deliberately* didn't tell you."

A muscle in my jaw twitches. Am I alarmed by that? More annoyed.

The man tasks me with protecting his family and assets, yet he goes out of his way to consult with a rival faction and keeps me out of the loop while doing so. He isn't petty, so this stems from more than our previous spats over Vanici. It's calculating, designed to make it clear that, at least for now, I'm being kept at arm's length. I suspect this meeting isn't the only thing he's concealed from me.

"May I ask why?"

He stands, putting his back to me as he glares from the window overlooking the property's western half.

At its core, the manor is a beautiful house, nestled in the countryside, surrounded by rose gardens, rolling fields, and gently sloping stone walls.

At the same time, it is a fortress. I've never worked in a place more fiercely guarded, but I've admittedly never worked for a leader more constrained by his emotions. My last boss was a man so cold I doubt the near-death of his wife and child would interrupt his routine dinner, let alone drive him to the brink of war.

Mischa Stepanov's heart *is* his family. What will he do when the very thing he cherishes most is threatened?

I know the answer—become reckless. Tactless.

Vengeful.

The complete opposite of everything I've trained myself to be. Still, I can admit that I never assumed him capable of intentionally cutting me out of the fold. There has to be a reason...

Though something warns me that I won't like what it is one fucking bit. An image comes to mind, but I banish it before it can unfold in full. I merely see a body. Green eyes. Sweet smile.

A hole where her throat should be. She wasn't the only one. I blink, and behind my eyelids, I see them all—each bloodied, lifeless face my burden to bear.

"You're unnerved," Mischa says, drawing my attention back to him.

I shake my head to clear it. "Sir?"

"By my actions," he reiterates. "I can sense your judgment."

"This isn't like you," I counter, shifting my stance. By uncrossing my arms, maybe I hope to detract from the defensive tone sneaking into my voice? "Sitting here, talking to a slave trader. We should be out looking for Willow—"

"You know damn well where she is!" He lashes out, striking the desk so hard it skids across the floor. The monstrous sound rips through the room, but it's not loud enough to keep him from pacing. Violent enough. His hands form fists as if he has to stop himself from hitting it again.

I clear my throat. "Mischa…"

Blazing like fire, his eyes cut to mine, more piercing than ever. In them, I see something I never thought I would, usually glimpsed in men with far less restraint.

He's breaking.

"She's strong," I say as gently as I can. "There's been no sign of her yet. I suggest we stay focused. Search Vanici's known whereabouts—"

"Fuck, you might be right," he says, pushing away from the desk. His hand tears through his hair, his dark eyes fixed on the scenic view beyond the windows. "But in this moment, I don't want your fucking logic."

His still clenched fists make it obvious what he desires.

Vengeance.

"You really want to start a war with Donatello Vanici?" I ask him quietly.

Donatello, a man who—as of a week ago—was little more than an investor of no particular importance who had one piece of real estate worth having—the city harbor.

Until the day he supposedly kidnapped Willow Stepanova out of the blue.

I didn't buy it then, and I don't buy Mischa's caginess now. There's more to this.

"Tell me what happened between you," I say, as close as I've ever come to an outright demand of him.

"A war?" Mischa questions as if I never spoke. "No. I want safety." He eyes his left hand, where a gold ring adorns the third finger. "I want my wife to live. I want my son to have use of his arm again. I want…" His voice breaks, and all I can do is stare. Emotions don't factor into my skillset. Not pain. Not love. Not agony.

I can't face them the way I could an attacker or a logistical problem.

The man sways, overwhelmed by all three at once.

Finally, he regains control, his eyes blazing. "I want my baby girl to have been born without having to fight for her life. I don't want a war, Evgeni. I want *blood*."

"Blood can have a higher cost than you expect," I warn through gritted teeth. "I heard your feud with the Winthorps had a particularly tragic aftermath."

"This is different," Mischa growls. "The Winthorps don't have my daughter, do they? Vanici's gone underground. Only God knows what he's done to her…"

For a second, I can glimpse beneath the rage to the real emotion driving him. Fear. For Willow. For his wife and son.

I'd probably feel sympathy if I had anything in my life worth comparing those relationships to. Luckily, I don't. I am what I'm paid to be—a soldier with no emotional investment, able to stay objective.

"My men are in the process of tracking him down," I say. "He couldn't have gone far."

"You underestimate him," Mischa snarls. "I can assure you that he's not sitting around pining for peace, either."

"So what will you have me do?"

"Go back to the hospital," he says, returning to his desk. "I heard you rearranged the detail on Ellen. Why?"

I swallow hard before answering. It's a switch I hoped would go unnoticed, but one that would hopefully prevent another surprise visitor, Briar Winthorp or otherwise.

"I believe Kristoph will be of better use here on the property. Danil has a better bedside manner."

Mischa's eyes cut to slits. "But you will take the lead," he insists. "I want you there now. Eli can come home tomorrow. He's safer there until Vanici is found."

It's a strain on our detail, but I have enough sense not to say as much now. "How are the children doing?"

A rare softness seeps into Mischa's expression. "As well as can be expected. They miss their mother, and brother, and their sister."

"I should check on Eli while I'm there," I suggest. "Maybe knowing his progress can help lift their spirits a little?"

"I want you there overnight," Mischa says, his head cocked. One look at his face, and I know that this is the real topic of our conversation. He's just waited until now to broach it. "Peter will head my personal detail from now on."

Peter. The rookie, untrained and undisciplined—yet eager to please. He won't ask questions.

"Can I ask why?" I can't disguise my irritation. Disagreements or not, Mischa has never intervened in my staffing before. Not once during all of my employment.

This is personal. I'm sure of that even before he strokes his jaw with a knowing nod.

"I don't want your judgment," he says simply. "You are a good man, Evgeni. But in this world, good men can rarely stomach the actions necessary. And given your history..."

He stops himself from saying more, but he doesn't have to.

So *that* is what this really is about. Trust in the context of "my past." That's his excuse anyway—because he doesn't trust me.

Not anymore.

"Don't coddle me," I snap. My tone slips, harsher than it should be. For a heartbeat, respect isn't a factor. An insult is still an insult, even if coming from an employer. "So you know my background. You've known it for years. That's never interfered with my duties before."

"And I know where you hesitate," he counters, raising his voice to match the volume of mine. "Donatello Vanici will not play by your rules."

My rules.

My creed. A low blow considering I've all but broken them for this family already.

"If we were playing by my *rules*, you wouldn't have gone after Vanici first," I point out. "You would have been honest with me from the start. If I were playing by my 'rules,' Mischa, I wouldn't still be here."

I've gone too far. Despite knowing that, the closest thing to an apology I seem able to muster is clearing my throat.

Mischa's lower jaw twitches, the only warning that I've hit my target. "Is that how you really feel?"

I nod. Even so, quitting isn't even on my mind. "Sir…" I force some semblance of normalcy back into my tone. "This is about *Vanici,* not me. I still think we should figure out his motives. Why would he—"

"You should go," Mischa says over me. Anger ripples through his voice but controlled enough that he doesn't shout. "If Ellen wakes up, I want her to be near a familiar face."

I can't escape the thought. Familiar like her sister's?

I should mention her now. First, an attack on Ellen and her son. Now a Winthorp returning out of the blue. She could have heard of the attack and come out of genuine concern.

But I don't buy it. Last I heard, the woman left the country. Returning in less than seventy-two hours seems a stretch. Unless she was already nearby.

"Evgeni?" Mischa demands.

"I'm on my way out," I say. "Good evening, sir. I'll return to the hospital. I wouldn't want my *past* to affect my judgment."

He says nothing as I storm into the hall.

He knows better.

Some lines you don't cross.

And some events aren't worth dredging up, even to prove a point.

12

DON

It's a big, bad world, sonny boy, Giovanni told me once. *You're going to do shit that you wouldn't have dreamed of just a day ago. Horrible shit. But if it makes you feel better... Somewhere out there, another man is doing something ten times worse.*

As per usual, the son of a bitch was right.

And he was *wrong*. There can't be anything much worse than goading someone else into doing the unthinkable. Forcing them to watch you do it. Looking into their eyes, seeing only your blood-soaked-self staring back...

And loving every minute of it.

Is that what Giovanni felt? The old man was fucking crazy, but this feels beyond insanity. Twisted. The more I scour those old memories of those days, though, the more obvious it becomes that he never forced me to do a damn thing. I was a willing soldier every step of the way. An enthusiastic one. We were drawn to each other, some might say, speaking the same language of ambitious, selfish men.

Vin never spoke that language—but I should have made him learn it. Pressured him to hold a knife to a man's throat and make him cut. Deep down, I know it would have been pointless.

When he was a kid, barely taller than my knee, he used to wake up every night screaming, convinced a monster was hiding in his closet. I'd never find anything there, but it was real to him. So real, he'd sob until his entire body shook, and it damn near broke my heart. One night I went into his room with a gun, intending to convince him I'd scare the *"monster"* off for good. The show of force was meant to comfort him more than anything.

But good old Vin… He cried even harder at the sight of the weapon and begged me not to hunt his monster down. As tormented as he was, he didn't want vengeance. *Shoot me instead, Uncle Don,* he demanded, his eyes welling with tears. *It's not the monster's fault that he's scary.*

God, he was such a wholesome kid. Never, not once, did I ever see the darkness in him that I always felt lurking inside myself. Even Mischa had his own unique brand of insanity, different from my own. No one's quite meshed with my sick fucking mind, except perhaps Giovanni, and now…

Her. It could have been a trick of the light, that spark in her eye. That gleam. But fuck, I felt something stir in my soul like I never have. Curiosity. Maybe a little irritation, too. Of all people, a little blond spoke my language, if only for a fucking second…

And it was music to my ears. Unlike Vin, she didn't want me to shield her monster. Oh no, she wanted me to gut it right at her fucking feet. Those eyes told me how, even if she wasn't aware of it. The way they narrowed as I cut. Widened when the man's screams finally fell silent.

Fuck, she told me exactly how she wanted it done. And it was wrong. Disgusting. Sick.

Because all I wanted to do in that moment was make her keep talking to me…

Cold air hits like a slap, and I blink to find myself stumbling from a side exit, dripping liquid too frigid to be blood. I look up and realize why—it's raining out. The sky above is a lighter gray than it'd been earlier. Hours must have passed, though it feels like an eternity.

Behind me, I hear a door open with a rusty squeal, followed by footsteps hurrying in my direction. "Don?" someone shouts. Luciano? "Where the fuck are you going?"

That's a damn good question. The knife is still in my hand, but I let it fall into the mud as I keep walking without bothering to look back. Soon I'll confront Mischa with what I learned. Make him pay.

At the moment? The only thing that seems to matter is moving. I spot a building up ahead and stagger toward it, with no aim in mind.

In my wake, those trailing steps continue—softer, too soft to belong to a man—but I don't look back.

Giovanni—and I after him—kept an apartment in this outbuilding. We probably slept there more than in our own homes. Days off weren't a factor with the livelihood of the entire *famiglia* at stake, such is the life of a leader. They don't tell any ambitious cuck gunning for the top position the truth—much of it is spent on a hard ass mattress alone.

For that reason, the old man kept the furniture simple. Utilitarian. Years into my tenure, I realized why. The shitty bed and bland furnishings made the few moments we spent away in our own homes with our respective families all the sweeter.

Sweet enough to tide us over as we went back and fought ten times harder. We were men who valued the business above all else.

So, predictably, Antonio Salvatore gutted the place. I know that even before I mount the outdoor steps leading to the entrance and find the door unlocked.

The fucker had the plain white paint replaced with ornate black wallpaper like something out of a sleazy hotel suite. The floors are polished wood, and the sturdy old leather furniture has been replaced with black suede and fur-covered bullshit.

The motherfucker installed a minibar at least, in the same spot where Giovanni would spend hours contemplating the various deals he had with the Colombian cartels. Things were dicey in those days—you got in bed with the wrong associates and could easily wake up with your cock missing, and a blackmail notice shoved down your throat.

Antonio seemed to enjoy having things shoved into his orifices even while at the office. The bedroom is too much of a shitshow to even dissect at the moment. Sex toys lay out in the open near the massive bed, and the dresser across from it is covered in an array of condoms and women's makeup.

Disgusted, I cross over to the closet and find a decent black suit hanging amongst a random assortment of clothing. Judging from the ludicrous level of tailoring, most were Antonio's, but the few dresses—all different sizes—reinforce that he didn't adhere to the "leaders sleep alone" creed.

His renovations of the bathroom were at least more practical, replacing the simple shower with a full bath and a walk-in stall.

I peel my clothing off and stand beneath the spray, letting the water pelt me from above, as hot as I can stand it. In here, there's no one to pretend for. No kingdom to guard, no lies to maintain.

No innocent blond to butcher a man in front of.

I wince at the reminder. If I dissect the emotion swirling in my gut, it could be guilt. Or concern that I'm too tired to feel in full. Logic is telling me to go back. She could have run off for all I fucking know. Good riddance. Let her scurry back to Mischa, having learned one final lesson.

A caged bird should stay in her cage or wind up devoured.

Or...that same bird becomes a predator herself.

Groaning, I brace my hands against the smooth black tile and watch the water pouring off me circle the drain. This shower is as gaudy as the rest of the apartment, too sleek and modern to match the grim seriousness of Giovanni's old hideout. I bet Antonio took glee in erasing any trace of our old boss. In addition to the silver fixtures, he had the base of the stall made of white marble, making it the perfect backdrop to spotlight the rust-colored liquid washing off my skin. So much red.

Too much...

The hue triggers a million twisted images that dance through my skull. I see Vincenzo, my boy, bleeding from his head. Then Antonio, greedily gasping for his last breath. Paulie Vanetti, sliced to pieces.

Last of all, I see her, the beautiful little blond, watching me work without a drop of crimson on her. My chest swells with so much rage it's painful. *Her* blood deserves to paint this shower floor, not Vin's.

And it's not her connection to Mischa that makes her worthy of death. Violence is just the way of this brutal world we live in. I could have accepted her deliberately turning against me. Wanting me dead. Wanting me to suffer.

Knowing her role.

Her real sin?

Rather than let me die in peace, she returned to gloat over the broken pieces. Back to watch me burn…though, when it came down to it, she couldn't even let me strike the match.

So what was her motive?

More images flood my skull to feed the rage boiling beneath my skin. I see her face. Her tiny hands wrenching at mine. Her desperation to keep me from striking a single match, even before I attempted to set her alight as well.

That final look on her face is what does it, though. Enrages me to the point that I plant my fist against the wall of the stall and howl in irritation. That look causes the most pain. The most hate.

Because in that moment…all I saw in those eyes was pity. Concern. As though she didn't want me to die. Not out of sweet, innocent mercy, either.

This life? It's worse than any hell. Only someone especially cruel would force me to live it, and then watch me suffer.

Ironically, if she were here now, she'd get her wish. The water itself feels hot enough to burn me alive more thoroughly than any fire. I hiss through my teeth, surrendering to the assault for what feels like an eternity. When I finally shut the water off, I'm still whole, though. Not ashes.

What a damn shame.

But in the absence of the spray, I finally smell the scent flooding the room, and my body goes rigid with the threat of an entirely different punishment. That smell... I inhale it again, recognizing it instantly. Roses and lighter fluid. *No.* I shake my head, unwilling to trust my own senses. *I've gone crazy...*

But I haven't. Her presence infects the air like poison, impossible to ignore. She's *here*, having followed me across the complex, presumably alone.

"What the fuck do you want?" I demand, wrenching my gaze toward the source of the stench. Even expecting her, the sight of that lithe figure watching from the doorway knocks the air from my lungs. I blink, expecting her to vanish, a figment of my imagination.

She doesn't.

Her face is partially obscured by the steam coating the glass barrier between us—but nothing could ever disguise those eyes. They bore into me as I use my hand to clear a section of the door.

She is here, but I suspect she saw more than she bargained for. Pink spots dot her cheeks, and a quick swallow distorts her throat. For all her bravery, she's still just a woman. A *young* woman, one I know for a fact, has never experienced a man.

Has she even seen one like this before?

The distraction is too tempting, and my tired brain latches onto it greedily. I grip the handle, testing the give of the metal. Slowly, I apply pressure and push the door aside, watching her expression all the while.

"Did you come to wash the blood from your hands, *principessa*?" My taunt falls flat—her hands are pale, utterly clean. Though while that damn stare remains constant, her body...

That body betrays her.

Trembling fingers grip the front of her dress. The bulk of it disguises most of her shape, but what little of it I can see— shapely, pale legs—make me exhale through my teeth.

Shoving the door open wider, I watch her nails dig into the fabric of her dress as if it's armor against me. And it is in her mind—as long as she's wearing it, she's untouchable. Funny, considering she's robbed me of *my* stability, following me even here.

Why should I allow her the same mercy?

"Take it off," I command.

She flinches, her tongue flitting across her lips. Triumphant, I advance, letting the water drip from me freely, slicking the floor with every step. The closer I come, the smaller she seems. The stranger, the less recognizable—and a wave of relief almost knocks me to the ground.

I can dominate this woman. She won't control me.

"The dress," I snap, coming within arm's reach of her. Those eyes are a mirror, and I see myself reflected in them. Every dark, twisted, cruel bit—and it's a relief in a sense. *This* is the Donatello I know.

A monster.

That reflection becomes even clearer as I finger the fabric of the delicate neckline. A quick swallow contorts her throat, and the reaction lights the fuse leading to a part of me I'm desperate to unlock.

Enough wallowing. Enough regret.

I want to feel…

Anything else.

So I keep tugging. Those sharp swallows come even faster, her small chest heaving beneath the cotton. Intoxicated, I feed off every frantic breath, growing bolder with each subsequent pull.

She starts to resist, stiffening her limbs against me, keeping the dress in place the best she can. Even so, a sliver of her breast peeks beneath the neckline, and an answering sound rumbles at the base of my throat. *Enough.* My fingers clench as if of their own accord and pull.

Her eyes cut back to mine, and she's a different person in an instant. A little girl, watching me with raw betrayal etched in her delicate features. A pain that I know in my soul I will never be able to erase no matter how many years pass.

I'm back there all over again, a slave to my own twisted need for revenge. It damn near killed me to do it, but I did.

All I *could* do in that moment was turn my back on her and keep walking.

No! Gritting my teeth, I rip my gaze from hers, hunting for any tether to the present I can find. Slim fingers fill my vision instead, and I fixate on them. Long. Slender. Those of a woman at my mercy.

This *body* is at my mercy, like nothing from that memory. Shapely. Slender. Beautiful.

I know that much even before I grip both sleeves of her dress and rip it from her. Split down the middle, the entire garment comes away, and belatedly I realize it's because she didn't put up a fight this time.

I still don't look at her face, choosing to focus on the pale collarbone prominent beneath her skin. The swell of her small breasts, each capped by a dusky nipple. I cup the globe of one and groan through my teeth at the feeling—a sensation I haven't felt in so damn long. Too long.

Something other than drunkenness, or rage, or hate. And it's potent enough to overlook everything else. Everything.

Like her pink lips open and parted. Her pulse surging beneath her skin. The way her body recoils against my touch, trembling and fearful...

"Fucking hell!" I release her and stagger to a row of counters, bracing my hands against them. A mirror hangs above, and I glare at the man watching me from the surface of the glass. Even without the blood, he's a wreck. The sallow wreckage of a fallen soul.

But with her scent in my lungs, it doesn't seem too damn bad to fall.

"Get in the shower," I snap, but I don't turn to see if she obeys me.

I don't have to. Her silence is a weapon, utilized more effectively than any screaming or pleading would be. It rings out, deafeningly loud, until she chooses to break it with a single, soft footstep.

Then another.

Shame sears through my gut before pure greed replaces it. Her body enters the range of the mirror, and the round swell of her ass is a pathetic distraction, but a welcome one.

"No," I warn as she reaches for the sliding glass door.

She freezes, her chin raised, eyes staring straight ahead. In them, I don't find the fear I suspect I should in a woman forced to strip before a stranger.

Because you aren't a stranger to her, you sick fuck, a part of me snarls. *And you know it...*

But even the old, guilt-ridden Donatello has no power here. Not anymore.

She isn't Safiya; I know that now.

The little girl is dead. Whoever remains in her place is a phantom, one I have no loyalty to. Owe nothing to.

Can demand everything from.

So, I demand, "Turn on the water."

She cocks her head, and as my voice echoes back to me, I realize why—that growl sounds nothing like me. Old, groveling, whining Donatello. He, too, is dead. My reflection proves it. Glaring at the monster in his place, I bare my teeth and bark, "I said, turn it on."

She reaches for the faucet, flinching as the spray pelts her. It must be cold. Frantic, she twists on the dial.

"Turn it back down," I snap without understanding why. Maybe it's the rare way she displays unease—jerking motions she can't control. It's as addictive as a sip of booze, and I'm sick enough to push her further. Make her squirm. "Keep it cold. As cold as it can go."

Confusion mingles with alarm, contorting her mouth before she bites her lip, squashing it into a firm line. Again, her face does the speaking for her—*Are you really this petty? This cruel?*

I am.

And for the first fucking time, she falters, her fingers frozen over the faucet.

"Did you hear me?" I question.

Her eyes widen a fraction, and it's like I hit a fucking bullseye. That grim satisfaction in me grows. Her unease is a drug ten times finer than the best damn whiskey. Heady and rich, every ounce floods my blood, drowning out the rest of the world.

Just this remains—her and me.

And my cock. It stirs as I turn around and face her directly. Her own reflection doesn't do her justice. Slender and naked, glistening beneath the shower spray, she's…indescribable.

I think I've stopped myself from truly appreciating her body until now, unable to shake that lingering hate. Strip her of that, and she's worlds apart from any other woman.

She's beautiful.

Her body rides the line between too thin, with just enough curves to entice. Her hips narrow into shapely thighs, crowned by a thatch of golden curls. But as beautiful as she is, one feature draws my attention more than any other.

Those eyes. Those rich, deep, incredible fucking eyes. They cast a spell. I stare into them, and the world stares back, or how I see it anyway. Cold, unwelcoming to me. Distant. Unafraid. Uncaring. Cruel.

She stands tall, seemingly unbothered by my presence or the water raining down on her. Until I cross over to her and reach out. She flinches, her lips parting before pursing together as those eyes flicker away from me. Then downward.

And my cock betrays me in every fucking way, twitching. Regaining control is as easy as reaching past her head, gripping the faucet, and wrenching it downward.

The water goes cold damn near instantly. I'm close enough to feel a few stray drops speckle my skin as I withdraw my hand.

But her? She jumps, her eyes widening. That brief break in her mask allows me inside her head as she wrestles with the instinct warning her to move. Her arms twitch as if she has to stop them from shielding her chest, keep her spine from contorting.

Savage pride counters any remorse I might feel. I've won. Her lips press together with the knowledge of her defeat, and I feel mine widen. Break apart. Smile.

So much for her childish little grasp at control. I rake my gaze over her, savoring every sign of unease. I almost miss the moment her eyes flutter, doing the same to me. They find my chest and linger there.

Too late do I realize why.

She's reading, tracing the name forever etched into my skin. Every letter she spies does something to her. She stiffens that spine. Her chin goes back into the air.

She's defiant again.

I swear I can feel her tiny hands, grappling for the upper hand the same way she fought me for the matches. The alarming part? I feel my hand flatten against my pec, obscuring her view. She's damn near winning...

Rage robs me of any mercy. I hear my voice bounce off the interior of the stall before I even register speaking. "Wash yourself."

She blinks again, her eyes gazing past me. The world transforms in the absence of her attention. Those whispers grow louder, the shadows looming nearby loom larger.

Like an addict, I crave another hit.

So I extend my hand, brushing my thumb along her chin, and I receive what I seek tenfold. She quivers against my fingertips, but it isn't enough. I feel the need to push her further. As hard as I can. "Did you hear me, little wife? I told you to wash yourself."

Her eyes fly back to me, and I overdose on the sensation of her fear. What the hell did I even call her? That's right, the promise I made half-drunk, numb with grief. A madman's crazed boast.

Make her give me an heir to replace Vincenzo.

Did I mean it then?

It's not like she'll stay here long enough to find out. As soon as it's feasible, I'll send her back to Mischa. Her life for Vin's…

But fuck it. A part of me loves making her squirm in the meantime. It's the one thing other than booze capable of helping me forget. God, I need to forget.

"Show your future husband what he has to look forward to," I tell her. "Do you even know?"

She doesn't. Good old Mischa kept her sheltered, from the ways of women and men. I can tell just from the color that paints her cheeks. Hell, I felt it for myself days ago in Havienna. That offending finger burns with the memory of her, and I almost can't control the heat surging right between my legs.

This isn't about sex. It's about power—and I have the lion's share merely by toying with her ignorance.

"Do you?" I taunt.

She swallows, her breaths feathering for a reason that I suspect goes well beyond the frigid water she's under. *Now* she's afraid. Horrified.

I press on her pouty lip, hard enough to sense her teeth chattering beneath. "Of all the ways I could use this mouth…"

She inhales, and just as it had in the barn, her face betrays her—*You're insane, Donatello. And I hate you.*

"Good," I tell her out loud, startled by how deep genuine relief resonates through my voice. "Hate me, little wife. Hate me so much you can't fucking stand it. Hate me. Hate me!"

I'm shouting.

She's gritting her teeth, looking past me again. Again, the loss of her gaze stings. Like an itch that doesn't cease itching until I can make her look at me again. Speak to me again.

Her silent fucking lips have conveyed the truest shit I've heard all goddamn day.

"*Willow*," I snap. Like magic, her eyes dart to me, and it's clarity, so sharp I could get high off of it. I already am. Drugged off the rage burning in her eyes. Beautiful, life-giving rage transforms her into this unknowable creature—because the longer I hold her stare...the more I realize that it's not my treatment of her that has her so angry.

It's that I'm not doing it *well* enough. All this time, I've been toeing the line when it comes to her—only someone who knew me well enough would be able to tell.

Restraint.

I'm just playing with her—I haven't *tortured* her.

As insane as it sounds, I think she's furious at me for holding back, because as long as I do...

She isn't fully in control of me.

"You like power, do you, little wife?" I risk submitting my arm beneath the chill of the spray a second time to grip the faucet. I wrench it high, too high. Steam hisses from the spigot, and if she had a voice, I know she would scream at the shock. Instead, her lips part, her throat contorting around a silent gasp. Just as quickly, she wrestles her limbs into control, standing stiffly even as her pretty skin turns an ugly shade of red.

The sick fucker inside me should take pleasure out of this and rejoice at her faltering armor. Instead, I lower the faucet —all the way down.

Biology is a tricky thing. Even if the mind remains strong, the body can't disguise its instinctive reactions quite so well. She lurches to the balls of her feet, sucking in a startled breath as the steam dissipates and the water temperature plummets.

Still, I have to give her credit. Written across her face is a single daring proclamation—*Do you think this will break me?*

"I don't want to break you, little wife," I tell her, meaning every word.

Being this close to her makes it somehow easy to set aside the rage for an instant and think differently. Mischa would love it if I ruined her. Tortured her. Like a hero, he could rescue her and put the broken pieces back together, then use her downfall as an excuse to drive me right into the ground.

That's probably been his plan all along.

And, if I were truly sick, I'd use that arrogance against him. Play into the narrative that her coming here perfectly illustrates—he loves her, protects her.

But I *have* her. I'm in her head, pushing him out. She'll leave his perfect life behind just to follow me. A sick son of a bitch would test just how far she might go…

I won't. Still, I want to hear how it sounds out loud. "I'm going to hone you," I say. "I'm going to bend you to my will, little bird. I'll erase any identity you've had before me. As long as you're here. You're mine…"

She frowns, trying to puzzle the meaning of the words. Hell, I don't understand them my damn self. Inane ramblings of a mad man, but at least I'm still sane enough to recognize as much.

She drives me *mad* with those watchful little eyes. They strip me down to nothing—in them, I'm none of my past selves. Not the fearsome *Il Mostro* or the Butcher. Not Donatello, the family man. Not even the dutiful Don who cared for another man's child out of what little kindness dwelled within his heart.

To this woman, I'm just someone to hate, and there's freedom in that. And damn, she does hate me. With every word, her lips go flatter, thinner. Her gaze turns cutting. She becomes an open book.

"You're fantasizing about killing me now, aren't you, little wife?"

She is. I can see the images flicker in her mind like I'm watching a fucking slideshow. She hates being powerless. She hates how easily I can make her feel that way.

I step back, taking her body in fully. The chill of the water forces a reaction from her I doubt I'd otherwise see. Her skin is so pale the bluish veins peek from beneath, feeding that frantically beating heart. Pink nipples stand erect, bared freely as she lowers her hands to her sides.

If I wanted to mistake the action as out of fear, those eyes would prove me wrong. They cut into me, unafraid, blazing like coals.

I don't look away from them as I cross to the counter and fish a rag from a rack by the sink. Before I fully think the thought through, I throw it at her.

"Wash yourself."

She crouches slowly, grasping the white cloth within her slim fingers. My breath catches—not because of her body. Just her expression. That face is more damning than the mirror, a broad reflection of everything I am. I'm in control of how she sees me, and I want her to gape. To stare open-mouthed as I lean against the countertop behind me and hold her watchful gaze.

Though they aren't true, I want her to believe every word I said.

"Wash yourself, little wife," I say, palming my hip with one hand while the other grabs my cock. I grunt, alarmed to find it already stiff as fuck. My eyes drift down to those breasts; they're shapely enough to explain it. But no. I meet those eyes again and grit my teeth as a wave of fire centers right beneath my fucking hand. Fighting to keep my voice steady, I dare her, "Make it worth my while."

A good captive would cringe and shield herself—that's what she is, after all. My captive. *Mine.* Though one determined to avoid the pretense of being my property.

Holding the cloth securely in one hand, she inches backward just enough to grab the bar of soap from a built-in shelf along the wall. The same soap I used. Laboriously she lathers the rag, taking her time with no hint of fear to quicken her movements. Though she's shivering from head to toe, it's the water doing it to her. Not terror.

If I doubted that, her eyes find mine through the damp strands of blond hair clinging to her forehead. Slowly, she drags the cloth along her body, jumping with every motion of the wet fabric against her skin.

Only a monster would get off on this. Her gentle movements. Her tiny form that makes the stall I just stood in seem massive around her.

Only a monster would want more.

"Turn around."

After a second's hesitation, she does. With her back turned, I can fully enjoy the sight of her. Without her judgment. Without that constant, blank stare.

Unashamed, I lean back, resting my head against the mirror, and let my hand work. Slow strokes. Then harder, gripping my shaft to the point of pain. The longer I watch her, the more I can read her, even with her ass to me.

Stripping her naked and on display for my benefit is one thing, but she hates this. The little witch loathes being out of control. If she can't see me, she can't manipulate me. As if aware of that fact, she inclines her head, and those eyes find mine again. In them, I see her anticipating my next words before I even voice them. Hell, she's taunting me, goading me to say them.

"Turn around—"

"Donatello?"

A knock resonates from the door of the suite, and I hiss through my teeth at the sound of that voice. Luciano. From his tone, I can tell he won't be turned away so easily.

But a flicker of motion from the woman draws my attention back to her. She stiffens, the rag falling from her fingers to slap against the floor of the stall, and I lean forward, my jaw clenched. I can sense her fear even as she turns away from me.

I can see her naked, but she's wary of someone else doing the same.

As she should be, a part of me growls. I ignore it. I don't owe her a damn thing.

"Come in," I call, loud enough for Luciano to hear.

In the meantime, I cross over to a larger rack and grab a white towel for myself. Trust Antonio to waste money on a damn good towel. As I wrap it around my waist, I eye her again, my trapped little bird. She doesn't beg me with her eyes this time. She doesn't cower. Not even as Luciano's steps advance swiftly through the suite.

"Where are you?" he calls.

"In here."

He's paces away, his heavy sigh preceding him. With every inch he gains, the woman grows paler. Her hands creep along her ribcage, drifting toward her breasts, and a bitten lip betrays her rage at herself—she hates this weakness.

"Here." Another towel is already in my grasp. I throw it at her, not intending to watch her cover herself with it. I do anyway. She scrambles to wrap the material around her body just as Luciano coldly remarks from the doorway, "At least you finally took a shower."

He hasn't seen her yet—a fact I'm sure of just from his tone alone.

"Wait for me down the hall."

"Will do," he says, already retreating. "I brought you some clothes, and something I found for your…'friend.' I'll leave them by the door."

For me, he left another suit in a hideous shade of gray. Regardless, it fits well enough. As for what he brought for the woman…

The style and cut leave nothing to the imagination as to the kind of women Antonio himself preferred. Black and velvety, it's short with thin straps. Lucky for her, she's small enough that the dress will cover far more than the designer intended.

But is that a good thing?

No, I tell myself, clenching the damn thing in a fist. I should be parading her before these men, humiliating her in any way I can. Because regardless of who she is, only one identity she possesses matters—daughter of Mischa Stepanov, the man who tried to kill my son.

I drop the dress, watching it hit the floor. Then I step over it and head down the hall, joining Luciano in the gaudy entryway.

"I would be lying if I didn't say that I might be doubting this little deal with a devil." He sounds so damn serious. I have to laugh. Then I sigh on my way to the minibar. Liquor is a better vice than any woman. I grab a bottle at random and take a sip without bothering to read the label. It's strong—but it would take the whole bottle at least to get me back to my usual mind state—numb, dumb, dulled to my darker impulses.

I set it down without drinking more. Still, the burning liquid searing down my throat gives my senses enough of a bitch slap to refocus.

"I knew you were a sick bastard," Luciano remarks from behind me. "But damn. I don't think the rumors did you justice."

"Justice," I parrot the word as though it's a foreign term. Maybe it is. I've never felt it for myself. I've chased it.

Waxed poetic about it once upon a time. Dreamt of earning it for myself. Only to come to one brutal realization.

"I don't believe in justice."

"Okay," he says mockingly. "Think I might have figured that after what you did to Paulie. Shit, man. He was a dick, but no one deserves that—"

"Didn't he? Taking a gun to a pregnant woman and child may be a cut above ripping apart said child killer."

"Don't bullshit me, Don. You don't give a flying fuck about the Stepanovs. That was personal. So now that you got off on torture, what the fuck now?"

"Now?" I raise an eyebrow. "Isn't it obvious? You had it recorded like I asked?"

He nods, wincing.

"Good. We send it to Mischa as a little present—along with an ultimatum."

"The girl in exchange for the hospital?" Luciano suggests.

"Eavesdropping prick." I don't even have the energy to scowl. "How much did you hear?"

"Enough to trust your crazy ass plan," he counters, crossing his arms defensively. "You aren't suicidal. You've got something to live for, at least. There's a slim damn chance that you aren't just trying to get us all killed in some last crusade."

I scoff, though hell, he might be right. Something to live for…

But it wouldn't be Vincenzo—I always gave him everything, and it wasn't enough. He deserves far more than me. But Mischa?

He is something to live for. I'll fight for every last breath until the moment I can see him suffer. He got cocky, living his life at the top of the food chain. And he'll live long enough to see his own slow crawl right back to the bottom.

"Is everything ready like I asked?" I question, switching back to the task at hand.

Luciano nods. "You mean your little 'present'? It's ready. But first… You might want to see this." He pulls a cell phone from his pocket. It must be his own, a different model from Antonio's, already displaying a video on the screen. It looks like a newsreel from early this morning, and the chyron flashing across the bottom of the picture tells me all I need to know.

Fire blazes through Hell's Gambit harbor.

"Fuck." I don't even have enough energy to put shock into my voice. Maybe because it's been a long time fucking coming. Mischa was bound to make a move like this at some point. Better the harbor than Fabio.

"It seems like Mischa didn't take kindly to you reneging on your harbor sale. Don't worry—" he adds as I lurch for the door. "He hasn't struck anywhere else. Yet. But if you aim to put your plan into action, I suggest you do it now."

I sink onto the nearest leather armchair.

My plan.

"Send a copy of the Vanetti recording to Mischa."

"And if he doesn't buy it?" Luciano counters.

"Then we'll send it to every faction with even a sliver of influence in this city," I say, ticking the names off on my fingers. "The Saleris. The Sigerellis. Every fucking MC and every potential ally. I want them all to know that Mischa acted on faulty intel."

"Done." He starts for the door, adding over his shoulder, "Then what?"

"Then... We make the rounds," I say. "If I were Mischa, I'd already be trying to cultivate an army to my side. We need to head him off."

"Anyone particular in mind?"

I swipe at my chin, thinking. "Gregori Saleri," I state out loud. "The hospital is in the heart of his territory. If I were Mischa, I'd already have invited the bastard over for tea."

Luciano skeptically cocks his head. "You think?"

"Hell yes." I rake my hands through my hair and wind up running them over the front of my borrowed suit. It's too small on second thought, constricting my forearms. I feel like a sausage shoved into it, just like I did during that fucking debutante ball, all in a bid to impress and pander. *Fuck it.*

I shed the jacket and throw it on the floor. One by one, I attack the buttons of the dress shirt, ripping them open and leaving my chest bare. Now, I can breathe.

And think.

"There is a reason Mischa isn't setting fire to the entire city looking for me. No…" I approach a window, bracing my hand over the glass. My outstretched fingers slice the view beyond into portions, much like the political layout of the city itself.

"He's biding his time, trying to smoke me out," I say through clenched teeth. "If he can rob me of allies, I'll have nowhere left to hide, in theory. He knows the hospital would be the one place I'd risk trying to infiltrate."

"Because of your nephew," Luciano says softly. "But you have his daughter. I'd personally hunt you down and cut your balls off if I were in his position."

He isn't Mischa Stepanov, a rumored brute, vicious and more than capable of doing a hasty castration—but you don't get to the top by acting primarily on impulse.

"He thinks I won't hurt her," I say, still thinking aloud. "He's counting on that. She'll be traumatized, maybe battered, but alive. He has a bigger goal in mind than merely finding her. I'm guessing he only needs her to hold out another day at most. Then he'll make his final play and come for her."

"Why the delay?"

I exhale, thinking it through. "Why?"

Because old Mischa isn't trying to punish me for these recent events—this is deeper than that. Personal. He wants to save his daughter from her nightmare once and for all as any father would. Drive me from the city. Crush me into dust.

Destroy every trace of all Vanicis.

Me. Vincenzo. He wants us gone.

Much like Vin's imaginary monster haunted him, his precious Willow can't live her life if we're still here.

The sheer cruelty of it hits like a punch to the chest, flipping my stupid hope right on its fucking head. If I go to Mischa now, even with proof that I wasn't behind the attack, it won't matter. He might let Vin be admitted to the hospital, if only to have direct access to kill him later.

It's what I would have done. Hell, I *have* done it. Some crimes can't be punished merely with death, but with brutality.

Gino Mangenello is proof of that.

This war has its roots in what happened seven years ago. I hurt his daughter, and by merely existing, I threw that pain back in her face. In Mischa's thinking, I struck first; therefore, anything is justified.

I could always fight fire with fire and launch a full-out war on the *mafiya*.

Or better yet, I can turn the tables on Mischa and beat him at his own fucking game.

I can make his daughter the perfect weapon.

"Change of plans," I say as the plan begins to unfurl in my mind. "We won't wait for Mischa to come for the girl."

"What do you mean?"

I lick my lips in grim anticipation. I can't even say it out loud. Yet. "You'll find out soon enough. In the meantime, set up a meeting with the Saleris."

"When?"

"As soon as you can. Tonight," I say, heading down the hall. "Just give me an hour."

It's time to drop the pretense of captor and captive. Giovanni had it right from the start—life is all a fucking game.

So I'll let Mischa's daughter decide for herself. To remain a pawn? Or become a more powerful piece...

A queen—one fully under my control.

13

WILLOW

I know pain. I know agony. I've seen horrible things in my life, and throughout it all, I've survived. Scarred and battered, but still alive, only there are no wounds as proof of this most recent ordeal. No blood to clean that is my own, at least.

It's all in my head, and that's how he wanted it. Mental scars inflict the most lasting damage—he taught me that.

Fittingly, all there is to mark this moment is my own reflection watching me from a bathroom mirror, my skin pink and tender.

The sight chills me more than any scar would.

This woman is a stranger to me, her brown eyes wide with shock, her lips pursed in a perpetual frown. The ill-fitting dress she's wearing hangs off her lanky frame, highlighting the dichotomy within which she finds herself.

Captive and toy.

Accomplice.

Murderer.

Tears glisten in her eyes, reinforcing the terror written across that face. Inside, however? I feel nothing to match her outward expression. No prickling behind my eyes to herald the moisture falling down my cheeks. Nothing aching in the pit of my soul.

Of everything I've been through in my life, this feeling is the strangest to grapple with.

Numbness.

Emptiness.

Nothing.

But as if to mock me, my ears pick up a distant sound—a footstep—and a million conflicting emotions flood my veins. *Fear. Unease. The building horror that I'm trapped...*

Another heavy footstep echoes off the cavernous walls, creating a cage more binding than this structure itself—but it's invisible, entirely of my own making. The reality is that I could have run from here all along. I didn't have to follow him into this building, this room. Didn't have to submit to his torment, or wear the dress he left for me.

In theory, I don't have to stay here now, and yet with every additional step to break the silence, I'm frozen, unable to move a muscle.

While I may be paralyzed, the face in the mirror isn't. With every step to draw nearer, that pink mouth tightens. Throat quivers. When the footsteps finally stop? Her tongue flits out along her lower lip, and her dark eyes widen as a masculine laugh catches the air.

She can instantly identify the culprit.

His shadow paints the floor beside the doorway, but he doesn't enter. Yet. He wants me to sense him first. For my nostrils to flare with the faint scent of musk that precedes him.

He wants me to remember, every grisly, twisted memory. Not just what happened in the shower, either. My skin is overly sensitive, speckled with throbbing scarlet blotches, but I'd rather be boiled alive than relive the previous moments.

I can barely admit it inside my own head—I watched him kill a man. Butcher him. Take pleasure in doing so…

But you watched, a part of me taunts. *You didn't look away.*

Not even when he met my gaze, his fingers dripping blood. For a second, he'd sported that grim, knowing smirk—as if he were seeing inside my head.

And what he found…excited him.

"Look at yourself, *principessa,*" the present Donatello demands, maneuvering to appear in the mirror's view, leaning against the doorway. He isn't fully naked, at least, wearing a pair of black pants, but his chest is exposed, each letter of the tattoo clearly visible. In this moment, I take the time to examine them in a way I couldn't before.

Each sloppily craved letter looks fresh given the coloring. As if he wrote them all in blood.

SAFIYA.

They do the one thing I can't do with my own voice—prove him a liar. The girl he claims meant nothing? The past he's tried to ignore...

It's here. It's *always* been here. My fingers twitch at my sides as if aching to reach out and touch one of those marks. Graze that lopsided A with the tip of my nail and force him to acknowledge me. How would he react? It's not hard to imagine.

With rage. With scorn and hate.

But we'd both know the outcome, in the end...

I'd gain the upper hand.

"Look at that face," he taunts, drawing my attention back to his mouth. Then my own. "Those eyes. In them, you see the same thing I do."

Does he see horror and despair?

He should.

"You know what I see? Nothing," he says, countering that hope. "You don't regret what we did, do you? I can see it all over your face. You enjoyed it."

Enjoyed. Is that the emotion to describe my blank expression or the pink cheeks streaked with tears? I shake my head, responding to my own question rather than him.

He laughs again, and those steps echo louder, playing a twisted melody off the walls. As his reflection appears behind mine, I suck in a breath.

Throughout my life, I've witnessed various iterations of Donatello Vanici. The stoic protector. The playful guardian. The vengeful betrayer.

Never before have I faced this specter. His eyes are so dark they gleam like coals, enhancing the hollow planes of his face. Dark stubble coats his chin like an embodiment of the shadows behind him. The most alarming feature of all? Myself, reflected in his gaze, different from the woman in the mirror. Distorted by the hue of his irises, she looks cold. Unbothered. Unafraid.

Just like him.

"Don't," he warns, before I even register looking away. Too late. A span of tile holds my attention now, even as thick fingers harshly grip my chin, wrenching it back to face the mirror's surface.

"You watch," commands the gruff voice dripping into my ear. "You see the truth there, written across those pretty lips. You may not be able to voice it for yourself, but I can tell— you enjoyed this, didn't you, little *principessa*? And I'm not talking about the shower. Telling me where to cut. Hearing him scream—"

My hand flies out, landing flat against the counter, serving as a protest I can't voice—*No!*

"Oh yes," he says amid a low chuckle. His fingers creep along my jawline and graze my throat. In the mirror, two dark eyes watch me mockingly, ablaze with fire. Then little by little...any humor vanishes.

I close my eyes to shut him out. Banish the memories—the blood. The screams. I shove them all as far as I can to the darkest depths of my psyche.

But not far enough.

"We're the same, hellcat. Both sick, pathetic creatures who thrive on pain. Accept that—" What feels like his thumb ghosts the swell of my cheek, lingering near the corner of my mouth. "We are. But you never need to feel guilty around me..."

His voice hitches, touching on an octave deeper than I think he meant to. I reopen my eyes, and even his frown can't disguise the fleeting expression to cross his face. Alarm —as if the words leaving his throat startle him just as much as they unnerve me.

"You can coddle yourself with lies, if you want," he says, raising an eyebrow to become mocking once more. "I won't. You've been sheltered long enough, *Willow*. It's time to face the world."

Before I can recover, he muscles in beside me and turns on the sink faucet. He takes his time wetting his hands before bracing them, still wet, against the countertop. Maybe he did it to draw my attention to them.

They fan out over the dark marble, gleaming like tarnished gold in comparison. Dangerous, thick digits capable of so much violence—the proof of which still smarts along my throat, burning in the heat of his breath.

To counter any self-pity I might feel is a grim satisfaction as my eyes flicker up to his jaw and the two lines sliced there, one a few days old, the other fresh. Both wounds look worse from this angle, even more vicious than the bruises left by his hands. I got my revenge.

"You hate me," Donatello murmurs, but his gaze is distant. Years in the past, I suspect, reliving the very reasons why. Slowly, he nods. "You should hate me. I want you to. Look at me... Look!"

Our gazes meet over the mirror's glass, and the rest of the world fades to a dull hum. His voice alone is powerful enough to rival even thunder. Somehow, his stare is even louder, outlasting the thrum of the still running water and my own frantic breaths. I can't look away.

I can't breathe.

"Hate me," he warns. "If that will make you feel better. Hate me all you want. I'll allow you that much."

If I want. He'll allow. I almost can't track the irritation flicking through me until it's too late.

As if he has any right to accept my rage like it's a mercy.

He chuckles in triumph at the response—my lips twitching, eyes narrowing. "You want to learn something, *principessa*? A great, universal truth?" He positions his face near mine, lips inches from my earlobe. "Your hate? It doesn't mean a damn thing. Though, I'm sure you think it does. If you hate me enough, it will somehow matter. Your hate doesn't mean shit. You know what does?" He leans closer, his gaze unreadable. "Power. You need power to get anywhere in this fucking world. Even as a woman, you have what you need."

I stiffen at the reference, but he doesn't sneer to punctuate the punchline. He isn't joking.

"You just never learned to use it," he adds. "You never will. Why? You were always sheltered in the grip of power, never expected to amass your own. What I did to you was *evil*, I'll admit that."

Rare sincerity ripples through his tone, and some part of me cringes in response. It's like a wall gives way, and for a split second, I feel everything…

The pain. The hate. The fear—god, that *fear*. My knees buckle, forcing me to grip the edge of the counter for stability. Back then, I had nothing to rely on as the gravity of what he did to me sunk in. He was gone.

I was alone.

The tears spring to life before I can hold them back, searing the corners of my eyes, unwilling to fall. Yet. Gradually, I get a grip on my emotions—smother them back where they belong, and as I do, I realize something.

His face... If I trusted the honesty in his tone, his eyes are cool enough to suck any warmth from the words.

"It was evil. But it wasn't enough to teach you what you should have learned... Your hate doesn't mean shit in the long run. Real revenge? Real retaliation? You can only garner that from power, and just by being here alone, you've given up any you ever had. Do you understand?"

I grit my teeth and eye the basin of the sink rather than face him. His expression sneaks into my mind anyway. That smug smile. The sly arrogance in his posture betraying that he thinks he's right. He takes pride in being right.

Even now...

I don't mean anything to him.

"Who you are now. Who you used to be..." He trails off. "Truth be told, *principessa*—I can't feel a damn thing. No love. No hate. All I feel?" He brushes his hand over his chest in the vague direction of his heart. "All I feel is pain. Sorrow. Emptiness. So hate me all you want. Maybe one day I'll let you act on it? In the meantime, I've figured out your real use to me."

Fire floods my cheeks, painting them red in the mirror. I can't stop my gaze from darting to his fingers, still braced over the counter, dangerously close.

"You think I aim to fuck you?" I flinch as his lips brush my ear, still moving. "I could. Does that scare you? I *could.*"

I wrench away from him, recoiling against the nearest wall. My shoulder throbs with the force of the collision, but I'd propel myself through the barrier if I could. His eyes narrow, tracking my reaction as the words sink in.

He could...

"If you mattered in this game, *principessa*? I'd consider it." He doesn't laugh. Doesn't flinch.

He means it. And I can tell from his low, slow exhale next that he means what he's about to say even more. "But you don't. Hear that now. A smart girl would take comfort in hearing that."

He leans against the counter, examining his curled fist. A muscle in his jaw twitches, undermining his careful, level baritone. "All that matters is Mischa. You heard the truth for yourself. What he did?"

I bite the inside of my mouth so hard I taste blood. I heard. Mischa attacked Vincenzo believing Donatello attacked him first—but he was wrong. Played by faulty information

And you knew it all along, a part of me snarls. *You never questioned it...*

"With you here, there are a million ways I could punish him," Donatello points out, watching me with his head cocked. "You realize that, don't you?"

I do. Yet, I force every muscle in my face to go still rather than show it.

"I could rip you apart. Let every man here take a turn. String you up for the hell of it and send you to him in a box."

He could. Worse things have happened, circling the manor as rumors. Mischa wasn't always a family man. I saw firsthand the way he used to live. Violently. Recklessly.

"He probably expects as much," Donatello admits. "But I know what will punish him more. What he truly deserves."

He lets the seconds pass, ramping up the tension the way a dramatic pause would in a drawn-out sonata. Finally, he moves to capitalize on the moment, advancing to the sink to shut the water off. Facing me from over his shoulder, he says, "I'm going to use *you*. He thinks I dragged you here, but I'll let him know the truth. You came to me willingly. You always came to me. Why? I have a hold over you he never will. Power over his precious little girl. You gave it to me—"

He reacts before I even realize what I'm doing—lunging at him with a fist brandished and no idea of where I'm aiming it. His chest. My knuckles ricochet off the scarlet F carved over his ribcage with a sickening thud—over and over again.

If I had that letter opener, or my knife…I'd use it.

Slice into him just to prove one point—he doesn't control me.

He has *nothing* over me.

"Enough." He grabs my wrist, still chuckling in that insufferable way. "Oh, little hellcat, I'll let you assault me all you want. *After* our wedding night, my body will belong to you after all."

Wedding night. The threat hits me like a slap, and I stagger back, tripping over my own feet. A firm grip on my forearm is the only force saving me from a nasty fall. Eyes wide, I gape at the tan fingers coiled against my skin. Like so much of my interactions with him, the sight is familiar, while the sensation—his actual touch—is so *wrong*. Foreign. Unnatural.

Heat radiates from him like fire, burning through my brain's pathetic attempts to remain unaffected.

"Did you hear me?" he goads. This time, he doesn't withdraw—instead, he tightens his grip, drawing me closer with a ruthless flick of his forearm. His opposite arm goes around my waist, setting off a million different reactions.

Air sticks in my throat as shock paralyzes me. Intentionally, I suspect. He wants to unnerve me.

He has.

His nearness assaults me from every direction. His body is an inescapable prison. So hard. Solid. My fingers scramble to find purchase against his chest—to shove him away. Then a sudden shift in his skin texture has me fanning my fingers out, seeking more. Parts of him are so scarred, so rough they hurt to touch. *Here* especially...

Rippling flesh, rugged and jagged.

What the hell happened to him?

I look down and see for myself—I'm grazing the outermost edge of the tattoo. Up close, the scarlet shapes reveal a viciousness you can't see when farther back. This wasn't the typical application—it was violent. Something ripped the skin apart, staining the flesh underneath. It took days to heal, if not weeks, such painful, deliberate marks. I can't resist flicking my tongue along my lower lip as I study them, unsure what I feel. Triumph? He lied—his unimportant SAFIYA left her mark on him, alright.

He immortalized her himself—and he wanted it to hurt.

To bleed.

To scar.

I barely get the chance to track the shudder running through him before he shifts, sinking his free hand into my hair. My reaction is exactly what he wants—I flinch.

But I don't pull away.

"You're not afraid to marry me," he deduces as though I've said as much out loud. But I haven't—I don't even know what my own thoughts convey, let alone enough to portray it.

But somehow, he still claims to know it all. What I'm thinking. What I fear. What I hate.

"Isn't that right, little hellcat?" His finger flits along my lower lip, raising chills in its wake. "No. You're afraid about what that might mean—that you *aren't* afraid. Don't tell me you enjoy playing with danger?" He strokes my jawline as I grit my teeth.

"I could leave you guessing as to what I intend to do to you. I could feed you a million senseless fears. Torment you through vague taunts and threats..."

He fingers a lock of my hair, winding it around and around the width of his finger.

"But I won't. I'm going to marry you. In front of your father and God, I will marry you. You'll consent to every step along the way. I'll become *your* monster to protect. You'll have no choice."

My monster.

I don't know what he means, but his eyes are even darker, his mouth the closest he can come to a smile. Even in obvious madness, he sounds so serious. Too serious. A million thoughts come to mind, each more dangerous than the last.

"Oh, don't look at me like that," he warns, lifting my chin against his calloused palm. "You think I'm going to ravish you, little hellcat? Rip you open over nice, white bedsheets and then display them in the morning for your father to see?"

I can't resist the imagery sneaking into my skull, illustrating his words. The heat in my cheeks turns searing.

"I won't," he says belatedly. "That would be too easy. Too merciful… And if there is one thing I am tired of being, it's merciful. You see, mercy is what got me here."

His tone rings with a double meaning—*here*, standing in an enclosed room with a figure from his past, he thought long dead. Here, proposing insanity with a dangerous smile.

"I am through with mercy," he says, using his grasp on that strand of my hair to climb higher. Soon his fingers scrape against my scalp, guiding the position of my head until I have no choice but to look at him. "I am going to marry you, little hellcat, but do not worry. Our union will not last long."

The way he says those words triggers a wave of unease that rides my spine.

"You're wondering why? Am I threatening you?" He laughs again, but his gaze becomes distant. Colder, if it's even possible. "No, little hellcat. I've decided to warn you—after our wedding night, your fears when it comes to me will be moot."

My dread must show on my face, feeding the slow, ripe smile to shape his mouth. The same emotion I felt when I lashed at his face strikes again. Burning. Blazing. But this time, I don't hit him—my teeth snap instead, barely missing the tip of his thumb.

He frowns, withdrawing his hand. I caught him off guard. Frantic, I realize it's the only way to fight against him.

React.

Already he's recovered, fingering a strand of hair a safe distance from my mouth. "Until then, I'm going to become your monster, little hellcat. Lurking in your closet—and you are going to shield me from Mischa. Corrupting you will be his punishment."

He's speaking through me, his gaze distant, even as his fingers work through my damp, tangled hair. "Get dressed."

Abruptly he pulls back, letting me go. His eyes rake over the black dress I'm wearing now. He lumbers into the hall, returning a second later with something he must have already had at the ready—a black case that he throws onto the counter, spilling its contents as a result. Makeup, all different brands, seemingly collected by the various women who might have stayed here at one point.

With him?

"Play your role, hellcat," he cautions, distracting me from the thought. "Good enough, so even I believe it. I won't waste my breath threatening your life, either," he warns, entering the hall. "I don't want a captive bird. But in case you do need some motivation, think of *her*."

The little girl—but his disinterested tone betrays the threat for what it is—hollow. His real tool to motivate me is something far more intangible than another life.

Pride.

Do I have what it takes to play his game?

Or will I cower in wait of rescue like the little girl he thinks
I am...

14

EVGENI

After the way our last meeting ended, I don't expect Mischa to call me back to the manor so soon—and definitely not hours into my shift covering Mrs. Stepanova.

I know the second I see the succinct text—*You're needed at base, now*—something's wrong.

My mind races with potential reasons, Willow first among them. As I park near the front walkway, I sense the mood shift before I even step foot inside the house. Unease tinges the air, affecting everyone on the property.

Case in point? The first man I pass on my way inside has a gun drawn out in the open, a sight so galling, I do a double take.

"What the hell is wrong with you?" I demand, snatching for his wrist. "Have you lost your goddamn mind?"

I glance at the house where the children could be watching through any one of the windows. Mischa may ensure that his property is well patrolled, but the foremost rule is to never reveal the true nature of that presence to his children.

The man before me is well aware of the rules, and yet he shrugs me off, still brandishing his weapon. "New orders from the boss himself," he explains. "We're to stand at the ready. At least until his 'guest' leaves."

"Guest?" The hairs on the back of my neck stand on end. Few "guests" could warrant this kind of vigilance. Donatello Vanici, for one...

Or someone far worse.

"Are they in the study?" I start forward, my shoulders tense.

The man shakes his head. "The main hall."

Shit. My alarm only grows, and I have to stop myself from running the entire way there.

The hall is where Mischa holds court only for the most joyous occasions—or the most grave. The man he loved like a father's funeral was here. His wedding took place in the same space. More recently? His daughter's debutante.

And now?

The drastic difference in attendees is one startling change. Instead of well-dressed socialites, Mischa alone dominates the room, flanked on either side by two guards, along with another figure I don't recognize.

Perhaps, because he's in pieces.

Someone delivered them in what once might have been a large blue box delicately wrapped and adorned with a white bow. Hell, it could have been mistaken for one of Willow's debutante presents at first. Instead of the typical necklace or bauble, a severed head lies within on a bed of tissue paper, along with a bloodied hand presumably from the same unfortunate individual.

"Who ordered this open?" I demand, scanning the box intently. I don't see a name or other identifying feature. "Was it even searched properly—"

"I did," Mischa says. One look at his face, and I suspect the delivered body parts are only partly the cause of the tense mood in the air. I can only name one other time he sported this pained grimace, that being when his wife and son arrived at this very home barely alive.

"This came with it," he says, presenting a tablet, sporting a blurred image of several figures in a room. A warehouse? Taking it from Mischa, I press play.

A man's voice rings out from the device next, cold and booming. I recognize it instantly—Donatello Vanici's.

A high-pitched cry answers, and my blood runs cold before I note the low pitch. Not a woman's, at least. Not Willow's.

But then I see her. She's visible for just a second, her back to the camera, blond hair loose. Her dress is filthy, but otherwise, she seems unharmed. As the video continues to play, I start to question for how long. Is this a recording of her death?

That fear only grows when the camera pans over Vanici's face. Despite the video's poor quality, it's easy to read the murderous intent in his eyes. Instead of Willow, he's fixated on another figure, however. Someone out of view.

"This is him," a man behind Vanici says. "Paulie Vanetti."

I cut my gaze over to Mischa and find him watching as well, his face stone. I can't tell if that name means anything to him, but it triggers a vague sense of recognition in me. *Vanetti.* I've heard rumors of a mercenary like that, prized for his ruthless skill.

When I return my attention to the video, I can barely make out the figure in question, kneeling on the floor. Bound?

"So this is the man Antonio contracted?" Vanici asks.

"It's him," the first man replies. "He's been cagey on the work he did. I don't think he'll tell us freely."

"There is no need for threats." Vanici crouches on one knee, inspecting the man before him. "Was it you?" he asks softly, flicking his thumb along the other man's cheek. "The Stepanovs. Were you the man Antonio hired to do his fucking dirty work?"

Recognition washes over me, and I almost can't keep myself from blurting my observation out loud—I was right. From the corner of my eye, Mischa remains impossible to read, his eyes fixated on the screen.

"Let's hear it," Donatello demands, yanking the man's gag free. *"Speak. Were you the lapdog Tony sent to do his bidding?"*

"Go. To hell," Vanetti croaks. *"Where the fuck is Tony? I'll teach that son of a bitch to—"*

"Tony's dead." Rising to his feet, Donatello flicks the discarded gag aside and clasps his hands behind his back.

"You answer to me," he says, towering over the captive man. *"Did he hire you to do it?"*

"The fuck is this?" The man's eyes continue to dart warily around the room. *"What the fuck is going on, Luciano?"*

"Luciano," I echo. This name I recognize. *"Famiglia* agent."

If that surprises Mischa, his eyes reveal nothing. I get the sense that he's focused on something else entirely. "Keep watching," he says.

"Tony paid me over a hundred grand for it," Vanetti stammers. *"I just did as I was told, okay? It wasn't nothing fucking personal."*

"Personal," Vanici snaps. *"Oh, but this* was *personal. If you won't take my word for it, then take hers."*

He inclines his head to a figure barely visible behind him.

"This is the man who attacked your mother," Vanici tells her. *"The reason why your father tried to kill my son. Did you know that? You knew. Didn't you? Is that really why you came running to me, little principessa?—"*

"Son of a bitch," Mischa growls, slamming his hand against the desk.

He's already seen this, I suspect. But despite it all—his daughter captive, standing so close to a madman—this is the part that unnerves him the most. Her, standing toe to toe with Donatello Vanici as he taunts her. But not just any taunt—*principessa*, said with such scorn there's no doubt that he means it as an insult.

"Let us not forget... I didn't drag you here as my captive. You came to me," Vanici growls.

I'm so busy watching Mischa, the next parts of the video register only in the broadest terms. Vanici extorts supposed proof from Vanetti that he was responsible for the attack on the Stepanovs. Anger burns hot in my chest, and I'm already planning a full on assault on Antonio Salvatore and his assets—dead or not.

Even as I do, I keep glancing back at Mischa, alarmed to find that he doesn't seem to feel the same. This video proves that he—literally—jumped the gun. He potentially waged war against the wrong man.

But as his teeth pull back from his upper lip, I realize that something more egregious than that is what really has him on edge. A sight that enrages him beyond Vanici's supposed guilt in harming his wife. A crime that outweighs the man's supposed innocence.

He approaches Willow, speaking to her in a low, unsettling tone. "You feel it too," he murmurs. "Hate. That sick need for revenge—and not mere 'justice,' either... You want pain. You want him to suffer, just as you suffered. Am I wrong? I can see it written all over your face... The hate—and not just for me, either. How should we punish him?"

Alarm builds in my gut. "What the hell is he doing?"

"Watch," Mischa warns.

"Don't deny that you want to," Vanici tells her. "So what will it be? A slit throat? A beheading? Name your choice, principessa. You wanted to play in our world, so play.

Willow's face is barely visible from this angle—a dark brown eye blazing fearlessly, riveted to the man before her.

"He threatened your family, your mother, your brother. You want more than just his pain. You want more than justice, don't you?"

Vanici turns to one of the men nearby. "I asked for a knife."

"Shit!" I rock on my heels, my jaw clenched to the point of pain. Will he hurt her? Are pieces of that morbid "present" from Willow herself? Again, Mischa's face doesn't give me an answer, but he's more animated than before, his gaze blazing.

Warier than ever, I force myself to keep watching as Vanici is finally given a blade. He raises it...

But I sway with relief when he turns away from her.

"You're going to tell me how to kill him," he says. "Every cut. Every scream. It will be all on you. Your face tells me everything

I need to know. Your eyes... I see the hate in them. You want this—Don't! You watch me. You watch all of it. Now... Where should we begin? Ah, of course. We need a name," he suggests, toying with the blade. *"Should we start with his tongue?"*

It's a cruel, sadistic mental game. One I know all too well, and a skill Vanici masters—manipulation. It's all in his tone —a mocking, stern rasp that can make the insane seem logical.

The unconscionable bearable.

The kind of charm that can sway a young, stupid boy to commit the unfathomable.

"You promised me your loyalty, Geno. Do you want to live up to your father's legacy? Then stop questioning..." The voice echoes through my brain as if spoken aloud—but not by Vanici. Regardless, I tear my gaze from the screen for a split-second, eyeing the doorway as if expecting someone else to come strolling through, his features untouched by time.

My heart races, and I have to grit my teeth to refocus. Vanici is my current target, and I wrench my gaze back to the video.

"I said watch me, Safiya."

A part of me reacts to that name before I realize why. He knows Willow's name. Why call her that? Safiya...

"This is your game, after all. Tell me where to cut him. Play your role. Look at me!"

"The son of a bitch," I croak, forming a fist though I know it's a futile gesture. It's all I can do, digging my nails into my palm as he makes her watch. He toys with her. Taunts her while threatening to kill a man.

But it's the familiarity between them that alarms me. An unspoken weight that enhances every glance they share between them, Willow and Vanici. It's uncomfortable, triggering an unease I can't name.

"You're angry. You have every fucking right to be. But you're suppressing it. Bottling it up nice and neat. Why?" He leans closer, bringing his mouth near her ear...

Mischa hisses in a way I've never heard, his eyes slits. Still, his restraint is remarkable—especially when Vanici shoves Willow to the ground, placing his knife against her throat.

I grit my teeth, lurching on tip-toe as if I could leap into the recording itself and stop him.

"Wait," Mischa says. "Keep watching."

Watching as Vanici continues his sick game, playing with Willow's head, goading her into cutting the man. Killing him. Until finally, he grows bored enough to do the job alone.

"So you choose to be a puppet. Fine. You can watch. Hold her," he snaps to one of the men who grabs her arms. "Don't let her turn away. Not for a fucking second."

By the video's end, several points are painfully clear. The first was that Antonio Salvatore ordered the hit on the Stepanovs, not Vanici, or so this stunt was meant to prove.

That should be a good thing, right? It follows what I've suspected all along, but I don't feel pride in this moment. Disgust rips through me as I glance at the "present." The head is distinctly masculine—not Willow's. Still, the implied threat is obvious.

That bastard's gone insane.

And he's hellbent on taking Willow right along with him. If I didn't suspect as much before, I do now—there is more between them than some silly debutante ball. A history, that Mischa is fully aware of.

An accusation of as much is on my lips. Only prudence holds me back—there are more important things to worry about for the time being.

"Who sent this?" I demand, though the answer is obvious. "How did it get through?"

"I allowed it," Mischa says tiredly. "That's not all that came."

He gestures to a corner of the room I previously overlooked. There a pile of documents lies discarded. Warily I cross to them, and at a glance, I instantly come to a conclusion that has me cursing under my breath.

"You were right," Mischa calls from over my shoulder, narrating what I've been able to read. "Vanici didn't order the attack. Supposedly this is what's left of the man who carried it out at least—" He nods to the grisly box. Presumably, he's the man from the video. "And I already confirmed that Salvatore is dead."

"So you believe it," I suspect. "Salvatore set up the hit along with someone else. Not Vanici."

Which leaves the origins of the attack even murkier than before. The only lead? A figure mentioned briefly, J.W.

"Yes." Mischa nods, hands in fists, teeth bared. "The bastard sent those documents to verify. Bank transfers. Phone records." He inclines his head, stroking his chin thoughtfully. "I hear from my contacts that he's already in the process of contacting the *famiglia's* old allies."

"Fuck," I say. The part I hold back is the kicker—in most men's eyes, Vanici has every right to. Still, I'm in no mood to gloat. I was right. Mischa was reckless.

All that matters now is Willow's safety, and the rest of the family's. "Do you think Vanici will mount an attack on his own?"

This time he'd have more than enough cause—a life in exchange for his nephew's.

Mischa's expression wavers for a split second before his frown becomes a terrifying smile. "Let him try. Attack aside, he still went after Willow. Only God knows what he's done to her."

Real concern breaks through his stoic façade. Despite everything, the man loves his daughter.

And he's right. Only God knows what's been done to her already. I eye the tablet still in my grasp, stroking that faint glimpse of blond hair.

"Do you know where this was taken? If Donatello went to the *famiglia*, maybe—"

"You are needed at the hospital," Mischa says over me. His eyelids lower as if he remembered something. Something he doesn't want me to know.

"Sir, I think I should be here—"

"I want security on my wife tripled," he commands. "Eli is being brought home tomorrow, and he and Anna are to be protected around the clock. I want you to split your best guards between them."

Reluctantly, I nod. "Of course. But…"

He cocks his head, raising an eyebrow. "Is something wrong?"

"Antonio Salvatore ordered the attack? You think he would really mount something like that alone? With no motive other than maybe gaining the harbor?"

"According to Donatello Vanici," Mischa says coldly.

I look over at the so-called evidence again, but see nothing definitive beyond numbers and inferences. Antonio Salvatore ordered the hit, but was he working entirely out of his own interest? Vanici's proof alone suggests he wasn't.

"The bastard just went by J. W. That's it! That's all I know. I swear to fucking God..."

"Sir—"

"I thought I told you to handle the arrangements for the hospital?" Mischa snaps.

"Yes, sir. But... The man in the video mentioned someone else. What if there was another motive to the attack, apart from merely harming your family?"

A motive that a certain Winthorp returned from obscurity to hint at.

Mischa hisses. "What? Forcing my hand so that I look like a goddamn fool?"

"No," I say softly. "But what about any other leads? I think your wife was connected to the Winthorps. Could they have a motive?"

One in particular. Her name is on the tip of my tongue, but for whatever reason, I don't voice it. Yet.

"The Winthorps?" His eyes narrow. Does he find such a theory plausible? His expression is nearly impossible to scrutinize.

"Most of them are dead," he says finally. "And those who aren't don't have any claim to any influence, let alone money."

It's a fair point, one that festers as I mull over the potential reasons. All of them, I suspect, lie within the mind of a certain Winthorp.

"What about Ellen?" I ask, still on the man's heels. "Didn't she have a sister? Briar, I think, was her name."

He scoffs. "She ran off with one of my men seven years ago. There's been no word of her since, but I frankly don't give a damn. You know who does have my full concern? My *wife*."

I nod in respect. "Yes, sir."

But I've been in Mischa's employ for too damn long. I know when he's reaching the end of his patience—and I know when he's deliberately provoking someone. He wants me gone, and quickly. Why?

The state of the guards outside might give me a clue.

"You're expecting someone," I say softly. "A visitor?"

Or a potential ally. If Donatello went to the *famiglia* alone, he wouldn't bother with reinforcements—the *mafiya* outnumber the dwindling outfit by more than two to one. But if Donatello managed to sway others to his side, Mischa might be driven to only one person.

Someone he swore to never associate with.

Rather than dance around the suspicion, I voice it outright, "You summoned Nicolai Baryshnikov—"

"I would summon the devil if it meant protecting my daughter," he bellows, his voice booming.

Instinct—and common sense—warn me to pause. Tread carefully.

But I can't. Not when *that* bastard is the topic of conversation. "I think Willow would prefer you work with the devil instead."

"What did you say?" He stiffens, his hand forming a fist. Honestly, I wouldn't be surprised if he did strike me. A part of me braces for the blow. Instead, he turns to me directly, his expression strained.

"I trust you, Evgeni. Above everyone else, your opinion is the one I trust—"

"But not on this," I interject.

"No." He levels me with a piercing stare. "I think your past is clouding your thinking. I've never ordered you to commit a massacre, have I? I'm not ordering you to stay, either."

I blink. It's the first time he's ever directly mentioned it. *I never ordered you to commit a massacre...*

Because one man did—but Mischa doesn't give a damn about the blood that may or may not be on my hands. He references it merely to prove his point. That's why he doubts my resolve. My ability to be trusted. My loyalty.

"If you mean my past when it comes to Nicolai Baryshnikov, then I don't think that is a bad thing." Anger tinges my voice, and I can't even begin to hide it. The memories swarm on the fringes of my psyche. It's harder than ever to push them back. Forget.

"I have always been able to rely on you," Mischa says with a sigh. "Always. But I've learned throughout the years that there are some lines certain men cannot cross. No matter the price, no matter their loyalty, and I am sorry, my friend, but when it comes to protecting my family, I will be cowed by no one."

"Is a war really what you want?" I ask. "Even if it's against the wrong man?"

He places his hand on my shoulder, letting the contact linger before he finally turns away, crossing to the center of the room. "Show me the man who has my daughter in his grasp, and I'll turn my attention to him," he says. When I remain silent, he gestures to the doorway with a violent slash of his hand. "Now go. From now until further notice, the hospital is your main post."

His tone alone makes his motive painfully clear. Whatever he's planning, he doesn't want me anywhere near it.

Because he knows I'd try to stop him.

15

DON

*N*o one spared their praise while I was rising in the ranks of the *famiglia*. I heard it all, from mindless worship to having grown men pledge their lives to me.

Fuck modesty—it felt good to be king.

No one warns you what happens when you fall from that high perch, though. Life isn't the same at the bottom as it is on top—and sure, you thought you knew that from the outset.

But you didn't.

The truth is that hardly anyone experiences what it's like to have it all, and fewer understand the pain of losing it. Not just the money or the prestige—that shit is secondary. It's the stuff you put by the wayside on your ascent that you miss the most. The people you took for granted, the memories you minimized, and the lovers you exploited for your own gain.

Their silence is deafening, and no amount of money or power or booze can fill the void.

All you can do is bury the agony and fixate on useless distractions. Like plotting your ascent back to the top, even if you gotta kiss a few asses on your way there. Or stab them. Butcher.

Bloodied hands are a sight preferable to an empty house and full graves any day.

I lack the foresight of a Giovanni Rossi this time around, though. Forget power and influence. My focus is restricted to one target—*Mischa*. Now that I have his daughter in my grasp, the world is figuratively mine to take all over again via checkmate.

I could always kill her to achieve that aim—or go a step further and bind her to me in a way that humiliates him more than her death would. I could marry her...

A part of me scoffs at the notion, though I'm the one who proposed it, initially as a way to fuck with her head. But now? It's an insane gambit. Only a true madman would actually go through with it—a wedding for my new bride with her father as the honored guest. You can't make that shit up.

Forget her. I shove the Stepanovs aside for the moment, returning my focus to Vincenzo. His safety is all that matters tonight, dominating my thoughts as I exit Giovanni's old apartment into the cool night air.

I've wasted enough time already. The "one hour" I promised Luciano unintentionally stretched into several—all spent staring at myself in the closet mirror, pondering the figure staring back. Who was that bastard?

A stranger I barely recognize with the face of an old man and the eyes of a murderer.

I've spent seven years too drunk to function, but sobriety feels more disorienting than the worst hangover. It's like my entire body is a shell that no longer fits, though I could blame the discomfort on my clothing. Antonio's old suits just enhance the feeling of wrongness I haven't been able to shake since losing Vin. I can't even keep the days straight anymore. Or the time.

"You're late," a voice calls disapprovingly. I look down the wooden steps leading below, surprised by the change in the landscape. It's dark out now, and Luciano stands near the railing, his expression barely visible in the absence of sunlight.

"Got caught up," I lie, smoothing my hand over the front of my jacket. "I'm ready."

"It's about damn time," he remarks. He's changed, wearing a suit, his hair slicked to his skull. It's a throwback to the old days and the dress code Giovanni preferred. *Professional,* or so he called it. *You may act like an animal, but you dress like a man.*

Two other men lurk behind him, similarly dressed. Parked a few yards back is a car that looks like it was taken from

Antonio's harem of them. While I've been daydreaming, Luciano's been busy putting the plan into action—it's time to go on a field trip. If I'm going to make headway against the *mafiya,* then I need an audience with the Saleris.

Putting that aside, for now, I refocus my attention on the task at hand—getting there in one piece. "Is everything in place?"

Luciano nods. "This is Ash—" he points to a man beside him with black hair pulled into a ponytail. "And Sanders," he adds, gesturing toward another figure standing further back. "They'll play point on your crazy ass fucking trip."

I feel an eyebrow go up. "You aren't coming?"

He shakes his head. "I'll hold down the fort here. That is if you aren't blown apart by Mischa, in which case, I'll be waiting my turn." He laughs before clearing his throat. "Saleri is at a club he owns on the Strip—"

"*Felicità,*" I say, running my hands over the front of my suit. I swapped the gray for the black, and I prefer the fit. Tucked in the inner pocket is a certain knife, along with a pistol stolen from a stash Antonio kept behind his minibar. The drinks, however, I left untouched. My brain buzzes in the absence of alcohol, my thoughts clearer than ever. Sharp. This has to be the longest I've been sober in…

A long damn time. I inhale, relishing the tension in the air. Much like tonight's unofficial dress code, the mood reminds me of the old days. The perilous calm before preparing to do a job, knowing that the only thing at stake is power.

The one currency every man puts stock in.

"Don?"

"Yeah," I say absently. "I remember the place."

"Then you know security won't be a walk in the park—but it's neutral territory. If you can meet Gregori in person, maybe he *won't* shoot you on the fucking spot. Let's hope he hasn't realized what happened to his granddaughter."

My eyes narrow at the thought of her. *Kisa.*

"She's safe and sound," Luciano says as if reading my mind. "I suggest you use that fact to your advantage."

I raise an eyebrow. "I thought you might be above such a threat."

He shrugs, his expression suddenly serious. "That's the language the Saleris speak, those crazy motherfuckers. Threats. I hope you remember that. Anyway, you'll take this car—" he gestures to the red one. "The men will take the front and the rear. Now, what about your other guest…"

He trails off, presumably for the same reason the hairs on the back of my neck stand up. Said "guest" picks this moment to make her appearance, exiting from the apartment without being called. I don't look back, taking the stairs as if the devil is on my fucking heels.

She could be to blame for why my head feels so damn screwy. Hours in that suite with her and it's like recovering from a hangover to reenter the world again. A world that doesn't smell like roses, untainted by that childish fucking presence.

My reprieve won't last long. Just the time it takes to set off for the Saleris'. There, I'll have no choice but to endure her, *without* the benefit of being in another room.

"Let's go." I snatch the keys Luciano hands to me and enter the car. As the seconds pass, I wind up eyeing the dashboard, forced to wait. For her. Ten seconds. Twenty. A full minute…

It's like she's *intentionally* aiming to piss me off.

Or it could be that I'm not giving her enough credit. She might have run? Just as I start to scan the yard beyond the windshield, a flicker of movement catches my eye. When the passenger's side door finally opens, I say nothing, letting my hands palm the steering wheel. Though fuck, I should throw her in the trunk.

She must have showered again. Her skin carries a freshness that floods the car's interior as she settles onto the seat, closing the door.

Just like that, I relapse on roses. On *her,*

The only acknowledgment of her I allow myself is a single glance in the rearview mirror. Instantly, I regret it. She's ready for me, meeting my gaze without a hint of fear. Those eyes gleam, seemingly larger than usual. *Makeup,* I suspect. Thicker lashes and a line of dark kohl enhance the depth of her irises. They're endless.

Ripping my attention away, I focus on the road and hit the gas, following the van in front as it takes off toward the main gate.

I don't owe her a damn thing, not even an explanation—but if I want to play this right, I have no choice but to gauge her mental state. Did my words from the bathroom truly stick?

"I'm only going to tell you this once," I warn, fighting to keep my tone level. "You wanted to play this game? You play. If you're planning to escape, I suggest you think twice. That little girl…"

I hear rather than see her stiffen; the squeal of leather gives her away.

"Her life is on you," I say to twist the knife. Surprisingly, that's where I let the threat die. Why? Mentioning the Salvatore child at all is merely a formality.

I know that now, just from the stubborn tilt of her chin I catch when I sneak another glance her way. She'll accompany me if only for one reason, and what a childish reason it is. With her this close, I can't ignore her. She's aware of that. Fuck, I know she is—relishing the way I eye the road rather than look at her directly. Even as I do, my nostrils flare, swollen with her scent. Given the state of her, I might be imagining it, floral somehow without the aid of perfume or scented soap.

Roses. Goddamn roses.

I'd rather suffocate than breathe it in.

Unfortunately, dying isn't part of my plan. To outwit the Saleris, I'll need her on my side. We'll have to play the political games I used to hate. To his credit, I'd rather face Mischa than Gregori Saleri.

Mischa at least claims some semblance of honor to live by. The Saleris only understand greed, a philosophy that's allowed them to wrestle control over much of the city's central territory despite the *mafiya*. Aware of their dwindling share of power, they lord over what remains with an iron fist.

I've been to *Felicità* a few times, none remembered fondly. Smack-dab in the heart of the city's wealthy entertainment district, the strip club serves as a notorious front for the Saleris' rumored trafficking operation. The catch? The place is also the preferred haunt of politicians and businessmen alike, leaving no mystery as to why they've gone so long without being raided by the police.

Gregori Saleri must have studied at the same school Giovanni Rossi did when it came to maintaining a façade. No one, short of the *mafiya*, has a better operation.

Or a more tentative grasp on sanity Known for both his ruthlessness and unpredictability, Gregori is an opponent I can't afford to underestimate. Unlike Antonio, he doesn't surround himself with five toy soldiers and a little girl, either. His men are well funded and expertly trained.

It'll take tact to circumvent them. There's no chance in hell I could fight them one on one. Sneaking in is also out of the question. No point in using blackmail either if my aim is to forge a peaceful conversation—leaving only one entry route.

To go in through the front fucking door and pray that Mischa or his *mafiya* aren't already inside.

On that point, at least, I have one note of reference to rely on—Mischa, the family man, wouldn't be caught dead in a skin bar while his wife is still in the hospital. No, if he met with Gregori, it had to be somewhere far from here, but that within itself presents another obstacle.

How to state my case *without* getting my head blown off, for one, and then there's the small detail of the woman…

Her scent floods my lungs, fighting for attention. It's harder than it should be to block her out. Hell, I'm edgier than I've been in years without a sip of alcohol to numb the anxiety —but the feeling isn't all bad. The adrenaline shooting through my veins recalls my early days in the *famiglia*. Back when Giovanni would throw me into the deep end, unconcerned whether I sank or swam. Survival depended solely on my own instincts back then. On my gut.

And right now? Every ounce of intuition I have tells me that the woman beside me holds the key to everything. Punishing Mischa. Reclaiming my throne.

Staying alive.

If only I can suppress the urge to wrap my hands around her neck.

She's too comfortable here. Despite sitting stiffly in her seat, there's no fight in her. We might as well be on our way to tea, given how she stares dispassionately from the windows.

It unnerves me to think that I might know exactly why she's so calm—for the same reason I am. Beneath the jittery tension fogging my thoughts lurks a chilling, ironclad patience I haven't felt...

Well, since I strangled Antonio Salvatore.

Could the little hellcat feel it too? I've never actually seen her under Mischa's spell or with her family—just a picture, that of a woman who seems worlds apart from the creature near me now. Oddly enough, I have no trouble envisioning how she must have looked.

Tense. Uncomfortable. The way I feel when shoved into a suit, attending some fancy fucking soiree when I know it's not where I belong. A caged bird never acts the way a wild one does—it can't. Life in false security robs it of the one thing it needs to feel alive—danger.

You set a dove loose, and it might fly right into the mouth of a wolf—but was it because life in the cage made it too naïve to the danger? Or was it just *that* damn desperate to feel the fear? The thrill. To tempt the forces, it was born to tempt.

My little bird? She's fluttering just beyond the reach of my mouth, too prideful to admit that's why she's really here—to watch me snap.

"Listen to me," I catch myself growling before I manage to wrestle my tone into some semblance of calm. "I could kill Mischa. Blow his fucking brains out."

She doesn't move a muscle, but I know she's listening.

"Or he can stay alive if you play your part. I could drag you in there, make those men think I ripped you from your safe little bed. I could…"

And she expects as much, her head held defiantly high. I lick my lower lip in anticipation of uttering the typical threat. *If you don't obey, I'll kill you.*

It's the only language anyone else would understand.

Not her… I suspect she's fluent in another tongue. One relying on subtler imagery. Taunts. Games. Hell, after her reaction in the barn—when I killed a man in front of her eyes—I think it's a dialect we share.

"You want to know how this story ends?" Dropping all malice from my voice, I speak to her the same way I'd talk to Vin. No…

I speak to her the way I'd talk to myself.

"You play the captive, Mischa comes for me—and I kill him. God, I want to. You *know* I want to."

From the corner of my eye, I watch her turn to stone. She can hear the honesty in my voice. The excitement too.

"But what would be the point? Your pretty little family gets torn apart," I add. "But mine already has been.

227

Vincenzo…" God, it stings just to say his name. "You want to help undo the damage Mischa's done? Then help me save his life. He's still alive."

Her sharp inhale triggers a reaction in me I don't expect. Surprise? I swallow hard, forced to admit that she might have some interest in saving him as well. Good. I've been wasting too much time, getting distracted at every fucking turn. He needs a hospital, and by God, I'll get him one.

"If you want to help him, then hear me out," I say. "When we get in there, follow my lead." I grind my teeth as if to stave off the words I wind up hissing anyway, "Want to prove your worth to me? Then save your family. Play the game."

As the words leave my mouth, I park. We're here, but I wrench open my door without giving her further instruction. Deep down, I already doubt this plan. I should make her squirm. Cry. Run.

By making her effectively a partner, I'm giving her a taste of power. And I'm fully aware that she might get addicted…

"So what's your plan?" one of the men calls from the van up ahead. I've parked on a side lot across from the building, forcing them to find their own spaces nearby. As they do, I try to come up with an answer to that very question.

"We go in through the front," I finally say, tugging at the collar of my suit jacket. "One of you comes in. The other stays out. Keep close, don't draw so much as a pair of nail clippers without my say so. Understood?"

The look they share between them speaks volumes—*This fucker is crazy.*

Without giving them the chance to argue, I step forward, jerking my chin toward the club. "Let's go."

"What about her?" one of them, Sanders, nods in the direction of someone behind me.

The soft thud of a door shutting is the only clue I have that she left the car. Her steps punctuate the air next, and I realize that I've yet to look at her fully. Is she wearing heels? She must be, enhancing her height enough to explain the warm breath ghosting the back of my neck.

What about her? My thigh twitches, desperate to keep moving without bothering to see if she follows. Let her run into the street. Fly away.

Let the little bird prove my point—that's exactly what she is.

Still, I find myself extending my hand out to no one anyway. A dare, perhaps. Or a test. As only cool air lashes at my palm, I get the response I want. Nothing. "Let's go." Curling a fist, I start walking.

A flurry of motion flashes in my peripheral vision. At the same moment a touch softer than silk brushes my hand— slim fingers boldly intertwining with my own. My first impulse is to jerk back before I come to my senses, snatching that grasping hand in a loose fist. Far from a romantic gesture, but at least my fingers aren't around her throat.

Voice rasping, I repeat my last command, "Let's go."

The men say nothing as I start forward, pulling a smaller body along. There's no need for stealth. I'm sure the second I cross the street that the entire place has already been alerted.

Predictably, the show of Saleri force is visible even from outside the building. Two men stand guard near the front door, with several more no doubt lurking nearby. Despite the intense security, it's telling that this place lacks the long lines that form outside the rest of the clubs on the Strip. One can't just enter *Felicità* uninvited. Only those who run this city have that privilege.

I rarely took advantage of that right. Even so, my reputation must proceed me. As I approach the nearest guard, his eyes narrow, his hand moving toward the inside of his suit jacket, presumably for a weapon.

Shit.

"Your boss is expecting me," I say before he can draw his gun. My tone alone makes him blink, fumbling for his headset. I hear a faint voice come from the other end, muffled and distorted. Barely recovered, he tries to wipe the shock from his face and nods. "You can head in."

His eyes dart from me to the woman by my side. I tighten my grip, hauling her through the glass doors, framed in gold, that make up the entrance. Does he recognize her? I can't tell, and I'm not inclined to find out.

Any second I expect to feel a bullet go through my skull—but at least one thing is on my side.

Optics. Shooting me here wouldn't go over well with the wealthy guests, and the Saleris subscribe to a different brand of extravagance than Antonio Salvatore. One that relies on maintaining a certain image.

Even if a rival barges inside unannounced.

Up ahead, a beautiful redhead stands guard beside a doorway leading to the main floor. She murmurs something worriedly into her headset. In the time it takes to approach her, I finally observe the figure to my right.

Fuck. Appreciation swells in my chest. Or shock. I could cruelly describe her image as a good girl obeying my wishes, but I'm not that cocky. Or stupid. She's an opponent, wearing the armor the war demands.

Beauty aside, I can now admit why the others reacted to her as they did. The dress suits her, even if it's too damn big. Paired with black heels, the effect isn't quite so glaring. She managed to dry her hair, letting it tumble freely down her shoulders in wild, loose curls. The makeup from this angle enhances her delicate features, adding an unexpected hardness to them.

She's more hellcat than dove, if only for a second.

A flurry of commotion draws my attention back through the doorway where a man now stands, his suit a deep shade of navy, his green eyes honing in on mine.

Son of a bitch. Rather than alert their security, they've sent out the welcome wagon.

"Donatello Vanici," the man coldly greets, his arms crossed. "You have some damn nerve showing your face here."

I notice he doesn't pair that statement with a threat—yet.

"Mateo Saleri," I reply, matching his icy tone. "Last I saw you, you were still in diapers. Don't tell me your father upgraded you to his doorman. I want to speak to him."

His eyes narrow. "Bold words for a wanted man." As he speaks, his attention flits to the woman, and his tongue traces his lower lip. "You even brought a diversion."

I tug her closer before I realize why. Not out of possessiveness, but prudence. To accompany nearly every rumor about the Saleris and their chosen business, is a horror story or two starring Mateo.

He's a fool, but a dangerous one.

"No time to share tonight," I warn.

"That's a damn shame." His gaze slithers over the woman again, but then he shrugs, turning on his heel. "This way."

He marches through a doorway leading onto the main floor. It's designed like a billiard room, with plush forest green carpeting and gold filigree wallpaper to complete the effect. A mahogany bar lines the back of the room, and positioned on either end of it are raised platforms where two beautiful women gyrate beneath the golden glow of a chandelier. My little guest falters, and I have a suspicion as to why.

"You're blushing," I warn, lowering my mouth near her ear. "Don't tell me. You've never seen much beyond your little school."

Apparently, the women in Stepanov manor don't prance around in tight black G-strings, their tits bared. An amusing suspicion sneaks into my skull—has she seen another *woman* naked, let alone a man?

To her credit, she keeps her face positioned away from me, and I shift my energy toward taking stock of the battlefield.

Apart from the main attraction, the layout of the club floor is nothing special. Men in leather armchairs watch the show from various positions as more women—clothed in black uniforms—circle around with trays of drink.

Giovanni brought me here once. Young as I was, I remember palming the ass of a dancer who jumped so violently she tripped, spilling her tray of drinks. No one ever had to convince me the rumors were true. I only have to remember that woman. Her eyes. I've never seen so much terror in one person.

To credit whatever good remained in my black soul, I kept Gregori and his brood at arm's length during my time at the helm of the *famiglia*. Any man rumored to trade in flesh and bone, isn't one I'd eagerly climb into bed with.

To be fair, he's done well enough without me.

Just as he had over a decade ago, the man himself sits at the very back of the room in the center of a leather booth built into the wall. Like a king, he lords over his domain, stuffed into a navy suit, his graying hair neatly combed. Nearly every fat finger sports a gold ring, his wrists dripping with diamond-encrusted cufflinks. His prized adornment at the moment is a brunette in a red dress lounging across his lap, lighting the cigar sticking from his mouth.

When his eyes settle on me, he undergoes an almost comical transformation. He huffs, his cheeks flushing red, and I spot at least ten men stiffen, instantly at attention.

Shit. The back of my neck prickles, and I curl my free hand into a fist to keep from drawing my weapon. Coming here with only two men for backup was a brazen move. Even more brazen? Parading Mischa Stepanov's missing daughter on my arm.

She draws notice from every direction as we cross the room, my own included. There are a million other things that should consume my interest—staying alive for one.

Even in this unfamiliar realm, her eyes blaze with irresistible fire, her red lips pursed in contemplation. Her mind is an open book, mine for the taking. I can read her the same way I did in the barn, crouched over Paulie Vanetti. Like me, she sees the folly of this plan.

Do you know what you're doing, Donatello?

I don't. Though I can only blame myself if this backfires. Or *her*—the innocent Stepanova is a factor I haven't seriously assessed until now. A girl who's never ventured inside a club before, let alone seen a man. It's pure insanity to expect she could play along.

"Wait." I release her hand, tracing a path up to her shoulders as I bring my mouth near her ear again. "This is your moment, hellcat. Prove me wrong. You're loving this, aren't you?"

Her answering shiver ripples through my tentative grip. *Yes.* She's excited, though she flattens those red lips in a vain attempt to disguise it. Intrigued, I risk ignoring Gregori and his brood to step closer to her, leveraging my weight against her slight frame.

She shivers again as I swipe my thumb through her hair, tucking a strand behind her ear. On this battlefield, it would only make sense for her to falter, woefully unmatched.

But I swear I catch her inhale. See the muscle rippling in her shoulders as she keeps her head high. Her eyelids flutter, and I can envision the mental commands she must give herself, a list of them—*Focus. Breathe... Fight.* As unmatched as she is, she proves to possess her own weapon in this war with one simple motion. The art of surprise. She leans into my touch, and I'm the one caught off guard.

She looks at me directly, and my breath hitches in my chest, a guttural sound revving in my throat. In her eyes is a simple challenge as clear as day—*You don't own me. You don't control me.*

And there's more.

You don't scare me. Give me what you promised—Mischa alive, a bloody war subverted.

She's right, but for a second, I forget why. I'd allow for an entire bloodbath if only to clear my fucking head. In her eyes, I lose track of everything...

Until they narrow, cutting away from me toward a figure watching us both.

"Donatello Vanici," Gregori says, now holding the cigar between two fingers, each capped by a fat gold ring.

Shit. I grab her hand purely out of instinct—a response to the possessive stare I sense grazing her body from head to toe.

Unlike his son, this man knows better than to openly show his unease. He forces a smile instead, revealing a missing front tooth beneath his graying mustache. Word on the street is that a rival knocked it out in his early days, and despite his wealth, he never had it fixed.

Perhaps for the same reason Giovanni openly sported a scar on his throat, left by a would-be murder attempt. *If anyone ever manages to get that close to you, they deserve to leave a scar,* he used to say. *Let it serve as a reminder—don't let it fucking happen again.*

I'm suddenly aware of the marks on my face, left by a writhing hellcat. They burn in her presence, and I feel the animalistic urge to return the favor. Mark her. Make her bleed...

"To what do I owe this visit?" Gregori asks. With a wave of his free hand, he sends his companion scurrying, but at least four men appear nearby to replace her. They merely watch.

For now.

Every passing second enhances the tension in this room. My gun is a lead weight in my jacket pocket, my fist a useless display. Forcing the fingers of that hand open, I tighten the opposite one, trapping the fragile digits caught within it. In essence, *she* is the only weapon I need.

"Don't tell me you came for the hell of it," Gregori taunts when I remain silent. "Or maybe you wanted to enjoy the show? Though, you always seemed too high and mighty to have your cock stroked—"

"I'm here about Mischa Stepanov," I correct, stepping forward to take the hand the old man offers me. I shake it once, but when he turns to the woman, I decline for her. Who knows where that hand has been.

"Dear Mischa?" Gregori raises an eyebrow. "You have my attention."

"I'm sure Mischa's already come to you with some sordid little story meant to provoke you into joining his crusade against me," I say, cutting to the chase. "What was it? That I'm a kidnapper? Attempted child-murderer? Outright asshole?"

"Among other things," Gregori says offhandedly. He leans back against his leather seat, inhaling from his cigar. A gold ashtray sits next to him, and he casually flicks a heap of ash into it. "Though who the fuck cares what the truth is? Mischa has money and power on his side. What do you have?"

Always to the point he was. Our dealings weren't many, but after every one, I distinctly remember the feeling of being fleeced, and the sudden need to take a shower.

"I'll tell you—" the old man pauses to take a puff from his cigar. His next word punctuates the cloud of smoke he exhales. "Nothing. Your harbor just went up in flames. You have no ties to the *famiglia*. From what I hear, you're a wanted man with a price on your head. Stepanov promised to make it worth my while if I helped him find you. I just never thought you'd stroll right up to me and present your fucking neck." He snaps his fingers, and one of his men takes a menacing step forward.

I think my laugh is what startles him into backing down. Hell, the sound startles *me*, so rich it's damn near genuine.

"Is that all? 'Worth your while'?" I parrot. "I think I can do a bit better than that."

"Oh?" Gregori inclines his head, his beady eyes narrowing. "You seem rather confident for a dead man walking, Vanici."

"Confident, yes," I counter. "Dead? Well, the devil must be shit at his job because as far as I know, I'm still fucking alive."

Painfully, goddamn *alive*. Even while Vin treads somewhere in limbo, wasting away while I waste more time.

"Hmph," Gregori huffs. "You and I both know that fact depends on how long you manage to stay out of *mafiya* hands." He drags on his cigar before tossing it aside for good. With both hands braced over his knees, he sits forward, his beady eyes suddenly flashing with interest. "You think you can offer me money? I doubt you have enough to outbid Mischa. Besides, I wouldn't be fool enough to stand with you alone. Even your reputation isn't quite that fearsome. Stand against the *mafiya*, and you'd be dead before you opened that smart fucking mouth."

"Funny," I snap. "My mouth is open now."

"Smart-ass." He goes red, his cheeks puffing. I glance at his men, but none of them move—a fact that doesn't comfort me one damn bit. I've already boxed myself in, and I'd bet my ass that Mischa Stepanov is on his way here.

It's killing me not to grab my gun. Desperate to do *something*, I grip my tie and tug. As I do, the hand in my other grasp flutters as if to remind me of what little power I do have.

"You're right," I admit. "I don't have a lot of time, so hear me well, Gregori. You say I have nothing? You're wrong—I have all of the *famiglia* at my back."

"The *famiglia*?" Gregori snorts, slapping his thigh. "Even after all these years, your sense of humor is legendary, Donatello. Antonio's a stupid cunt, but he's not that stupid. No way would he welcome you back."

I smile wide. "You're right. It's a damn good thing then that Antonio Salvatore is dead."

The reaction couldn't have been scripted to have more impact. The entire room goes silent. You could hear a pin drop—or Mateo Saleri grunt as he rushes to stand beside his father. Gone is his smug sneer. His eyes home in on mine, openly suspicious.

"You?" He laughs. "I don't buy it."

"You should," I say, letting my voice carry throughout the entire room. "Antonio took money to 'buy' a hit on the Stepanovs. He set me up, and I have his patsy on video admitting it all. Mischa has it as well, by the way," I add. Predictably, Gregori pales with horror. Whether he believes me or not is beside the point. If Mischa didn't confront him with this information, there had to be a reason.

Smiling, I voice it out loud, "Do you really think he'll believe Antonio acted alone? Like you said, he was a stupid son of a bitch. Too stupid to come up with something like that without help. Now his father-in-law? I don't think anyone would call you *naïve*, Gregori."

He sputters, his cheeks turning even redder. I think he'd launch himself at me if he could, which makes the fact that he isn't more glaring. Another telling sign is that his men still don't make a move.

"If Mischa's not suspecting you now, it's only a matter of time," I say. "We both know Antonio was too greedy for his own fucking good."

"Where is your proof that he's dead?" he demands, throwing his bejeweled hands into the air. "Are we just supposed to take your word for it?"

"Go to his mansion and see for yourself," I say. "His body should still be there."

"What?" Gregori nearly falls out of his seat. "You went to his home?" Suddenly, something seems to dawn on him. His eyes go wide, his jaw slack. "Kisa—"

"Your granddaughter is alive," I say. "For now. I shouldn't have to add that threat, but if you wanted a reason not to attack me, there it is."

The man sputters, turning five fucking different shades of red all within the span of a few heartbeats. "You bastard! I should—"

"I have a man with a blade at little Kisa's throat, waiting for my signal. If he doesn't hear from me, the knife bites deep. I can assure you, you won't find her in time."

His eyes bug as he mulls whether I'm bluffing or not.

I am. But he doesn't know it.

Neither does the woman. Her fingers buck against mine, desperate to wrench away in disgust. I have no doubt that she'll whirl on me, brandishing those hellcat nails with righteous indignation.

"Trust me," I hiss through my teeth loud enough for only her to hear.

She goes still, and I barely refocus on Gregori in time to catch the moment he nods toward one of his men, who finally reaches inside his suit jacket. *Shit.*

"You can kill me," I say quickly. "Or you can prove that you're smarter than Antonio. I don't want a war. Not even with Mischa."

Mateo raises his hand, and his man stands down. "So what do you want? You think Mischa will take the time to hear your threats before he runs you through?"

I force a harsh laugh. "Mischa needs to stop and ask himself why he truly attacked me. Faulty intel? Or the pride of a man too stubborn to admit that he can't even control his own daughter?"

The father and son share a glance. Mateo returns his attention to me first, an eyebrow raised. "From what I heard, you dragged that daughter from her own fucking birthday party and did what men like you do."

I laugh again even as the fingers in my grasp turn to stone. "And what was that?"

He demurs with a smile that doesn't reach his eyes. "I'd rather not say in front of the lady."

"*This* lady?" I tug her forward, surprised when she obeys, coming to stand before me. "You mean Willow Stepanova, unharmed and un-assaulted?"

Even before the words finish leaving my mouth, my eyes go down to her neck, but the bruises I expect to find have vanished. Makeup, I realize, even before I settle over that red mouth, unable to suppress my own confusion. She covered them. Why?

Belatedly, I remember my warning to her—*Play your role.*

"You are a fool," Gregori snarls, lurching to his feet. "To parade the girl here—"

"Parade?" I grab her shoulder, feeling the delicate bones flex beneath my grip. It's not a restraint—but a warning to the men who advance. Sure enough, they stop short, but one of them finally draws a pistol from his jacket pocket. I'm painfully aware of the time it would take to grab my own. Too long. *Fuck.*

All I can do is keep playing the long game.

"You believed Mischa's fairy tales without stopping to ask yourself how I could break into his manor and drag the girl out not once but *twice*," I point out, thinking fast. "You've been to Stepanov manor. I'd need an army, which you just pointed out I don't have."

The two men share another searching look, but I don't miss the overriding emotion they both sport in the end. Greed.

"But you know what I do have?" I add, sliding my hand over the soft collar bone beneath it, grazing a trembling throat. "I have Mischa's daughter, in love with me despite her father's disagreement."

I don't look at her face as I spout that bullshit lie. Instead, I slip my fingers into her hair, controlling her scalp. Despite the contact, I still expect her to run. Wince, anything.

Anything but remain by my side, seemingly endorsing the lie.

"Love?" Mateo sneers, drawing my attention. "Isn't she a bit too young for you?"

"The last time I checked, nineteen wasn't the age of a child," I counter with a confidence I don't feel. Against my palm, the brush of her skin contradicts me—soft. Fresh. Innocent. My throat goes dry, and I force a swallow. "Mischa's pride has made him desperate to start a war. Do you really want to align yourself with him all in the name of a petty feud? I'm not asking for your loyalty."

"So, what do you want?" Gregori demands.

"It's simple—stay out of my way."

Mateo hisses. "And if you're the liar? How the fuck do we even know you're telling the truth? I'm of mind to think you did rape the girl—"

My pulse surges, drowning him out. I can't resist the allure anymore—my eyes are on her. Her mouth. Those lips. If only I could make them talk to parrot whatever I want. Her silence is my limitation, and a paranoid part of me wonders if the little witch was banking on that.

I can't make her say the right words, so what use is this ruse?

I'll always be the monster in comparison. Perhaps I should fall back to plan B instead? Make it known that she's my captive, my hostage—her life is mine until my demands are met.

But then I see those eyes. They flit up to mine, smugly aware of my shift in thinking. She's too coy to smile in triumph or savor her victory some other way. She just stares, a corner of her mouth tilted in silent admonishment.

You were wrong, she taunts with that expression. *Wrong. No one would ever believe I'm in love with you. No one.*

My hand is against the side of her throat before I can stop myself. *Good.* Choking her out would be a decent step toward plan B. Her eyes widen as if she's reading my mind, and I can only stare as she comes up with her own strategy on the spot.

It's so predictable. I called her maturity into question. So, like any child desperate to participate in a round of chess, she clumsily reaches for the nearest piece she can touch, knocking over everything else in her path.

In this case? Her piece is me.

Her fingers splay against my wounded cheek. Before I can even tense to avoid her attack, she lunges, lurching onto the tips of her toes, narrowing the distance between us.

My breath hisses through my teeth. *Damn her.* I know her aim the second her eyes go to my mouth—but I'm even more sure of the fact that she won't carry through. She'll cower in the end. Slap me. Try to run.

Those lips won't brush mine with a hesitance that fractures my resolve more than a bullet to the head would. It's like I *have* been shot. My mind goes blank. Her breath is on my skin, her mouth so soft it's like fucking silk…

My lips part, drinking in her taste however faint it is. Like fire and spice—the very embodiment of the lighter fluid I doused myself in at Havienna. Only in this instance, she's both an accelerant and a match.

An inferno.

A drug.

A low grunt catches in my throat, my fingers grasping for a slender hip to steady her as I inhale, our lips a breath apart. She deliberately lingers here, daring me to react.

Because I've already failed. Her scent is a poison, made ten times more effective by her nearness. I'm struck by both. Defeated. A surge of lust overwhelms every other thought. I want more. Crave it.

Until I remember who she is. What she is.

I recoil from her so violently she staggers. I only have a second to remember where I am. What I'm doing. Reflexively, I snatch her arm, keeping her close, but it's too late. I'm off balance.

Any second, the Saleris will attack, unconvinced by the charade.

But they don't…

It takes me a second to realize why. She may have been foolish, but her childish, idiotic move did what I don't think I could have achieved short of snapping her neck—it got their attention.

"I'm warning you now, you don't want part of Mischa's family feud," I rasp, looking up to find them still watching. "Stay out of it."

"Or what?" Gregori purses his fat lips, grasping for another cigar from an ornate box beside him.

"Or you'll get the same treatment as Antonio," I reply without a hint of irony. "Little Kisa's already lost so much… I'd hate to see her suffer any more."

"Bold words," Mateo snarls. "What's to stop me from ordering my men to put a bullet in your brain now, taking the girl, and calling your bluff?"

Nothing, I realize. Still, I smile.

"I'll tell you what you stand to gain instead—leverage. Mischa went after me out of spite and nearly killed my nephew in the process. Do you really think that you can stand in the way of what he truly wants? He aims to cement power for himself. Seize the moment and seat himself at the head of the table. By staying neutral, you can leave two men to settle our differences and keep him in check."

"Don't tell me peace is what you're after," Gregori spits. He's fully righted himself, his brow furrowing. If he didn't believe at least half of what I've said, I doubt I'd still be standing here. "What do you really want?"

My brain spins its own answer to that question—*Dark eyes on mine, the scent of roses in my lungs, the taste of spice on my tongue. Her. As much as I can take…*

What the hell? Blinking, I swat the images aside. "I want your men to stand down so I can return to my operations at the harbor," I insist. "I don't want an alliance—but I do want reassurance and the ability to move freely throughout your territory. Your voice alone can sway the less powerful factions."

"That can't be all," Gregori spits.

I nod. "I want you to put out the word that Mischa is reckless, and you're staying out of his fight. Let the *mafiya* stand on their own. You can see for yourself that his crusade was based on a lie—" I jerk my chin toward the girl.

The action should seem performative at best. There's no way in hell we've convinced them. No way.

But Gregori's eyes betray none of the doubt they should. Scowling, he strokes his chin. "So what? You fuck Mischa's daughter and expect to fend off a war? I heard you were one of the few men who *don't* think with your cock."

When I snatch the woman's hand this time, it isn't for show. I crush her fingers. If she had a voice, she'd cry out.

"I'm going to marry her," I declare. The conviction in my own voice shocks me, but there's no point in playing coy now. "Let's see how far her father is prepared to go. He can hunt me down, but she'll be in the crossfire."

My voice bellows throughout the room as if I suspect the *mafiya* is already lurking inside, listening to every word. I hope so. I hope Mischa has a bird's eye view.

"And," I add. "If Mischa is willing to own up to his mistake and aim for peace, I'll be waiting."

Gregori is the one smiling now, but it's one of grim admiration. A wolf in grudging respect of another who took down a prey item everyone else was too afraid to.

"You twisted son of a bitch. You have balls, I'll give you that."

I force my lips into the shadow of a smile. "I'll send your invitation in the mail."

He sputters, and I have enough sense to read the room. *Times up.* I spin on my heel, heading back through the showroom, woman in tow. During our friendly conversation, the place has all but cleared out. It's a bad sign. If I were a betting man, I'd suspect that if the *mafiya* isn't already outside, lying in wait, they're not far off.

Fuck.

"What about my granddaughter?" Gregori asks as we near the exit untouched. Apparently, that threat hit its target. "If you touch her, I swear to God I'll gut you like a pig—"

"You can see her at my wedding," I counter from over my shoulder. "Have a nice night. In the morning, I expect your men to stand down. I'll send your regards to little Kisa."

Only now do I realize how big a fucking gamble I took by coming here—and for nothing. That show alone shouldn't have been enough.

Any second, I'll feel a bullet in my back…

But I don't. Not when we enter the lobby and not even as I push through the main doors, finding the street beyond deserted, but devoid of *mafiya* soldiers.

There's always the chance for a sniper. Taking cover should be my primary concern—not vengeance. The longer I remain sober, the less my brain seems inclined toward logical thinking. Rage wins out.

Growling, I tug the girl closer, bringing my mouth near her ear. "Don't you ever do something like that again. *Ever.*"

Fuck the game. She's banned from playing. My mouth stings with the remnants of that little stunt, and I know damn well why she did it. The answer glints in her gaze even now.

I'm going to play, she seethes. *You motherfucker, I'm going to play, and make you regret ever letting me touch a single piece. You can't control me.*

I shove her away, heading toward the car without bothering to see if she follows. She will. After all, she's made herself a vital pawn. My willing little fiancée.

It's one thing to taunt her with that future. Torment her with it.

It's another thing entirely to have her turn the tables. The worst part? It could fucking work...

Mischa can't hide behind the shield of being a vengeful father anymore. To anyone on the outside, he'll appear to be merely an obstacle, lashing out at a man he doesn't like over the affairs of his young daughter's heart.

It's the shit tragedies are made of. Giovanni Rossi himself couldn't have come up with a better cover story.

And I hate the mere thought of playing along. Why?

It's her doing. *Her* game.

The little bitch attempted her own fucking checkmate. To keep the ruse going, I need to play my part, though admittedly only in public.

In private, she's still what I want her to be—an enemy. A captive. Mine. Bruises aren't all makeup can hide…

"Where to now, sir?" Sanders prompts. I almost forgot the man's been here all along. To his credit, he's done his job—having my back and staying unnoticed. "I don't like being out in the open."

He's right.

"We'll be followed, so we can't go back to West Helm," I say, crossing the street to where the cars are.

But there's a better option.

"I know where we'll go. Have Luciano meet us there with the Salvatore girl—" Approaching footsteps consume my notice. *Her.* Good. I want her to hear this especially. Inclining my head, I look dead in her eyes as I say, "We're going home."

WILLOW

A reprise—the repetition of several notes—is a hallmark of most musical compositions, one I always admired. When properly placed, the effect is a perfect illustration of the entire piece coming full circle.

I just never realized how horrible a concept it can be to endure in real life. To repeat, re-live and experience the same dramatic series of notes all over again.

Different and distorted but the *same*.

It's a vicious, twisted reprise to be here after seven years. Inside this house. In this small pink room that feels like a stranger's. In some ways, it is. Safiya no longer belongs to me.

She's become the creation of Donatello Vanici. Jealously, he hoards all memory of her. I can't even recall a single one without feeling like I'm intruding on someone else's life.

Someone else's pain.

Her room feels equally foreign, and that's exactly why he put me here. To hurt me. To force me to view the old, narrow mattress propped against the wall, and the bed frame coated in dust. To make me realize what he's done.

He owns her, reducing that little girl to nothing more than a series of stacked boxes. They take up a single corner and aren't labeled, but I know what's in them before I even peer inside the topmost one.

Toys, dolls, clothing—all of it.

The sight hits like a punch to the chest, and I grapple for stability, bracing my hand against the wall. These things…

He kept them all, letting them fester in this old, abandoned house, collecting dust and cobwebs. Why? My eyes water as I view this place for what it really is—my grave. *This* is his shrine to a dead girl.

This entire house has become nothing more than his crypt. Around me, the structure rattles to life, forced to accommodate living beings again. The walls are as ineffective as tissue paper against the sounds betraying the presence of at least a dozen strangers, picking their way through the various rooms, including the one next to mine. Vincenzo's old room…

"No!" A tiny voice seeps through the barrier between us, but I doubt I'm hallucinating. It sounded too soft to be from a memory. Not Vin. "I'm not sleepy," they assert.

The little girl? She sounds louder, insistent on that one point. Amid this insane ordeal, she doesn't want to sleep.

"Quiet," a male shushes her, his tone gentle. "You gotta try, honey. Just close your eyes…"

The genuine note of kindness differentiates this baritone from Donatello. Which one of these men took it upon himself to care for her? The gray-eyed figure?

My heart breaks as I remember that I'm not the only one captive to the whims of Donatello Vanici. I can only imagine how she's coping. Though how would any other little girl? I think of Aljona and Marnie and feel my throat thicken. I left them asleep in their nursery, but how did they react to wake up and find me gone? And their mother and brother?

Creeping in circles is the only way I can drown out the thoughts, letting my feet noisily prod the old floorboards— but I'm not alone.

Another set of footsteps ring out to echo mine, sounding just beyond this room. They're too heavy to be a child's. Unsteady. Their familiar cadence instantly brings a suspect to mind.

Donatello.

He's pacing as well. Each heavy footfall echoes off the walls, reverberating through the thin barrier between us. It's as fitting a soundtrack as any to mark this moment—steady, relentless, violent noise. In a sense, another sort of reprise, recalling the twisted events that unfolded the last time we were here alone.

Fighting. Struggling. Almost burning alive…

I shudder, ghosting my fingers along my throat, feeling the bruises throb. Some sting more than the others, and I prod those spots the most. I want to feel that pain.

Maybe it can distract from my mouth. My lips still burn with the heat of his breath. They ache, though barely touched in reality.

Damn him. My eyes burn, spilling fresh hot tears—but I don't know why. It's harder to breathe this dusty air. Harder to think. Frustrated, I cross the room, hammering my feet against the floor to drown out his noise. Reaching the nearest window, I throw it open and lean out, gulping at the night air.

All the bracing cold does is highlight my searing cheeks, no doubt blushing red. Not because of shame. I did what he wanted me to do. What he all but *threatened* me to do. I played along.

And he pushed me away, scolding my actions as though I were a naughty child. Not because I refused to take part in his twisted charade…

Because I played too well. I kissed him—and in the process, I made Mischa look like a fool. Mischa… One of the few people who has ever truly cared for me.

My breaths come faster when I think of him. To distract from the guilt, I eye the moon above, partially obscured by gently swaying trees. I'd give anything to know that Mischa's men were out there now, creeping closer to this embodiment of hell. Evgeni, his charming grin flattened into a frown—he'd lead the charge to rescue me.

I *need* to be rescued.

Ha, a part of me scoffs. *Donatello needs to be rescued. From you...*

I hate him. God, I hate him. Hate so potent I can taste it. Feel it. I dig my nails into my palms so hard I jump, but the biting sting isn't nearly sharp enough to counter the remnants of him.

On my throat. My lips. *God,* my entire body hums with the aftereffects of Donatello Vanici in some way or another.

Damn him.

I bare my teeth, wishing with all of my soul that I could scream. He couldn't ignore me then. If I could throw his own silly hypocrisy in his face, he'd hear me. If I had a knife, I'd lash at his skin and carve my new name across his chest...

Perhaps he'd acknowledge the truth.

If either of us has a right to torment the other, it's me. I'm the one with the right to strip *him* naked and subject him to torture. The one with the right to shove a blade in his hand and taunt him with how far he's willing to go.

I'm the one with the right to hate him.

Damn him!

I push away from the window, glaring at these pretty pink walls with even more disgust. Once, they made me feel so safe. So protected.

It horrifies me to remember that he even painted them himself.

And now? They make for the worst kind of prison. Bars would be preferable. Locked in a cage, I'd have an excuse for staying this long.

My heart pounds with renewed purpose as I scan the room in a different light. I should run now, taking the girl with me. Traversing the woods on foot should be a fate preferable to Donatello Vanici any day. The window is an option, but risky in the dark.

The easiest way out is right through the front door.

Let him try to stop me.

I take a step purposefully toward the hall. At that exact moment, a different set of footsteps advances in my direction. The ominous thud stops me cold. A coincidence? I tiptoe closer to the door, only to hear those same footsteps echo me in tandem.

Step.

Thump.

Step.

We're in a silent game, my noisy shadow and I. By the time I reach the door, the tension is palpable. My racing heartbeat ticks the seconds down like a metronome.

Tick, tick, tick…

Feeding on the anxiety, my opponent waits until I brace my hand against the doorknob to finally speak. "Now, you want to hide, little hellcat? Don't tell me you've changed your mind."

I stiffen. *Changed my mind.* Like I ever had a choice.

"You weren't afraid before," he adds. *Before*—standing in a realm of strange men with him at my side. Performing the very damn act he wanted me to. *Play*, he said. And I did.

But it wasn't good enough for him.

"You don't get to hide now," he warns. "So you've changed your mind? Come and face me."

His taunt slithers through the barrier of the door and into my head, impossible to ignore. "You've stayed this long," he points out softly. "But it's good if you run now. I've scared you. At least let me see that fear for myself."

The door flies open without an attempt on my end. Donatello stands behind it, still dressed in the pristine suit he wore to the club—but his expression? His eyes blaze, set in his skull like burning coals.

I shock myself by meeting those eyes without flinching. Outwardly, at least. For once, intimidation isn't his aim. Narrowed, he drags his attention lower, fixating on my chest. I flinch. It's like he sees through flesh and bone right down to the rapidly beating heart beneath.

"Do you want to know why I brought you here?" he asks.

I make my entire body rigid, depriving him of an answer.

"As proof," he says simply. "You may look like Safiya. You may share her memories—but you are not her."

Each word lands like the cruelest foundation of a sick joke. That perfect, innocent little girl he knew once upon a time. The one who loved him so damn much. The one whose innocence he shattered.

This, I realize, is his method of punishment for my actions at the club—using memories as his cudgel. Not only will he deny me my past identity. He still cherishes her.

"You can't be."

He's in front of me before I can fully recover. Throat tight, all I can do is stare as he reaches out, cupping my chin against his palm. Without warning, his thumb shoots along my lower lip with a precision that stings.

"She wouldn't kiss me," he declares.

So that's what this is really about. I kissed him, and he makes it sound so vile an act. As though I wanted to. As though I enjoyed the feeling...

I almost can't process the sickening insinuation. My mind goes blank as I try. Thoughts shut down.

"Do you deny it?" His eyes trace my mouth as if the flesh alone contains the truth. *No.* "Don't tell me that was your first kiss. Wasted on a silly little stunt."

The reproach in his voice comes as a shock. I grit my teeth, glaring in a way that I hope conveys the obvious—*no.*

"Liar," he scolds. His nostrils flare, eyes narrowing a fraction of an inch. I've angered him. "I was the first man to kiss you. Wasn't I?"

The first man to kiss me. To see me naked. To taunt me with the nature of my sex and lord my ignorance over me. He's the first, alright. The first to force his way inside me to test my purity.

But when utilized against *him*, my maturity is a step too far.

Poor Donatello. I've insulted his sense of decency.

"Did you think that was funny?" he demands. "A little game? Next time, I suggest you not flaunt yourself in front of goddamn sex traffickers. Did you hear me?"

He's closer. Too close. Distractingly, his thumb returns, drifting up to my cheek. With a subtle bit of applied pressure, he manipulates me into facing him fully.

"You realize what you've done? Don't ignore me," he warns as my eyelids threaten to lower. "Don't hide from it. You can't. I should know. I've spent nearly a decade hiding."

It's the first time he's directly referenced the past without hate or pain in his voice. Just emptiness. *Damn him.* He doesn't get to do this. Ask probing questions as if he's entitled to any answers.

I wrench away from him to eye the wall. His laughter, however, chases me.

"You think I've gone insane," he declares, once again worming his way into my skull unbidden. I can feel him in there, slinking through my thoughts as boldly as he pleases. His fingers seem determined to do the same to the rest of me. One captures my chin while the other strokes the hair from my face, leaving nothing to obscure my view of him.

A stern frown makes his point painfully obvious—my body is *his* tool to utilize. Not mine.

"Don't you? You think I've lost my mind, but you haven't stopped to consider the obvious, little hellcat? You're just as insane as I am," he says with a venom reserved for the nastiest of insults. "I can smell it on you. That anger. The rage. You feel it creeping through your soul no matter how hard you try to ignore it. That pretty life as a safe little musician never suited you, did it?"

Hooded, his eyes toy with my frame, hovering over the parts of me that make my cheeks flame more than when he had me strip for him.

Not my breasts or my hips, but my hands. He inspects them in that way only he has ever been capable of—this peeling, constricting ability to reduce anything before him to the barest bones.

"These hands…" He moves too quickly to counter, grabbing one of them. Deftly, he displays my palm, pressing his thumb against the center of it. His gaze cuts up to mine, ablaze with mocking. "These hands weren't made for music."

He manipulates my fingers as I watch, contorting them to press against his chest.

"I know how you really want to use these pretty hands, hellcat," he gloats as I struggle in vain to pull away. I can feel the coiling muscle beneath my touch, dangerous and thick. His warmth. The surge of his heartbeat, hammering against me as effectively as any weapon.

Thump. Thump. Thump!

"To kill," he says over the pulsating noise. "Maim. Rip me open. Go on. Do it."

I'm in that open room again, crouching near a puddle of blood as he shoves a knife into my hand. *You want pain,* he taunted. *You want him to suffer, just as you suffered. Am I wrong?*

Maybe he wasn't. In that brief moment, I had felt something stir to life inside me that I can't deny. Curiosity.

And I feel it now, building as he lets me go.

"Do it." Stepping back, he extends his arms in welcome while I stumble to find my balance. A smile shapes his mouth, but it's wild. Crazed.

"Don't tell me that you need your little weapon—" he reaches into the pocket of his jacket for an item I instantly recognize. My knife. He dangles it between two fingers before tossing it into the air and catching it by the handle. Smiling, he presents it to me flat against his palm.

"Don't be shy. Take it. Now."

I'm not given a chance to refuse. He lashes out, seizing my wrist. My breath sticks in my lungs as the edge of the blade grazes the flesh of my forearm. Gently, but the warning is unmistakable.

"You want to hurt me, hellcat," he goads. "So go on, then. I'm sure you could make a mark if you tried."

And he wants me to. I can see that desire flashing clearly in his eyes.

He wants the fight. The thrill.

But most of all, he wants me to forget the only weapon I've been able to effectively wield against him—*myself.*

The longer I face him, the more unsteady I feel. Like a fallen soldier lost amid a minefield. One wrong move may be my last, but I have no choice but to navigate a way out.

He wants me to stab him? I feel a desperate urge to do the opposite. Deny him the pleasure of predicting my actions. Controlling me.

He can't.

At first, I don't understand why I slide my hand along my waist, cinching a fistful of my skirt. The fabric is so thin that the excess material clings to me, enhancing my body's curves.

And he notices, recoiling a fraction of an inch.

"Enough!" Already, he's recovered, sporting that judgmental sneer. "You hate me, little hellcat. Don't go out of your way to claim mercy now. Finish me off. Now! Do it!"

He raises the blade again, offering it hilt-first.

I don't move.

"Take it!" He grabs my wrist, wrenching me against him. His other hand sinks through my hair, seizing a fistful to keep me in place as he lowers his mouth to my ear. "Any innocent, childish fantasies you still harbor? Forget them," he snaps. "I won't hesitate to hurt you."

And yet, his touch doesn't match his words. Firm but not painful. His fingers shake, entwined within the strands of my hair as if he wants nothing more than to pull away.

He can read me so easily, but I marvel at the fact that, even after all this time, I can still interpret some piece of him, however small. His heart doesn't lie. I reach out willingly this time, finding the same spot on his chest he made me touch a minute ago.

It thrums with a steady pulse, so strong my fingertips burn in the aftermath. This simple melody sparks a revelation inside me. No, he doesn't like it when I touch him.

He doesn't like when I kiss him.

He doesn't *like* when he can't predict me…

He craves it. All of it. More than the violence, he craves the chaos.

As if to validate that notion, he raises the knife, bringing it near my throat. Merely to watch me react, I suspect—and I reward him with a trembling breath. "You want to play? Then let's play."

Alarm grips my spine as the edge of the blade kisses the skin above my pulse point. He lets it linger there before moving it up, up…above my head entirely.

"A real game this time. Which one? I know, hide and seek," he decides, letting me go, knife in hand. "Let's play it now. I'll hide this blade, little hellcat—and you better pray that you find it. I'll even give you time to search. Turn around."

My breathing hitches, my knees locking in defiance.

He laughs, and this unsteady display of noise reveals his true feelings better than if he spoke them explicitly—he needs me unnerved. He needs me to fear him. It's the only way he can remain in control.

"Turn around, hellcat. Do it—"

I spin on my own, robbing him of the chance to fully voice the command. His harsh exhale betrays his disappointment. He didn't predict that.

Nonetheless, his steps track his journey across the room. Toward the pile of boxes in the corner. Curiosity itches my brain, and I have to dig my heels into the floor to keep from watching him.

Already, he's moving away, heading for the doorway. "Find it," he taunts. "I'll be waiting when you—"

I lunge so quickly the rush of air racing through my ears drowns him out. I practically throw myself in the corner he just vacated, preparing to rip open a box and hunt. I don't need to. *There...*

He left it out in the open, daring me to claim it.

I snatch the blade, shivering as my thumb grazes the name etched into the handle—*Mouse*. That sheltered, rescued girl, daughter of a crime lord. She's as distant to me now as Safiya. A mask. A role I had to play.

Stripped of both identities, who am I?

That question feels unanswerable as I whirl around to find a monster lurking in the doorway. As I brandish the blade, he smiles, and my stomach lurches. God, he craves to fight me so badly. To have me throw myself at him. Claw at him. Scream for his attention.

This time, I don't. I slash the blade at my own throat, and I couldn't begin to predict his reaction—rage.

"No!" He roars, lunging toward me. "What the hell is—" He practically skids to a stop when he realizes I'm not bleeding.

I didn't cut my skin…and yet, the cool air assaulting the left side of my chest stings just as much as any stab wound. The thin strap has been cut, letting the material dip without support. I shiver, hating my body's instinctive reaction. The bastard probably thinks it's because of him.

The goosebumps that prickle my flesh. The tightness in my chest.

All because of him.

I don't let myself think it through as I snatch the other strap of this dress. Meet his gaze.

Cut.

Triumph is a fitting antidote to fear. I'm in control of my own body again—and I intentionally let the dress slide from my body to pool on the floor. On trembling legs, I step from the material entirely. I'm naked before him all over again.

And the more I watch him…

The better I feel.

He teased me for thinking I had power over him?

Well, now I do. Power so fearsome he staggers back in the face of it. His throat works noiselessly, but the only sound ripping from it comes out too growled to be words. He can't fathom this form of defiance.

One by one, I force my fingers to release the knife and let it fall, unconcerned as it skitters across the floor.

And he nearly trips in his rush to back away, out into the hall. His lips part, eyes blazing. The sad part is that shock almost humanizes him. *Almost* makes everything he's put me through worth it. Almost…

Attacking him with a knife failed to get this reaction out of him.

Speechless, shocked, alarmed. Fearful, even.

But then he turns on his heel, breaking my hold over him, and nearly runs into another man whose arrival we both missed. Luciano. His gray eyes widen as he sees me, and I feel my cheeks flush. Frantic, I try to use my hands to shield what little I can.

However, Donatello goes rigid. A muscle in his throat works, and I think he might strike something. Me? Luciano?

When his hand lashes out, I'm holding my breath.

But all he does is snatch the doorknob and slam it shut, trapping me in here.

"What the hell do you think you're doing?" Donatello's voice resonates through the very walls. Only the physical barrier of the door between us gives me a reason to suspect he's not talking to me.

"I came to check on *Kisa*," a man replies, his tone carefully straddling the line between respectful and irritated. "Little girl. Saw her father die in front of her then got shoved into a trunk. Ring a bell?"

"Don't forget what I fucking told you—"

"About you being the only one to see your little friend? Touch her? Yeah, I remember. Though maybe you should tell *her* that? Having her walk around naked might make your little directive harder for the boys to abide by."

Tension crackles between the two men, palpable even isolated from them in here. In the resulting silence, my brain dwells on that choice of words—about you being the only one to see her? Touch her?

Would even someone as domineering as Donatello resort to such a base command? Yes, a part of me whispers. The man who rages when I kiss him wants me only to himself.

His toy to break.

To corrupt.

My cheeks flame at the thought, and I nearly miss what Donatello says next in a tone marginally calmer. "Just… Get her some fucking clothes. The girl too."

He must be responsible for the furious stomping that rattles the staircase next, followed by an exasperated sigh I assume comes from Luciano. He leaves next, traveling further down the hall. In the absence of defiance and fear, I sway, eventually leaning against the wall for stability.

Gradually, it sinks in that despite that stunt, nothing's really changed. I'm still here. I'm still naked, shivering in the night air drifting in through the still open window.

He's still in control.

But as footsteps advance in this direction, I lurch to my feet with a savage desire to face him again. If he thinks he can manipulate me, he can think again…

A soft knock rattles the door, and all tension deflates from my body. I can tell from the pressure alone that my visitor isn't Donatello.

"I brought you clothes," a man says, his voice vaguely familiar. "It's stuff I found in one of the rooms," he adds.

I wait until his steps finally retreat before I creep to the door and crack it just enough to spy a small cardboard box resting in the hall.

I drag it inside, bracing my back against the door as I close it. Even in the dark, I suspect who the owner of this clothing might have been. Her smell outlasts time, connected to a million different happy memories.

My connection to her wasn't as strong as it was to her husband, but I still remember her fondly. And I know that Donatello didn't send these items to me himself.

Like Safiya, this figure is another one he's claimed.

Olivia.

17

EVGENI

*U*nfortunately for Briar Winthorp, she has to battle with another woman for my attention—though both present real threats to the Stepanov family. Just in very different ways.

Willow's fate remains at the forefront of my mind... Forty-eight hours into her disappearance and I feel no less responsible. Could anyone blame Mischa if that were his real reason for exiling me to the hospital?

It's my fault she escaped. *Again.*

Though maybe escape is the wrong word to use. I'm no fool. All of the signs point to one obvious conclusion—she left on her own. Willingly. The main question is, why? I suspect it has everything to do with Mischa's hostility toward Donatello Vanici, even before his so-called first assault on the girl.

It makes sense. She's drawn to him. Enough to forsake her home and protective family. Enough to have Mischa on edge, ready to go to war.

Enough to confront a madman by herself. If anything, Vanici seems to reciprocate that unsettling draw between them. What did he call her? *Safiya...*

No matter the reason for Willow's lapse in judgment, it's not like I can blame her. Temptation is an insidious thing, creeping into your thoughts and teasing answers to questions better left unasked. Such as why Briar Winthorp returned from obscurity after so long.

Or why I haven't mentioned said return to Mischa more than a day later.

His feelings on the Winthorps aren't exactly a mystery. I suspect he has no love for any member of that family, sister of his wife or not. No wonder she hasn't attempted to visit him directly.

Though Mischa certainly has his hands full.

It strikes me as funny that even while at the manor, Mischa still withheld information from me. Word of a fire at the harbor reaches my post in the hospital hours later—but that's the telling part. I had to hear it secondhand from a pair of nurses walking by rather than from my team. Mario doesn't answer his phone when I call for more details. I'm left to hunt for information on my own. Even before I look up the reports in detail, I suspect that it wasn't a freak blaze.

Key details from the headlines prove it—done seemingly at random. No witnesses. Carefully controlled burning and a fire that managed to stay contained to its target… It has all the hallmarks of a *mafiya* strike.

Son of a bitch. It's a bold move, coming from Mischa—but setting fire to a port is a long way from painting the town red with Vanici's blood. No, he's waiting for something. The real question is what?

Not that I can ask him directly. That much is made obvious when Mario finally sends me a text message, but it only conveys Mrs. Stepanova's current condition—no change—and nothing else. When I send a reply, prodding about the harbor, he doesn't respond. I decide to play coy, responding with a direct question about Vanici.

Still looking, is his reply. Nothing else. Sloppy on his part, but effective enough to get the point across.

Where Mischa is concerned, I've been cut out.

The feeling itches at my skin until I have to move, walk, run —anything to distract from it. Rather than rest before returning to my post in the wing, I patrol the building's outside perimeter on foot. As long as I keep moving, churning blood through my system, I can keep the irritation at bay.

Mischa's secretive planning aside, his attack turns the hospital into a topmost target should Vanici seek to retaliate. Begrudgingly, I wonder if that's why he really stationed me here—in anticipation of the fallout.

The only upside is that I doubt Donatello Vanici would be bold enough to mount a strike. Though hell, he might.

After all, madness has no boundaries.

Concern for Willow eats away at me in the rare moments when I'm not stewing over everything else. Such a situation should be handled delicately, but I suspect that delicate is the last attribute Mischa has in mind. The more I think it over, the harder I find myself running until I'm in a full sprint.

No matter how hard I breathe, I can't ignore one glaring fact—I'm worried. Violence doesn't scare me, but brutality does. Cruelty. I know firsthand the damage that can resonate when a man loses his soul—Mischa himself threw as much in my face.

I know the aftermath of vengeance.

And I know the limits of sanity. How far a man can be pushed to the brink before he snaps. Mischa? He's almost there, and I pray he doesn't cross that line.

If he hasn't already.

But he's not the only one acting out of character. I lied to him, obscuring the identity of the woman from the hospital room. Why?

Perhaps because I knew she wouldn't be satisfied with just one visit...

And, this time, I'll be ready for her.

After another lap, I reenter the building, dripping sweat beneath my gray jacket, breathing heavy. I don't bother to rest or change. I head straight for the private wing intending to take over for Danil. Even before I enter the hallway, I sense her—a presence that permeates the crisp, clean atmosphere of the hospital proper.

She infects this space, tainting the air with the stench of perfume. I don't have to see her to suspect she's near, but she's good. Subtle. As I draw up beside Danil, his expression doesn't reveal the stress it might if he'd dealt with an intruder.

He eyes my forehead with a frown, noticing the sweat drying there. "Ev. Did you rest at all?"

"I'm fine," I say, shrugging off his concern. "Any visitors while I was out?"

He shakes his head. "No, sir. The doctor's last update was an hour ago. After him, there's only been a cleaning lady."

"Good." I start forward, only to stop short. "Cleaning lady?"

"Yeah. Not one of the usuals, but they were out sick. There's a reason I noticed *her*, though." He chuckles, winking. "A bit too pretty for the profession, but who am I to judge?"

My breathing picks up in a way that has nothing to do with my run. "Is she still here?" Gritting my teeth, I can barely keep my voice steady.

He nods, frowning. "Is something wrong, sir?"

I head for Mrs. Stepanova's room without a reply, reaching for my holster. Paces from the doorway, my nostrils flare, confirming the suspicion building in my gut. *Perfume*, growing more potent with every step I take. I can taste it on my tongue as I round the corner and peer inside the spacious suite.

Mrs. Stepanova lies in bed, unmoving and unconscious but alone. Her progress from the other day is apparent in the color returning to her skin and the easier pace of her breathing. Even so, the relief I feel isn't enough to prevent me from continuing down the hall past the vacant rooms that make up the rest of the deserted suite.

As predicted, they're empty, and I hiss out a sigh, leaning against the nearest wall. Mischa's edginess has made me overly paranoid. And reckless. If the intruder is a spy or an assassin, I've given her more than enough time to wreak havoc. In blunter terms, I've been gambling with Mrs. Stepanova's life.

All in the name of what? Unraveling the mystery of a long-lost character from the Stepanovs' past?

I'm starting to believe that the lack of sleep has led me to spin my own fairy tales. Make my own mistakes, or punish Mischa by keeping him in the dark. Perhaps the boredom of this monotonous post is addling my brain?

To be on the safe side, I continue down the length of the hall, checking for anything out of place.

As I start to turn back, I see it—a metal cart of cleaning supplies positioned just beside a nearby door. Whoever put it there didn't even bother to hide it, and perhaps that's why I didn't notice it until now. It's bold. Then I hear a noise equally as blatant—faint whistling, musical and feminine. The song itself has no real tune, just random notes strung together.

Or the contented purr of a cat too arrogant for stealth. I wonder if she heard me, tearing up and down the hall while smirking at the brilliance of her hiding place—within plain sight.

I start to grab my pistol, but I round the doorway of the room without drawing it. She leans against the wall near a row of windows, presenting a far different picture than the other day. Her blond hair has been swept into a low bun, her expensive outfit replaced by a simple light blue uniform.

As Danil remarked, her beauty clashes with the disguise. With that bold smirk, no one would mistake her as someone accustomed to lurking in the background.

"I'm surprised you aren't pointing that gun at me," she declares, hands on her hips. Confidence radiates from her posture—until I reach her eyes, that is. They flicker nervously, taking stock of the nearest exit.

"You and me both," I retort.

She exhales, carrying on as if I never spoke, "Or launching into some cynical, threatening speech meant to send my poor heart into a flutter. Your man there—" She gestures in the vague direction of Danil. "He didn't recognize me. Not to mention my photo wasn't plastered all over the walls of this damn hospital. Don't tell me that you kept our naughty secret?"

Despite her smile, she doesn't sound thrilled at the idea.

"Does that upset you?" I enter the room fully, closing the door behind me—not all the way, just enough that she stiffens. That act alone tells me more than I think she realizes. She's smart for one, but guarded, all while maintaining the illusion of confidence. It's an act. But for whose benefit?

"It intrigues me," she says, addressing my question. "Why a big bad man such as yourself would be so lax in my dear sister's security. If my intentions were nefarious, you would have given me ample time to harm her."

She's right—and I don't know what irritates me more. The fact that she knows as much, or that I've willingly taken such a stupid risk.

Time to reconcile both failures. I advance another step, keeping her cart between us. "So, what are your intentions?" I ask.

"What else?" She shrugs but quickly inches back, disguising the motion with a yawn. "To reunite with my beloved sister and nephew, of course, especially in their time of need—"

"So you break into a private wing under the guise of being a custodian?"

"This?" She fingers the hem of her blue uniform shirt. "I did this for *you*. I thought you would appreciate the effort." Her eyes dart to her cart, and I suspect she has a weapon hidden there.

Aware of that, I position myself in front of it.

"By 'appreciate the effort,' do you mean alert Mischa of your presence and have you barred from the property?"

"So why haven't you?" Her tone stays entirely level, but I don't miss the subtle inflection. Or how she flinched at the utterance of a certain name.

So I say it again. "Mischa. You're afraid of him."

Her hard swallow tells me all I need to know. She is. Because she knows what I suspect—Mischa wouldn't welcome such a reunion. Not now. Which only deepens the mystery of why she chose to return at all.

And Ellen to target, unconscious or not.

Time to ask her outright. "If you intended to visit as you claim, then why not go through Mischa directly?"

Her eyes narrow. She doesn't like having her little game turned on its head. "Let me guess, he's lurking in that hallway behind you, ready to kidnap little old me? At least this time, he might get the right sister."

It's a reference to the events preceding the end of the *mafiya*-Winthorp feud—Mischa attacked the family directly, kidnapping who he thought was Briar Winthorp. In reality, he took Ellen, his now-wife, unearthing a wealth of family secrets in the process.

"Ah, so you aren't as ignorant as you look," Briar snipes. "I'm sure you know the stylized version of events. Your wonderful Mischa rescued his lovely bride from her evil half-sister and my vicious monster of a brother, raising the son of his enemy as his own—"

"You toy with me," I point out, ignoring her original question. "But you're smart enough to avoid notice. Why is that?"

Her smile widens, and devoid of the red lipstick, it's still disarming.

"Why not?" she asks. "Perhaps, I was 'smart' enough to do my research, Evgeni Volkov."

I can't resist the grin that contorts my mouth—or perhaps it's a snarl. "I doubt you could learn much from merely my name."

She laughs, inclining her head with a knowing smirk. "You'd be surprised what information someone can garner. Especially with a few greased palms—the right palms. You are a hard man to understand, but shrewd. No wonder you were drawn to Mischa. Working for a murderer is par for the course for you. Do you think you find peace in it? Serving one happy family when you've slaughtered so many others—"

"You don't know a damn thing about me." I grit my teeth before I can stop the reaction, sending her grin widening further. She won that round. But I've gleaned a revelation of my own. "It's not every woman who could come across such knowledge."

I'm being polite. The few people who could have enlightened her don't deserve the effort. Child killers.

Murderers. The kind of men I refuse to associate with. Anymore...

"Who are you working for?" I hunt her gleaming eyes, scouring them for any hint of weakness—and I find plenty. But not in the form I expect.

"I'm working in the interest of my own bleeding heart," she sneers, crossing her arms. Those eyes dart again, more wildly.

Especially when I take another step.

"Your bleeding heart," I echo. "Or an opportunity?"

Her tongue flits across her lower lip, stealing the smile in its wake. An answer to my suspicion is written across her face —*the latter.*

"You must like me, soldier," she says in a simpering tone meant to charm. "To risk provoking the wrath of the man holding your leash, not once but twice. Quite the feat. I'm starting to think you enjoy our little clandestine meetings."

"I'm starting to think you don't give a damn about meeting with me at all. And...you don't," I suspect out loud—her swift frown confirms it. "You *want* me to alert Mischa about you. Why?"

She shrugs with a sigh. One I'm now close enough to feel sear my cheek.

"Why would I want you to alert a dangerous madman that I've returned in my estranged half-sister's time of need, you ask? Word of advice, Evgeni, if something sounds as ridiculous out loud as it must when thought inside that devious brain of yours, maybe it's just that? Ridiculous—"

"Don't play coy." My hand is on her wrist before I even realize it, gripping so tightly I can feel the slender bones beneath. For all her bravado, she's slight. Weak. Just a woman.

A desperate one. The cadence of her breathing falters despite her confident smile. The stench of perfume can't hide the faint scent of sweat, and that pretty makeup can't disguise the dark shadows beneath her eyes.

She hasn't been sleeping. Judging from the pallor of her skin, she hasn't been eating much either, and even as brazen as she is, I doubt any woman in her position would prance into a hostile environment twice in as many days.

Not unless she wanted something. Desperately.

"What do you want from Mischa?"

She wrenches away from me while taking a step back, effectively placing herself against the wall. Her hand slips into her pocket, and I stiffen with the realization that she could have a weapon.

But even as her pulse flutters madly at the base of her throat, she doesn't draw it.

"Let me ask *you* a question. Why haven't you alerted your employer that your security has failed to protect my sister, more than once? You haven't dragged me before him kicking and screaming. Are you afraid of the punishment you might receive for such a failure?"

Her tone is sufficiently cutting. I figure any other man would miss the hitch in her voice.

She's more than desperate. She's terrified.

"What are you after?" I demand, taking another step toward her.

It's a mistake. She's thin enough to slip past me and pivot on her heel, betraying a lithe grace that reveals some level of training. Not in fighting, but something more feminine. Dancing?

"I told you," she says, her hand still in her pocket. "I'm here only to reunite with my dear, ailing sister, though maybe it is time I contact my brother-in-law directly? We're all so long overdue for a reunion."

Her threat would be convincing if it weren't for how she tenses, her right foot twitching against the floor.

With one shift of my stance, I move to block her in.

"Give me a reason," I demand. "Is it money you want?"

"Do I look like that much of a cliché?" she murmurs, insulted.

She doesn't. "Women like you typically sport tans this time of year, but you aren't," I point out. "Your nails are unpainted as well. Either you've come into hard times, or you are a very frugal heiress."

Or, she's been too busy for those small luxuries. Busy running from something.

Or someone.

"You soldiers, so astute," she simpers, batting her eyelashes. "Though should I say *mercenary,* in this case? Seeing as how the man you take orders from is no ordained government. This time. Though that means he's prone to chasing after dead ends. Ignoring the real threat until it's too late—"

"A woman who consults with child murderers and the criminal underbelly," I say coldly—the only people she could have learned this information from. "Those aren't the sort to populate some high-class ball."

"I haven't been to one myself in a long time," she counters in a softer tone. "But even I know when something seems too good to be true."

"So what are you saying? Someone else attacked Mischa?"

"No." Her eyes dart to the doorway and back to me. "I'm saying...what if Mischa was *never* the intended target?"

I feel my brow furrow. "Mrs. Stepanova?"

She scoffs, tarnishing her cool façade. "As if Ellen could ever make herself relevant enough to be targeted by anyone. I want you to think bigger, Mr. Volkov. Colder. Everyone in this business is no more than a snake—so slither into your deepest darkest impulses. Think of it this way—it all has an...*air* of mystery about it, doesn't it? Now, if you'll excuse me, I'm late for my next room."

As she starts past me, I snatch her arm, surprised when she darts out of reach. She's quick, and I feel the knife she pulls from nowhere biting against my wrist before I even see the blade itself.

"Play nice," she warns in a trembling voice. "I may not be a soldier, but I suspect that you wouldn't like it if I hit this security button and cried rape, sending the entire hospital running, now would you?" She wiggles her other hand, now in her pocket, presumably poised to strike the alarm.

Son of a bitch. She's smart, and I'm not in the position to assume she's bluffing.

"Fine." I step back, keeping my hands in view. "So you've done your research on me," I admit. "But I've done my fair share on you. I will say there isn't much news about the Winthorps recently."

She chuckles without any amusement reaching her eyes. "No. But I wouldn't be so naïve as to think the Winthorp name ended with my brother Robert. Don't tell me Mischa is? His wife had a child by another man, as did our mother. Surely he knows that husbands and wives stray from their marriages. I wonder if *he* has bastards running around behind my sister's back?"

"He may," I concede. "But I have to confess that it is odd behavior for a woman so concerned for her ailing sister to mock her marriage."

"Right you are." Pink paints her cheeks, and her nostrils flare. Her frustration is ugly. Raw. And yet, I can't help thinking the realness suits her better than the fake grins.

"So allow me to cut to the chase as any concerned family member would," she snaps. "While Mischa is chasing phantoms in the shadows, the real threat is growing stronger. The next time they attack, I can assure you, the victims won't land in a hospital. If there is anything left of them to bury, that is."

"Is that a threat?"

She laughs. "No. It is an honest warning. You're a bodyguard, aren't you? Shouldn't you be acting on intel like this to…I don't know. Guard bodies?"

Her seething rage hits a target. How ironic that she understands my job better than Mischa seems to.

"But let me guess," I say. "You're willing to divulge all you know of this mysterious threat, but only if rewarded. What's your price?"

That coy smirk returns. "My apologies, *soldier,* but I don't bargain with the help. Anything I know goes only to Mischa."

"Mischa, who would rather run you through with a blade than hear a word you have to say, is that right?"

The corner of her mouth falls, but the expression reveals another hint of the real woman lurking beneath her mask. Someone with so few options, she's already seriously considered that possibility. She's still determined to go down this route anyway.

"That's where you come in, dear soldier. *You* convince him not to."

"Tell me what you know," I suggest, making my tone softer. I try to, anyway. "And if it's convincing, maybe I'll let you take your chances."

"Oh no," she scolds, waggling a finger disapprovingly. "And spoil my own fun by letting you take all of the credit? I will speak to Mischa on my own—"

"But you need a way to get to him," I interject.

A muscle in her jaw twitches. Just as quickly, she disguises the unease behind another blinding smile. "Perhaps I do need to change my tack after all. While we're busy playing word games, the threat to all of you grows more real by the second. I can assure you that the next attack won't end in a near miss."

"Is *that* a threat?" I demand, reaching for her again.

She easily evades my grasp, pivoting on her heel. "No. Think of it more like a friendly warning. The game is only beginning, Evgeni. Will you let your employer be caught unaware simply because you have too much pride to act on the intelligence provided by a woman? I don't even know if I should waste my breath on stating the obvious of what will happen if you don't."

"*Intelligence* you don't find fit to share with just anyone but the person who destroyed your family?"

Her lips press together so quickly I almost miss it. That's the third time her mask has slipped. Sparkling blue eyes blaze with more than enough pride to outlast the mistakes, though.

If she's good at anything, it's acting.

"You don't believe me," she says calmly. "I wonder how your boss will feel if the worst happens and he finds out that his most valued lackey withheld information from him that could prevent it? Trust me, you have no idea as to the forces at play. What happened to my sister and her son? That was merely a gentle opening salvo. You can take that as a threat, if it will help you listen."

Her tone is convincing enough. Too convincing.

"You want an audience with Mischa, but I think he'd be more skeptical of you than I am," I say, turning on my heel. "As for me, I've decided that you have nothing. You think you can convince or blackmail Mischa? Do it. Maybe he'll give you the pennies your family left behind—"

"As if that bastard has any right to control my family's estate!" Real anger colors her cheeks red, and her free hand curls into a fist I doubt she's even aware of making.

"Give me something," I tell her, done with this game. "Something to pique my interest. Something other than vague, half-empty threats and a mysterious bogeyman. Then you can leave."

Slowly, she rebuilds her armor, swapping a glare for a stern frown. "Here—" She reaches into her pocket before I can stop her. Rather than a weapon, all she holds is a slim slip of paper.

"I'll do both," she snaps, shoving the paper toward me. It's a card, printed with the address of a nearby motel. "The name is Alexander, and his life is just as important as your precious Eli's. Do you want the lives of *two* children on your conscience?"

"Two." It could be a boast. A sick attempt at manipulation. If it weren't for her eyes. They blaze with a raw hint of an emotion I haven't seen in her until now. Honesty?

"Who is Alexander?"

"I gave you something worthy of piquing your interest," she says, pushing past me. "Now, you uphold your end of our bargain. Let me speak to Mischa. Keep him on a leash. I get what I want, and you can sleep peacefully at night knowing that you subverted a war."

"And if I don't?"

"The blood will be on your hands. Given your past, I don't think you can live with that. Can you?"

"Enough!" Anger flares, unfolding across my expression before I can suppress it, and she pales.

A good man would ignore the way she shudders. The sight wouldn't make his heart race, his mouth dampen. A good man wouldn't imagine how far such a woman's expression might transform when she's in the throes of true fear.

It's a way I haven't thought in a long damn time. Like a predator. To suppress it, I think of my freedom. My future. I think of sanity.

The feeling subsides.

"Did you hear me?" Briar asks. I blink and find her watching me, an eyebrow raised. "I must not be such a threat, after all."

She stands on tiptoe, bringing her face near mine. I should recoil. I don't, and she inches even closer, swiping her lips across my cheek. "Remember our bargain," she murmurs. "Once you decide to stop playing the obvious game, come find me. I think you'll know how."

She saunters from the room, leaving her cart behind.

"Wait!" I start after her, but she's already exiting into a stairwell. By the time I snatch the handle, it's locked.

"Sir?" Danil calls from the front of the suite. "Is everything okay?"

"Fine," I reply. I know that even if I were to run for the opposite stairwell and try to head her off, she'd be gone.

She's smart. I can't shake that assessment as I move to take Danil's place. Smart, coy, and—I rub my hand across my wrist—dangerous.

Her words keep echoing in my brain. *An air of mystery…* The way she stressed that word clashed with her crisp accent. An excess of emphasis, almost as if she meant another word entirely.

Heir? It could fit. Technically, Ellen would be heir to Mischa's fortune should he die, but the woman had scoffed at the suggestion of her being the target. Which would only leave…

Eli? He may be Mischa's oldest child, but—while it's not common knowledge—his father was another, as Briar so politely insinuated. Her brother, Robert Winthorp.

And given that as far as I know, the elder Winthorps are all dead, that would leave the boy as the sole heir of that particular fortune.

And a worthy target of someone looking to claim it.

"Sir?" Danil's voice chases me as I exit the suite before he can.

"I'll have someone sent to relieve you," I call over my shoulder, taking the steps two at a time. "Send word to the manor. I'm taking a break."

"No one can fault you for getting some sleep, finally," the man says.

But sleep isn't on my mind.

Briar Winthorp is, just as she intended.

18

DON

*R*age is addictive, a harsher vice than the cheapest alcohol. Pervasive, it overwhelms the body like a poison—or, to be more specific, like venom. One injected by a viper with a malignant aim—to penetrate deep and contaminate anything it contacts.

Thoughts. Feelings. Emotions. All become corrupted by the fervor sowed by one little witch.

The only antidote?

Get drunk off of it, in my opinion. Keep doing the same damn thing sowing the pain until you overdose. Drown in it. Then brutally smother every ounce of surviving emotion until it's finally gone. Snuffed out.

Only then can you find relief.

So by God, I drown out thoughts of *her* with dangerous fantasy. In the confines of my brain, I lose any sense of decency, envisioning every vile thing I could do to her.

Ways I could hurt her. Slowly. Methodically. The sicker, the better.

But not sick enough. Even in my mind, she remains unfazed by the worst shit my brain comes up with. Through the darkest thoughts, her eyes glint with a taunt—*You won't hurt me.*

You can't touch me.

And she's right. Hell, I gave her every chance to mount her own attack, get this hate out of her system. Rather than try, she stripped herself naked just to reinforce the hold she thinks she has over me.

And it worked.

When she stupidly offered up her body on a platter, I couldn't touch her, and she capitalized on that moment to wield a very different kind of weapon. It struck true, just like she wanted. The shock lingers even now as that scene replays inside my skull, over and over. Her defiant posture. Those slight curves and flawless skin...

An artist couldn't design a better body to both entice and repel. Because despite that beauty, every inch of her seems hell-bent on resisting me. Taunting me. Daring me to look away—but I couldn't.

My brain hoards that moment jealously, pouring over every damn frame. Breasts small enough to fit in the palm of my hand, hips so narrow they might snap if I mount her. Those eyes... How enticing might they be if I take her up on her dare, damn my own hesitation? I try clinging to my anger, that intoxicating rage, but biology betrays me. My cock throbs with each slow instant replay, and I lose track of the rest. Everything but her…

"Are you alright?"

The voice comes from the doorway, jolting me awake. At first, I don't recognize the room around me, trashed and covered in dust—my old study. I must have slept here, slumped over the desk, but the pale light ghosting through the windows is just enough to illuminate the aftermath of my last visit.

Oily splotches coat the desk's surface, and one of the chairs has been toppled over. That's not all. A pair of two distinct sets of footsteps mar the dusty floor, mine and a woman's. If I breathe in deeply enough, I'm sure I can still smell her. Roses and hate.

"You look like hell," Luciano adds, entering the room fully, dressed in a black shirt and slacks. "Don't tell me you're rethinking your fucking insane plan. I know I am."

"No." The only thoughts in my head center around a woman standing defiantly as black fabric pooled at her feet.

And Luciano's face when he saw her.

I eye him critically, wondering if he's stuck on the same memory. "You remember what I said about the girl?"

To his credit, he keeps his expression blank. "Off limits," he recites. "Yours alone. Am I missing anything?"

Yeah. That I'll cut your eyes out if you so much as look at her again...

Fuck. It's not jealousy. I write off whatever ripples through my gut as pure irritation. I'm sure she allowed him to see her on purpose, like a child playing with matches, hoping to see a spark. Fortunately for her, I am not the Saleris.

Sex isn't my preferred currency. For his sake, Luciano's better not be either.

"As for my insane fucking plan," I say, returning my attention to his original statement. "Did you make the arrangements I asked for?"

He nods, reluctantly if that. "I did. Though, I have to admit that I'm partially convinced you won't go through with it. I heard that you had balls, even back in the old days. But this..."

I have to laugh, though there's no humor in the sound. "Oh, I more than intend to go 'through with it.'" I'm no longer looking in his direction. The view from this window overlooks a muddy expanse of earth. Over the years, the yard has become overrun with neglect, choked by weeds. Not the grandest of venues for a wedding.

"Antonio's mansion, did you secure it?" I ask, picturing the gaudy property in the hills.

"Yes," Luciano says. "Though honestly, *famiglia* accounts pay for the damn thing. Antonio never had shit in his own name."

"Send your men to patrol the property. I want it ready to stay in."

I look over to see him raising an eyebrow. "I didn't take you as the decadent mansion type."

"Clear it out," I add. "Burn the shit inside if you want. The furniture doesn't matter. I just need the space."

"For what?"

My jaw aches before I realize why—a real smile shapes my mouth for the first time in days. "Just do it. And I want you to do something else for me. Fabio Botelli—" my smile falls flat. Fab—understandably—is beyond pissed. Only God knows what he's already learned, but it's time to face the music now and cut him in on the plan. I can't hide from him forever. "Track him down and tell him where I am."

"Is that smart?" Luciano replies. "Can you trust him?"

"Trust him, yes." As for the smart part, not contacting Fab from the outset was the dumb move. He won't like playing catch up, but there isn't time to feel guilt.

Speaking of which…

"Where is the Salvatore girl?"

Luciano juts his chin. "You mean, *Kisa?*"

I wince hearing her name spoken out loud. In addition to Fabio, she's another reality I'll have to reckon with. "Yes… Kisa. You seem protective of her."

He looks away, his jaw clenched. "Yeah, well, someone had to be."

I fixate on his tone—cold. Hard. "I'm guessing Antonio wasn't father of the year?"

Luciano scoffs. "I wouldn't use the term 'father,' to describe him—" He stops short, his eyes narrowing. He said more than he meant to, a slip-up he covers expertly with a shrug. "She's in one of the rooms upstairs, next to your...guest. I found clothing for both, by the way."

A part of me reacts to that statement with an unexpected sense of relief. Ignoring it, I refocus on the task ahead. "I'm going to need your help when I'm ready to head out," I say. "Bring as many men as you can while leaving the house secure."

"Can I ask where we're headed?"

I thread my fingers together, mulling over the plan. Finally, I say, "The hospital."

Enough games. It's time to test the Saleris on their own turf, and come through for Vincenzo. Sure, it's a risk, but the hospital is the one place Mischa wouldn't mount an outright attack.

That's the gamble, anyway.

"The hospital..." Luciano cocks his head, his expression carefully blank. "Do you think that's smart?"

"The Saleris will let me pass," I point out, though I'm not entirely convinced of that. Mateo and Gregori don't exactly have a track record built on honesty and goodwill. I have to trust that my bluff put the fear of God into them.

For now.

"No one's going to go against the *mafiya*," Luciano points out. "Whether you have proof of your innocence or not."

"You don't know them like I do," I counter. "Everyone has a price. Everyone."

And everyone has a breaking point. Mine feels imminent—that indeterminate action from which there is no turning back. She's pushing me there, that ghost from my past, mocking me with every breath.

We're both bound for hell, it feels like.

In the meantime, I might as well enjoy the ride.

⁜

*F*abio arrives within the hour, driving himself in a black car identical to the one I stole and subsequently totaled. I make a mental note to cover the damages, but guilt isn't what churns my stomach as he parks paces from the house.

He's alone.

I don't know why I keep staring at the empty passenger's seat. Maybe I expected to see Vin sitting there, sporting a Band-Aid but lucid. Alive.

What a naïve fucking hope. Fabio's appearance unnerves me more than Vin's absence, though. He looks ten times worse than he sounded on the phone. A wreck. I've never seen his hair so disheveled, his chin coated in auburn stubble. His suit jacket is rumpled, the white shirt beneath stained.

I have no doubt that his lapse in self-care is a testament to his concern for Vin. The second he climbs from his car, he meets my gaze.

"He's alive," he says in a rush before he seems to realize where we are. His eyes dart around the yard strewn with *famiglia* vans and Antonio's red sports car. He's not stupid. I'm sure he recognizes them. Nonetheless, he turns back to me without saying as much.

"Hello, Fab," I croak.

He scoffs. "Vin's alive, but I don't know for how long I can say the same thing about you, you idiot!" As a credit to his resolve, he sounds only half as scolding as usual. "I almost didn't want to come. I'm sure Mischa is watching me now —" he shoots a glance over his shoulder as if he's afraid the *mafiya* will surge from the trees at any second. "You know it's only a matter of time before he finds you here, of all places… But I knew you wouldn't rest until I told you in person. He's still critical, but alive, Don. Vincenzo's still alive."

I wait for the news to affect me like it should. Only a few minutes ago, I would have assumed with tears. Unending relief. Gratitude. As it stands, I only feel the chill of the morning air on the back of my neck. I only see the empty car behind Fab. I keep hearing that goddamn word —*critical.*

"It's about damn time you told me where you were. Have you come to your senses, at last?" Fab demands, cocking his head to eye me critically. "It's not ideal, but if you give me an hour, I can get you out of the city and on a plane. Maybe to Mexico? I hear it's wonderful this time of year—"

"Not necessary," I say, turning to pace this small corner of the driveway. It's an overcast day, cold as shit. An icy wind cuts through the clearing, enhancing the grim fucking mood. What feels like a raindrop splashes on my forehead as the words I prepare to say ring truer than ever. "I'm done hiding."

"D-Done?" Fab sounds stunned as he blinks his bloodshot eyes. This close, I can smell the cigarette smoke wafting from him—he's fallen back on his old vice hard.

"You practically have scorch marks on your lips," I scold. "I think you should kick the habit."

Of all things, he laughs, but his eyes widen as if he's as shocked by the reaction as I am. "You don't get to crack jokes, you son of a bitch! After everything you've put me through. Like you look any better? You look...." His eyes narrow, scrutinizing me closer. "Sober."

He makes it sound monumental. More shocking than singlehandedly turning the entire *mafiya* against me. He makes it sound like something to be proud of.

"I am," I admit, though my mind sober isn't anywhere near the calm, logistical state of someone like Fabio. My brain *needs* impairment—something to weigh it down. Without that handicap, too many dangerous ideas seem possible.

Like tormenting a woman with golden hair in every way imaginable.

I forcefully shake my head to clear it. "Where's Vin now?"

"Vin..." His entire expression hollows out, becoming pained. "For now, he's in a private clinic somewhere in the suburbs. He's stable. I'll spare you the gritty details."

He doesn't have to; I can read in between the lines. Vin is stable but requires access to adequate care if he hopes to have a shot. I've been down this road before...

But this time? I can actually do something about it.

"Can you move him?"

Fabio frowns. "He's not up to go gallivanting to Mexico if that's what you mean."

"No. Can you move him to the hospital?"

Anger always looks so dignified on Fab. He doesn't snarl like I do or glare. He only has to incline his head to get his point clearly across. "For what? So you can taunt Mischa and have Vin die in a shootout for real this time?"

"No," I insist. Weighing my words, I try to pick the most tactful way of phrasing it. Something other than—*Fuck Mischa.* "So that he can be admitted and treated. I've already cleared it with the Saleris. Mercy hospital is in their territory. The *mafiya* can't do shit without Gregori's backing—"

"And Gregori Saleri is a deceitful fucking snake," Fabio snarls so forcefully spit flies from his mouth. "There's no way he would… You're serious—" he runs his hand over his face, shaking his head in disbelief. "Fuck, Donatello. How the hell did you secure something like that? Or *think* you did, at least. What did you do?"

I take in his gaunt appearance and jump to the conclusion that perusing the local gossip hasn't been at the top of his priorities. "You haven't heard." It makes sense—primarily explaining why he's nowhere near as edgy as he should be. Or as angry.

He doesn't know.

"Heard what?" He shoots me an incredulous look while smoothing his hand down the front of his suit as if hunting for something. A heartbeat later, he fishes a cigarette from his pocket along with a gold lighter. "You want to know what I do know? That I'm tired, Donatello. Every fucking waking moment that I'm not with Vin, I'm spending it on the phone trying to cover your ass with any neutral party I can. You know what that comes out to? Hunting down everyone that might be able to give you an alibi during the Stepanov attacks."

Apparently, he hasn't been completely out of the loop.

"So tell me, Don," he demands, propping the butt of the cigarette in his mouth. "What *don't* I know?"

"That I love Vincenzo more than anything, and that you might be a close second. You are my brother, Fabio, if not in name, then in every other way that matters. Do you trust me?" I hold my hand out.

With a heavy sigh, he takes it, shaking it firmly. "Of course I trust you, you dumb son of a bitch."

"Good. Then trust that I'm doing what needs to be done," I insist. "That's all."

"You always were so fucking sentimental." He scans my face while fumbling to light his cigarette. After taking a deep puff from it, he sighs, flicking the ash onto the pavement. "You scare me when you look like this, you know. It's been years... But I still recognize it, that dangerous gleam in your eye. Just like I recognize that these are *famiglia* men—" he nods to two figures lingering on the porch, standing guard. "I doubt Antonio Salvatore would join forces with you—or that you would let him. So what have you done?"

His eyes plead with me to reassure him. Lie?

"I need you to trust me, Fab," I say instead. "And I need you to have Vincenzo transferred to the hospital. I'll meet you there. No one will dare touch him or you. I promise."

He eyes the structure behind me with open revulsion. "I don't like that you're back here," he admits. "*This* house of all places—"

"It's safe," I counter. "Mischa wouldn't expect me to return."

"Bah!" He exhales a cloud of smoke. "I'm worried about *you*, Donatello."

"I don't need you to be worried." I try to grin, but I can't raise my lips high enough. So I shrug. "I need you to trust me."

"Fine." He takes another deep drag from his vice. "I'm too tired to ask questions. I'll just pray that you've made up with Mischa and all is well. You might be a crazy son of a bitch, but you'd never put Vin in danger. Never." He waits as if expecting me to counter that fact.

When I don't, he tosses his cigarette and grinds it into the dirt with his heel. "I'll meet you at the hospital. In the meantime, I think I'll do my own research. Though, something's telling me that I don't want to know half of what you've been up to."

With one last wary glance my way, he climbs back into the car and drives off.

As I head back to the house, I spot one of the men standing guard nearby, Sanders. "Tail him," I say, nodding toward Fab's retreating car. "Make sure no one else is. Have his back. If you see so much as a hair out of place, you call me, understood?"

He nods, setting off. Inside, Luciano lingers in the front hallway. His guarded expression makes me wonder if he stood here, purposefully listening in. Or... If he crept upstairs and into a certain room. Would the woman inside strip so eagerly again?

"Don?" Luciano waves his hand before my face.

"Get ready," I tell him, putting everything out of my mind but this—getting Vin to safety. "I want to be at the hospital within an hour."

"You're really going to go through with this?"

I don't bother to soften my tone. "Is there a reason why I shouldn't?"

He opens his mouth as if he means to say something else, but winds up nodding instead. "Okay then. Want me to retrieve your guest?"

I choose to overlook what could be eagerness in his voice. "No. Get ready to head out. I'll meet you near the car."

He retreats deeper into the house, shouting for the others as he goes. Belatedly, he calls back to me, "Someone will stay behind with Kisa."

"Good." I turn my attention to the staircase, but despite the urgency in the air, I take my time mounting it. In contrast to Antonio's, this house was always small. Modest. Just five rooms in comparison. *Hers* is near the end, beside Vin's.

A thousand different admonishments run through my mind the closer I come to it, warning me to turn back. Have Luciano drag her downstairs instead. Hell, I can smell her through the fucking door. Roses and sweat.

The aroma conjures an image of her in my brain before I can quash it. She's standing tall, I bet, waiting to face me. Her hair will be down, and Luciano probably found a dress for her. Tight, with a neckline that might display her throat. I can almost hear the thump of her heartbeat surging with every step closer I come.

I finally grip the doorknob, hesitating for a fraction of a second. Maybe she followed through on our little game and took the knife, preparing to use it this time? Of all things, a smile tugs on my mouth as I push the door open.

God, I hope so.

As predicted, she's standing near the bed, one hand tucked behind her back, the other at her side. If she's holding the weapon, I lose track of the ability to care.

"What the hell…"

Luciano gave her clothing, alright. A deep blue dress that fits her surprisingly well, far more modest than the black ensemble. The primal part of my brain drinks her in, noting how the color sets off her hair and those eyes…

But a different emotion from lust overrides the appreciation —shock. I grapple for the edge of the doorway, gripping it tight. That's no random outfit—I've seen it worn a million times, just on a different woman.

It was Olivia's.

"Take it off!" I barely recognize the voice ripping from my throat. "Now. Take it off!"

At the back of my mind, I know she didn't pick it—still, that doesn't matter. I start forward, intending to rip it from her, my damn self. "I said…take…it…off—"

She doesn't move, but I go still regardless. Those lips are slightly parted, her chin held high, and those eyes… They stare straight ahead, boring into mine like goddamn lasers, tempered by nothing. Not fear. Not hate.

She's daring me to break my own fucking rule. Touch her.

Luciano may not know the history of that dress, but she does. Wearing it is just the opening salvo in our latest battle of wills. Fuck me, she's already scored.

One round won.

"You…" I clench both hands into fists just to keep from reaching for her. Instead, I turn and enter the hall, descending the steps two at a time.

Before I know it, I'm in Antonio's red car, gripping the steering wheel so hard my knuckles are white against the dark leather. Without thinking, I put the engine into drive, ready to pull away. *Forget her.* Forget the plan. Forget everything.

The door opens before I can hit the gas, and I don't have to look to identify the culprit. She climbs in, settling quietly beside me, her scent a fucking vice around my throat.

I could tell her to get out, but that's what she wants.

To be acknowledged. To be seen. To take precedence in my mind, if only for a second…

So I deny her.

I just drive.

*Luciano was right—it takes balls.

Not to come here—that could be explained by insanity. Or perhaps stupidity. No, as I walk through the main lobby, head held high, even I can admit that it takes balls to figuratively sport Willow Stepanova on my arm.

Like it's real. Like she's here of her own free will, and there's no threat of war hanging over our heads. It takes balls to go into battle with her and resist the urge to look over my shoulder every five goddamn minutes. Not for Mischa.

For the knife, I'm sure she still has.

To her credit, she doesn't bolt the second we're in public. She doesn't stab me either, but I'm not cocky enough to believe fear is what keeps her in line. No, her *pride* remains her strongest armor.

The only hint of unease is the slight quiver in her throat. Though, I can admit that her emotion could be caused by a myriad of other reasons. As far as she knows, her mother and brother are still under care in this facility, along with the latest Stepanov newborn. Should I feel some semblance of sympathy at that?

I'm too sober to care, entirely fixated on the layout of the building.

Surprisingly, Mischa *isn't* waiting in the lobby. It's spacious with plenty of room to maneuver in the event of combat, but apart from wandering nurses and the average visitor, it's relatively empty. We approach the receptionist without incident, but I'm more on edge than ever.

"Welcome to Mercy." The woman seated at the polished desk flashes a grin. "How can I help you?"

"I'm waiting for a transfer. Vincenzo Vanici."

She swallows hard, clearing her throat, and turns to a computer monitor. After a second of scanning the screen, she nods. "Yes, all of the arrangements have been made. You can head up to the fourth floor."

God bless Fabio. I have no doubt that this is all due to him. The real question is whether I can uphold my part of the bargain by protecting them both.

"I'll keep watch from here," Luciano says, Ash behind him. They're dressed so as not to arouse suspicion, any weapons discreetly hidden.

Assuming Sanders is still shadowing Fabio, that leaves just one man to cover me on the way upstairs. I'll be outnumbered when Mischa shows up—and it's only a matter of *when*, given that his wife and children are in this building. Luciano could be positioning himself to cut and run.

The second I see his face, the paranoia dies. The bastard's more alert than I am, darting his gaze suspiciously toward every potential entrance and exit.

"Alright. We'll head up now." Inclining my head toward the girl, I start for the elevator. "Let's go."

"I should go first," the remaining *famiglia* soldier says, surging ahead to claim the empty elevator. "To make sure it's clear."

I let him take the lead, waiting in the lobby with the girl for the elevator to return. When it does, she enters without resistance. Her silence feels heavier than usual. I look over, and she's facing forward, her shoulders squared. Is it the ruse that has her so wary?

Or the sliver of space separating us…

As the doors slide shut, the authority I have over her sinks in. By pure physicality alone, I could overpower her. Even if it's the dumbest fucking thing to do in this moment, I want to. Test her. Taunt her. Watch her squirm.

Regain the upper hand in this game.

"I warned you." I'm surprised how guttural my voice comes out sounding. Furious.

Does that startle her?

Yes. She keeps her face turned from me, but the elevator's polished door serves as a mirror. I can clearly see those eyes, glinting with stubborn pride. That pursed little mouth tightening, her defiant posture wavering.

"Did you hear me, hellcat? I mean…*wife.*" I grab her wrist before I can even process the motion, dragging her closer. "There are lines you don't want to cross with me."

Like stripping naked just to get a rise. Letting another man see her. Flaunting herself—not because she craves the attention, either. She's too fucking naïve to realize the enormity of the fire she's playing with.

That's it. No other reason could explain her boldness... Like *wanting* me to see her. She wouldn't even know what to do with me if I did lose control.

To prove it, I shove her back, pressing her small body into a corner. It's too easy. Just for a second, I let my brain off its leash, relishing her reaction—a shudder. A swallow. A wary glance at my hands.

I flex them, unconcerned by the threat the gesture might convey—the complete opposite of my "you're here willingly" spiel to her. This is a lesson she needs to learn. Power, and who between the two of us truly has it.

I do.

Aware of that, her teeth clip together, the only audible sound she makes as those eyes dart fearfully up to mine, her fingers flying to my chest to push me off.

"Do you think I won't do it? Touch you?" To prove the opposite, I reach out, ghosting the top of her shoulder. "Do you think that just because you're in on this game, I won't force you to play your role if I have to?"

Her eyelids flutter, her cheeks pink.

Satisfied, I start to pull back. "I thought so—"

Her fingers find mine before I've gone a full step. Boldly, they curl around the width of my hand—but her nails graze the flesh deliberately. Hard.

A grunt revs in my throat as everything leaves my skull, but this—she's testing me—*purposefully* testing me. I try to wrench my hand back. She bears down harder. Tighter.

A question rips from my throat, "Do you really want to fight me?"

I jerk my head around just to see her response—more defiance. She squares her chin without an ounce of fear.

It's the worst thing she could do.

My next reaction is born purely out of instinct. I snatch at her throat with my free hand, leveraging my weight against hers. A million warnings race through my skull, but it's already too late. Her chest slams against mine as she tries to push past me, but she's no match. I wrestle her body into submission with barely any effort.

But she fights me every step of the way. Kicking. Writhing. Struggling. *Fuck.* Every point of contact feeds the dangerous tension building in my abdomen. My slacks tighten uncomfortably. Too fast.

"Stop!" I snap, pulling back as far as I can while keeping her restrained.

She relents, breathing so heavy the cadence plays like a fucking song. Helpless, I flex my hand, sensing tender bone and delicate muscle beneath. I could choke her again. Strangle her finally and send her body to Mischa.

But the second those eyes meet mine, all other thoughts go blank. Her scent dominates, her heat so intoxicating I groan. My mouth is against her jaw, I realize, able to sense the tension coiled beneath that silken skin. I could kiss her now. Claim those pink lips for my own and show her how a kiss should be. With teeth. Pressure.

Hard enough to hurt. Bleed…

Another woman would let me have that moment. Seize it. Anyone other than this stubborn little princess so determined to not be relegated as a mere pawn in this game of power. No, she wants control by any means. Again, I can almost feel her grappling for it, figuratively wrestling for the upper hand.

My attention is the match in this equation, ripe for the taking.

Already, she's inclining her head, putting her mouth beyond reach, daring me to close the gap. Daring me to chase her scent. Daring me to ignore my own goddamn boundaries.

Those eyes meet mine fearlessly with an intensity I shouldn't find. She should be cowering, not confident, her pink lips glistening, so fucking tempting. Restraining myself is an exercise in self-control unlike any I've ever experienced—no other vice holds quite the allure she does. Not alcohol. Not heroin.

Just when I think I can withstand her, she flits her tongue across her lower lip. My brain goes blank in the aftermath. The next thing I know, is fire. That wetness is on my tongue, her heat like a match. I lurch forward, nearly crushing her against the wall just to seek out more. Take it.

But when a quivering tongue prods my mouth for entry, it hits me that I was never in control of this game…

Suddenly, the elevator doors part, and I barely have the sense of mind to let her go, staggering to put distance between us. It's like surfacing from underwater to snap back to reality. Focus. I'm in the hospital again, and the *famiglia* agent is standing at the mouth of the elevator, his expression blank.

"Sir." He nods respectfully. "They're here."

Here. His tone isn't quite grim enough to be referring to the *mafiya.* For the first time in days, the full extent of everything that's transpired hits me all over again. All of it. *Vin…*

My chest fucking aches at the thought of seeing him finally.

Ignoring the woman nearby, I start walking while hunting for what little positives I can find. This ward is secluded, for one, semi-private. Even the staff seems discreet, unsurprised by our arrival. Trust Fab to cover all the bases.

He stands near the last room, somehow seeming more exhausted than he did over an hour ago. A few paces back, I notice Sanders posted against the wall. Spotting me, he nods before returning his attention to the rest of the hall.

"Took you long enough," Fabio says with a sigh. "Now… You should brace yourself, Don," he warns as I approach. He already has another cigarette in hand, but a sharp glance from a passing nurse makes him shove it back into his pocket. "Most of…*the stuff* is just as a precaution. Once he has the surgery, they can stabilize him—"

I stop listening, entering the room without giving myself the chance to falter. This is it. Days of thinking the worst only to culminate in this moment…

My first thought is that the room is nice. Fab came through again, getting him one with a view of the city. It's large with calming white walls and a bed positioned in the center.

But the figure lying there, with tubes sticking out of him, isn't my boy. Not my Vin.

He can't be.

This figure is a ghost. A shell, so pale I can see through his skin to the blue veins beneath. A machine breathes for him in a slow, ghastly rhythm. His eyes are closed, his mouth absent that beautiful smile.

And all the lies I've fed myself fall flat.

Mischa Stepanov isn't the only one to blame for this.

I am.

This is *my* fucking fault.

19

WILLOW

I never knew it was possible to actually taste the pulse surging in your throat. Mine carries the distinct flavor of copper, *blood*; I've bitten my lip, but I can't move. My entire body goes rigid, electrified as though I've just stuck my finger in an outlet—or witnessed the unthinkable…

Donatello Vanici facing a reality he can't sneer down or brutalize.

This moment humanizes him like nothing else, highlighting the gauntness of his once handsome features. Robbed of all bravado, he's a ghost, thriving on the darkness the shadows provide, clinging to life like a zombie animated by only one stimulus.

Pain.

At the sight of Vincenzo, he staggers, threatening to collapse. His hand shoots out, gripping the back of a nearby chair, but the weight of his body nearly topples it. Like an old man, he hunches over, helpless…

My legs twitch, lurching into motion without permission. I'm already reaching for his shoulder before I can process the cons of the action. Plenty.

His heat scorches me through the cotton of his jacket. Instinctively, I try to draw my hand back—but his clamps down on my wrist before I can. I stiffen, expecting him to shove me off, but he tugs me closer, using my body to steady his. God, he's heavy. Firm.

But his weight feels different when he isn't leveraging it like a weapon. He clings to me with an amount of care that shocks me. Gentle. When I finally see his face, I realize why —he's distant, miles away, too far gone to give a damn about me. I've never seen any man so lost. Vacant. For an instant, those piercing dark irises serve as a mirror, reflecting my own expression back—and it's terrifying to see myself as he does…

Devoid of hate in exchange for concern.

For him.

He blinks, seeming to realize where he is. Shrugging me off, he keeps moving, eventually sinking to his knees beside the bed. The sound he makes next… I'll never forget it—a wordless howl that floods the room.

No matter my feelings toward him, even I'm not immune. My heart aches, but for the wrong reasons. Is this how he mourned for his precious Safiya, after he left me—*her*? It's sick to think this way. Selfish. And yet…the thoughts keep coming.

Did he cry out like this? Sink to the floor as if every ounce of strength left him, driven out by sorrow? Did he crouch over those things in that pink room and sob openly?

Tears blur my vision, and I lose track of the comparisons. All I can do is watch the scene unfolding, as disconnected as an outsider. For as long as I can, I prolong my own reckoning with the figure in the bed.

Until I have no choice.

When I finally look at Vincenzo, I choke on another wave of conflicting emotion. It's strange how he looks the same, even after all this time. Even with his head wrapped in bandages, his skin so pale it's see-through in places.

"He hasn't regained consciousness yet," a man declares from the doorway.

Only slightly taller than me with a head of auburn hair, he's dressed in a tailored suit, his posture conveying authority. Another shocking wave of recognition hits me. Once, I called him by another name. *Uncle Fabio.*

He stares past me without an ounce of recognition, speaking to Donatello. "The doctor assures me that there is brain activity. He requires surgery to relieve some pressure on his brain, but if all goes well, his status will improve—"

"Whatever it takes." In the blink of an eye, Donatello is on his feet. He's cold and composed once more, but his hand still grips Vincenzo's, his thumb stroking the pale skin. "Whatever the cost. I don't care. You have them do it."

"Of course." Fabio nods. "But who did you..." He trails off the second he sees me, grappling for a nearby table just to keep his balance. Dismay constricts his features, and I'm sure that he knows who I am. "Jesus, Mary, and Joseph, Donatello Vanici," he croaks. "You didn't. Tell me you didn't!"

He spins to confront the taller man, his expression horrified. "Are you insane? After everything I've done for you? For Vincenzo? This is what you do? You bring the daughter of the *mafiya* here?"

I was right, I realize. He knows who I am—just not the identity I expected him to.

"As what?" he demands. "Some kind of fucking hostage! Have you lost your mind—"

"Look at her, Fab," Donatello says quietly. Despite his insistence, his eyes are on the wall. "Look."

"I'm not blind, you stupid bastard. I can see this situation for what it is—insanity—"

"I said *look at her*, Fabio!" Donatello lunges toward me. Snatching my arm, he spins me to face the other man's inspection. Gone from his touch is any of that previous warmth. His hand gripping my chin might as well be a manacle. "Look at her! Really look. I'm sure you see it now."

"What are you…" Fabio blinks, shaking his head. If possible, he turns even paler before finally exhaling a sound in between a sigh and a groan.

"You aren't blind," Donatello says in a tone so cold I shiver. "I'm sure you knew before I did. I'm sure you *always* knew who she really was. You just kept it from me. For what? You thought I'd go after her then?"

For what it's worth, Fabio looks shocked into silence, still eyeing my face.

Donatello grunts, unsatisfied. His fingers grip me tighter, his breaths searing my neck. "It doesn't matter. Fuck, you doubt me now of all times? I would die for Vincenzo!"

His voice rings out, and Fabio flinches, startled back to the present.

"I know that," he says faintly. "I know that."

"So trust me. I didn't kidnap her. In fact, I didn't do a damn thing to her!" One by one, he pries his fingers from me to illustrate as much. "Mischa jumped the gun. He struck first."

"So, what do you plan to do?" Fabio demands tiredly. "Threaten the girl as retaliation? Trade her life for Vin's? Is that the real reason you got safe passage here? Just to lure Mischa Stepanov?" Raw pain laces his voice, and Donatello flinches.

"I'm not going to hurt her." He returns to the bed, lifting Vin's limp hand with both of his. "I'm going to marry her, Fab, and end this feud before it even begins."

"You…what?" The man staggers to the wall, bracing his hand against it. Nonetheless, he sinks to his knees with a faint sigh. "Jesus Christ, you've gone insane—"

"I haven't," Donatello snarls. "Think about it for a second. Use your head and fucking *think*. I marry her—"

"And Mischa kills all of us!"

"No," he snaps. "I marry her and beat Mischa at his own game. The bastard thinks he owns this city. He wouldn't have come after me, otherwise. This is personal. So I make it so fucking personal he has to face me on an even playing field."

"And what about her?" Fabio gestures to me. "I'm sure you've threatened her. God, don't tell me you raped her—"

"I never have to touch her," Donatello declares. He sounds so damn confident of that. "I haven't, by the way. You want to know why? All I need to do is show her with me *unharmed*. All I need to do is make her my wife and dangle that goddamn ring before Mischa and the world. If it looks like she's willingly mine, he can't touch me."

"You realize how you sound," Fabio croaks, letting his mouth hang open. "Do you? You sound insane, Donatello. You sound like you've lost your damn mind—"

"I have." He sounds so calm. So unconcerned by the grit in his own voice. The coldness. "I have lost my mind."

For the first time, I hear his words—truly hear them. He's not proposing a marriage. He's not even proposing a twisted hostage scenario. He's proposing, in essence, a sick reversal of his original crime—throw me away again. Only this time? My soul is what gets sold. My humanity.

I'll be reduced to a lifeless husk sporting a ring, no better than Vincenzo.

As Fabio insinuated, a life for a life.

"What would you have me do, huh?" Donatello questions as if arguing directly with my thoughts. "Sit idly by and let Vincenzo die? Sit by and watch Mischa Stepanov lord his power over me as though I'm some patsy he can step on, even if he fucking crushes me in the process? No..." His laugh will haunt my nightmares. "I can't let that happen. I refuse to."

"So you what? Turn into the same sort of tyrant you used to scoff at? This isn't you, Don," Fabio pleads. "Not anymore. Trust that I love Vin as much as you do. I would have found a way. I would have done something. Something that doesn't result in you with your boot on the neck of Mischa Stepanov."

"Well, it's too late." Donatello faces him, his head held high, shoulders squared. "So what are you going to do now?"

"Damn…" The man sighs heavily, rising to his feet. "You swear on your life that you haven't touched her? Not so much as a fucking hair?"

Donatello makes a motion in between a nod and a shake of his head. "I haven't seriously harmed her—"

"And you won't," Fabio warns. "Not a hair. You don't harm her. You don't touch her. You don't fuck—do anything other than *look* at her. Promise me."

Donatello's eyes narrow. Finally, he nods. "You have my word."

"I better," the other man insists, wagging a trembling finger. "I mean it. Now, as for your insane, ridiculous plan that I in no way endorse…it just might be crazy enough to work."

He starts to pace, instantly transforming from frantic to composed. With one hand, he strokes his chin, mulling over the thoughts he proposes out loud. "I assume there's more to this—you'll need to catch me up on the politics of it all."

"You don't know the half of it," Donatello warns. "To cut to the fun bit, Antonio Salvatore is dead, I'm in control of the *famiglia* now, and I found proof that Mischa acted on faulty intel. Someone else wanted his family attacked."

Fabio sways, his expression shifting from alarmed, to horrified, and then resigned all within the space of a second. "Who?"

Donatello shrugs. "Didn't get that far."

"Typical," Fabio snaps. "You always jump the damn gun. Right. Aside from that, you might be on to something. Cooling things down now could ensure peace with Mischa and avert an outright feud. You make it known that you haven't harmed her. She's here of her own account. And you won't go any further than marriage as a show of good faith. It could buy you time. And, of course, I can help spin the narrative. Put things into motion. Spread the publicity. Mischa may control the criminal underbelly, but he has nothing on the public front. With a few well-placed phone calls, I can make this the talk of the fucking city. He'll be boxed in."

"I'm not asking you to make yourself a target, Fab," Donatello says.

"Stop right there—" Fabio raises his hand. "You don't need to ask me to do a damn thing. Everyone knows we're connected. I don't have a choice but to fix this mess. Now…" He folds his hands behind his back, continuing to pace. "A long engagement would be the best course of action. An actual marriage might not even be necessary—"

"The legal protections are what matter," Donatello interjects. "Mischa can rage all he wants, but there are rules that even men like us are forced to follow."

"What a twisted world," Fabio laments. "Maybe you're right, but only to buy enough time for you and Mischa to hash out your differences without putting bullets in each other's brains. In that case, a brief ceremony. We'd need to arrange for the right guests. The right optics to make this as convincing as possible. Even the *mafiya* can't challenge public opinion." He reaches into his pocket, withdrawing a cell phone. "I need to make some calls. Give me some time. And don't worry about Vin," he adds more softly. "That's been arranged too. Just try to stay out of trouble for five minutes."

He leaves the room, the phone attached to his ear.

In the resulting silence, Donatello returns to Vin's bedside, taking his other hand. "Don't look at me like that," he warns.

Considering that Vin's eyes are closed, it's obvious who he's speaking to.

"This way, you keep your family alive. Vincenzo alive. You get to go back inside your perfect little cage and—"

I back away from him so violently I nearly trip. I brace my hand against the nearest window to steady myself, overlooking a lonely gray parking lot, the city in the distance. The sight is surprisingly reassuring, a desolate landscape partially populated. It reminds me of a world far from the machinations of men like the one behind me.

If I really were the bird he mocks me to be, I'd fly away now.

Fast.

"Don't pretend like this isn't the best fucking option," he warns, advancing too quickly to evade. "You stay alive, and I get the best chance to save Vincenzo. Look at him—"

His fingers latch onto my throat, forcing me to face the bed. "Look at what your beloved father did. You want his blood on your hands? Then refuse to play along."

I grit my teeth, my eyes watering. Maybe he's right? In his cruel, sick sense of logic, this is probably the far less of multiple evils. Merciful. After all, he once sold me intending to let me die.

The only difference now is that he gets to inflict the damage himself. He gets to steal the pampered, polished life Mischa provided and relegate me to insignificance all over again.

His life becomes my new prison.

And I'd rather be left for dead.

I'm crying in earnest. Tears paint my cheeks in steady strokes, but inside I'm woefully numb. The medical machinery and noises around us create a twisted sort of melody—a mocking rendition of what I have to look forward to.

A dead-end—being technically alive, but in essence, just existing. Breathing. A shell.

"Don't you dare think you can run now," Donatello cautions as I remember how to move and wrench out of his grasp, staggering to put distance between us. "You wanted my attention? Well, now you have it."

I could laugh. Scream. Rip him open with my nails or stab him with my knife.

I could. But that's what he wants. To lord this prison over me. To gloat. To have me writhe on his hook so he can forget who truly caused this mess.

He did.

Focus! It takes everything I have to wrestle my rage into submission. I'm shaking with the effort, choking on the air in my lungs as more tears blur my vision. When I finally regain control over my breathing, I meet the gaze of the man before me, putting everything I have into my expression, if only to convey one point. One last threat.

I'll play his game, alright.

And I'll make him regret ever asking me to in the first place —not through violence. Something far worse.

I'll become *his* prison.

I'll make his life a living hell.

I'll make him writhe on my hook, and in the end, he'll be the one to turn tail and run.

I'll make him pay.

His gaze hardens as if he's aware of every plot and scheme taking shape. "Fair enough." His mouth flattens into a hard, stern line, but his raised eyebrow makes my pulse race. It's amused. A dare. I swear I hear him murmur, "You think you can try? I want to see you do it—"

"Sir!" A man staggers into the room. I vaguely recognize him as the figure stationed by the door when we arrived, now grim-faced, his hand ominously inside his jacket pocket. "*Mafiya* men spotted entering the hospital. They're on their way here."

"It was only a matter of time," Donatello murmurs, but I marvel at the levelness of his tone as he enters the hall with a galling sense of calm. I scramble after him, my brain struggling to reconcile his myriad of clashing responses. When I strip for him of my own accord, he rages, but in the face of a different kind of enemy?

He's damn near poised. The stark contrast highlights just how unsure I am of my own feelings. Doubt gnaws on my nerves with every step I take. Mischa is here… I should feel relieved. I *am*. My heart swells, and I ache to see him. Try to explain. Apologize.

Maybe I could end this just by facing him, finally?

The thoughts barely finish forming, when a commotion cuts the tranquil quiet of the ward, alarming the few nurses and medical personnel. Slamming doors. Shouting. My stomach contorts into knots as my head swivels along with everyone else's toward the source of the noise. Instantly, I'm forced to reconcile my wishes for what they are—childish fantasies.

Mischa *is* here, barging through a door that I assume leads to a stairwell, but instead of relief, fear floods my body. It's so strange how a few changes in demeanor and clothing can drastically alter someone.

Gone is the jolly fellow who I've witnessed read fairy tales to his young daughters and play tag with his sons. Hate strips any ounce of warmth from his features, and I'm not immune to the effect he has on those caught in his path. I stiffen, my eyes glued to him, my body tensing with instinctive alarm, sensing the danger in the atmosphere.

His blond hair is gathered loosely at the nape of his neck, enhancing the angular planes of his face and the dark eyes ablaze. If it weren't obvious until now, the piercing glare he sports makes it clear—this man isn't here to make nice. He's ready for war. Dressed head to toe in gray fatigues, he embodies the frightening image of the *mafiya* leader the world knows him to be.

But another figure stalks past me to meet him fearlessly, easily drawing my attention away. Remarkably, he undergoes the same drastic transformation as Mischa, but in reverse—from stiff with grief to electric. Wearing a black suit, his dark hair mussed, he seems like an unlikely match compared to Mischa's bulk—but no less intimidating. Shadow in contrast to fiery gold. Light against darkness. When viewed together, the effect they have is chilling.

Two equally powerful pieces fighting for control over a dwindling game board. The sole piece deciding said fate? A lone, insignificant pawn caught between both sides. That designation feels cemented by the way Donatello positions himself—near enough to grab me.

"Are you really going to shoot me here?" he demands of Mischa, outstretching his arms in a grand gesture. "Right here? Then do it, you son of a bitch."

The vitriol seems honed like a volley of arrows into an advancing army. Undeterred, Mischa merely slows his pace as a cruel half-smile tugs on his mouth. At least six men lurk behind him, a mere fraction of what I know his security force to be. At a glance, I only recognize a few faces, none of them Evgeni.

"You dare show your face here," Mischa growls, sounding more incredulous than enraged. "I should—" his gaze meets mine and his entire expression shifts, his eyes widening. "Willow…"

"Not so fast." Donatello places a hand on my shoulder, locking me in place before I can even think to move. "I want to hear you say it," he demands. "What are you here to do? Plan to shoot up a hospital? Finish Vincenzo off? Don't be shy with your plans for vengeance now."

A shadow darkens Mischa's expression, harshening the rage already apparent. "I'm the one who should be asking you that fucking question." He inclines his head, his eyes slits. "Let me hear you say it—are you threatening her?"

I shrink beneath the weight of attention as several pairs of eyes turn to me.

"You haven't heard?" Donatello scoffs, tightening his grip on me. Ruthlessly. His nails bare down on the thin material of the dress, threatening to pierce the tender flesh beneath. It stings, but I'm more alarmed by the suspicion that pain isn't his aim this time. For once, he *sees* me, but only as something to claim. Own. "I'm sure you have. Your friends, the Saleris haven't told you?"

He waits, but Mischa doesn't react—which is exactly what I think he was counting on. I glance over to see him practically levitating with arrogance. With a dark eyebrow raised, he says, "I plan to marry your daughter, Mischa. As a show of goodwill and to acknowledge her affections after you viciously mounted an attack on my family. Consider yourself lucky that I'm more interested in peace than revenge."

Silence falls with a deafening impact. All I can hear is my pulse racing as my heart pounds so hard I feel it jolt up my throat. I can't even look at him—but as I cut my gaze down to the tile flooring, I'm acutely aware of the man behind me. His touch is violent, his breath fire against my cheek. His stance unnerves me more than his hate does—it's possessive. *Confusing.*

Finally, he withdraws his hand, but the sensation hits like a slap. It's jarring, recalling the torment he put me through in the shower tenfold—unbearable heat switched to sudden cold.

"Threaten me if you want," he taunts, facing Mischa. "It will only serve to prove my point—you're too power-hungry, caught up in personal grievances to see reason. Don't tell me this all has to do with the harbor?"

That dangerous silence lingers for a second longer. Another.

"You know damn well what this has to do with," Mischa growls in a tone so guttural I feel it in my bones. Finally, I lift my head to face him, unprepared for the man I see. For a moment, I'm twelve again, viewing him as a stranger whose motives I couldn't fathom. Would he be just another monster?

As he sees me, however, the spell is broken. He's the man I've come to trust once more, though furious as he eyes the place Donatello held me. "How dare you even touch her—"

"Let's ask her if I forced her here," Donatello counters with a false sense of calm. "If she's so battered and broken, let her run to you. Go!"

His hand slams against my back, shoving me forward. I stumble, my eyes riveted to Mischa. God, I never knew how much my heart could hurt. Physically throb as if stabbed. Beaten. Broken. Deep down, I know exactly what will make the pain go away—run.

Hide. Forget Donatello, damn the consequences of what might happen. In this moment, I want nothing more than to do just that—go home to my family.

I even take a step, but then reality cruelly sinks in. The man on my heels didn't release me out of kindness. He's merely testing the invisible binds linking us together more tightly than any chains. Pride—I refuse now; I'm playing right into his depiction of me. That as a selfish little girl. And I'd prove him right, Vin's death would truly be on my hands.

And I would be *his* pawn to conquer.

If I were hoping otherwise, Mischa's expression gives a clear roadmap about how this will end. In violence. The sheer depth of the rage written across his features is breathtaking. So much anger. Hate.

As his hard mask returns in full, I barely recognize him.

"I guess that's settled," Donatello remarks, forcing me to realize what everyone else has. All this time, I haven't moved.

Smug, my captor appears at my side, snatching my hand—but I can sense the tension coiled in every thick finger. Despite his outward composure, he's wary.

As he should be.

"We should discuss this over lunch, like men," Donatello suggests. "I'll send you the information—"

"You go to hell," Mischa snarls, his eyes flashing. With every word, his accent thickens, coating each syllable in malice. "You want to hide inside a hospital? Use a woman as a shield? I knew you were a coward, but this... It's pathetic."

"Tomorrow," Donatello cordially replies as if never interrupted. "We can discuss my nephew's medical bills, which you will personally cover."

Mischa growls, sounding more animal than human. A wolf, snarling for blood. "You—"

"And, as a show of faith, you will have access to the Vanici harbor enterprise," a different voice interjects, throwing the tension on its head. Fabio. Almost comically, everyone whips around to find him standing in a doorway roughly in between the two men—a symbolic placement if there ever was one.

In his hands is a small notepad and pen. I have a strange thought of him patiently taking notes all this time.

"This will be a union of two families," he says, seemingly the voice of reason amid this unfathomable chaos. "As a show of faith, I'm sure we can come to other agreements. Donatello has assured me that your daughter has not been harmed in any way—"

"Perhaps you want to examine her yourself," Donatello interjects with a hint of menace. "At least before you go crying rape. Just know this—I have no intention of ever laying a hand on your precious daughter—"

"She has always been *my* daughter," Mischa snarls, his hands fists. "Always. Never will I forsake her. The same can't be said for you, can it?"

"No." Donatello's voice is unchanged. "But I guess I can take those words as your blessing?"

A ripple goes through Mischa's men as their leader cocks his head in warning. "My blessing?"

He seems to teleport; he moves so fast. Air whooshes past my ears, and I only see a blur of motion before a force shoves me aside, ripping my hand from Donatello. I crash against the wall, scrambling to spin around.

A sickening thud shatters the silence, followed by a masculine groan. Another. It happens so quickly I can barely track it all. Men scramble in every which direction, while—at the center of it all—Mischa grapples with Donatello, his hands around the other man's neck. With a violent thud, he shoves him against the wall, and I know in my soul he won't stop there.

"Enough!" someone shouts, their voice drowned out by another groan. "Not here! Jesus Christ—"

My pulse surges, deafening me. I'm only aware of moving blindly with no real aim in mind. Just shoving my way through the fray, against a wall of writhing bodies. Reaching out. Grasping at a muscular arm and tugging.

The figure in question jerks, his eyes finding mine. Mischa. A flicker of emotion flits across his gaze too quickly to track. The rage contorting his features doesn't diminish, but he steps back just enough for the man in his grasp to break free.

"It's about damn time you attacked *me*," Donatello rasps. He staggers to regain his balance, swiping at his nose. Blood flows freely from one nostril, speckling his chin and white shirt, not that he seems to care. He's smiling wide, his teeth painted scarlet. "Do it again. Hit me. Shoot me! You know you want to. At least we're finally man to man." Another manic grin contradicts any fear that he might be truly in pain. With a start, I realize this is the most animated I've seen him since that horrific moment in Havienna.

"Attack me," he hisses. "Not a *boy*. You're luckier than you know, Mischa—" his eyes cut to me, devoid of an ounce of warmth. "I could have killed her. God, the things I could have done to her..."

He sounds annoyed that he *hasn't* done those horrible things. Sure, he's considered them, going so far as to taunt me with the threat. But he hasn't crossed the line. The only sense of comfort I can find is that the other night I realized why—he's *afraid* to.

"You won't ever touch her again." Mischa surges forward, grabbing my arm to pull me against him. His strength is a battering ram, both a comfort and a restraint. "You're lucky I don't castrate you with my bare fucking hands," he says to the man watching us.

Donatello doesn't react, still sporting that gruesome smile. I can't escape the creeping sensation that he's in my head again, boldly reading my mind.

And whatever he finds emboldens him more. "Not being able to touch her might make our wedding a tad bit more difficult—"

"Marry her?" Mischa scoffs. "I'll kill you first—"

"Don't tell me you're making the choice for her?" Donatello's smirk widens as he licks the blood from his lips. "You don't trust your little girl, Mischa?"

"Come near her again, and I will kill you." To his credit, Mischa doesn't take the bait this time. Gesturing to his men, he conveys the reason why—this fight was never fair from the outset. "Stand down now, and maybe I'll let you live for the time being," he says. "I'm taking my daughter home."

He turns back the way he came, maneuvering me to follow. He's too strong. Too fast. It takes effort to dislodge my arm from him. Desperation. Wrenching on my shoulder isn't enough. He doesn't react when I paw at his wrist with my free hand, either. In the end, I have to grab the edge of a nearby doorway and leverage my body weight against him. He tightens his grip at first until, with a shocked grunt, he loosens it just enough.

The second I pull free, it's as if all of the air is sucked from the room. My skin burns in the absence of Mischa's touch, and this time I can't escape his expression.

He only stares, his gaze devoid of emotion. No anger. No hate. No pain.

And I'd prefer he shout. Yell. Rage at me.

In his silence, I break. Internally fracture, held up only by muscle and bone. Like a coward, I wrench my gaze down to his chest, but the sight isn't a comfort. I swear I can see his heart pounding madly beneath his jacket, assaulted by both shock and rage.

Or maybe a different emotion, one that softens his voice just a fraction as he asks, "Is this what you want?"

What I want. There are too many nuances to that statement to parse over. The only one that matters is the grim suspicion that, just like Donatello, he knows me too well.

My impulsive answer? *No.* I want to go home. See my family. Know for sure that Ellen and Eli are okay. Forget what's happened.

Ignore the past.

Instead, I look up and try to tell him everything I can through my expression. That I love him—so much. That I would never willingly turn against him…

He holds my gaze unflinchingly, every bit the stoic figure I've come to respect. For a second, I swear I see a grudging frown tug on his mouth. Acknowledgment that he at least understood, even if he doesn't quite understand…

But I'm too much of a coward to be sure. I look away and catch Donatello watching me, his mouth in a flat line. I'm struck by the sense that he knows what I'm planning even before I do. Gradually, I regain my balance and start toward him, but his blank expression doesn't waver.

Though he at least has enough tact not to gloat now. There's no point. As far as his twisted game is concerned, he's already won his round.

The pawn is his to claim.

Walking toward him is like wading through quicksand. I fully expect Mischa to grab me again. Lunge. Fight. But it's as if the world is paralyzed in this moment. I'm the only person alive able to move. Walk. Breathe.

And I can take some small shred of smug pride in watching Donatello's expression. The hard mask slips for a heartbeat.

I know he's holding his breath, cocking his head warily as I reach out, grappling for a fistful of his suit jacket. I raise it slowly, dabbing at the blood streaked across his face.

As I do, I meet his gaze, and I let him in. I let him see every thought circling my brain.

He thinks he's in control of this game? He's wrong. So wrong. Now more than ever, am I determined to punish him for everything he's done. Death isn't good enough.

I want him to thoroughly know the pain that comes from doubting your own identity. From having someone else consume who you are and spit out a mockery.

I want him to suffer just as I did.

And I make a mental note to do whatever it takes. I strip myself of any past hesitations or modesty, and I dive right into the only weapon I have that's ever truly seemed to affect him.

He vows never to touch me? Well, I didn't promise to show the same restraint. As our eyes meet, I let my thumb graze his jaw just once.

It's a warning. Unexpectedly, he nods, having understood me clearly. "Play with fire if you want, hellcat," he murmurs for only me to hear. "Play. I'll gladly watch you burn—"

"Willow?" Mischa's voice is ice.

I turn to him as Donatello shrugs me off, but gently, maintaining the ruse that I am his willing fiancée.

"Lunch, tomorrow," he says to the figure behind me. "Bring your fists if it will make you feel better. I'll make sure to find a place public enough to cause a scene—"

"Fuck you."

"Your daughter won't—the least I can do," Donatello says quickly. My cheeks flame at the rare note of honesty in his voice. I don't think he even realizes it himself. "Until our wedding, at least. Though maybe I should change my mind?"

The tension cracks, and I brace for another assault.

"Enough," a quiet voice demands. Fabio. "I suggest we settle this for now," he says, smoothing his hand down the front of his suit. "Not here. Both of you have family trying to rest and heal. Let's not forget that, shall we? Who knows what amount of stress this little argument might cause them? As Donatello suggested, you should meet tomorrow at a restaurant of my choosing. All necessary documents will be agreed upon then."

"You're just as insane as he is," Mischa growls.

"I am insane," Fabio says with a respectful tone and a slight nod. "I've spent the past three days trying to hold my nephew's brains in with bandages while hunting for a hospital safe enough for him to recover in. If you think Donatello is the only one with a grievance to leverage, think again. You've seen the proof of Antonio Salvatore's crimes. Maybe you should spend your time finding out who really set this mess into motion. *Both* of you."

Again that rare note of authority slips into his tone, hardening it.

"A wedding honestly sounds reckless and contrived, but damn it, if it keeps my nephew alive and puts an end to this before more damage can be done, I will shove them down the aisle myself. As you can see, the girl isn't a prisoner. I'll vouch for Donatello's behavior—she'll remain intact and safe before any vows are uttered. Now, again I suggest you leave while I try to head off any publicity that might arise, yes?"

I never actually hear Mischa acquiesce. Like a coward, I face the wall, and it feels like an eternity passes before the *mafiya* finally retreat. Their heavy steps are my only clue, along with Donatello's weary sigh.

"I owe you, Fab," he rasps with genuine gratitude. "I mean it—"

"You're damn right you do," Fabio snaps, jutting his chin. "Whether you put a fucking chastity belt on her or lock her in a room, she better be unharmed. I mean it, Donatello—"

"She's a child, Fab," he says offhandedly.

"Hmph." Fabio's eyes narrow to slits. "You almost sounded convincing. Now get the hell out of here. Think of all the bribes I'll have to hand out to keep the staff quiet, in addition to arranging for increased security—those *famiglia* aren't nearly enough."

"That's another thing I wanted to talk to you about," Donatello suggests. "Antonio wasn't exactly a champion of employee retention. I need help tracking down the old crew to replenish ranks."

"I did notice the entourage seemed a little anemic," Fabio says. "But this was never my realm, Donatello. Never. I always kept my nose out of *famiglia* business, and you never had a problem with that before. Why should I change what I think in hindsight was a very prudent decision now?"

"For me," Donatello says simply. I marvel at this vulnerability. This raw, open pleading. If he had asked me to participate in his scheme like this…

Would that have made any difference?

"I need you, Fab," he says, his expression stern once more. "I need you."

"Fine." Sighing, Fabio rakes a hand through his graying auburn hair. "I'll hunt down some old contacts—but my one stipulation is some new recruits. I think I know of a small outfit you might be able to absorb. They're scruffy and will need some shaping up, but I think in this instance, the more, the merrier."

Donatello scoffs. "Don't tell me you've been rubbing shoulders with lowly criminals, Fab."

"You don't know the half of it." The man shoots him a guarded look. "Anyway. Go get cleaned up. I'll stay here for a while. I think they'll schedule the surgery for tonight— but I don't think you should be here."

Donatello's entire posture shifts in the blink of an eye. He hunches, the color draining from his skin. I sense my heel twitch against the floor at the fear he might collapse again.

"You think I'll let him go under the knife alone?" he asks.

Fabio doesn't even flinch. "I think you should let the team work in *peace.* Let Vin rest without worrying about another visit from the *mafiya*, hmm?"

"Don't use him as your excuse," Donatello growls, drawing himself back to full height. "What? You think I'll be too emotional?"

"That's exactly what I think." Fabio crosses to him and places a hand on his chest. "You need to stay focused, Don. Keep your head clear. The best thing you can do for Vin is to make things as safe as possible for him. He should be your primary concern right now. Not Mischa. Not anyone. So go home. Wait for my call on his status. Don't drink, and keep your head clear. Think of the man you want Vin to see when he wakes up. You, covered in blood? Or you, dressed nicely in a suit, not smelling like drink for once, with a safe home for him to recuperate in? I'll leave you to make that choice."

He returns to Vincenzo's room, smiling weakly at the startled nurses and medical personnel peering from around corners.

"Fuck." Donatello eyes his bloodied hand, shaking off fresh droplets of blood. Shoving that same hand into his pocket, he meets my gaze and inclines his head toward the elevator. "Let's go."

He lumbers down the hall, leaving me to follow. At a glance, Mischa's men appear to be long gone—but my guilt isn't. It pools in my blood, growing stronger with each beat of my heart. I swear I can hear it, morphing from noise into a guilt-ridden taunt—*I failed him.*

I failed him…

There is no pretty way to say it. No heroic words to soften the blow. I chose Donatello Vanici over the man I love like a father. The man who saved me. Who has always protected me.

I turned my back on my family.

For what? The whim of a monster.

"You played your part, little wife," Donatello remarks from inside the elevator.

I flinch, hating how he can read me so accurately. He leans against the wall, his eyes unsettlingly dark. "I'm sure your Mischa will be angry, but I think you'll agree that it is better to be angry than dead."

Is it?

My body chooses to answer for me where words can't. I step back just as the doors start to close.

"No!" He's too fast, shoving his hand between the barrier before it can fully seal. Eyes flashing, he starts toward me, but I'm already turning my back to him, retracing our path through the hall.

He's hot on my heels, raging. "What the hell are you playing at?"

It's the wrong terminology. This is so not a game.

It's a war, and I'm tired of cowering behind the trenches.

Increasing my pace, I practically sprint to my destination, expecting to feel a wrenching hand on my shoulder at any second. Just when I swear I see movement in the corner of my eye, I enter a room where the only conscious inhabitant looks up, puzzled by my appearance.

"Can... Can I help you?" Fabio asks, rising from a chair beside Vin's bed.

"What the hell are you doing?" Donatello snarls, storming in a second later. He doesn't reach for me. Yet.

Ignoring him, I approach Fabio, making my expression as pleading as I can. Truth be told, I know nothing about him. He could be just as dismissive of me as Donatello, but when I raise my hands and mime for a pen and paper, he nods, fishing both from his suit jacket.

"Here." He gestures to a small table nearby, clearing a space for me to write.

"What are you doing?" Donatello demands as I start scribbling. I can sense him reading over my shoulder, but I don't bother to disguise my words. As I pen my first line across the page, he scoffs.

"A list of demands?" Fabio interprets.

I nod, gripping the pen so tightly it shakes, smearing ink. If this were a game, as he claimed, the rules could be easily broken. But in war? There are more rigid norms to follow.

Or so I hope.

"Does the heiress think she gets to stomp her foot and get her way?" Donatello mockingly snipes. The venom in his voice is a shock. Not entirely due to anger, I suspect. Fear?

Once again, he hates when I foil his expectations of me.

"You've had your say. Let's see her speak for herself." Fabio gestures to the page. "Well, let's see them then—"

"Fabio, are you seriously entertaining this?"

The man raises an eyebrow. "Is she your *willing* fiancée or not?"

Donatello says nothing, but I can feel his gaze boring through the back of my neck.

"Well then," Fabio says in the resulting silence. "Let's see her demands."

I only have four—just a small list in the grand scheme, composed with one aim in mind. In what way can I claw back a pathetic shred of power for myself?

The first step is to remember who I am—a Stepanov. Ellen and Eli are in this very building. I can't leave without seeing them, so I write.

1. I am allowed to see my family.

"Now?" Fabio sounds wary, but Donatello snorts.

Or maybe he growls. "No. Hell no—"

"Perhaps once everything is set in writing," Fabio says over him. His lips contort into a strained smile purely for my benefit. "I'll see to it personally."

"So she can go prancing back to Stepanov manor and return leading an army of guards?" Donatello snipes. "Hell no."

"If we make the proper arrangements, I don't see why not," Fabio says tacitly. He taps the paper, eyeing me expectantly. "What else?"

2. I have my own guard stay with me. Evgeni.

It's the only option that seems capable of making Havienna somewhat bearable—a piece of my new life. Someone to ground me in the world of Donatello Vanici. He may have consumed Safiya, but I refuse to let him destroy Willow.

"Think that's a proper 'arrangement'?" Donatello snipes.

Fabio furrows his brow in concentration but merely nods. "What else?"

My hand shakes, but I force myself to finish.

3. I have unlimited access to my own financial accounts.

That draws an even more violent scoff. Unbothered, I keep writing.

4. I am allowed to pick my own clothing.

He doesn't challenge that stipulation. For the first time, I look back to find him leaning beside me, his hand braced on the table, his eyes dark in thought. A shudder runs through me that I can't explain. Rather than inspect it, I turn back to my paper as Fabio gently takes it from my hand.

"These all look agreeable to me," he declares. "I'll have them drafted into the final agreement you'll present to Mischa—"

"No!" Donatello grabs for the page, but Fabio pulls it out of reach. "Have you lost your mind?"

"You want this to seem like an equal partnership, right?" Fabio eyes my list and nods, folding it. Meeting my gaze, he tucks it into his pocket. "These sound reasonable enough. Consider them done—" He turns his attention to Donatello, unfazed by the glower the other man shoots him. "I suggest you start making your arrangements. Think of it this way, Mischa has less to counter if it's clear she's let her own voice be heard in this matter. Which brings me to another point…" He eyes me as if considering whether or not to voice his concern. After a second, he squares his jaw. "The matter of her 'virtue.' Call me old-fashioned, but if you haven't touched her as you say, then we should codify that. Have it cemented in stone so that no one can accuse you of taking advantage. Besides, if your *love* is so pure, you

"Knock it off." Donatello casts me a glance of disgust. "I have no intention of ever fucking her if that's what you mean."

My cheeks flame—a reaction I have no control over. It's purely instinctive and not at all a response to the sincerity in his voice. Sincerity that so vastly contradicts the way he touched me only a few moments ago. When his mouth had been inches from mine, and I could see it in his eyes...

He wanted more.

"Good," Fabio says. "Then put your money where your mouth is. You break that—in any way. If she winds up... scandalized in your care, you forfeit everything. I'm sure you have no trouble agreeing to that."

Donatello noticeably hesitates, his eyes flicking in my direction. Just when I think he'll argue, he nods curtly. "Fine. Let my little wife have her stipulations." Pushing back from the table, he stalks from the room, his voice a parting slap. "Come."

"I'll make sure these are drawn up," Fabio insists. He opens his mouth as if he means to say more. Instead, he nods. "Good luck."

I take a steadying breath before turning to the doorway, but a childish urge to linger here in Fabio's orbit swamps me. With every inch I stray from him, the shift in the

352

atmosphere becomes more apparent. It's a feeling like that of being adrift in a boat with no oars.

And my destination is a waterfall certain to dash me to pieces.

More than that, Donatello Vanici is a storm unto himself, swirling madly just beyond the door.

I could run and cower from the resulting tempest. Or step right out into the thick of it, unbothered.

He stiffens when I enter the hall and find him waiting, standing tall as a nurse scurries past him, looking so small in comparison to his bulk. In his eyes, I expect to see that simmering anger—and I do. But mingled there amongst it all is an emotion I wasn't anticipating.

Grudging respect?

It gleams for just a second from the overall darkness before he blinks and inclines his head. "Come. Little wife."

I stiffen, inhaling a shaky breath. His tone says it all—he'll make me pay for my little play for power.

But this time?

I'm ready to do battle—and I have more than a knife to counter him with.

20

EVGENI

*B*riar, in all her mystery, continues to surprise me. I expect the card she gave to lead to some grand hotel. A backdrop elegant enough to fit the allure of a disgraced heiress.

Instead, I find myself before a motel in the part of Hell's Gambit aptly called the "shitty end." In a city where crime runs rampant, it's only fitting that the district deemed the very worst fits all of the most glorified stereotypes.

Two women stand on the corner across the street, and their outfits make it obvious what wares they're selling even in broad daylight. Further down the block, a man stands wearing an oversized jacket, his gaze darting around the few people passing by.

Inside, the place's quality is even more apparent with peeling tile and creatures scurrying in the shadows. My my, the Winthorp heiress has fallen from grace.

Her room is on the second floor in a slightly better location that overlooks a vacant parking lot rather than the main street. I knock once, expecting a haughty silence from the other end.

Anything but a cheerful, purred, "Just a minute."

Amusement mingles with an emotion I can't decipher, and both make me raise an eyebrow with one realization—she's expecting someone.

Just as I start to wonder who, the door opens, ushering a cloud of perfumed steam into the hall.

"Oh," the woman remarks, sounding mildly surprised. "It's you."

I blink to find her standing on the other end with her back to me. Her bare back. A towel slung around her waist barely covers the curve of her ass and the rounded tops of her thighs.

Everything else is on stark display. Modest doesn't seem to be her default setting, so I suspect her appearance is entirely by design. To intentionally distract me.

Perhaps from the fact that a male was here. Recently. I mentally parse through the stern, gruff figures I passed entering this establishment, none of whom seem to be an aristocrat's preferred company. Perhaps this woman has fallen further than I realized?

"Do tell me you're here for a reason," she prompts.

"That depends. I hope I'm not interrupting something," I counter.

"I promised one of the girls downstairs some of my old clothes," she says coyly before slinking around a corner, presumably into a bathroom given the steam wafting from that direction.

I picture her tailored red dress and the janitorial outfit. "I don't think your style fits with their line of work."

She laughs, sticking her head out from around the corner. Her blue eyes gleam, and I'm once again struck by how similar she looks to Ellen Stepanova.

And how different. It's as if someone took Ellen and stripped the warmth from her gaze, leaving only cold, serpentine mystery. This woman is as similar to her as I assume Eli is to his murderous, bastard of a biological father.

So tread carefully, a part of me warns. *Even if your cock insists otherwise.*

I blame biology for the tightening in my abdomen. I'd have to be blind not to notice her beauty. Luckily, those same eyes spot the gun lying on a dresser across the room. I don't miss the distinctive hint of masculine cologne underneath her feminine smell, either.

The lone bed in the center of the room is empty, apart from rumpled white sheets. A few paces away is a closed door, I assume leads to a closet. Could the culprit of the scent be lurking there, waiting to spring an attack?

Though hell, I couldn't blame anyone but myself if this is an ambush. I'm the fool that blindly entered it without even alerting my men of my location.

Almost as if I know how stupid it would sound out loud. To come here on a whim. Even rookies know one simple rule—never meet an enemy in their den, especially not alone.

But here I am, so why wait for the tables to be turned?

The room is small enough to cross in just three strides. From here, I have a clear view into a narrow bathroom where she stands with her back to me, sans the towel.

Gritting my teeth, I rip my gaze away and wrench open the door, palming my own gun in its holster.

Inside, all I find is a leather suitcase and a simple array of clothing hanging. At a glance, none of the items, in particular, look like they could belong to a man, from the slender red dress to a simple coat and a few blouses.

"Don't tell me you intend to interrogate my luggage?" the woman purrs from the doorway of the bathroom.

I turn to find none of the playfulness reflected in her gaze. Her eyes warily track the return of my gun to its holster while her arms hold a thin towel around her. The dampness of her hair reinforces the fact that she took a shower, and I interrupted. But was she alone?

Unapologetic, I surge forward, surveying the narrow bathroom before glancing into the shower.

It's empty.

"Should you strip search me as well," she remarks coldly. I glance back to find she's pressed herself against the wall. "Maybe I have a weapon hidden on my person? Make sure you're thorough."

Sarcasm laces her tone, but I recall her trick with the blade at the hospital and back away, keeping her hands in view.

"Maybe I should?"

Amusement mingled with irritation flickers across her gaze. Then she shrugs. "Oh, all right." With an exaggerated sigh, she lets the towel fall, stepping into me with her arms outstretched. "Take your time," she taunts.

Something that could be alarm makes me grit my teeth, but I take another step, switching to the mindset of a man who can't afford to take a chance. Not even if it's offered mockingly.

I let my eyes sweep her body with a scrutiny usually reserved for the days I'd scan the landscape for enemy soldiers or active threats. Instead of underbrush and sky, I make a mental map of pale skin unmarred by so much as a pimple. The only flaw I find at all is a series of linear, faded scars along the inside of her wrist—which she quickly contorts from my view once she catches me staring.

Other than that, some men might deem her…perfect.

Perfectly dangerous in my book.

"Satisfied?" she snaps once it's clear that she doesn't have a weapon within reach. I wouldn't put it past her type to smuggle a knife in one of the few crevices available on a human body not visible to the naked eye.

A flush spreads across her cheeks as if she can read my mind, but her smile is shameless.

"I think you've seen enough." She stoops, grabbing her towel from the floor. Casually she drapes it around her, and I'm finally convinced that she's alone. "What brings you here? Let me guess. You intend to lure me into a trap at the behest of your employer?"

"No," I snap. "I came to listen. Who is Alexander?"

She laughs while slinking past me for the closet. From it, she grabs the red dress and drops her towel again in favor of it. From over her shoulder, she chirps, "Don't tell me you believe me, now?"

"I don't," I counter. "But even if you are lying, I'd still like to know your aim."

"But don't you already?" She whirls around and props her hand beneath her chin. Slowly, her eyes rake me over, and she nods once to herself. "Spoiled little rich girl, desperate for money. My aim is to fleece Mischa by threatening his wife or holding whatever information I may know about my family over his head, yes?"

She smirks knowingly when I don't respond.

"Oh, Evgeni, Evgeni…" Arching her back, she eyes herself in a dingy mirror hanging on the wall and runs a hand down her side. "Of course, there's always the possibility that I've already decided what type of man you are and have arranged everything perfectly to exploit that knowledge."

"Oh?"

Her smile widens. "That you are the bleeding-heart type ripe for the manipulation by some poor, downtrodden woman you deem in need of saving. That by luring you here with the promise of information, I've only managed to provoke that sense in you. Once you see my living arrangements, you'll be driven to protect me."

It's an unnervingly specific plan. "Then you've sorely misjudged me," I say.

"Ah, but did I?" She nods in the general direction of my gun—while I notice she's inching closer to the one lying on the dresser. "Don't tell me you bring that on all of your social calls."

"Only when I'm meeting with someone who has already proven themselves dangerous."

She shrugs and switches tack, throwing herself onto the mattress. Fluttering her lashes, she eyes me through them. "Well, I must have made quite the impression for you to come so armed just to meet one lone woman. If I do tempt you enough to take a shot at me, do use a silencer, or you might spook the drunk next door."

"A drunk, huh? Is *he* responsible for the smell of cologne in here?"

Her tongue flits across her lower lip—I caught her off guard. "As you can see, I'm all alone, soldier," she simpers.

It's a lie, but I can't fathom her reasoning.

"Right. One lone woman," I parrot.

"Ah!" Her upper lip quirks into a smug grin. "So you do have a sense of humor. You could have fooled me—"

"Talk," I demand. "Or lose your chance. Given your family history, I think you know a thing or two about loss."

Her smile falls, and something in my chest twinges. Regret? I don't decipher it.

With a heavy sigh, she hauls herself upright and spins to face me while still seated on the edge of the bed.

"You're right," she snaps. "I do know a thing or two about *loss*. Especially loss derived from the pissing contests of two arrogant men. Your Mischa? I've been on the receiving end of one of his grudges before. I'd rather not be in that position again—" the shudder she suppresses seems genuine enough. "So arrange a meeting between us like a good dog and everyone is happy. Trust me, I think he'll want to learn what I know."

"And what is that?" I demand. "You should be careful throwing around the term 'dog.' I've known some men who train their animals to rip their enemies limb from limb."

"And I'm sure Mischa has trained you well," she says softly. "But before you rip me apart, you should know one thing."

"What?"

"I'm the only person standing in between him and a bullet aimed for his skull—and not just his. Those sweet little girls of his. The boy? Eli? Would you see them all dead because you were too arrogant to listen to what I have to say?"

I take a step toward the bed. "I suggest you say it now."

She swallows, her eyes darting to my side again. "Alright. Mischa is in danger—"

"And how do you know that?"

I can't tell if the emotion flitting across her gaze is unease or pride. "Because I'm the one who brought the hoard right to his door."

Her words take a second to process. "What are you—"

My phone buzzes in my pocket, an occurrence so abnormal I reach for it automatically.

"Volkov?"

"You should get here," a man warns, his voice vaguely familiar. Usually, he isn't whispering.

"Mario?"

"Just get back to base," he insists. "Now. Mr. Stepanov is not happy."

His stern tone is the only trigger I need to lurch into action, heading for the door.

"Also, while this may not be the best time to mention it," he adds in a rush, "I found something you might be interested in. It's not much, but I think you're smart enough to make use of it. I'll send it all in an email. Keep in mind it won't lead back to me, and if anyone asks, we never had this conversation."

He hangs up before I can even question. For once, Donatello Vanici isn't at the forefront of my mind.

"Leaving so soon?" the woman simpers, crossing her arms as I open the door. "Don't let me stop you. I'm sure anything at all must be more important than—"

Pivoting on my heel, I snatch her arm, yanking her from the bed mid-word. She covers her fear easily, trying to pull her hand back with a smile.

"Let go of me—"

"You wanted your audience with Mischa?" I snarl, satisfied when she falls silent. "Well, you've got it. I'm taking you to him now."

Surprisingly, she doesn't argue as I haul her from the room.

And I can't resist the paranoid suspicion that she was ready for just this very scenario.

Ready for me.

*B*efore I even go through the main gates, it's apparent that security is at an all-time high. The typical detail looks to be at least doubled, with more men than usual milling alongside the road, eyeing me warily as I approach the house.

I drive straight to the front of the manor, sensing the urgency in the air. Mario wasn't exaggerating. Something is wrong.

My body feels electrified by the charged atmosphere as I park just beyond the front steps. For the first time, I have to resist the urge to grab my gun, sporting it out in the open.

"Stay here," I warn the woman huddling in the passenger's seat. "Though hell, you're stupid enough to run, try it—" I nod to the nearest agent standing guard near the entrance. "While I'm inside, I'll give them permission to shoot if you step so much as a hair out of this van. Got it?"

"Of course." She flashes a disarming smile, but I'm not the only one affected by the heightened mood. She seems paler than ever, her eyes glued to the manor house in a way that could be politely deemed as "disgusted."

"In the meantime, I'll run over my heartfelt entreat to the man who killed my brother and destroyed my family," she adds absently.

Real hate tinges her voice, and for the first time, I mull over the sheer stupidity of bringing her here. I didn't even think to blindfold her—a breach of protocol too glaring to interpret as of yet.

Instead, I leave the van and instantly feel all eyes fixate in my direction, but not in the typical greeting. They're on edge, eyeing me warily as I start inside.

"What's going on?" I ask one of the two men posted by the main entrance.

He shrugs, avoiding eye contact. "Mr. Stepanov is in his study—"

"Something happened at the hospital," another man interjects. "You weren't there."

Alarm runs down my spine, and I'm already lunging forward. "Mrs. Stepanova? Is everything alright?"

Rather than answer, both men push open the door, ushering me inside.

The trip to the study feels longer than ever, populated nearly every step of the way by a guard standing at attention. Either they're readying for something or...

They've just returned.

The answer is made clear the second I near the door to the study where Mischa stands, shrugging off his jacket.

"Where the hell were you?" His voice is chilling, bellowing throughout the room. I've never heard this tone directed my way before—a guttural baritone previously reserved only for Donatello Vanici.

"Sir. I had to step out. I informed the other men on duty..." One look at his face, and I sense the need to drop all protocol. If there were ever a time for honesty between us, this is it. "What happened?"

"Donatello Vanici strolled into the hospital where my wife is. Where my children are. *That* is what happened." He slams a fist against his desk with a sound like a gunshot. "Do you have any idea the danger they were in? Do you?"

But more than that is angering him, evident in his tense posture, crackling with barely concealed aggression. I only know of one topic capable of stirring this kind of reaction. "Willow," I say thickly. "She was there?"

"Yes." Mischa cocks his head, his expression suddenly ice. That look alone tells me that this reunion with his daughter wasn't a particularly happy one. "Do you want to know what that bastard claimed? Do you?" He hisses a chilling imitation of a laugh. "That he was going to marry her."

"What?" I feel my brows shoot up. "That's—"

"Sick," Mischa says with a grudging nod. "That's exactly why he thought of it."

"But Willow…" I bite my tongue, trying to choose my words carefully. If Mischa is this angry, but Vanici isn't dead, there can be only one explanation as to why.

"Did he threaten her?"

Mischa looks away, glaring through the window, and I have my answer.

"She stayed with him." It feels strange to say out loud, but in my gut, I suspect it's the truth even before I see Mischa's jaw tighten in acknowledgment. He whirls back to face me, and I'm struck by just how angry he truly is.

Not all of it might be directed at Vanici, I suspect.

"She didn't have a fucking choice, did she?" he counters. "Vanici threatened her. The bastard probably got a kick out of it."

"Did she look injured?" I press, trying to wrap my brain around how such a meeting went down. I can't imagine Mischa standing aside while Vanici pranced off with his daughter—and he wouldn't. Unless something convinced him to, and I doubt Donatello Vanici would have that sway. Only one person could make Mischa show that kind of restraint. Willow. Which means...

"She...wanted to stay?"

"I know her," Mischa insists. "She wouldn't submit to that motherfucker without a reason. That son of a bitch!" He slams a fist against his desk, and the conviction in his voice would be enough to convince anyone else. But I remember the way they interacted in that recording, how Vanici seemed to worm his way inside her head. It was obvious from day one—the bastard has a hold over her.

"I should have been there," I admit.

"Damn right you should have," Mischa growls, turning the full brunt of his gaze to me. "I hope your diversion was worth it."

A part of me reacts to that word choice. Diversion? Did he have me followed? Know where I'd been all along?

Or is his caginess feeding my own budding paranoia? Even so, one fact remains clearer than ever.

"I would have been there if I were on your detail," I point out. "Like I should have been. In fact, if you told me the connection between Willow and Vanici from the start, we might not be having this conversation."

"You don't know Vanici," Mischa warns, his eyes slits. "And I suggest you drop this topic. It's done. I've already sent Mario to replace your post at the hospital—"

"So you continue to shove me aside," I say, alarmed by just how much that angers me. Rage coils through my bloodstream, red hot and searing. "Vanici? Maybe I don't know *you*. I thought Willow was your focus. Not some childish feud." The words are out of my mouth, and it's too late to take them back.

"What did you say?" Mischa steps from around the desk, his head cocked in a warning.

Any other day I'd adhere to my creed. Bite my tongue.

Today? I'm too damn tired.

"I said you brought this on yourself," I say, holding my ground. "All because you were too damn stubborn to listen —" Within the space of a second, he's within striking distance, and I don't even see the punch coming.

My vision goes black as pain shoots through my jaw. Groaning, I blink to bring the room back into focus. Mischa's back is to me as he paces, anger radiating from him like heat.

"Get out," he growls. "You're done."

"So you won't even talk to me about this? What is really going on between Willow and Vanici? They knew each other, didn't they?" I taste blood. A lot of it. I have to spit at my feet just to keep speaking. "Mischa—"

"Don't make me rethink my leniency, Evgeni," he warns.

"I'm not doing anything but trying to reason with you." I spit again, fighting to ignore the fire lancing through my jaw. "Just hear me out. I'm sorry I left, but I think I learned another lead—"

"Get the fuck out." He isn't even looking at me anymore, marching toward the desk. "Now. Before I change my mind on letting you leave peacefully."

"Peacefully?" I scoff at the word, holding my ground even as he whirls around, ready to strike again. Anger simmers just beneath the limits of my control. I cling to every ounce of restraint I have, but when my lips part, I can't contain the words that spill out. "You call what you've done 'peace'? Vanici is no Saint, but if you would have listened to me from the outset—"

"You'd have me roll over like a fucking whipped dog," Mischa counters coldly. "Because that's what you are, isn't it? I knew you were gun-shy when I hired you, but there comes a point when 'peace' can't be fucking *wished* for. I won't sit by and let my daughter be taken from me."

"Because that's what I did? Sat by?" I don't even recognize the sound of my voice. I hear it as if I'm miles away, and for a second, I don't even see Mischa. I see blood. Lifeless faces staring up at me. I see death…

"Don't judge me," Mischa cautions in a voice so harsh it snaps me back. I blink and see him clearly again, his eyes like coals. "Don't you fucking dare. I'm no 'saint' either, but I never massacred women and children under the guise of following orders. These should be simple for you—get the hell out."

I say nothing, eyeing the man I've followed faithfully for over six years.

He's barely recognizable, but deep down, a part of me acknowledges the subtle changes. His coldness. The vicious tension lacing his posture. His rage.

Fear will do that to a man. Consume him until it's all he can see. I know that firsthand. It's why I've come to trust my simple creed before the Stepanovs, and it's the only thing I have left to rely on now.

Loyalty first. Survival second. Never get too close.

Still stroking my jaw, I head for the door, passing the man standing guard. My surroundings blur as I navigate the house, exiting what feels like an eternity later. Out front, my van still waits untouched.

"Don't tell me he's not home," Briar snipes as I open the door, climbing into the driver's seat. Her sly smile is comically easy to see through now. Fake. A thin veneer against her fear.

She's terrified. Hell, she reeks of it.

But I don't feel a damn thing. Just a persistent, pulsating sensation near my hip. Without thinking, I swipe my hand there, striking something hard. My phone?

"Evgeni?" Briar prods, her voice trembling slightly. "What are you doing?"

Her eyes are on the hand I slip into my pocket, but I don't answer, withdrawing my cell phone. I narrow my eyes at the notification flashing on the home screen—an email from an unfamiliar address. Belatedly, I remember Mario's parting words. He found something.

In the end, it isn't much—a single name that nonetheless triggers a wave of haunting recognition.

Safiya Mangenello.

I heard it before... When? I wrack my brain until the answer hits me—straight from Donatello Vanici's mouth. The name he called Willow.

"Where are you going?" Briar demands, her fear even more apparent. Her eyes are saucers, her lips pursed, her hand reaching for the door on her end.

Stowing the phone, I put the car into drive before she can get it open, slamming on the gas. As I peel down the driveway, I don't look back at the manor once.

Mario was right. Even a name is enough to set me on the right path. If Mischa won't listen to reason, then I'll follow another avenue if I have to. Anything to protect Willow.

At least I have two potential veins of information to tap—Briar Winthorp and Safiya Mangenello.

One of them holds the answers. Only this time?

I refuse to be restrained by any sort of creed.

21

WILLOW

*R*eturning to Havienna feels like leaving the real world for a shadow realm. One in which up is down and down is…

Pain.

As the sun makes one final stand against the evening cloud cover, the sunlight bathes the walls of the old house like firelight, and apprehension rips through my body, dissolving every ounce of resolve. I was wrong. Shadow realm might have been too kind a term—it's hell, a reality made perfectly clear the closer we come to it.

The devil himself sits beside me, itching to reclaim his domain.

He doesn't speak as he parks in the driveway, flanked by two vans. Without so much as a word to me, he exits the car, leaving me to follow as the men we went with fall into step behind us.

Inside the house, I shiver, hating the painfully familiar feeling that shoots through me as I cross the foyer. The past battles with the present, and I'm nearly overwhelmed by the conflicting emotions. All I can do is grit my teeth and dart my gaze without settling over anything for long.

I still notice when Donatello barrels past the stairs, heading in the direction of his study. Preferring to extend the distance between us, I scramble up the stairs, aimlessly wandering the hall, unwilling to enter that pink room just yet.

I stop short just beyond it, startled to find someone watching me from the doorway to Vin's old room. Not a ghost, though she's pale enough. My heart breaks at the sight of those wide eyes staring blankly. Someone found clothes for her at least, but I recognize them with a chilling jolt of *déjà vu*.

They were mine. Hers. Safiya's.

The little pink shirt has faded slightly with time, but it and a pair of jeans fit the girl perfectly.

I approach her slowly, all thoughts of Donatello forgotten. The same person who procured the clothing is presumably responsible for arranging the room as comfortable as possible given the circumstances. They made up Vin's old bed, and the small collection of toys scattered around also seem familiar.

The girl watches me warily, her thin arms crossed over her chest. Raising a dark eyebrow, she inclines her head. "I want to go home."

The pleading note in her voice breaks me. I wind up staggering toward the bed, sitting on the end of it, feeling more helpless than I did even before Mischa. It's not her fear that rips through me like a lance. It's her hope. Like I might help her achieve her only goal. To go home.

When in reality? I'm no better than the madman holding her captive. Unlike her, I always had a choice whether or not to be here.

I don't know what it is about my posture that draws her closer. Silently, she sits on the floor nearby and picks up a ratty doll with a sigh. "Luca said you can't talk," she says in a near whisper.

Luca? I picture the man always near Donatello with the watchful gray eyes. Luciano. Has he been taking care of her?

She doesn't say. When I nod to confirm her insinuation, she returns to her doll, absently twisting its stringy hair around her finger. Something in her dejected expression chills me to the bone. There's a familiarity in her posture. Like this isn't the first time she's had to submit to a horrific situation and distract herself with play.

I think of my sisters, Marnie and Aljona, even little Ivan. They wouldn't be half as calm as she is. Where did Donatello find her? I wrack my brain and recall a name he's said before. Antonio. Antonio Salvatore.

Was he a different monster than Donatello? I can't ask her. But as I watch her fiddle with the doll, I recall another memory—this time not one of Safiya's.

I had already shed that identity by the time I came under the care of someone other than Donatello Vanici. A gruff man with long, wild blond hair and flashing dark eyes. Early on, he proved himself different from the man I'd been sold to. He gruffly procured clothing for me and taught me how to braid my hair. He teased me with his rare smile and snuck me sweets.

In that short amount of time, he set himself apart from any other father I knew.

Without thinking, I reach for the girl, tentatively stroking one of her black curls. It's soft, the color a beautiful raven hue. She stiffens, her eyes cutting cautiously to mine. When I run my fingers through her hair, she doesn't withdraw.

So I stroke until she lets me inch nearer. Then, once I gauge that she won't withdraw, I braid her curls as slowly and methodically as Mischa once did for me.

*t's pitch dark when I startle awake, sensing a smaller body curled alongside mine. It takes me a second to realize where I am—still in Vin's old room. A sliver of moonlight drifting through the window illuminates the little girl, asleep near the head of the bed, her hair in a neat braid.

Whatever woke me hasn't disturbed her, at least. She lies still, her chest rising easily.

I can't say the same. My heart stutters, my breathing heavy. Anxiety eats at my fraying nerves, but I don't know why. Then I hear it—a faint noise resonating through the walls in addition to the typical creaking of the house. It's deeper, unsettling in pitch. Guttural. Howling.

An animal?

Cautiously, I rise to my feet, feeling my way to the door. When I open it, the hall is deserted but silent. I wait, straining my ears. Could the noise have been a trick of the wind? Just as I start to retreat into the room again, I hear it. Definitely a low cry, coming from the end of the hall.

Curiosity drives me forward. Or recognition…

The closer I come, the less that sound resembles random noise until I can clearly identify it. Human. A man. One crying out in utter agony.

Before I know it, I'm standing near a partially closed door, sensing the hair on the back of my neck stand on end. Every cell in my body throbs, warning me to back away. Better yet, take the girl and run for good.

I push on the doorknob instead, peering into a room I vaguely remember from another life. I rarely came in here, even back then. It was a mysterious realm where adults retreated at night and children were banished from.

It smells like him. Like pain and sweat, and other intangible scents collectively deemed *masculine*. Loud, his breaths rasp on the air, unsteady and disjointed, undercut by the creak of the mattress. He's moving, but I doubt he's awake, merely tossing and turning. Writhing.

"God," he rasps, shocking me into stopping cold. A frantic heartbeat later, I realize he's still asleep, shouting only at nothing. Just phantoms. "Fuck... No. No!"

I freeze, paralyzed by the same feeling I felt in the hospital. Helplessness, like a bystander forced to watch a tragedy unfold, unable to do a damn thing to help.

If I heard him, I'm sure the others in this house have as well. Preserving his modesty could explain whatever impulse drives me to close the door without leaving.

Or cruel voyeurism. For once, I get to see him tormented, but the sensation constricting my heart isn't anything close to pleasure. I'm not happy as he cries out wordlessly to no one. I'm numb.

He excels so well at turning his pain into rage that it's easy to forget what it stems from. *Pain.* An agony few can fathom. It marks those who suffer from it like scars.

My feet inch closer to that bed of their own accord, while my heart beats frantically as if protesting every step of the way.

Go back.

Go back!

Too late. I'm near enough to see the sweat glistening on his forehead and the sheets tangled around his frame. My bare foot strikes something soft, and I look down, making out the vague outlines of clothing. His suit jacket, shirt, and finally his pants. As my gaze flits back to the bed, my cheeks flame as I register the bold outline of his body.

He's naked except for a pair of boxers. His bare chest heaves as he claws at the sheets tangled around him, and I have my clearest view ever of the tattoo.

The name blazes as if on fire, the letters bold enough to make out in the dark. I don't know what possesses me to reach out, brushing the end of the final A.

He groans, his eyelids fluttering, lips moving wordlessly. A silly thought strikes me—braiding his hair won't soothe him.

But I don't know any other methods.

I should leave. Avoid him. Run. The same way I should have stayed in Stepanov manor the night I heard about Vin. The same way I should have avoided him at all costs from day one.

Where this man is concerned, I do nothing at all that I *should.*

So, instead, I sit on the end of the mattress with my back to him. Before long, my fingers shoot out as if of their own accord, landing over that telltale jagged strip of flesh so different from the rest of him. It's like I've already mapped it inside my head without meaning to, able to navigate every ridge and curve without having to see what the shapes form.

Her name.

Absently, I trace the letters over and over the way I would the notes printed on a sheet of music. And as if his body is my instrument, it plays along. His groans lessen while his heavy breaths paint the air in a twisted, unstable melody…

One so beautiful and so haunting it deafens me to everything else.

Even the part of my soul warning me to run.

22

DON

This fucking house is a prison—both hers and mine. The calculus of bringing her here was that the environment would give me the edge, but now?

I couldn't give a damn about exerting my influence over the little Stepanova. I'm too tired. The kind of bone-melting exhaustion sleep can't fix. I've forgotten what it feels like to experience it. Or to dream, for that matter. Whenever I close my eyes, I do neither.

Instead, I get a taste of what true hell is. Emptiness. Loneliness. Nothing. A darkness where the loss of everything and everyone ever stolen from me looms, and I'm powerless to run from it anymore.

Who needs hellfire? Guilt is searing enough, blazing through my chest, impossible to douse.

For Vin. Olivia. Safiya…

I still see them, lurking just beyond reach. I can hear them calling for me. Condemning me. Dooming me. Their cries tease me on the edge of consciousness, impossible to escape.

Screw Fabio's praise of sobriety; I'd kill for a bottle. Booze would be enough to dull the clamor and let me sink into oblivion. It's gotten me through the past seven years, after all.

Damn, it's been so long since I've laid in this room. Fuck, this might even be the same bed I shared with Olivia, feeling her soft, warm body against mine, her voice in my ear. The memory feels more real than ever. I can hear her, *"Wake up, baby. It's late. I told you that another round would exhaust you, old man…"*

Her warmth breaches time and space, heating my skin. I swear I feel her hand on my shoulder…

But it's not.

I jolt awake, fully aware that the warm fingers grazing my chest are too small. Too textured. Olivia kept her hands manicured, but these…

They've been used. Worked, but in a delicate manner different from the callouses that harden mine. *Music,* a part of me suspects, even before I open my eyes.

Pale moonlight drifts through the singular window, adding vague definition to the master bedroom, though now emptied of everything but the bed. Bathed in the glow is a lone figure perched on the end of the mattress, her back to me even as her fingers trace the expanse of my bare chest. She could be a twisted figment of my imagination if it weren't for her smell.

Roses.

I sigh, eyeing the ceiling, too tired to mull over her motives this time. She could be a masochist, driven to find me always at my fucking lowest. Her mind is a landmine I'd rather not maneuver. Instead, I remember…

How it felt to have a body next to mine. A feminine scent flooding my nose. With Liv, I only felt a constant current of love. Trust. Obedience.

With her?

There is no warmth, just a cruel need to test her presence. Exploit it. In the absence of liquor, she's all I have—so I take it. She doesn't expect the second I snatch her hand, lifting it for inspection. There's always the possibility that she's not here. Experimentally, I flick my thumb across her palm, sensing the shudder that runs through her. She's real, all right. To her credit, she doesn't pull away.

Or to her detriment.

I've changed my mind. Fuck sobriety. Her fear is a fitting substitute for liquor, and I'm too weak to resist.

So, I tug, dragging her closer until she's almost lying on her side. Those eyes flit up to mine, but if I expect to find a motive in them, she denies me that much.

Her gaze is unreadable.

But I've already learned how to make her react. With a shift of my weight, she's beneath me, and I get my wish—her slender throat jerks around a hard swallow. Inhaling, I savor the slight tinge to her scent. How those eyes widen and her teeth seize her lower lip in alarm.

Finally, she gives me something to interpret—fear. I crave the shiver that wracks her spine as I deliberately run my finger across her chest, copying the same path she traced over mine. Her heat distracts me from everything. So warm.

But her scent is a gut-punch, so sharp I find myself leaning down, inhaling as much as I can. It's the wrong move. Intoxicated, I close my eyes, extending this dangerous position a second longer. Another.

Nothing compares to feeling her body against mine. For a moment, I can pretend I'm back there, with the weight of the world on my shoulders but a loving woman in my bed.

It's funny how that intangible concept can change every fucking thing. *Love.* One kiss can soothe the blood-soaked memories. The act of it can even make a new life.

And one fucking second can rip it all away.

When I open my eyes, the figure staring up at me isn't my sweet Liv. She's a different creature entirely, with dark eyes so huge they swallow me whole. Pink curved lips. A gaze that doesn't flinch.

Not from me, or the open hostility I don't bother to hide. She takes me in as though it's all entertainment just for her. She won't admit it out loud, but this is why she's here. Why she's *always* been here.

My descent into madness amuses her. Why wouldn't it? It's guaranteed vengeance, and she doesn't even have to wield a blade or pull the trigger to carry it out.

My own brain will destroy me in the end, and her presence is the catalyst.

I choke out a laugh, eyeing that pretty mouth. The least I can do is give her a good show.

"Do you enjoy your taste of power, little wife?" I'm surprised by how calm I sound. Inside? My heart is ramming against my ribcage, my breathing heavy.

Oh yes, she's enjoying this.

Instead of a verbal answer, she inclines her head, sending that hair fanning out around her. Her eyes flicker, processing the question, but she's unsure. Unprepared. Damn, there's something irresistible about catching her off guard. Making her squirm.

"You like to exert control over me?" I ask her, letting my gaze travel down her face and lower, glimpsing the flesh bared below the neckline of her dress. It's wrong. But what the fuck do I care?

This moment is a thin, fragile barrier keeping the past at bay. I'll deal with the consequences later...

When her breasts aren't separated from me by a thin layer of fabric. When I can't feel her heartbeat hammering away. Or every twitch and jolt of her muscles as she fights her body's own instincts to lie still.

My brain does what it does best and conjures up dangerous images—like of her splayed in her bed back in that perfect Stepanov manor, naked and alone. It brings up a very good question…

"Have you ever touched yourself, hellcat?"

That lone question has the same effect as gasoline dangled over an open flame.

Her skin ignites, flushing red in the silvery lighting, her lips twitching as she swallows again. Her fear is one thing, but this is the real addicting aspect of her—this supposed innocence. A girl who grew up in the heart of the *mafiya* but never saw a man's dick in person. Yet, she dangles her sexuality when it suits her.

Which brings up an irritating point—it suits her. Stripping naked when it gives her an advantage. Playing coy when it doesn't. Insisting on her own stipulations and most egregious of all…

Seeming offended by my insistence on one point—I don't want her.

Not this body. Not those eyes watching me grip her wrist, pressing the slender limb against the sheets. She stiffens, her breaths coming faster. *Good.* I should only want to push her this far.

Nothing more.

Until I do. It's like another part of me takes over, bypassing all logic, driven only by curiosity. How far can I make her go?

Her eyes track every movement of my head as I bring it near hers. Letting my lips brush her earlobe, I test that theory with a simple statement. "You don't know the first damn thing about what really happens between a man and a woman. You've never fucked…and I'm assuming the answer to my question is no. You've never touched yourself, either."

Her body always betrays her. That slender throat quivers as her heart beats so rapidly I can hear it. I could dance to the melody if I wanted—fitting given her music background. She may be silent, but terror makes her sing. A symphony of physical tells, too beautiful to resist.

I feel my grip on her arm tighten. Before I know it, I'm dragging that hand across the sheets, down to her waist. Then lower.

Sensing my intention, she starts to struggle, kicking with her legs. The pressure of one knee is enough to pin her down. She tries clawing at me with those hellcat nails, but if she pierces the skin, I don't feel it. I don't feel a damn thing. My entire focus centers on the thin wrist in my grasp, manipulating it against her will until her fingers brush her hip.

She goes still, her lip between her teeth, her cheeks flushing a deeper scarlet even in the dark. Beautiful. And dangerous.

I'm fully aware of the line I'm toeing. The risk I'm taking by playing this game. In another time, and another place, I'd heed the warnings blaring through my veins.

But I'm already addicted to this…

Her defiance. Even now, she doesn't shy from my gaze. She holds it, daring me to push her harder. Test her. Break her.

So I blurt the first thing that comes to mind, damn the risk. "Do you want me to teach you?"

Bingo. She sucks in a breath, though I realize I've done the same. Her fingers twitch, inching between us as I goad her on. My cock twitches, but I drag her hand right past it, urging her lower.

Lower.

Her eyes stare resolutely past me, up at the ceiling—but her body is an inferno. A rigid mass of twitching muscle. I close my eyes again, breathing her in. Her legs twitch, fighting to resist the pressure of her own hand inching between them. The air wheezes from her lungs, her pulse a fucking symphony.

My thoughts flash back to how she reacted as we stood before the Saleris. How she looked at me then. It wasn't her audacity to kiss me that irritated me. Still does… It was the way she did it. Her expression, so quick I doubt she was even aware of it.

The same brief glimpse of terror I saw in the study when I tried to strike a match, and again in the hospital with

Mischa. I don't care that she's the catalyst for my impending war with the *mafiya*—that's not what condemns her.

This one look has always been her original sin.

Concern for me.

"You still care about me, hellcat?" I croak, hating the raw pain in my voice. Because it's a lie. It has to be... But like any addict, I chase the illusion.

Even when it stings.

"Then show me what I'm missing," I rasp. "This is how you can hurt me. Show me what I'll never have."

I open my eyes just in time to see her eyelids lower as she registers that statement. Does it empower her? *No,* I decide. It annoys her. I'm giving her permission to torture me.

She hates being controlled, so fucking stubborn she'll do anything to defy any attempt to. Like stop fighting me, letting her hand settle exactly where I aim it.

Fire washes through my abdomen, heralding a volatile reaction. Fabio's warning echoes faintly through my skull, but I'm inclined to ignore him. If I pretend this is a dream, nothing that happens fucking matters. There are no consequences if I'm imagining all of this.

And I have to be.

Because otherwise, the little hellcat wouldn't look so... eager? Her nostrils flare, her eyes darting back up to mine.

I slide my fingers over hers, painfully aware of the searing heat building between us. Sweat slicks her soft skin, enhancing every little tremor to shoot through the tender muscles and fragile bones. If I weren't sure before, I am now —she's never done this.

So I bear down harder.

At the same time, our gazes meet again, but it's different. I'm inside her head, clearly seeing every thought to cross her mind. Confusion. Sweet, fucking *confusion*.

How could something so debasing feel so fucking good? It's a question I'm wrestling with myself. Finally, she takes over, resisting my grip.

"Do it."

Her eyes blaze, accepting the challenge.

And she does. Her lips flutter, pursed over gritting teeth, and it's all the proof I need. Damn. I'd kill to see her fingers make contact for the first time—but nothing comes close to watching the realization spark within her. The pleasure that can come from a simple touch. A sensation sharp enough to blind her to everything else. The world. Shame. Me…

"Look at me," I goad before she completely goes vacant. I'm here with her.

And, fuck, it's hell. It's heaven.

"Keep going," I grate through clenched teeth.

Her eyes narrow, but I sense her hips arch. Buck.

"More."

Her eyelids flutter as her head rears back against the pillow. Her teeth seize her lower lip, her breaths feathering.

I rock against her, torturing myself with the feel of her moving hand and twitching limbs.

I make the mistake of watching her again as those eyes go to my chest. Her throat jerks around a swallow, her hand moving faster as she traces the letters tattooed there.

I know the second she comes. She can't disguise it.

Her entire body radiates pleasure, her lips parting, body glistening with sweat.

It's incredible.

Terrifying. I'm struck through, mortally wounded the second she goes limp. Her scent teases the air, sharp with pleasure, and I'm dying a slow, vengeful death.

The little witch has won another round.

And she found a weapon better than a knife.

"*W*ake up!"

I startle to awareness, groaning as my head pounds. A cool, wet sensation hits me full in the face, snapping me awake. Water? I sputter, wrenching my eyes open to find Fabio standing over me, an empty glass in hand.

"What the fuck?" I croak, spotting the dampness coloring the sheets around me. He spilled something on me, alright.

"Considering the fact that your entire fucking life depends on you making this meeting with Mischa, I assume you don't want to be late. You wouldn't wake up." He leans over me and sniffs. "What? Did you drink an entire fucking bottle?"

"You're cursing," I point out—a rarer occurrence than even his smoking.

"Fuck you," he bites back.

"Fuck me," I rasp. My head pounds violently enough to be explained by a hangover—but even that can't explain the erection threatening to rip through the front of my goddamn boxers. It's an almost painful state of lust. Beyond blue balls.

I grapple for a handful of sheets to haul myself upright, and I remember the source of the discomfort…

Fuck, the sheets are still warm. Like she slept here afterward —my innocent little fiancée who fingered herself beneath me for the first time. Climaxed, her dark eyes so wide with the newfound sensation it's like taking an entire cask of whiskey straight into the vein.

"Jesus, Don!" Fabio's tone drips with disapproval, and he crosses to the window. With his gaze on the view, he fishes a cigarette from his pocket and lights it up in the same breath. "Just tell me—how drunk are you?"

"Not drunk," I admit, hauling myself into a sitting position.

"You sound like it," Fabio snipes. "You sound like hell."

"What time is it? How is Vin?"

"Vin is fine," he says, his tone softer. "He's recovering well. No complications. You can see him later. Now, I need you dressed, along with your pretty fiancée, and across town within the hour to meet Mischa on time."

"Fuck." I swipe my hand across my bare chest. The skin there burns as if ignited—all because a little minx wanted to see my scars as she came.

I groan, swiping my hand along my face as if I can physically wipe the memories away.

"Are you sick?" Fabio asks, a hint of sympathy leeching into his tone.

"No." But I am.

Sick enough to toy with fire and enjoy the searing burn. God, I can still smell her. Feel her.

"Well, if you aren't sick, we need to move. Here—" he throws a handful of fabric at me, dry at least. "Get dressed. I have a car waiting. You have five minutes. I assume your

lovely fiancée is somewhere safe and sound in this house..."
He trails off, his expression shifting from anxious to
horrified. With a forced cough, he heads for the door. "I'll
find her."

I wonder if he will, "safe and sound" in that pink fucking
room.

I can't seem to move, eyeing the black suit Fab left as
though dressing is a foreign concept.

My innocent little fiancée...

Even if I wanted to fuck her—hell. My cock throbs, and I
drop the pretense, at least in my skull. I do. I crave her if
only to get her out of my system for good.

But I can't touch her.

"Don? Change of plans." Fabio storms into the room,
scoffing when he sees I'm still not dressed. Rolling his eyes,
he inhales on his cigarette. "Mischa's called off the
meeting—"

"Son of a bitch!" I lurch to my feet, already spinning toward
the window. I expect to see a hoard of *mafiya* vehicles
peeling down the driveway. If not now, then soon. "I should
have known this fucking plan wouldn't—"

"Oh, the plan is still on," Fabio insists in that superior tone
he rarely uses. The one that signifies when he's fully in
"accountant" mode and the world around him becomes
reduced to numbers and profit. "The arrangements are

already being put into place as we speak. Your wedding, by the way, will be within a week."

My head spins, and I wish I truly were hungover. I'd be too numb to fully feel the consequences of those words and what they represent.

My wedding, to a woman I can't ever fully claim.

I grit my teeth so hard my jaw cracks, snapping me back to the present reality. "So why did Mischa call off the meeting?"

Fabio huffs on his cigarette and then sighs. "His wife is awake. I thought it prudent to allow him some time to help her…adjust."

Namely to the reality that her daughter is being married off and an attempt had been made on her life.

"So what now?"

"You still get dressed. I've been pulling some strings to help you get the *famiglia* back underway—"

"Thank you."

"Don't," he says. "If you do anything illegal, I don't want to know. But I figure keeping you busy minimizes the risk of you going on another killing spree."

"There's another thing," I say. "Antonio was set up by someone else. I need to find out who."

"That could be a nice way to segue your relationship with Mischa away from murder."

"It could," I admit.

A happy family on a mission of revenge.

It's the shit warm, fuzzy fairy tales are made of.

~ The story continues in Shattered Throne, Book three in the Mice and Men Series ~

AFTERWORD

You have finished book two of Donatello and Willow's story. Do you want to see where it all began? Check out the War of Roses Trilogy!

XV: Fifteen: War of Roses Trilogy Book One

Kidnapped, Ellen must do whatever it takes to survive her cruel mafia captor, Mischa. Will he break her— or will she outsmart him?

WHEN HATE BECOMES OBSESSION…
Mistaken for her beautiful half-sister, Ellen Winthorp is taken captive by a madman who declares that she will be his "fifteen": the fifteenth victim of a vicious mafia blood feud. Armed with only her instincts, Ellen must resist her captor for as long as she can—which is easier said than done the more she's exposed to the complex man beneath the beast.

Because Mischa Stepanov isn't a mindless monster—he's a wolf, and she's the unwitting doe caught in his midst.

Unraveling the torment of his past may be her only hope of salvation...

Or the secrets uncovered may destroy them both.

CHAPTER 1 OF XV: WAR OF ROSES TRILOGY BOOK 1

Noise...
Chaos...
Briar...

The first thing I'm aware of is that I'm blindfolded—a fact that could be a blessing in disguise as my thoughts blur and jumble together. Only one coherent question escapes the fray: *Where am I?*

No answer comes to me immediately. My straining ears can make out only a few words muttered nearby in unfamiliar voices. Deep, *masculine* voices.

Various smells irritate my nostrils as well: sweat, body odor, male. *All* male. God, *where am I?*

I try flexing my shoulders only to wince. My hands are impossible to move, tied behind my back with something rough. Rope?

Oh, God.

Familiar terror gnaws at my belly as moisture gathers in my armpits and sweeps across my palms. At least, now, I have an inkling of my fate. I'm trapped in another one of his games. My nostrils flare with renewed purpose: seeking out *his* scent.

He must have hired lackeys this time; foreign body odor drowns out the stench of his cologne. I can't smell him.

But you can survive this. I fall back on the mantra that has gotten me through every day for sixteen years. *You can survive, Ellen. Focus, Ellen. Breathe, Ellen.*

Ten hours—that's how long I endured last time. My resolve had nearly splintered by the end. I'd almost given in. Almost.

But even psychological wounds eventually heal and leave tougher scar tissue behind. I can last another ten hours with Robert. My brain makes that distinction as the barrage of scents dissipates, revealing one that overpowers the rest: a man's. I taste the nuances in his stench rather than smell them—he's *that* potent, composed of a multitude of different things.

Cigar smoke.

Vodka.

One scent in particular makes my heart stop. Salty and sweet, it's almost as familiar as the flowery perfume wafting from my skin now. *Blood?*

Robert never smokes. He doesn't drink. Whenever he hurts me, he always washes his hands before and after. It is our routine, and he is nothing if not predictable.

No. This is someone new. Someone taller, whose shadow completely blots out what little detail plays across my blindfold. His footsteps are steady. Heavy.

"This her?"

I sense the outline of his fingers before the callused edge of one grazes my forehead.

"You made sure?"

His voice is deep. Almost *too* deep to be intelligible: a series of grated, rumbling notes. There's an accent tucked among them—something thick. Eastern European? Briar had a maid from there once. Sonja.

Sonja liked to read Jane Eyre. She liked scribbling love notes to Robert Sr.'s men before fucking them in the broom closet late at night when she thought no one was looking. Sonja liked a lot of things before Robert took a liking to her.

But another figure from my memory possessed this accent as well. Even though his words were hissed in a whisper, I still remember. *Breathe!*

"Bring her."

Those two words snap me back to the present. Unfamiliar hands grab my shoulders, cinching the soft silk of my blouse. *Briar's* blouse. She dressed me in it lovingly, remarking on how the color complemented my eyes. Our eyes, the same shade of light blue.

"Move!"

A tug on my shoulders hauls me upright and unseen hands shove me forward. Every sound echoes. Four footsteps, including mine. The biggest man takes the lead, I suspect, his gait rhythmic against creaking floorboards.

In contrast, the men holding me dig their nails into my skin and scurry toward an unknown destination. A rusty squeal seconds later conjures the image of an old door opening, and the footsteps trail off.

"Move!"

Something rams into my side and I stagger for balance until my cheek strikes a hard surface. It's warm. *Human.*

"Get her on the bed."

Those harsh hands return to my shoulders to fulfill the command.

"Sit her on the edge...like that. Cut her hands free."

A metallic hiss sends a shiver down my spine—then *pain!* Fire courses through my fingertips as circulation returns to them. I long to flex each one, but I know better. Instead, I keep them close, settling them onto my lap.

These men kept my skirt on, at least. Her skirt. The hem comes down past my knees, and I've never been so grateful for four inches of satin. It will buy me more time.

Ten hours. I've already lasted ten minutes. *You can do this,* the courageous part of my soul whispers. But then that voice dies in the wake of two more words uttered in that guttural cadence.

"Leave us."

The two smaller men scatter in the direction we entered—but it's all wrong. No. No. I don't smell Robert, and he'd never leave me alone with another man. Not his lackey. Not even his own father.

Most alarming of all, this man certainly is no Winthorp. His voice isn't familiar and this house doesn't smell like any property on the familial grounds.

They took me from the motorcade...

Fire sears through my skull as memories return in snatches. The clearest one is of her face. *Briar.* So beautiful, dominated by that pure, sweet smile. "I want you there," she insisted. "We're sisters, after all."

Sisters. I cherished how that word sounded in her soft cadence, tucking that moment inside myself like one of the trinkets hidden in my secret cache. Love was more precious than a button or rock I'd stolen away. Those four words meant everything. *I want you there.*

But the memory of that moment serves as a weak antidote to the terror paralyzing me now. More bits and pieces come back.

I was in the car—the beautiful limousine for once, instead of one of the servant vans that took up the rear. For part of the way, I was even sitting beside her while she braided my hair. "We look alike now," she wistfully remarked, beaming at our reflections in the polished windows.

We look alike. The phrase haunts me. As if I could ever look like Briar, with her lighter ringlets and her creamy skin. The only feature we truly share is our eyes. Our mother's eyes. Large, round, and blue. In every other respect, she takes after her father, with a beautiful aristocratic nose and a graceful neck. Every Winthorp possesses the same subtle characteristics—markings of the blood, they like to claim. Good blood. Blue blood.

I take after my father, whoever he is.

Briar loves to tout our tentative resemblance anyway—especially to her benefit. *I* am the one the maid saw sneaking out back two summers ago. *I* am the one who scurried out of the room of that visiting businessman one winter.

And now...

We look alike.

"Take off the blindfold." That voice...

I swallow hard, uneasy. Robert has found a new monster to play with. Someone who shares his flair for the dramatic. *But where is he?* My tormentor always relishes this part of the game. How he enjoys savoring my fear as I try to piece together where I am. Admittedly, it wasn't this hard before; he never strays too far from the property.

His favorite lairs are the boathouse, or the deserted crypt, or the east wing. I could always hear the bluebirds chirping throughout the grounds, no matter which corner of the estate he deemed my chosen cell.

My ears strain, searching for that faint, familiar song. This time of year, they're nearly deafening, able to be heard in even the farthest reaches of Winthorp Manor.

Two seconds. Three.

I hear nothing.

"Take off the blindfold."

The harsh rasp of syllables steals my breath away. I know anger on Robert. On Robert Sr. Even on Briar. They stutter. They shout. They scream.

None of them ever exude their impatience to the point where I can sense it in the air. Or taste it: copper on my tongue. This man isn't a Winthorp.

The realization coaxes my body into action. My sore fingers finally contort, trembling after what must have been hours of captivity. Whoever tied my blindfold snagged bits of my hair in the process and every tug on the knot at the base of my neck rips tiny strands loose from my scalp—comparable to my pathetic hopes being ripped from underneath me one by one.

I don't hear the bluebirds.

I can't smell Robert's favorite cologne.

When I finally get the knot loosened enough to uncover my eyes…

I see hell.

Mother used to say it was beautiful, forsaking the teachings of the local priest. "Hell is a rose," she used to murmur, her gaze turned inward, wistful and distant. "A flawless one, with all the life sucked out of it. The thorns have become knives. Its leaves have swallowed up the stalk. It's grotesque. It's deadly. But never forget that, underneath the violence, it's still beautiful."

He is beautiful. Or he was once. Blond hair draws my attention first—a sun-kissed gold in places, darkened with age in others. It's been clawed back from his face into a ponytail longer than mine was before Briar trimmed it. His eyes are that dangerous color between blood and brown. Like a flame, they catch the light filtering in through a sloppily boarded-up window beside him. His face is angular. Chiseled. Stone. Every feature is sculpted to convey just one emotion: determination. The way an owl might watch the mice scurrying underfoot in the stables. Or the way Robert used to look at me.

The way the devil looks, I presume, as if he has all the time in the world. More than ten hours.

An eternity to torture me.

~ Continue Reading XV ~

A WORD FROM THE AUTHOR

Hey there!

Thank you so much for reading! If you enjoyed the story, please leave a review and recommend the book to any friend you think would love this twisted world. You'd have my eternal gratitude. Even a short sentence goes a long way!

Then, come join the rest of us dark romance lovers in my Facebook Group where you can get snippets, sneak peeks of upcoming books and even help vote on aspects of future novels.

Come to the dark side:
https://www.facebook.com/groups/lanasbeautifulmonsters/

WANT MORE STUFF TO READ?
Join my newsletter and get a **free book**! Plus, you get to stay updated with any new releases, random giveaways and exclusive sneak peeks!
https://www.lanaskybooks.com/newsletter

Other Novels: https://lanaskybooks.com/

FREE BOOK - JOIN MY NEWSLETTER

DARK, TWISTED ROMANCE

Join my newsletter and get a **free book**! Plus, you get to stay updated with any new releases, random giveaways and exclusive sneak peeks!

https://www.lanaskybooks.com/newsletter

ABOUT THE AUTHOR

Lana Sky is a reclusive writer in the United States who spends most of her time daydreaming about complex male characters and parenting her Cockapoo Joey. She writes dark, twisted romance across several genres. Her titles include everything from mafia romance to vampires.

facebook.com/AuthorLanaSky

twitter.com/lanasky101

amazon.com/author/lanasky

pinterest.com/lanasky101

goodreads.com/lanasky

instagram.com/lanasky101

bookbub.com/authors/lana-sky

tiktok.com/@author_lana_sky

ALSO BY LANA SKY

For more titles by Lana Sky, please visit:
https://www.lanaskybooks.com